THE MT. ABRAMS MYSTERIES

Volume One

A Mother's Day Murder
A Founders' Day Death
A Killer Halloween

by

Dee Ernst

A Mother's Day Murder Copyright © 2015
A Founder's Day Death Copyright © 2015
A Killer Halloween Copyright © 2016

235 Alexander Street

235
ALEXANDER
STREET

ISBN 13: 978-0-9970154-5-2

If you'd like to learn more about Mt. Abrams, including other books in the series, please visit https://mtabrams.com

To find more of other Dee's books, go to www.deeernst.com

Comments? Questions? An uncontrollable desire to just chat? You can reach me at Dee@deeernst.com

*This is for my mom,
who introduced me to Archie Goodwin
and pretty much set me on my way.*

A Mother's Day Murder

A Mt. Abrams Mystery

by

Dee Ernst

CHAPTER ONE

MOUNT ABRAMS WAS EXACTLY THE kind of quaint, close-knit community that people dreamt about. Everyone knew everyone else, people smiled and rescued kittens, childhood sweethearts lived happily ever after, and everyone who lived there, when asked, would all say the same thing—"Yes, it's a lovely place to live. Nothing ever happens here."

Everyone who lived there was, of course, lying. Mt. Abrams was exactly the kind of quaint, close-knit community where everything and anything happened, quite often, and to lots of people. There were moms who drank too much wine, kids who did drugs and shoplifted makeup from Lord & Taylor, adultery, vicious gossip (much of it true) and worse.

We all thought that a certain wife kept falling down the stairs way too often. And the single mom with the drug problem kept sending her kids away to her "grandparents," and we all smiled and nodded and ignored the child services worker who came every week. And, of course, there were "characters." As my very good friend Shelly Goodwin often said, Mt. Abrams seemed to have a disproportionately high percentage of drunks, assholes, and whack jobs.

But the myth persisted. Nothing ever happened there.

Until Lacey Mitchell dropped off the face of the earth.

For me, Ellie Rocca—divorced, working from home, and in a little bit of a rut—it became almost a challenge to figure out where she'd gone, and more importantly, why.

Routine meant a lot to the people around here. Just like any small town, people liked things to stay pretty much the same from day to day, especially when kids were involved. The morning bus stop ritual, for example, was sacred. So when Lacey Mitchell did not walk with her boys to the bus stop one Monday morning, we all noticed. Lacey usually stood with her two sons, David and Jordan, smiling faintly from a short but significant distance from the main group. That morning, her husband Doug did the honors. I smiled and waved, and immediately started to wonder—laziness? Doing her roots?

"Hi, Doug, is Lacey all right?" I called over. He was standing as far away from the bus stop as was humanly possible without actually being on another block.

The two boys both turned and looked up at their father.

"She's fine," Doug said. He smiled briefly. "Her father is ill. In Buffalo. I drove her to the train station Saturday."

Jordan, the older of the boys, tugged on Doug's sleeve and muttered something, but Doug shook him off without even glancing down at his son. "Don't know how long she'll be away."

I nodded. "Oh. Well, give her my best when you talk to her. Do you need any help with the boys?"

Doug flashed another smile. "No, thanks, ah, um…"

"Ellie," I reminded him.

Another tight smile. "Right. Ellie. We're good."

I turned back to the circle of moms, eyebrows raised. "Buffalo?" I whispered.

"I never realized she had a father in Buffalo," Sharon Butler said.

"I never realized she had parents, period," Shelly Goodwin muttered, and the group burst into smothered laughter.

"Come on," I said. "Lacey isn't that bad."

Maggie Turner made a noise. "Yes, she is. She's like a mom-bot, all perfect and polite. Him too. They're like Stepford people."

She did have a point. They were a beautiful couple—tall, lean and vaguely Nordic, with fair hair and pale blue eyes. They both had a certain look, as though they'd met while modeling for Abercrombie & Fitch. They looked like the type of people you couldn't imagine doing anything even vaguely distasteful, like throwing up in the back seat of a car. Their sons were equally good looking and polite, and managed to never get their clothes dirty.

The bus pulled up, and the sounds of the engine and cries of good-bye drowned out all conversation. I gave ten-year-old Tessa a kiss and waved as my beautiful, fearless, and way-too-stubborn little girl climbed on the bus.

The bus chugged up the hill, and I turned to Shelly. "Ready?"

Shelly nodded. "In fifteen?"

I nodded and watched as Doug got into his Camry to drive away, and then trudged up the hill to home. In fifteen minutes I'd be back down with Boot, the most spoiled cocker spaniel in the world, and a Thermos mug of coffee for a morning walk around Mt. Abrams. It was all the exercise I got these days, and since I was on the slow rise after fifty, I made the effort, even on days not as perfect as this beautiful May morning.

When I came through the door into my kitchen, there was no blare of hip-hop or garbled television noise from upstairs. Cait was still asleep. Caitlyn was my other beautiful, fearless, way-too-stubborn daughter. She was twenty-four. She was born in the first years of my marriage, when things between Marc and I had been great. Tessa was born in the last few years of the same marriage, when sex was the only thing Marc and I had left in common. Now Marc lived in a sleek two-bedroom condo in Hoboken with a view of the New York skyline. I was still in a slightly shabby, decidedly quaint Victorian on Abrams Lane, around the corner from the post office and town library, with a view of the lake.

Cait had just finished a very expensive graduate program with a master's degree in French poetry, with a specialization in early nineteenth century romantics. I figured she'd be switching from her part-time job waiting tables at a chichi French restaurant to a full-time job waiting tables at a chichi French restaurant any day now.

I filled my Thermos with hot coffee, then added way too much sugar and flavored creamer, and called for Boot. She skittered around the corner into the kitchen, ears perked, stump tail wagging. Boot is milk white with black spots and a single black paw. She sat patiently while I attached her leash. My phone made its *You've Got Mail* noise. A text from Carol Anderson. She'd meet me at the corner.

Carol was ten years older than I, with all her kids grown and mercifully out of the house. She'd lived in Mt. Abrams all of her life, having been born in one of the Victorian houses on the top of the hill, and then having moved into a more spacious Craftsman-style house after her marriage. She knew all the old guard, and as the librarian at our tiny local branch, she knew many of the newer residents as well.

I bet she'd know something about Lacey Mitchell.

"She rents lots of movies for the boys," Carol said. "Superhero stuff. She reads mostly nonfiction. I never see him at all." Carol treated her relationships with library patrons with the same confidentiality as a doctor or lawyer, often claiming you could tell more about a person from what they read than by any other means. She kept everyone's guilty secrets intact, for the most part, but was not above breaking her code of silence for a good cause. "Last week she came in on Thursday. That's the last time I saw her." She glanced down at me. "Father in Buffalo?"

I nodded. I never talked much when we walked. Carol was almost six feet tall and had legs up to her neck, and despite the few years she had on me, never seemed out of breath, even going uphill. Shelly was my height, almost five-six, but jogged everywhere and ran marathons in her spare time. I managed to keep up with them mostly because Boot pulled me up the hills, but trying to have a conversation anywhere but on a flat stretch of road was too much to ask, and both of them knew it.

We turned onto Morris, which was *almost* not a backbreaking incline. Shelly tugged on Buster's leash. Buster was a chocolate lab, and you'd think he'd love the great outdoors, but he hated the hills as much as I did.

"I bet there's something odd there," Shelly said. Shelly was five years younger than I, and my best friend in Mt. Abrams. Her youngest son was the same age as Tessa. I had met her during my first week in Mt. Abrams, when her previous chocolate lab, Bruno, wandered into my new house and refused to leave. Cait adopted him on the spot, and when Shelly arrived to claim her wayward pet, she had to resort to some quick thinking to get her back. Cait became her dog sitter.

I became her friend.

Shelly was average height with a flat body—no boobs, no butt, narrow hips. She was very healthy and fit and had a heart of pure gold.

Carol rolled her eyes. "There's always been something odd there. I mean, those kids come into the library and never speak unless spoken to. Not that I object. Those boys are model library citizens. But who has kids like that anymore?"

Maggie Turner came jogging out of her short driveway and ran around us, grinning. "Come on, Shel, let's take the next hill," she said.

Maggie was young, thirty-six, with way too much time on her hands when she was home. Her hair was bleached blonde, super short, and she had five visible tattoos. She was a professional musician, playing second violin in a fairly famous chamber group that gave concerts worldwide. When she was touring, during five or six months every winter, her husband Derek, an artist and cartoonist, cared for six-year-old Serif.

Who was a little girl, in case you were wondering. I know. Serif. That's a therapy session just waiting to happen.

Maggie was wearing high-cut gym shorts and a Guns N' Roses T-shirt. "Up the hill?"

Shelly tugged at Buster again. "Not today. What did you think of Doug?"

Maggie stopped bouncing and settled in beside Carol. "I think the two little boys were as surprised as we were about Lacey having a sick father."

I nodded. "Yeah, I noticed that too. And Doug looked awful, like he'd had no sleep."

Carol shrugged. "Maybe she left him. Maybe he threw her out. Maybe they were up all night having great monkey sex, and she couldn't walk this morning."

I was in the process of taking a gulp of coffee as she said that and spewed it all over the street. "Monkey sex?"

Carol nodded. "Yes. When you climb up the headboard, shrieking."

I licked coffee off my thumb. "Well, I wouldn't know about that. I've pretty much forgotten what sex is, even the non-monkey kind."

"Seriously, Ellie, I can introduce you to Martin," said Maggie. "He's first cello. Amazing guy."

I shook my head as we turned onto Davis Road. It was quiet and flat, lined with what looked to be Victorian dollhouses. Back in the late 1800s the lots had only been thirty feet wide at the street, so the homes were all narrow and deep, with tiny porches and lots of gingerbread trim. Kate Fisher was on her porch, as she was every morning. We waved and tried to hurry by, but we weren't quite fast enough. Kate was a talker.

"Ladies, good morning! Oh, I love spring, don't you? And this is the weekend I set out my impatiens. I hate to see the pansies go, but it's time…"

We walked on. Luckily, Kate never minded if no one answered her.

There were a few rental properties in Mt. Abrams. The general consensus was that renters did not make good neighbors because they didn't care how their properties looked. Even though she had only lived there a few weeks, Kate was quickly earning the respect of all of Davis Road. She'd painted all the trim of her tiny house herself, a bright white, and had filled all her window boxes with pansies. It was too bad she couldn't keep her mouth closed for more than seven seconds at a time.

We turned again, climbed another hill, and finally, spread out in front of us, was the lake. Beyond that rose the mountain that Josiah Abrams named after himself. My house was off to the left, across from the water. Josiah's original house had been expanded over the years to become the clubhouse, and come summer, the social center of Mt. Abrams. The Mitchell house stood on the opposite side of the lake, facing the clubhouse, looking pristine in the morning sun.

The whole vista was flushed with the first pale green of spring, and the reflection off the water was breathtaking.

I stopped to take it all in. I got to see this every single morning. What else could I want from life? Probably not a cello player. "No thanks, Maggie. I'm going to leave my love life to fate."

Shelly sighed. "Yeah. Good luck with that."

The community of Mt. Abrams was founded in 1871 by Josiah Milner Abrams, a Brooklyn-born merchant who made a fortune during the Civil War by supplying the Union army with saddles and bridles for its cavalry. He had grown tired of the city life, such as it was, so one day he got on the train in Hoboken and traveled due west into the untamed heart of New Jersey, looking for a little piece of paradise he could call his own.

Legend has it that when the train stopped at Lawrence Township, he stepped off to stretch his legs and started wandering up a nearby hill. He forgot all about getting back on the train, apparently overwhelmed by the natural beauty of the place. At the top of the hill was a crystal clear lake, and beyond that, a small mountain so green that Abrams fell in love and bought the whole shebang. Luckily for him, the small mountain was insignificant enough that it didn't have a name, so of course, he named it after himself. He started by building a grand summer retreat. He had dreamed of a quiet, private paradise for him and his family, but his heirs had other ideas, and most of them involved making more money by selling off everything Josiah had owned, including his land. By the time Marc and I looked at Mt. Abrams, it was your basic lakeside community. Quirky, yes, but hardly paradise.

When Marc and I moved there in the mid-nineties, he wanted a nice, modern bi-level, steps from the train station, so he could commute easily rather than try to drive every day into New York City. I fell in love with one of the original Victorians—not right on the lake, but close enough. Since living by the lake meant he had to walk ten minutes to the station instead of three minutes, he hesitated. Once he conceded that, from a resale perspective, lake view was a better location, we bought the house. Because it had been fairly neglected, we bought it for a song and spent five years in a state of continual rehabilitation. Not the best way to live, but Cait learned early on the joys of new sheetrock and that fresh paint smell.

I loved it. Marc did not. He tried, but he grew to hate the house—its quirky electrical system, uneven floors, and random fits of falling shingles. By the time Tessa was born he was done—with the house, the small-town living, and with me. He got a shorter commute. I got the house I'd always wanted, amazing friends I'd cultivated for years, and a king-size bed all to myself.

Small-town living isn't for everyone. I loved it. There was a real sense of community and safety that I felt comfortable with. I often left my door unlocked, and let Tessa walk to her friends' houses without any real worry. Caitlyn hated it. Everyone knew everything, she complained. People were always judging, she insisted.

And nothing ever happened.

CHAPTER TWO

WORKING FROM HOME HAD LOTS of advantages. I never had to worry about what to wear, for example, although some days I'd catch a glimpse of myself in the mirror and think that maybe, just maybe, I should rethink my usual uniform of yoga pants and T-shirts. But I needed to be comfortable. I was a freelance editor. I used to be a junior editor in a very well-known publishing house, right down the hallway from Marc's office. It was where we met, fell in love, and worked side by side for years. When Caitlyn was born, I took a few years off before returning a few days a week, then back to full time. Marc and I dropped Cait off at daycare and took the train to Penn Station together. I always took an earlier train home, got Cait, and began my second and third jobs as wife and mom. It worked out quite well for a long time, aside from the part where I was exhausted and grouchy and kept asking Marc when he was going to start to help around the house.

But after Tessa was born, several things happened at once. A larger conglomerate bought out my company, resulting in a huge promotion for Marc and a job elimination for me. Self-publishing started to pick up a little steam, and independent authors needed independent editors to work for them. And finally, Marc leaving forced me to rethink how I was going to support myself. Did I really want to find another NYC job?

So I went online and stalked writers boards and groups, and little by little, I started getting work. Self-pubbed authors had no real money, so I gave all my clients huge breaks on their first few manuscripts. Luckily, I managed to get quite a few good writers wanting my services, and soon they were making enough good money to start paying me good money. That, along with an excellent divorce lawyer, made me feel fairly secure moneywise. When my father died a few years ago, I got an insurance payment that allowed me to buy out Marc's share of the house and pay off most of the mortgage. I had no car payment anymore; Cait's education had been paid for by grants and scholarships, and I even had a savings account in case the roof collapsed or the furnace blew up. Living in an old house made for a long list of possible emergency scenarios.

My life was good. I had few complaints. I was even getting a little restless and—dare I say it—bored. The problem was I specialized in mystery novels. Cozies, thrillers, classic whodunits—my mind was never more entertained than when the dead body showed up. And I was good at finding plot holes, making sure the red herrings weren't too obvious, and tying up all the ends nice and tight. I was an excellent editor, if I do say so myself, because my brain was very good at the little details that made for a first-class mystery. That made my real crime-free life a bit dull. That's probably why when I got home that morning I went straight to my computer to Google Lacey Mitchell.

Doug and Lacey Mitchell came to Mt. Abrams last year, moving into the old Dwight house after it sat empty for almost six years. There were a string of owners before them, each one doing less and less upkeep until it was a sad, shabby wreck of a place. When we saw the Mitchells putting all sorts of time and money into the house, we were all pretty excited. And when the last of the painters and landscapers drove away, and the Dwight house stood at last, gleaming white in the summer sun, we all waited breathlessly for the first of us to see what the interior looked like.

We were still waiting. We knew nothing more about the family than we did when they first moved in. Hopefully, that was about to change.

There were more Lacey Mitchells than I could have possibly imagined. I narrowed the search to Lacey Mitchells in New Jersey. Nothing. I tried to remember if anyone had found out where they had moved *from* when the family moved to town.

I texted Shelly. She managed a very busy allergist's office, but I knew she constantly checked her phone. Sure enough, after searching fruitlessly for fifteen more minutes, I got a text back.

I think VA

Good. Lacey Mitchell, Virginia, and bingo—there she was.

Lacey Scott Montgomery, of the Fairfax Montgomerys, married Douglas Wade Mitchell, on December 24th, 2002. Mr. Mitchell hailed from Austin, Texas, where he was employed as an engineer. Ms. Montgomery recently graduated from Sweet Briar with a degree in public relations.

Public relations? Lacey needed to go get her tuition money back. She'd obviously learned nothing about PR.

Then I Googled the Fairfax Montgomerys. Yes, Lacey did have a mother. Millicent Clair Montgomery, nee Wilcox. She also had a father but not anymore. I read the obituary very carefully. Gerald Montgomery had died the previous February. It happened suddenly. He was survived by his daughter Lacey and two grandsons.

Wait. Why wasn't the wife mentioned? Had they been divorced?

I looked around the Internet. I was on a mission. No mention of divorce or separation, but I wasn't sure something like that was open information. Last mention of Millicent was the wedding announcement, back in 2002. Nothing at all since, not even in a Lifestyle section where the comings and goings of the Fairfax elite were carefully documented. Millicent had simply vanished. Much like her daughter.

There was another little snippet about Gerald in what looked to be an even more local weekly paper. There, nestled among pie contest results and advertisements for John Deere tractors, was a little article about the generous Mr. Montgomery and how he had used his family money to better the community by donating to various charities, including the library and Habitat for Humanity.

Hmmm. Family money. According to the *Fairfax Bulletin* his family money was estimated to be in the neighborhood of five million dollars. And without the wife in the picture, could Lacey have inherited the whole bundle? I sat back and stared at the computer screen.

So much for sick in Buffalo.

"Mom. Are you working?"

"Of course," I lied. I'd been in the process of trying to see if ol' Gerald had probated his will, how much was involved, and most importantly, who got it all. I minimized the screen and stared intently at the incredibly tedious cozy mystery I was supposedly copyediting. "What's up?"

Caitlyn Elizabeth Symons looked exactly like I would have looked at twenty-four if I had been six inches taller with a discernible waist, shapelier butt, and boobs. And a better nose. And red hair. She had her father's eyes and my chin, which wasn't a bad thing. She was a very pretty girl with a smokin' hot body and a potty mouth that could put a longshoreman to shame. She was also very smart about all sorts of things, but not necessarily common sense things. She made, at one point in her high school career, a small solar rocket that placed third in a national science fair. But for God's sake, don't let her near an iron.

She walked into my office, which was a sunroom perched in a corner of the second floor directly over the porch, and sank into a battered but cozy armchair I'd stashed in the corner for when I needed to relax my brain. She was sipping coffee from a very large mug.

"Would you kill for five million dollars?" I asked her.

"Depends. Why, did Grandma strike it rich?"

"No." I swiveled in my office chair away from my computer to face her. "You'd kill Grandma?"

"Of course not. Who has five million dollars?"

"Lacey Mitchell. Her father died recently and may have left her a bundle."

"Is there anyone in our family to leave us a bundle?" she asked.

I shook my head. "Nope."

"Oh. So *we're* going to kill Lacey Mitchell?"

I shook my head again. "Nope."

She sighed. "Why do you start these conversations?"

"You came up here, remember? I repeat—what's up?"

"I applied for a fellowship in French comparative literature. They want me to go out for an interview."

I think my jaw dropped open. I never imagined she'd find anything that was even remotely related to her chosen field of study. But wait—would she get paid for something like that? "Cait, that's amazing! Oh, I'm so happy for you. When?"

"The first week in June."

"Where?"

"Catholic University."

I made a face. "Well you know how I feel about being Catholic, but if they're willing to take you anyway, that's just great. Where is that, D.C.?"

"Lyon."

I stopped being excited. "Lyon as in France?"

She nodded.

"Oh," I said.

My office has floor-to-ceiling windows on three sides, and long gauzy curtains diffuse most of the light, but I swear the world got a little bit darker there for a second. "You're going to France? They hate us in France. And it's very expensive there. Finding a place to live is going to be impossible. Don't you watch *House Hunters International*?"

"First of all, the French do not hate us. And I've been saving money like crazy. You know that. I haven't bought so much as a new pair of shoes in three years. I've got lots of money in the bank."

I took a deep breath. Oh, my dear, sweet little girl. She was a *waitress*. She only worked three nights a week. I mean, really, how much could she have saved? I stood up, stretched, and then gazed out the window. "Exactly how much have you got in that little nest egg of yours?"

"Eighteen thousand dollars."

I spun around to gape at her. "*What*?"

She looked at me patiently. "Mom, I've been working for seven years. Since high school."

"But part time."

"Still."

She waited. I knew what she was thinking.

During her junior year of high school when she should have been traveling around to all the out-of-state colleges she was determined to get into, Marc left.

I was a mess. So was she, but for a different reason. She saw the writing on the wall just as clearly as I did. That was the summer she started working at Pierre's, and that was the summer she told me she could get just as good an education at Rutgers and live at home to save money, keep her part-time job, and help out with Tessa. So she'd commuted through a four-year BA, then a two-year masters program. She was done. I was no longer a quivering mass of depression and anger. Tessa was a serene and oddly mature child. Cait didn't need to be here anymore.

"Honey, they'll be lucky to have you. What an amazing opportunity. And you'll be able to live like a queen. Who knew?"

She flew out of the chair and into my arms, picking me up and hugging me tightly. "Oh, thank you, Mom. I was so afraid you'd freak out."

There were tears in my eyes. "I am freaking out. I will miss you terribly. But you deserve this."

She was crying too. "Yeah, I think so. So, which of us tells Tessa?"

Tessa only worshipped her older sister with a devotion formerly found in ancient apostles.

I shook my head. "Not me. This is your dance. You pay the piper."

She grinned. "Okay. I'll buy her pizza first."

I wiped the tears off my face. My little baby. All grown up at last and going off on her own. As much as she was often a huge pain in my butt, I knew I'd have a lot of emotional adjusting to do. "She'll want your room, you know."

Cait went back to sit back down, resuming her coffee sipping. "Well, she can't have it. Not yet. Now, who is this Lacey Mitchell person, and why do you think someone killed her for five million dollars?"

Cait's announcement distracted me from work—and Lacey Mitchell. We went out to lunch, stopped at the bank to take her passport out of the safety deposit box, and had our toes done. All that girlish bonding did little to make me feel any happier about the fact that my child, my firstborn baby, was going across the ocean to live in a strange country where even though she knew the language and loved the culture, she would be a complete outsider, alone, without her mother's advice and support.

"Mom, you know I rarely take your advice now," she reminded me, after I expressed my concern.

"I know. But I can give it to you. I can actually see you smile and nod. How can I do that when you're in France?"

"Skype."

Damn that kid. She had an answer for everything.

She dropped me off at the bus stop in Upper Main Park, then drove the car up the hill. It was about twenty minutes until Tessa came home from school, so I sat on a bench and quietly took in a truly beautiful spring day. The forsythia was in bloom, as were the daffodils. Birds were singing. A small bunny hopped across Marie Wu's front yard. I half expected a Disney princess to burst out from somewhere, singing at the top of her lungs and leading a conga line of dancing deer.

"So Ellie. What about Garden Club?"

Lynn Fahey probably worked for the CIA in a former life. She snuck up on me so suddenly I literally jumped.

"God, Lynn, wear a bell around your neck or something, please?"

She sat next to me, crossed her legs, and began bouncing her foot. She was always in motion. Barely over five feet tall, she was one of those aggressively busy women, running to meetings and organizing events. She was vice president of the Garden Club, a member of the Mt. Abrams Historical Society, was on the local PTA fundraising committee, and ran coffee hour at the Methodist Church. She also had two kids in middle school, and her husband always looked happy.

"I'm not joining the Garden Club, Lynn. For one thing, I don't have a garden." My house did have a yard, and there were things planted in that yard, but that had been Marc's doing. Cait weeded and watered things for me. I mowed the small patch of green that, I'm sure, contained a few blades of grass among the weeds. Tessa had a jade plant that I was trying desperately not to kill.

"You don't need a yard to be in the Garden Club, Ellie. You just need to love plants."

"I don't love plants, Lynn. I have a black thumb." I glanced at my watch. Eight more minutes until the bus.

Lynn tugged on the end of her braid. Her hair was long and light brown, barely streaked with gray. Her braid fell past her waist, adding to her hippie-chic fashion style. Today she was wearing faded jeans, a batik peasant-style blouse, six or seven long beaded necklaces, and Birkenstocks with argyle socks. "Ellie, please. Do you know what Mary Rose is planning? She wants to put pavers in the library park. Can you imagine?"

The library did not actually have a park. It did have a small grassy area by the entrance, where the Garden Club had planted a bank of hydrangeas a few years ago, and had recently installed a picnic table.

I could see Sharon Butler coming around the corner. Sharon was young, in her early thirties, with a six-year-old son. She was considerably overweight, probably close to two hundred and fifty pounds, but she trotted up the hill with a smile and no apparent shortness of breath. "Honestly, Lynn, pavers aren't so terrible. It gets really messy around there in the winter."

That was obviously the wrong thing to say. Lynn and Mary Rose Reed were as close to archenemies as one got in Mt. Abrams. Their wildflower garden feud had been epic.

"Pavers would ice over, and that would mean salt being put down. Salt would get swept to the side, all over the hydrangeas, and would kill them off in just a few years. Do you really want to kill the hydrangeas?"

"Of course, not. So, you want me to join so I can become part of the anti-paver voting block?" Sharon, now within earshot, made a sympathetic face. Lynn's strong-arm tactics were the stuff of legend.

Lynn leaned over to give me a quick hug. "Exactly. Meeting is Thursday at seven-thirty. In the firehouse. See you there." She bounced up, waved at Sharon, and then disappeared as quickly as she had come.

Sharon laughed. "Did she recruit you? Pavers?" Sharon was very pretty, always perfectly made up, and her hair carefully colored and styled. She worked from home too, but managed to get herself dressed in coordinated outfits with matching accessories. Today her earrings and necklace complimented the blue in her cotton sweater. She also always wore perfume. I was a tad jealous.

I nodded. The rest of the moms materialized, and seconds later, the bus pulled to a stop. Tessa was first off the bus, of course. She liked being first. At anything and everything. I liked to think that having big sister fed into her competitive spirit.

David and Jordan Mitchell did not get off the bus. They were obviously hanging out at the Mt. Abrams Elementary School gym, along with all the other kids in the after-school program, including Shelly's boys. The program ran until six. I had often seen Doug pull in as late as eight in the evening. I wondered what other last-minute arrangements he'd had to make.

Tessa lifted her face for a kiss and handed me her backpack.

"Good day?" I asked.

She nodded, standing patiently and waiting until Jerome got off the bus. Jerome's mom, Jessica, dropped him off every morning, and Tessa and I walked him to Bev Sutter's house every afternoon, who watched him until Jessica picked him up after she got off work. There were a fair number of stay-at-home moms in Mt. Abrams, but living barely thirty miles west of New York City made for a fairly high cost of living, and most of the families had both parents working.

Maggie came tearing down the hill, just as Serif hopped off the bus.

"Ellie, hold on a sec," she said. I motioned Tessa and Jerome up the hill, and Serif fell in beside them.

"What?" I asked.

Maggie glanced around, smiled briefly as the rest of the moms drifted away, and leaned towards me. "Did you know that the Mitchell house is for sale?"

I stopped and stared at her. "For sale? Since when?"

"Since yesterday. Viv told me."

Vivian Brewster was the local real estate agent. Just about every house bought or sold in Mt. Abrams was handled out of her office. She and Maggie, I knew, were not just neighbors but good friends. "Yesterday? Are you sure?"

Maggie nodded. "Yes. But get this. She told Doug she needed Lacey's signature on the contract, but he told her that he had been given power of attorney. He showed her paperwork. And there's no mortgage. Everything was paid off a few months ago."

"When her father died," I muttered.

"Whose father?" Maggie asked.

"Lacey's. Her father died in February. And left a lot of money behind. Five million bucks."

Maggie stopped and stared at me. "Her father died? You mean the one who's supposedly sick in Buffalo?"

"Yes," I said.

"Why would Doug lie?"

I shrugged. "I don't know. Lacey's mother still has a phone listing in Virginia, and when I called it yesterday, I got an answering machine."

We had started walking again, and Maggie poked me in the ribs with her elbow. "You actually called her? What for?"

"I don't know. I guess I wanted to see where she was. She dropped out of sight after Doug and Lacey's wedding."

"Maybe *she's* in Buffalo?"

I shook my head, not convinced. "There's something really odd here. And I think we need to find out what it is."

I had stopped eating real food about five months ago.

Let me take that back. I stopped eating food that tasted good and satisfied my various sweet/salty/spicy urges five months ago. Now, I only ate stuff that was good for me, which is why I did not go out with Tessa and Cait for pizza, although I was sure Cait would have appreciated the moral support. I, quite simply, could not be trusted anywhere that pizza or pasta was served. I had pretty much zero willpower about pizza and pasta.

When Tessa was born, I was forty years old. I also weighed almost two hundred pounds. My second pregnancy was quite different from my first. Not only did I eat for pretty much the entire nine months, I continued to eat the following nine months. Being over forty, I did not expect the baby weight to fall off as easily as it had the first time around, but I really hadn't counted on gaining *more* weight.

My marriage started to fall apart. I lost my job. Tessa was a bit whiney. Cait was a teenager—need I say more? I could often be found wandering up and down the aisles of the Stop and Shop, my cart loaded with frozen Sara Lee banana cream pies and bags of Oreos.

After Marc moved out and I started getting side jobs, I began to feel better about myself. When I finally took a cold, hard look at myself in the mirror, I decided drastic action needed to be taken. I joined a gym and tried different diets, with varying levels of success. Last year, when I could no longer kid myself about "baby weight"—after all, it had been years—I started walking every day with Shelly and Carol. My New Year's resolution was to lose the last thirty pounds.

I was almost there.

I was never going to be a size eight. I don't think I was a size eight *ever*. Not even when I was twelve. But my boobs were once again the only part of my body that noticeably stuck out, and I was happy with that.

So there I was, sitting in my kitchen, eating a cold poached chicken breast with a huge side salad and a single slice of cheddar cheese, when Shelly knocked briefly and came through the door.

She glanced around. "The girls?"

"Cait is going to France. Maybe for a while. She's breaking the news to Tessa over pizza."

Her shoulders slumped. "She's going to France? Oh, Ellie, are you okay?"

I nodded and gulped down some lemon-infused water. "Not really, but I'll cope. What's going on?"

She sat down across from me and folded her hands. "Tell me about Lacey."

I told her. Then I told her about what Maggie said. She looked thoughtful, nodding to herself.

"I saw Maggie earlier, and she told me what was going on, but I wanted to hear it directly from you. So, Lacey inherits millions, pays off her house, gives her husband power of attorney, then disappears?"

"To be honest, she didn't exactly disappear. We just don't know where she is," I said. "And I can't find out who inherited the money." I'd spent most of the afternoon reading through that cozy mystery and had decided, after reading the sixth or seventh red herring the author threw on the page, that there was usually a very innocent explanation to everything.

Shelly tilted her head. "We know that Doug lied. Why would he do that?"

"Maybe he was embarrassed. Or caught off guard. I mean, we don't know him at all, and here I was, in his face, asking questions."

Shelly still looked skeptical. "You asked one perfectly innocent and easy question. Was Lacey all right? If there was an easy or innocent answer, why didn't he give it?"

I got up, gathered my empty paper plate and napkin and threw them in the garbage. "I don't know, Shel, but honestly, what can we do? We don't know them at all. Maybe she goes off by herself all the time."

It was odd that living in such a small community for almost a year the Mitchells managed to remain such a mystery. The boys did not exchange play dates. Lacey had made no close friendships or shared any type of personal information at all. We didn't know her birthday. Or her favorite color. Or where she went every day between nine and noon. No one knew what Doug did all day, aside from putting on a suit and driving off every morning by eight-thirty, often returning quite late.

That was still okay. I mean, not everyone who lived in Mt. Abrams was as open and friendly as Shelly Goodwin or Carol Anderson. Or me.

I looked at Shelly. "So, what do you *think* happened?"

She frowned. "I guess I was hoping for a nice, juicy murder plot."

I laughed. "Where do you think we are, Cabot Cove? Listen, I'm joining the Garden Club to help Lynn fend off the evil Mary Rose. Come with me?"

She sighed. "They meet Thursdays, right? Yes, I suppose. Is this about the pavers?"

"I prefer to think of it as the mission to save the hydrangeas from death by road salt."

She stood up. "How can you support death by road salt? I'm in." She sighed wistfully. "A murder would have been nice."

I laughed again. "Not for Lacey."

She laughed with me. "You're right. When is the Cait thing happening?"

I shrugged. "She's flying over for the interview in June. She'll know by August. If she gets in, it's two years. If not, she'll be working at Pierre's forever."

"No, she's a smart kid. She'll figure something out. See you tomorrow."

She closed the door behind her, and I finished cleaning up my kitchen. When Marc and I remodeled ten years ago, we debated as to whether to try to bring the kitchen back to its original 1875 glory. I spent five minutes researching the Victorian kitchen, then ordered extra-tall cabinets and granite countertops. There's a lot to be said for keeping those important period details, but nobody wants three feet of counter space and a single cabinet for storage. We did find a killer vintage gas stove, complete with cast iron fittings and cute chrome knobs, but that was as authentic as we got.

The girls weren't back yet. That meant there was probably ice cream involved. I glanced down at Boot. "Walk?"

She perked up her ears, and we went out the back door.

After the warm day, the cool evening air surprised me. May was a fickle month in New Jersey, tempting you with sunshine then reminding you that snow before Mother's Day was not unheard of. I walked quickly towards the lake. About five minutes of this was all I was going to be able to take.

The Mitchell house was ahead of me. I headed towards it. The porch light was on, and there were a few interior lights on. I slowed as I got nearer. Was it possible to just take a peek inside?

I stopped myself. What was I doing? I may have been curious about Lacey, but not enough to turn me in to a Peeping Tom. Boot caught the scent of something and took off, pulling me up the Mitchell's driveway, past the wraparound porch to the detached garage in back.

The garage had been built later, of course, probably in the forties, and it had two doors that still opened manually, just like my garage. One of the doors was standing open, and I could see Doug's Camry parked between rakes hung on the interior wall and a row of garbage cans. Boot was heading straight for Doug's car until a small dark shape appeared out of nowhere and shot past us. Boot reversed suddenly, spinning me around and practically pulling my arm off.

As I turned, I got a glimpse of the garage interior. Something struck me as odd.

I jerked at Boot's leash and moved closer. I glanced at the house. The last thing I needed was Doug coming out and finding me prowling through his garbage cans and gardening tools.

I skirted the Camry and stopped.

There was a great big nothing where Lacey's Suburban should have been.

Doug said he'd driven her to the train.

I backed out slowly and turned again to look at the house.

If he had driven her, why was her car gone? That made two lies. In barely three sentences. Doug was starting to look a bit dicey.

CHAPTER THREE

WHEN THE GIRLS CAME HOME, Tessa was not happy. She stood in the middle of the living room, arms crossed defiantly, chin down, pouting. She was a mini-me, the same dark, curly hair, big brown eyes, and thick, straight brows. She was built like me too, skinny legs, narrow hips, and sturdy around the middle. There was always a chance she would grow into a long-waisted nymph like Cait, but I doubted it. My prediction was that she'd be carrying around a fireplug body just like mine for the rest of her life.

"I don't think Cait should go anywhere," she said with conviction. "She won't like it in France. She likes it here."

I pasted on a smile. "Tessa, this is a great chance for Cait to live someplace new and really cool, meet lots of amazing people, and she can work at what she loves."

Tessa glared. "Well, I hope they don't pick her. I hope they like somebody else better."

I put on my stern face. "Tessa, that's being mean. This is something your sister really wants. We should support her and hope for the best."

"Daddy won't let her go."

I glanced up at Cait, who stood behind her sister and rolled her eyes. "Daddy would never keep your sister from doing something she really wanted," I said.

Tessa was not giving up. "When I see him tomorrow, I'm going to tell him, and he'll make Cait stay home."

I sighed. Poor Tessa. Poor Cait.

Actually, poor Marc. He really was a good dad, spending lots of time with Tessa, even taking her on vacation with him to his family's cabin in Maine every summer. His relationship with Cait was different, of course. Father-daughter things were difficult under the best of circumstances, and there was a lot of baggage they were still filtering through. Cait loved her father and spent time with him. She had understood that although Marc had been the one to leave, every marriage—and divorce—was about two people.

"Maybe Cait can go with you and Daddy tomorrow. What do you think, Cait?"

Cait rolled her eyes again. "I'll tell Dad about France, and we can all talk about it together, okay?"

Tessa sniffed. "He won't let her go," she said again, then turned and marched out and up the stairs.

I looked sympathetically at Cait. "So, I guess this was not a fun girl's night?"

Cait threw herself into a chair. "How can one little kid be so smart? She came up with three really good arguments for me staying before she went into her *because I said so* mode."

"Well, let's face it, you both had exceptionally brilliant parents. I'd talk to your father tonight and let him know what's going on. If he gets blindsided by Tessa, he won't be happy."

She nodded. "Yeah, you're right." She was quiet. I picked up my book and started reading again.

"What if they don't pick me?" she asked finally, in a very small voice.

I looked over at her. "Baby, they would be complete fools not to pick you. You're a Renaissance woman, for God's sakes. You speak, what, three languages besides English, you're a literature wiz who's also a science geek, and you can talk the leaves off a tree. How could they not jump at the chance to have you on their team?"

She smiled crookedly. "Thanks, Mom." She pulled herself up and went upstairs.

I tried to get back into my book, but couldn't concentrate. Even though I read books every day for a living, I always chose reading over television at night to relax.

I closed my book and started turning off the lights. I looked out the window and over to the Mitchell house. The porch light was off. The first floor was dark. A blue flicker in an upstairs window told me that someone was watching television. Was it Doug?

No, it wasn't, because there was a light on in the next window, and a tall shadow crossed it. Again. And then again.

Someone was pacing back and forth.

I watched for ten minutes. What was I expecting? That Doug Mitchell would race down the stairs, across the street, and down the road to my front door, where he would tearfully confess that Lacey was stashed in the basement behind the old coal bin?

I shook myself, turned and went upstairs.

It was not unusual for my mother to call me at seven in the morning. In fact, it was typical. She knew I worked during the day, afternoons were usually spent with Tessa, then came dinner. Since my mother was usually asleep by eight-thirty, mornings were her best time. It wasn't *my* best time, but for Mom, I didn't have to be a shining star.

After my father died, Mom sold the house and moved into an assisted living facility. It made sense. We had already been joking about her faulty memory before Dad became sick. I think he convinced her, in those last awful days, that trying to live alone in a three-bedroom, two-story colonial on half an acre was too much for her. I had felt a momentary cringe at the thought of my childhood home being taken from me, but my younger brother, Ted, finished it for me when he drew me aside after the funeral.

"Listen, Ellie, I'm in Chicago," he said. "I can't help out here. Do you want to be the one running every time Mom can't find the remote?"

Mom had a large room in a very nice facility where they sang Broadway show tunes around a grand piano in the lobby every evening after dinner. They also organized weekly trips to Walmart and monthly excursions to museums, local theater, and craft shows. My mother loved her new life. No cooking, no cleaning, and someone else to drive her around.

I had to admit, I was a little jealous.

So when the phone rang in my house at seven-oh-five, I always knew who it was, even without caller ID.

"Hey, Mom, how are you feeling?" I always led with that question, so we could get the complaining portion of the conversation out of the way early.

"Well, you know, my knee." Ah yes, the knee. Cait jokingly referred to it as a "sports injury," as Mom got it when she fell trying to wrestle a Le Creuset Dutch oven marked down to only $150.00 from another equally determined customer at T.J.Maxx.

"Don't take too much Tylenol, Mom."

"Why, it might kill me?" I could picture my mother on her phone. She did not have a cell phone. The technological sophistication had proved too much for her very early in the game. She had a landline in her apartment and a very simple answering machine, and if she felt cheated of the latest marvels of Android and Apple, she didn't show it.

She had a phone chair. It was the same phone chair she'd had in the old house, as well as the same phone table. When she was on the phone, she did not watch television, eat, or do her beloved crossword puzzles. She was all about the phone call. She would sit upright, both hands gripping the phone, eyes closed in complete concentration.

"A little gas last night," she said and sighed. "I don't know why I eat broccoli."

I poured myself some coffee. I had always managed to combine phone conversations with other activities. "High in antioxidants, Mom."

"High in fiber. Mr. Milano almost blasted us out of bingo. What are we doing for Mother's Day?"

"I thought I'd pick you up early; we could have brunch here, then go to the Arboretum. They're having an orchid show."

"I killed the last one I bought," she said sadly.

"I know. You don't have to buy one. We can just look."

"That sounds nice. I hope my knee is better by then."

"It's a few days away, Mom. No tennis and you should be fine."

"You're not funny." She sniffed. "How are my darlings?"

"Caitlyn has a chance to go to France. We're all very excited."

"They don't like us there," Mom pointed out. "And there are bombs."

"Mom, there are bombs everywhere."

"They killed all those poor journalists."

I sipped my coffee, thinking fast. "Mom, she won't be in the journalism district."

"Oh?"

"She'll be in the literature district. Nobody gets bombed there."

"Oh. Well then, that's fine. Maybe Ted can fly out?"

Sometimes I shifted gears as quickly as Mom, and sometimes it took me a bit longer. After trying to picture

Ted in the literature district, I took three steps back in the conversation. "You mean fly here for Mother's Day? I'll ask him. He and Calvin would love the orchids."

"Why, is that a gay thing?"

My mother had a bit of difficulty with my brother coming out. She'd been raised in a strict Catholic Italian household, where homosexuality meant an immediate ticket to hell. She became gradually tolerant, even as her grasp on reality began to waver, so the ingrained mistruths of her childhood often became fuddled.

"No, Mom, it's not a gay thing. It's a cool and beautiful thing." Boot came and put her paw on my thigh. She seemed to know when Mom was on the phone and always offered moral support. "When is Walmart day?"

"Tomorrow. I need sunglasses. That damn Justine Caldwell keeps stealing mine."

"Are you sure you aren't misplacing them?" My mother was robbed of some personal belonging at least twice a month, and Justine was the usual culprit. Having met Justine, I doubted her guilt, as the poor woman was confined to a wheelchair and couldn't steal a cotton ball without upping her oxygen intake.

"No. She took them. I wish I had enough money to buy a nice pair."

"Mom, I told you, you have plenty of money. Just ask the aide. You have a spending account, remember?"

"I think Justine stole it."

Boot whimpered and wagged her stub of a tail. "Mom, I've got to go. I'll see you Friday."

"Okay, dear. Give my love to Marc."

That was always the saddest part. Even though Marc and I divorced before she started forgetting things, she had decided in her heart of hearts we were still married, and I'd long ago given up trying to talk her out of it.

Tessa came into the kitchen, face wrinkled with sleep. "Why does Grandma always call so early?"

"Because she knows that I'm usually not doing anything too important, and I can talk to her."

"Can I have some breakfast?"

"Of course. Cereal? Toast? One perfect scrambled egg?"

She slumped into her chair. "Cheerios. Do we have strawberries?"

"Yes. Coffee with that? A side of fries?"

She put her head between her hands in mock despair. "Mom, I'm not treating you like a waitress. I'm not tall enough to reach the cabinet yet!"

"Well, okay. Start growing. It's time you started earning your keep around here. Do a few chores, lift that bale, tote that hay."

She looked at me between her splayed fingers. "Is that a movie thing I never heard of or a Broadway thing?"

I poured her cereal in a bowl and grabbed the milk and berries out of the fridge. "Both. I think we have to start your classical movie education."

She groaned. "No, Mom, please."

"Cait loved classical movie nights."

She chewed. "Yeah, well, Cait's weird." She swallowed. "Did you know that Jordan's grandpa got killed?"

I tried to look completely casual. "Jordan Mitchell? No, I didn't know."

"Well, yesterday I tried to tell him I was sorry his grandpa was sick, and that my grandma sometimes didn't even know who I was, and he got really angry. He said his grandpa got killed."

I swallowed my coffee very carefully. "Really? He must have been very upset."

"He was. Mrs. Winship took him to the nurse because he started to cry. I felt kinda bad."

"Well, baby, it wasn't your fault. You were trying to be kind."

She shrugged and finished her cereal in silence. Then she went upstairs and left me with Boot. I looked down at her soft brown eyes, then I stood up and looked out the window at the Mitchell house.

What the heck was going on there? Where was Lacey Mitchell?

"I think you're being ridiculous," Carol said. We were done with all the hills, and were on the walking path around the lake. This was my favorite part of our walk, through the tall oaks that rimmed the water. Since the path was maintained by the county, the walking trail was wide and well tended, no ruts or sizable rocks to contend with.

"I think the whole thing stinks," Shelly said.

"Maybe," Maggie said. "But what can we do about it?"

"I was thinking about talking to the police," I said.

"And tell them what?" Carol asked.

I had no answer. I'd been running stuff over in my mind, and I had no idea what I thought, let alone what to do.

"Last night, you were convinced we were all overreacting," Shelly said. "Now you want to call the police? What happened?"

"Doug spent most of the night pacing around his bedroom."

Shelly raised an eyebrow. "And we know that how?"

I made a face. "I couldn't sleep. Every time I got up, the light was on, and I could see him pacing."

"Still," Carol said. "That means nothing."

"This morning Tessa told me that she tried to talk to Jordan about the sick grandpa, and Jordan got upset and said *his* grandpa got killed." I looked around. "And

I just happened to be walking Boot past the Mitchell house last night, and she was following something into the garage, and the one door happened to be open, and I saw that Lacey's car was missing."

"Grandpa got killed?" Maggie echoed.

"Lacey's car is missing?" Carol asked. "Now that sounds like something."

"Let's look at this," I said. "Lacey's father died suddenly, or was possibly killed, and left a lot of money to someone, maybe Lacey, because for some reason the wife wasn't even mentioned in the obituary. At all. Lacey is gone, and her husband lied about her whereabouts. Her car is gone. And he told us he took her to the train station. We heard him say that. Her sons are really upset about something."

"You might have something," Carol said slowly. "It's starting to get more complicated. Maybe you could just, you know, talk to a detective or something? In fact, you could go and see Sam Kinali."

"Who?" I asked.

She carefully stepped over a stray tree branch. "He's a detective with Lawrence Township. I've met him a few times. He presented a few programs at the main library, and he seemed very friendly. In fact, I'm closing today and don't have to be a work until four, so I'll go with you."

Going to the police. So, we were going to find out what had happened to Lacey and become neighborhood heroes, or we'd discover that nothing had happened at all and become neighborhood laughingstocks.

We walked a little farther, and Carol spoke again.

"So, I met someone on Fish."

Carol had started dating. Her husband had been dead for almost five years, and recently she'd decided to sign up for every dating site she could find. Her conversations were peppered these days with a sort of cyber-dating shorthand—Fish, JDate, FOB and SOH. Fish was Plenty of Fish, a dating site, as was JDate. FWB meant friends with benefits (a big no-no for Carol), and SOH meant sense of humor (a must-have).

"Leon. He's age appropriate and financially secure. He wants to meet for coffee."

"Excellent," Shelly said.

"I think so." Carol was the type of woman who still wrote thank-you notes and used linen napkins when she had us all over for lunch. She approached dating with the same efficient sensibility that she used for changing her seasonal house decorations, sending out Christmas cards, and having her tires rotated. For her, there was a proper time and place for everything. Right now, Leon fit in perfectly.

"Does he have a friend for Ellie?" Shelly asked.

"Ellie," I said loudly, "doesn't need his friend."

"Yes, you do," Maggie said. "Do you want to grow old alone?"

I slowed to give Boot the chance to pee all over a fallen log. "I have children, Maggie. I'm never going to be alone."

"Okay, then," she countered. "Do you want Cait choosing your nursing home?"

What could I say to these women? Sure, they were all my friends, and yes, I'd throw myself in front of a bus for them. But I could never admit, not even to these best of confidants that I was still madly in love with my ex-husband.

"I'm sure Cait will do an excellent job, but thanks for thinking of me."

We walked the rest of the way in silence. We all liked to talk, but we all also enjoyed that moment, halfway around the lake, when the only thing you could hear was birdsong and the sound of our breathing.

It appeared that any Lacey Mitchell conversation was closed until we found ourselves directly in front of the Mitchell house. We all stopped and stared.

"I wonder if her car is still gone," Shelly asked no one in particular.

"Are you thinking that someone returned it in the middle of the night?" Carol asked.

We all walked up the driveway. The left-side door of the garage was open, as it always was during the day. Yes, I suppose anyone could have snuck in and stolen any number of empty garbage cans or rakes or shovels, but that usually wasn't a problem in Mt. Abrams.

We walked into the garage. No Suburban.

We started back down the drive, when Shelly stopped short. "The back door is open," she said.

We looked. Yes. The screen was shut tight, but the actual door stood ajar.

"I wonder if somebody's in there," Maggie said in a somewhat hushed voice.

Shelly climbed the back steps, opened the screen, and yelled, "Hello."

Silence.

Shelly opened the door further and yelled again.

"What are you doing?" Carol hissed.

"Checking to see if everything is all right," Shelly said.

"What are you hoping to find?" I called softly.

She turned and grinned. "Who knows? But don't you really want to see what the inside looks like?"

Maggie bounded up the back steps. "Right with you."

Carol cleared her throat. "I refuse to participate in breaking and entering."

"That's fine. Then hold the dogs and yell if somebody comes." I handed her Boot's and Buster's leashes.

She glared at me. "This is actually illegal," she warned.

I climbed the steps behind Maggie and went into the Mitchell house.

"It's very clean." Maggie whispered.

"Why are you whispering?" Shelly asked. "No one is here, remember?"

"What if Lacey is tied up in the attic?" Maggie said, voice still hushed.

"Then she'd probably want to hear another voice so she can stomp on the floor and get rescued," I said. "Do you hear her pounding on the attic floor with her tied-up feet?" We all stopped and stared up at the ceiling. Nothing.

"Okay, then," Maggie said in her normal voice. "It's really clean."

It was. The kitchen had been redone in that pseudo-country style, with whitewashed cabinets, a farmer's sink, and butcher block on the large island. We walked slowly through the kitchen into the dining room, then into the living room, turned left through the hall to a small office, then back into the hall to the stairs.

"And it's pretty," Shelly said.

She was right. The rooms were beautifully decorated, but showed no personality at all. There were no framed photos, no kid art on the side of the refrigerator. The pillows had obviously never been used to smack a younger brother, and nobody had dared to kick at the rungs of the dining room chairs.

It was very quiet. I could hear a clock ticking somewhere, but that was all. All the windows were shut, and the air had a faint potpourri scent. "It's really quiet," I said. My house was always talking to me—a creak of the floorboards, the wind through an off-center window frame, the rustling of leaves against the side of the house.

"With two boys, how is this so clean?" Maggie asked. "Where are all the toys?"

"They must have a maid," Shelly said.

"Maybe they're waiting for *Country Living* magazine to come by for a photo shoot," I said. I put my hand on the stairway banister and looked up the stairway. "What do you think?"

"Well, in for a penny, in for a pound," Maggie said, pushing me up the stairs.

The landing was big enough to function as the family room, and it looked like people lived there. The remote control was on the floor, and video games were crammed into a very large, and I knew, expensive Longaberger basket.

"I'll take the master," Shelly called. "You guys take the boys' rooms."

I stared after her. "Since when did we become Charlie's Angels?" I muttered. Maggie giggled and slipped into a bedroom.

I walked into Jordan's room. I'd like to say I used a clever detecting technique to figure out whose room it was, but since his name was spelled out on the wall in large wooden letters, I couldn't boast too much. His bed was made. All his Legos were in bins, his completed sets on a shelf. There were lots of age-appropriate books on his nightstand and a very scruffy stuffed panda on the bed.

"Guys, come here," Shelly called.

I went back out and followed Maggie into the master bedroom.

Shelly stood in front of the walk-in closet. A walk-in? In Mt. Abrams? Most of the old Victorians had a single closet for the whole family. A walk-in was unheard of.

"Wow," Maggie said reverently. "Look at all that space."

I looked. She was right. There was a lot of room in the closet, because it was half empty. Only men's clothes hung there.

"Her clothes are all gone," Maggie said.

I turned and looked around. There was nothing on the vanity, no perfume bottles, not even a comb. I crossed the room to start opening dresser drawers. They were all empty until I came to one filled with men's socks.

"Nobody packs everything they own just to take a trip, no matter how long they think they'll be gone." I said, closing the last drawer slowly.

"Where did all her clothes go, if she didn't pack them in her car and drive away?" Shelly asked.

Maggie shuddered. "Let's get out of here. This place is too perfect. It's giving me the creeps."

As I stepped back into the landing, I looked up and saw the attic access panel. I stopped so short that Shelly bumped me from behind.

"What?" she asked, then followed my stare. "Do you think?"

I shrugged and reached up, grabbing the chain, and pulling open the attic steps.

My house had the same access. I unfolded the ladder, and we all looked up into the darkness.

"I went up the stairs first," I said. "Somebody else can climb up there first."

Maggie took a deep breath and climbed up the ladder.

I guess I was expecting her to scream in horror, or at least gasp. What she did is laugh and come back down the steps.

"Cleanest attic I have ever seen," she said, refolding the ladder and pushing it back up. "Neatly arranged file boxes and an empty clothing rack. Totally boring."

We went back downstairs and out the back door. Carol was sitting on the picnic table bench, a dog leash in each hand, and a disgusted expression on her face.

"Done? What were you all thinking, just going into that man's house like that? You should all be ashamed of yourselves. And I bet you didn't learn a thing."

I took Boot's leash and shook my head. "Wrong there. We did learn something. Lacey doesn't live here anymore."

Chapter Four

WE WERE IN MY KITCHEN, drinking coffee, not talking. I had three projects waiting for me upstairs, and I wouldn't get paid this week if I didn't finish them, but all I could think about was the empty dresser drawers in the Mitchell house.

Shelly had spooned sugar into her coffee and was still stirring it, and the spoon was making soft clinking noises as it hit the sides of the mug. I had been listening to it for what seemed to be ten minutes.

"Shel, stop stirring," I growled. "I think your sugar has dissolved by now."

She shot me a look. "What's with you anyway? You're a bit touchy."

"I think something awful happened to Lacey," I blurted out. "I can't stop thinking about her. Which is so weird, because I don't know her well and certainly don't like her very much. Carol, do you have a number for this Sam person?"

She shook her head. "No, but I can get one. I'll see if we can get an appointment later this morning." She pushed away from the table, got up, and put her mug in the sink. "Shelly, all her clothes were really gone? How very distressing. And before Mother's Day. Poor Lacey. And her poor little boys."

I could hear Cait on the stairs, and she came into the kitchen wearing a T-shirt and a thong. She froze, looked around, then glared at me.

"Gee, Mom, thanks for the warning."

I waved a hand. "Why are you worried? Shelly used to see you naked. So did Carol. You usually aren't up this early."

"Yeah, I know. It's weird. Hey, everyone, just comin' by for coffee." She waved and popped a pod in the Keurig. "Are you having a meeting or something? You look pretty serious."

"We're going to the police about Lacey Mitchell," I told her.

She nodded. "Wow. Well. Are you going to take it to Missing Persons?"

Carol shook her head. "No, dear, I know a detective there. Sam Kinali. Your mother told me about France. How very exciting for you."

Caitlyn actually blushed. Cait grew up loving words, and for her, the library was almost sacred, which put Carol on some sort of pedestal from which she would never be able to climb down. "Thanks, Mrs. B. Yeah, I'm pretty stoked. You make sure Mom doesn't go too crazy."

Carol smiled graciously and left. Shelly sat back and stared at Cait. "Are you sure this isn't about some boy?"

Cait looked at her in surprise. "Boy? You mean like go all the way to France just to be with some guy?"

Shelly shrugged. "Or to go all the way to France to *not* be with some guy."

My daughter turned beet red as she added cream to her coffee mug.

"Cait?" I stared at her, then at Shelly. "Who?"

"It's nothing," Cait muttered and practically ran from the kitchen.

I pushed my coffee away from me and glared at Shelly. "What do you know that I don't?"

Shelly looked very innocent. "Kyle Lieberman."

I frowned. "You mean Kyle Lieberman who was her best friend in third grade? Skinny Kyle with the awful nose and big blue eyes?"

Shelly was smirking. "Yep. Only his nose isn't awful any more, and his eyes are still as blue. Just graduated from Wharton. MBA. He's been coming home to pack up his things from his parents' house, and I know for a fact he and Cait were seen together down at Zeke's."

Zeke's was Ezekiel's Tavern, an old-style pub right next to the train station, with craft beers on tap and the best burgers in the county. It was a favorite of just about everyone in Mt. Abrams, not just for the food, but also because of its location.

I hardened my gaze at Shelly. "And you didn't tell me because?"

"I just heard last night. Honestly. I would have said something this morning, but the conversation got hijacked."

"Was that the guy in the beemer?" Maggie asked. She lived behind the Lieberman's house. "He was way cute."

My daughter and Kyle Lieberman. Cait, who according to our brief and infrequent conversations on the subject, had spent the last few years going from one casual hook up to another, was perhaps finally finding happiness with the boy almost next door.

Talk about the world being full of mysteries.

Lawrence Township may sound small and country-like, but it was in fact, a very large, sprawling town of over fifty thousand people in an area of over twenty-five square miles, thirty minutes due west of New York City. The police station had been rebuilt about ten years ago, and it was a large, imposing place adjacent to the municipal court right across the courtyard from Town Hall.

Carol and I walked through the glass doors into a small lobby, past the bulletin board to a thick window. A very young-looking officer behind the glass leaned forward to speak into a microphone.

"Yes?"

"I have an appointment with Detective Kinali," Carol said.

The officer nodded, spoke into a phone, and a few seconds later, the door clicked and swung open.

"Come on through," he said.

We walked through the door into a short empty corridor. A door on the other end opened and a man stood there, smiling.

"Mrs. Anderson. How lovely to see you," he said, and we followed him into the squad room.

There were a dozen or so desks, half of them empty, and a buzz in the room, but there didn't seem to be much actually happening. No jaded hookers slumped in a chair, no shivering junkies, not even a happy drunk. Crime in Lawrence Township appeared to be nonexistent. Detective Kinali led us to a small glass-enclosed room, held the door open, then closed it behind us and sat across the small metal table from us. He took out a small notebook and asked us for our names, spelled out, please, then our addresses and phone numbers. He closed his notebook and folded his hands in front of him. "Now, what can I do for you?"

I almost said "marry me." He was pretty much the sexiest man I had ever seen in real life, and I think my tongue was hanging down to the floor.

He was big. Not just tall, although he was probably over six feet, but big everywhere—broad shoulders and a barrel chest, thick neck and large, strong-looking hands. He was probably my age, maybe older, his hair turning silver, with a slight softening at the jaw.

And he looked…dangerous. He was dark skinned, probably Middle Eastern, with dark eyes and thick but beautifully formed eyebrows. There was an energy about him, as though he was ready to spring into action, but it wasn't a nervous kind of energy. Every movement he made seemed deliberate and necessary. His teeth were very white, and his hair was that shiny, almost slick kind of gray that made women want to run their hands through it just to see if it felt as thick and soft as it looked. He didn't have a mustache, but he should have.

"Detective, thank you so much for seeing us," Carol said. "This is my neighbor, Elizabeth Rocca, and she and I have a problem, and we need some professional advice."

He nodded encouragingly. I swallowed hard, but my mouth was so dry I almost choked.

Carol glanced at me. "Ellie?"

What, me? I was supposed to talk? About what? I had looked into Detective Kinali's eyes and completely forgotten why I was here.

"Ellie," she said, a bit more strongly. I tore my eyes from his face and looked at her. Carol. Oh—that's right. We were here because of Lacey Mitchell.

I turned back to Detective Kinali. "We believe something has happened to another neighbor of ours," I said. "We haven't seen her for a couple of days, and there are, well, circumstances."

He raised an eyebrow. "What kind of circumstances?"

I had a brief flash of this man dressed in robes, riding an Arabian stallion through the desert, sword held aloft, like a character from *Lawrence of Arabia*. "Her name is Lacey Mitchell, and she lived with her husband and sons in Mt. Abrams, and no one has seen her since last

Friday when she picked up her boys at the bus stop. Her husband says she's with her sick father in Buffalo, but he's lying."

He frowned. "Is he?"

"Yes. Her father died this past winter. Down in Virginia. Suddenly. Apparently, there was a lot of money involved. Millions. And there's a wife, but she wasn't mentioned in the obituary, which I find highly suggestive."

"Of what?"

"Of some sort of separation or divorce, meaning that Lacey would have gotten all the money."

He sat back. "And you know this how?"

I settled myself more squarely in my chair. "I looked it up. I found the marriage announcement, online of course, got Lacey's maiden name, and started looking for the parents. There was an obituary for the father and a small article about all the money. And the mother? Still has a phone in Fairfax, even though she didn't answer, and there's no trace of her online since 2002."

His mouth twitched. His lips were very full and soft looking. "Very enterprising of you, Mrs. Rocca."

"I'm not Mrs. Rocca," I said. "I used to be Mrs. Symons, but not anymore. Now I'm Miss Rocca. Ms. Rocca. Ellie."

"Ellie, then. You must be a very accomplished researcher."

I nodded. "I'm an editor. Freelance. I often have to do fact checking for my clients."

He tilted his head. "Really? Lucky you, spending all your time reading. Although, I imagine you have to read a lot of things that are not to your taste."

I rolled my eyes. "You have no idea. I'm almost done with this mystery and let me tell you, these characters are deaf, dumb, and blind. I figured out whodunit by the second chapter."

He threw back his head and laughed. His voice was so deep that he sounded like his laughter came from the bottom of a well. "If I ever write a book, I'll be sure you read it first. I wouldn't want *my* characters to be thought of so badly." Our eyes met.

Can I tell you? They were the softest, gentlest, most beautiful eyes I had ever seen. And they were smiling at me. The lines around them crinkled, and there was a warmth and spark to them that made my blood pound.

This was ridiculous. I didn't even know this man. How could I think he would be just perfect for me?

"I'm sure there's more," he said.

I leaned forward. "Her ten-year-old told my ten-year-old that his grandpa was killed." I sat back, feeling rather smug. Now that was a tasty piece of information.

"I'm completely unfamiliar with ten-year-old children. Can they be inclined to exaggerate?"

I shook my head. "Not my ten-year-old. So, you have no children?"

He lifted his shoulders, then dropped them. "No. It's better, perhaps. This job is not very family friendly."

"Are you married?" What? What did I just ask him?

He shook his head. "Like yourself, not anymore."

I leaned forward again. "Where are you from? There's a slight accent, but I can't place it."

Beside me, Carol shifted in her chair. I didn't care. I just wanted him to keep on talking.

"My family is from Turkey. I came to this country as a small child, and grew up in Queens. After law school, I went with the NYPD. Five years ago, I decided to look for a less, well, stressful position."

I grinned. "I bet Lawrence filled that bill. Nothing much going on here besides stolen BMWs and rich kids getting drunk. Bor-ing."

He laughed again. "Believe it or not, life out here in suburbia is much more interesting than you'd imagine.

In fact, I am constantly surprised at the beautiful and amazing things I come across every day."

He was looking at me. Yes, that's right. At me. And I didn't even blush.

"And now, the possibility of a missing housewife and mother," he said, after a moment. "Is there anything else?"

"Well, her car and all her clothes are gone," I told him. "And the house was just put on the market, and the realtor says Doug, that's the husband, had a power of attorney, and the mortgage was paid off in full a few months ago."

He raised his eyebrows. "You know, realtors don't usually give out that kind of information."

Carol cleared her throat. "That's generally true, detective, but Mt. Abrams is a very…well, close-knit community. The local realtor is a close friend of a friend, and that particular bit of information came to us—how can I put this?—on the sly."

Why wasn't he taking notes? He should have been scribbling madly in a moleskin notebook. Instead, he was sitting there, looking handsome and slightly mysterious and powerful and masterful and…wait. Let me just stop there.

He smiled and folded his hands on the top of the table. "May I ask you a few questions?"

I nodded. Of course he could. No, I wasn't seeing anybody. Yes, I loved walking in the woods and watching sunsets. Yes, I *did* like Italian food, and I'd love to have dinner with him this Friday…

"How do you know that all of Mrs. Mitchell's clothes were gone?"

Of course, he'd have to start with *that* question. I opened my mouth, but nothing came out.

He shifted his gaze to Carol. "I would hate to think," he said softly, "that curiosity caused someone to do something illegal."

Carol leaned forward. "Detective, I swear to you, I did NOT do anything illegal. That particular bit of information didn't even come from Ellie. It came from another source."

Carol managed to tell the absolute truth. Amazing.

He unfolded his hands and placed them, palms down, on the table. "Before I do anything official," he said, "I'll call down to Virginia and see if anything was suspicious about the father's death. I'll also see if we can find a plane ticket issued to Mrs. Mitchell in the last few days. There are all sorts of perfectly reasonable explanations for what is going on. The first thing that comes to mind is that she packed up her belongings and left her husband. Most of our missing persons have usually run away on their own."

Boy, did I feel like an idiot. Lacey left home. She took her five million bucks and just left. So much for my brilliant powers of deduction, honed by years of editing mystery novels. She left; he was embarrassed by it, and since the children don't know yet, he'd made up an innocent lie

Poor Doug. I glanced over at Carol and could tell she was thinking the same thing.

Detective Kinali smiled graciously. "Nevertheless, this is certainly interesting. Thank you, ladies." He stood. "Thank you for coming in."

He gestured towards the doorway, and Carol and I filed neatly out.

We were walking to the exit, and I felt like my head was going to explode. Lacey left Doug. Of course she did. And I had to go make a fool of myself in front of such an attractive man. I caught my breath. Where did this come from? I still had fantasies getting back together with Marc, yet, and here I was, practically paralyzed with what—lust, love, need, want? I remembered when I was sixteen years old, and Bobby McGowan walked into art class. I fell immediately in love. That's exactly how I felt, only, you know, with thirtysomething years of wisdom and experience telling me how crazy it all was. But—whatever it was, I could not ignore it.

I came to a full stop. "Hold on, Carol. Was it just me, or was there something going on between Detective Kinali and myself?"

She sighed. "Really? You have to ask? Good Lord, there were sparks flying across the table." She lifted her eyebrows and tightened her lips. "I half expected you to sit back and light a cigarette."

"I'll be right back." I turned to march back towards Detective Kinali.

Let me put this out there right now—I'm not brave. I don't take lots of chances. I'm also not very impulsive. So I cannot explain why I went back to his desk and sat down abruptly across from him, except that, if I didn't, I'd hate myself for the rest of my life.

He tilted his head and smiled at me. "Is there anything else I can do for you?"

My tongue was frozen to the roof of my mouth. All I could imagine were those strong hands around me. "Yes. Would you like to have a drink with me tomorrow night?"

His smile broadened. "As a matter of fact, yes. Nicola's at eight?"

I nodded, then bolted from the chair and practically ran back to Carol.

I was hyperventilating by the time I burst outside. Carol grabbed my arm and shook me, hard.

"Ellie, what happened? What did you say to him?"

"I asked him out. And he said yes."

She raised an eyebrow. "Good for you. That man is hotter than a witch's tit."

She patted down her hair and walked calmly towards the car.

Yes, he certainly was.

My work was finished. I had done a bit of snooping, satisfied my inner Nancy Drew, then gone to the correct authorities, and now the situation was in the hands of people who actually knew what they were doing and would probably find Lacey hanging around a pool in the Caymans with a studly twenty-three–year-old. So I did not spend the day not working, staring out the window, and thinking about what had happened to Lacey. I spent it not working, staring out the window, and thinking about Detective Sam Kinali.

I'd had this kind of blind, all consuming crush before. After Bobby McGowan set the bar in high school, at least three equally momentous attachments had followed throughout college. It all ended when I met Marcus Symons, three days after I got my first job as a very junior assistant to an assistant in a major publishing house. Right from the start, I knew Marc was different, because I didn't just want to spend all my time with him naked. I also wanted to talk to him. Marc had been the smartest, most interesting person I'd ever been close to, and talking to him became one of my life's real joys.

Now, I wanted to talk to Sam Kinali. I wanted to know if he'd ever been back to Turkey and what it had been like for him growing up in the United States with immigrant parents. Why had he become a cop instead of a lawyer? Why had his marriage failed? What was his favorite food?

I'll be honest and admit that I also wondered what he'd look like without all those clothes, if he'd be hairy—not that I'd mind—how his skin would feel, and if those lips were as soft as they looked. And all that controlled energy—how would *that* translate?

By the time I had to pick up Tessa, I was so hot and bothered I felt like I should take a shower.

"When is Daddy coming?" Tessa asked.

I swung her backpack over my shoulder. "When does Daddy always come?"

"Five-thirty."

"Okay, then. There's your answer."

She raced ahead. Maggie fell in step next to me. "How did it go with the police?"

I glanced around. No one was too close. "We gave all the info, and a detective said he'd check some things out," I told her. "His first thought is that Lacey packed herself up and took a powder."

Maggie made a face. "Yeah, I guess that's just as likely as Doug killing her, then packing up all her things nice and neatly, stashing them in her car, then driving the Suburban into the lake."

"The detective, Sam Kinali, is going to be my new fantasy boyfriend."

Her eyes lit up. "Do tell!"

"He's big and sexy and dangerous-looking, and his eyes are beautiful, and he's Turkish, so I keep imagining us in the middle of the desert somewhere in a big tent, drinking sweet wine and lolling around on pillows." I glanced at her. "I asked him for a drink."

She snorted. "Oh, Ellie, did you switch to editing romance novels? Is that where this is coming from?"

"No. I just finished a tedious mystery with no character development and a plot full of holes. If the author doesn't do a complete rewrite, she doesn't stand a chance of selling a single copy."

Maggie made a face. "Ouch. What happens when you tell a person something like that?"

I shrugged. "If they want to get their money's worth, they'll do what I say. If they want a cheerleader, they'll get another editor. I get paid to be a hard-ass."

She laughed. "And you're such a softie in real life."

I chuckled. "Yeah, well, that's because you don't get paid for real life. See you tomorrow."

I had not seen Cait all day. She yelled good-bye at some point in the morning and did not reappear until just before her father was due to pick her and Tessa up. Kyle Lieberman? I dared not ask.

Marc beeped from the curb, and the two girls tumbled out of the house and into his car. I waved from the porch, then walked over to Shelly's house.

Shelly lived a bit farther down the hill where the houses were still from the late 1800s but were smaller, with even more embellishment. In fact, her whole block looked like a Christmas card in winter, without the snow, of course, a row of gaily painted visions gilded with candles and gingerbread trim. Shelly lived in a long but narrow house with a deep front porch and double glass doors in front. I knocked, then pushed my way in.

Shelly and I had been going in and out of each other's houses for so long that our respective dogs didn't even bark anymore. I went past her sons, sprawled on the couch watching television, and back into the kitchen.

She was standing over the stove, stirring something and muttering to herself. She glanced up, saw me, and grinned. "So, you've hooked a hottie?"

I slumped against the counter and peered into the pot. "Chili? Are you grumpy about chili?"

"I'm not grumpy about the chili. I'm just grumpy in general. They're setting up a new billing system at work, and you know how I am about computers."

I did know. Shelly apparently had a special electro-magnetic force surrounding her that invariably infected every electronic device that came into her orbit. She'd been through so many cell phones that I wouldn't even let her borrow mine. The things that happened to her various computers and laptops would have sent all of Silicon Valley into a tailspin.

"Sorry," I said. "And yes, I have a date with a very sexy man, and I haven't dated in twenty-six years. Do you think much has changed?"

"Ask Carol. Then again, don't ask Carol. When I saw her earlier she was trying to decide what color panty-hose to wear to meet Leon. I didn't know anyone wore pantyhose anymore."

"Just Carol. At least I feel better about Lacey. I mean, this detective seemed to take us seriously. I think he'll really find something out, if there's anything *to* find. But I'm pretty sure he's right, and Lacey just…left."

"Yeah, I get having a bunch of money and leaving the old life behind, but her kids? She wasn't exactly the warm and fuzzy type, but I think she really loved those two boys."

I was trying to think. "How was she when she picked them up Friday afternoon? Do you remember? Did she seem like she was extra clingy because she was never going to see them again?"

"I'm not there for pick up, remember? Ask Maggie. As for you, you got a date out of it. Sounds like a good day all round. Marc has the girls, right? Want to stay for chili?"

I shook my head. "No, thanks. Celery and cottage cheese tonight. I have to save calories for tomorrow night in case things get crazy and there's an appetizer with the drinks."

"Well, it's paying off. You look really good. Pre-Tessa good."

I looked down at myself. "Thanks. I was going to fill you in on my day, but as usual, you know more about it than I do." I shot her a look. "What's with Cait and Kyle?"

She grinned. "Doesn't that sound so cute? Cait and Kyle?" She shrugged. "They've been seen down at Zeke's. A couple of times. That's all. Why don't you ask her?"

I shuddered. "Ask my daughter about her love life? Are you kidding? We agreed on Don't Ask Don't Tell when she was sixteen. Well, I'm outta here. See you tomorrow."

I walked back home, ate carrots, cottage cheese, and celery with all-natural peanut butter. I called my brother, inviting him to fly out for the weekend, but he was spending the day with Cal's mother. We talked for a long time. Ted was not just my brother, he was one of my best friends, and we always had lots to share. I finally hung up, and since I had gotten very little work done, I went upstairs and made it a point not to look out my window towards the Mitchell house.

I was in the zone when the girls came home, because I didn't even hear the car or the front door slam. I snapped out of a rather spicy interrogation scene and hurried downstairs at the sound of Tessa's yelling.

I turned into the kitchen and stopped short. Marc was there.

I hadn't been in the same room with him in over six months. When Tessa announced she was old enough to go from house to car door without an escort, Marc and I stopped needing any regular face-to-face interaction. But I knew why he was in my kitchen. Tessa was throwing a fit, and he was trying to calm her down.

He was on his knees in front of her, and she was yelling at him, her little face mere inches from his own. Cait was slumped against the doorjamb, looking miserable.

"Whoa, Tessa, stop yelling," I said, loud enough for her to hear. She turned and ran to me, throwing her arms around my waist.

"Daddy won't make Cait stay home," she wailed, then burst into tears.

Well, damn.

Marc looked up at me miserably. "I don't know what to say," he said over the sound of Tessa sobbing.

Tessa was getting tall and was all gangly arms and legs, but she was still my baby. I picked up my little girl and carried her up to her room.

She took a while to cry it out, but she finally settled into a hiccupping bundle, half on her bed and half in my arms.

"Tessa, honey, you are making us all very sad by acting this way," I said softly. "You're hurting Caitlyn and your Daddy and me. I know you love your sister and don't want her to leave, but this is important to her. And when you love somebody, you can't keep them from following their dreams."

She sniffed. "What about my dreams?"

I stroked her hair. "What are your dreams, baby?"

"That Caitlyn and I live together on a farm with six horses and a goat."

"Oh." I kissed the top of her head. "And when were you going to do that?"

"After I got out of vet school." She sat up and wiped her eyes. "And we were going to have lots of rescue dogs, and I'd take care of them for free."

"That's a great dream, Tessa. But isn't Cait going to have to wait an awfully long time for you to get out of vet school?" She nodded, then looked at me with narrowed eyes. She was a smart kid. She knew where this was going.

"So, while she's waiting," I went on, "shouldn't she be able to do what *she* wants?"

She took a deep breath. "But she'll be gone for two years."

I hugged her. "I know. I'll miss her too. But we can Skype and stuff. She can still text you all the time."

She buried her face in my side. "Not the same."

"I know. But it's what we've got."

She nodded.

"Good. Now go downstairs and say goodnight to Daddy, and then take a quick shower, okay?"

She uncoiled herself and slid off the bed and out the door. I sat there for a few minutes, looking around her room. She was still in the princess stage, the pink and purple stage, the stuffed animal stage. I knew that at any moment I would turn around, and she, too, would be going off on her own into the great unknown.

A few minutes later, Cait and Tessa came back upstairs. I got off the bed and met them in the hall.

"How are my favorite girls now?" I asked.

Cait gave me a hug. "She's a tough bug, but I think we're good." She glared at Tessa, who promptly stuck out her tongue and scurried to the bathroom.

"Dad's still downstairs," Cait said, then went into her room.

I went downstairs slowly. I could hear Marc talking, and I knew he was lecturing Boot. He had been crazy about that dog and would spend evenings lecturing her on various subjects, from proper canine behavior in public to how to properly clean her butt. Cait had especially loved those times, and she would be collapsed in giggles by the time Marc was done.

But tonight he was sitting alone in what used to be his living room, and I could hear him...

"And don't forget to go in everyday and smell Cait's room. You don't want to forget her," he said.

I paused to watch him, sprawled in the corner of the couch, Boot practically on his lap with her ears perked in intense concentration.

"Spend more time with Tessa, until she becomes a pain, then pee on the floor a little so she goes away on her own."

"Please," I said with a grin, "do not be telling that dog it is okay to pee in the house."

He looked up and smiled. "I told her just a little."

His smile could still make my stomach do flips. When he left, he had truly broken my heart. It had taken me three years to get over his being gone. I never got over being in love with him. Looking at him now, I could still feel his body against mine. I knew the way his skin tasted, and the sound of his breath in the night.

"How are you?" I asked. It felt easy, standing on the other side of the room. After not being alone with him for so long, I wasn't sure how I would feel. It wasn't bad.

"I'm good," he said, scratching Boot behind her left ear. "The babe is up and grown."

I nodded. "We'll get used to it, I guess. I'm really happy for her."

"How's your mom?" he asked.

I shrugged. "The same. Maybe worse. I see her every Friday for lunch." I had a sudden flash. "I'm taking her to the orchid show this Sunday for Mother's Day. Would you like to come? She always asks for you."

He smiled. "Sure. Since my own mother still insists on celebrating Mother's Day alone in the Caribbean, I've got nothing else to do."

"Great. I'll let you know the details. The girls will love it."

He was watching me. "You look really good."

I shrugged. "Yes, well, losing fifty pounds will do that."

He shook his head. "Not just that. You look happy."

"I am. Work is good, money's coming in, I've got friends. I've even got a date."

He raised his eyebrows. "A date? Good for you." He glanced around. "You painted the living room?"

"Last year. When Cait was around for Christmas break. We went for gray rather than the usual taupe. I like it"

He got up. He was not tall, barely five foot ten, and was slightly built. His hair was dark red, the color of fall leaves and copper wire tangled together. His eyes were a deep green, his skin fair and freckled. He had aged a bit, a trace of gray at the temples and a tired look around his eyes.

I suddenly thought of Sam Kinali, all big and dark and sexy. I blinked, and there was Marc again, hands in the pockets of his jeans, and he seemed suddenly frail.

"You look tired," I told him.

He shrugged. "Yeah, well, you know publishing. And right now it's even a bigger cluster fuck than ever."

I nodded. "I bet. I'm still in a lot of the loops. Still get *Publisher's Weekly*. Not a pretty picture"

He nodded a few times, looking down at the floor. That meant he was thinking, and thinking hard. "So, a date?"

"Yep. First date in a really long time."

"Well." He looked up. "I still love you, you know that, right?"

I think I stopped breathing. He what? He just said *what*?

I finally exhaled. "Yeah, sure. You're just not *in* love with me anymore, right? Isn't that what you said?"

He walked past me to the front door, turned around, and grabbed me by my shoulders and kissed me.

The feel of his lips on mine was such a shock that I almost fell to the floor. And it wasn't just his lips. I felt his fingers as they gripped my shoulders, and then the slim, hard line of his body pressed against me, and I opened my mouth to him as all sorts of things came crashing in—familiarity, lust, happiness, more lust, that oh-my-God-he-wants-me-back feeling.

I pushed him away and stepped back. "And what the hell was that?"

He looked down at the floor again. "I've missed you," he said at last.

"So? I'm sure you miss your brother out in San Diego. Do you give him a lip lock when you see him too?"

He shook his head. "No, of course not, but—"

"But what? We haven't been in the same room together for months, and you think you can just, well, what you did?"

He looked at me. His eyes were full. Was he crying? "I miss you," he said again. And walked out the door.

I put my hand to my mouth. My lips were still tingling. The rush I had felt had settled down in, well, you-know-where.

He still loved me. He missed me.

Damn him anyway.

CHAPTER FIVE

THE NEXT MORNING IT WAS raining, which suited my mood perfectly. I'd slept very badly the night before, plotting various forms of ecstatic sexual reunion and/or severe mental and physical torture, with Marc as the central figure. Throw in Sam Kinali and his incredibly gorgeous eyes, and it was a pretty disrupted night.

Sometimes, when it rained, I drove Tessa to the bus stop, but today brought a light, warm spring shower, so we put on matching yellow fisherman's slickers and walked down the hill.

Carol and Co. did not walk in the rain. Or the snow, for that matter, or when it was below thirty degrees. Taking Boot for a long walk to make up for the lack of exercise was out of the question. She did not like getting her feet wet. Yes, I know, spaniels are sporting dogs, and you'd think they would be fine in any weather, but—no. Not Boot. She started dragging her feet at the third raindrop. Puddles made her whimper. What a dog.

One of the advantages of the kind of community that was Mt. Abrams was that certain traditions remained intact. Marie Wu, for example, moved into the farmhouse style house across from the bus stop five years ago, and when she was told that her front porch was the spot of the school kids to take shelter during the rain, she just nodded and smiled. So there we were, crowded around Marie's rocking chairs and empty planters, waiting. Shelly was at the opposite end of the porch, so I couldn't fill her in on the latest Marc development, but I knew I'd talk to her later in the day.

The bus came and went, and I started back up the hill. It was raining harder, and I had the hood of my slicker pulled up over my head, so I didn't hear the car as it drove up beside me, not until a voice was calling my name.

"Ellie, how about a lift?" It was Doug Mitchell, his window rolled down, smiling at me.

"Ah…" This was odd. Doug had never said more than five words in a row to me. Was he really trying to suddenly be a good neighbor? Why? "I'm good."

"Ellie, it's pouring."

It was pouring. What could I say? "Sure. Thanks."

I ran around to the passenger side and jumped in the front seat. I was dripping all over his nice leather interior.

"Oh, Doug, I'm sorry. Everything is getting wet."

He was driving slowly. "No worries. I'm glad I saw you walking. I need to ask you a question."

I was busy with my seat belt. Yes, I was only two minutes away from home, but well, it was a thing. "Sure. What?"

"Why were you in Jordan's room yesterday?"

I opened my mouth. Then I shut it. I swallowed hard. "What are you talking about?" I said, very proud that my voice did not tremble, squeak, or crack. My heart started to beat a little faster. I was a terrible liar. More than that, I was guilty as charged.

"Well, you see, Ellie, when Jordan was little, he kept insisting that someone came in his room at night. So Lacey and I set up a nanny-cam, just to show him that it was only his imagination, you know? These days, I just automatically reset it every night for him. It's a very sophisticated piece of equipment. Motion activated. So imagine my surprise when I looked at the log and saw that the camera went on when no one was supposed to be home."

I stared straight ahead, barely breathing. His voice had started out calmly enough, but he was talking faster and faster, and his tone was changing. He sounded angry. He had a right to be.

I was trying to think a way out of this, but seriously, how could I? Caught on nanny-cam. I thought that sort of thing only happened on reality shows.

"We walk past your house every morning," I told him. When caught, try the truth. My father used to tell me that all the time. "And yesterday, Boot chased a rabbit into your yard, and we followed, and Shelly saw that your back door was open, so we went in to check to see if anything was wrong. It was a good deed sort of thing." Oh, God, that sounded *so* lame.

"I see." His voice was tight. "And you went upstairs because…?"

Very good question, Doug. I stared out the window. We were almost to my house. I could leap out of the car, run inside, lock my door and avoid him for the rest of my life.

"Did she send you?" he whispered hoarsely. "Did she?"

He suddenly sounded afraid. Of what? I turned to him. "Did *who* send me?"

His jaw was clenched, and his hands gripped the steering wheel like it was his last link to the real world. "I didn't think she made any friends, but of course, she'd use you against me." He seemed to be talking to himself more than to me. He was white as a sheet, and sweat had broken out across his forehead. "What did she send you there for?"

"Doug," I said slowly and a little loudly, because, honestly, I was starting to panic. He was freaking out about something. "I don't know what you're talking about."

He jammed on the brakes, put the car into park, and turned in his seat. He looked desperate, and I was suddenly afraid. This was not about me being in Jordan's room. This was a lot more than that.

"What did she tell you?" he asked harshly. "You know she's a liar, don't you?"

I laid my hand slowly on the latch to open the car door. I needed to be away from here. This had gone from embarrassing to scary to something totally beyond scary in just a few heartbeats. I lifted the latch gently, but of course, it was locked. "Doug, who are you talking about?"

He lunged forward, his face suddenly inches from mine. "She got everything she wanted," he screamed at me. "She said she would leave us alone." He had to be talking about Lacey. Why had she left? And why was he so terrified of her coming back?

I was done. My blood was pounding so hard I could feel it trying to burst through my heart and out of my chest. I looked down, found the lock button, pressed it, and pushed the car door open. He grabbed at me, caught my wrist, and twisted. There was a brief spurt of pain, but I jerked my arm, and his fist closed on the sleeve of my rain slicker. I pulled away, leaving him holding the empty slicker, and went running out into the rain and up the street towards my house. I was afraid to look back. He was in a car. He was obviously crazy. What if he tried to run me over?

I swerved off the street and jumped up on the stone wall bordering my yard. I immediately slipped, falling on my face in the wet grass, but at least I was on the other side. He couldn't run me over without plowing through hundred-year-old puddingstone and mortar. I struggled to my feet, soaked, sprinted through to the back yard, and then slowed enough to glance over my shoulder.

Doug's car had not moved. It was still in the middle of the street, wipers on, motor idling, my bright yellow slicker spilling out the open car door.

I ran through the lilac bushes, up the steps, and into the house. I locked the back door with unsteady hands. Then I raced to the front door and threw the dead bolt. I sank to the floor, shaking uncontrollably, breathing in great gulps, Boot whimpering at my side.

I had texted Maggie. I was still huddled on the floor when Boot started barking. Seconds later, there was a pounding on the door behind me.

"Ellie, are you okay?"

I struggled to my feet and unlocked the door. Maggie was standing there, Vivian Brewster behind her. She came in, grabbed my arm, and pushed me back into the kitchen.

"You need tea," she said. I sat down. My breathing was back to normal, but I was drenched and felt cold. I think I was shivering. Viv had been in my house enough times to know my kitchen, and she pulled out mugs and tea bags. Maggie had vanished, but returned with a throw from the living room and put it around my shoulders. I wiped my face with the corner of the throw and pulled it tightly around me.

There was silence, until a mug of tea was put in front of me. I took a grateful sip and closed my eyes.

"Do you want to call the police?" Maggie asked.

I shook my head.

"Ellie, you sent me a text that Doug was after you. Are you sure?"

I took another sip. "Is he still parked out front?"

"No," Viv said.

"He has my slicker." My teeth had stopped chattering.

"We'll get it back," Maggie said. "What happened?"

I told them. I looked into my tea, sipping it as I spoke. When I was done, I looked up at them. "What should I do?"

Viv sat back, folded her arms across her chest, and shook her head. "Girl, you are into *something* here."

Vivian Brewster, besides being a very successful business woman, was the kind of person you wanted in a dire emergency, because she never seemed fazed by events around her. A few years ago, when Hurricane Sandy came through and Mt. Abrams was without power for eight days, she got the key to the Josiah Abrams original summer retreat, which had become the clubhouse for the Lake Association. It still had gas for cooking and a fireplace in every room, and she set up a place where we could all come to get warm and fed.

She was also beautiful, with skin the color of coffee with a hint of cream, high cheekbones and wide dark eyes. She could have easily been taken for an African princess, but when she opened her mouth, Bayonne would come out.

She wagged her finger at me. "Breaking into that house? You both *know* those people aren't right. And now you have him goin' all kinds of crazy on you, and not in a good way." She shook her head again. "What *were* you all thinkin'?"

Just hearing Viv's voice made me feel better. I love Maggie to death, but despite her coolness and bravado, most of the time she tended to be useless in a crisis. Thank God for her husband, because every time Serif skinned a knee or bumped her head, Maggie would get hysterical while Derek applied first aid. With Viv in my kitchen, I wouldn't have cared if Doug came through the door with a machete.

"I think he was really scared of something," I said, putting down my mug and running my hand through my damp hair. "And who did he mean by *she*? Lacey?"

"I thought you all thought that *he* was the one to be afraid of," Viv said.

"I know," I said. "But who else could he have been talking about?"

We sat in silence. The rain had stopped, and the breeze coming into the house was warm and damp. I was feeling less chilled but needed to get out of my wet clothes.

"I'm fine now. Honestly. I was just, well, panicked," I said.

"I don't blame you. Doug doesn't sound very stable," Maggie said.

I shook my head. "No he wasn't."

"What are you going to do tomorrow morning at the bus stop when you see him? Pretend this never happened?" Viv asked.

I shrugged. "I don't know. I'll figure something out."

But I never had to. When Tessa came off the bus, she told me that Jordan was pulled out of class before lunchtime. The jungle drums sounded quickly, and by the time I was getting ready for my date with Sam Kinali, I got a text from Maggie. She had just left the library and had heard from Carol Anderson that Doug withdrew both boys from school. He told Denise Whitmore, school secretary and Carol's yoga buddy, that he and the boys were going to be staying with Doug's sister, beginning immediately, and for an indefinite amount of time.

Getting ready for a date when you haven't had one since before the existence of the Internet is not nearly as much fun as it sounds, especially when you can't fit into anything that looks even remotely sexy because all the sexy clothes are size ten, and you're not quite there yet. Tessa was of no help, because she didn't think I should be going out at all. Cait viewed the entire operation with ill-concealed amusement.

"It's only a drink, Mom. Or are you expecting something more?"

I tore my eyes from my once-again disappointing image in the mirror and glared at her. "No, I am not expecting anything more. But my generation has a different definition of the word *date*. We don't just accidentally bump into each other and decide to hang out or hook-up or whatever else you Millennials do. We plan ahead and try to make a nice impression."

I pulled off outfit number six, decided a skirt or dress was too fussy anyway, and started hauling out my dress pants. I knew I had black pants from the Gap that I'd bought last winter, but they were actually too big. I found a dark purple tunic I'd had for a couple of years with black embossing around the shoulders and a V-neck, and long flowing sleeves. A little hippy-dippy, but it fell midthigh and hid the fact that the pants were too big and were being held up by a bright green belt.

"You could wear leggings with that," Cait said. She was sprawled on my bed watching. I turned around and looked at myself from the back.

"Women with hips like mine should not be wearing leggings," I muttered. The bulk around my waist was noticeable. Just perfect.

"If you wear them with that shirt, you'll look fine," Cait said.

"I don't own leggings," I told her.

She got off the bed and ran out. I stared at myself unhappily for a few seconds, then undid the pants and let them drop to the floor. I was running out of options as I stepped out of the pants and kicked them to the corner.

Cait came in holding a jumble of black and her cowboy boots. "Here, put these on."

I held up the leggings. "You weigh, like, nothing. These will never fit."

"One size fits all," she insisted.

I sat down and started pulling them on. Yes the leggings were tight, but not uncomfortable. And I could feel where they were packing in all my flabby bits like sausage into a casing. I got up and looked in the mirror again.

"Wow. This might work," I said, surprised.

"Try the boots," she said. Our foot size was the only size we shared. The boots were black with deep gold embellishment, added a few inches to my height, and looked much cooler than I felt.

Cait grinned. "My work here is done. Some gold jewelry, and you'll knock him dead," she said as she walked out.

I looked at myself from the back again. Much better. I found a long gold necklace and some dangly earrings, and decided I looked just fine.

I had told Cait about what had happened with Doug, and although she did not seemed concerned, I did not want my two daughters home alone. On the way out I gave Cait twenty dollars, told her to head to the mall with Tessa, buy something for dinner, and plan on getting home around ten. Tessa's eyes lit up at the prospect of being out so late on a school night, almost distracting her from her disapproval of my date. I kissed them good-bye and drove slowly past the Mitchell house. There were no lights, and the left side of the garage was open and empty. Doug had not returned from wherever he'd taken his sons. Besides, I'd only be gone an hour.

Nicola's was on the other side of Lawrence, a nice Italian bistro with a very comfortable bar and live music on the weekends. I pulled into the parking lot, smoothed my hair, and went inside.

He was waiting for me, which made me smile. He had snagged a booth in the back and was nursing what looked to be a scotch. I slid into the booth and smoothed my hair again. It hadn't rained since the morning, but it was humid, and my hair had a tendency to frizz, even after being doused with Moroccan oil.

"Hi," I said, somewhat breathlessly.

"Hello," he said. "You look lovely." He raised his hand to signal the waitress.

"Thanks," I said. "My daughter is very good at dressing me."

He raised an eyebrow. "The ten-year-old?"

The waitress materialized. "White wine," I said.

She nodded. "Sure. Something to snack on? Would you like to see a menu?"

I would have loved to see a menu and would have probably ordered stuffed potato skins, loaded nachos and fried mac-and-cheese balls.

Luckily, Sam intervened. "Maybe just some spiced almonds, unless you..." he looked over at me, and I shook my head.

"That sounds great," I said to the waitress. She vanished, and I turned my attention back to Sam. "Actually, I also have a twenty-four–year-old. She's the one that contributed to this evening's outfit."

He smiled broadly and nodded. "I see. That must be interesting, two daughters so far apart in age. Are they much alike?"

I shook my head. "Caitlyn, she's the oldest, takes after her father. Redheaded, slender, freckles everywhere. And she's an absolute brain. Tessa looks like me. And she's just your average super-smart kid, which is fine with me. One genius in the family is more than enough."

He drank some scotch. "How long ago were you divorced?"

"Four years. You?"

"Seven." He stopped talking while the waitress set down my wine, then the almonds. "It was hard," he continued. "I did not want my marriage to end. But I could see her point. My job made things very...difficult. Shortly after that, I retired from the force and came out here. Life is much easier for the police here in Lawrence."

I took an almond and nibbled one end. "Speaking of which, did you find anything out? About Lacey Mitchell?"

"Ah," he said. "Yes, I did."

Silence. I sipped some wine. "And?"

"Really now, Ellie, do you think I should be telling you such things?"

"The thing is," I reasoned, "I am the one who came to you, remember? Maybe just a hint?"

He shook his head.

"Oh come on, just one thing, okay? Like, if Doug has ever been, you know, arrested for anything?"

"No, he has never been arrested," Sam said.

I made a face. "Well, I guess since this *is* a date, I'll stop pumping you for information."

He threw back his head and laughed. "Thank you. I'd hate to spend the evening trying to evade your clever and subtle questioning. I'm sure I'd find it exhausting."

I laughed with him. "Yeah, that's me. Clever and subtle."

He looked good. He was wearing a light-weight V-neck sweater over a T-shirt, a look I usually didn't think too much of, but on him...perfect.

"So," he said, "should we spend the next half hour bashing our ex-spouses? I don't have much to say about mine, and I'd much rather talk of other things, but I'll be happy to give you the opportunity." He spoke very carefully.

"Is that how most of your dates start off? Dragging exes through the mud?"

He shrugged. "It happens. Frequently. It seems you women have quite a lot to say about the men in your lives."

I sipped my wine. "That's interesting. I mean, that's what my girlfriends are for. I'd rather spend my time dazzling you with my charm, wit, and boundless sex appeal."

He laughed again. "Excellent. I was hoping you were different. So tell me something else. Did you have a happy childhood?"

"Very. My mom and dad stayed married until he died; my brother and I were very close—still are—and I even had a pony. No trauma, no drama, no secrets. How about you?"

"I was the youngest of six. My parents had no money when they came to this country, just a horde of children and the address of an uncle in Albany. He let us live in his basement until my parents found jobs. Our family's proudest moment was when we moved into our own three-bedroom row house. All of us kids worked; my father had two jobs, and my mother also worked and took care of us all. They never let go of their old ways, but made sure each of their children was one hundred percent American. The name on my original birth certificate is unpronounceable, even to me. My parents changed my name to Sam when they moved here. After Uncle Sam. We became citizens as soon as we could. I loved history, but I was encouraged to study only American history. Turkey's past is long and illustrious, but also filled with much regret." He shrugged. "My father was in the army when he was young. I imagine he did terrible things. That's probably why they left."

I was fascinated. "Did you ever ask them about the past?"

He shrugged. "They wouldn't talk about it, and we never asked. My oldest brother went back to Turkey and lived there for some time, but he eventually returned to the States. If he learned anything while he was there, he never said." He took a long drink. "We were a close and loving family, but there were boundaries. And as children, we learned to respect those boundaries."

I sat back. "It would drive me crazy to think that there was a family history that I didn't know."

He smiled. "It drove me crazy too. It still does. But my parents are still alive, and I will not disrespect them. When they are gone..." he lifted his shoulders, then let them drop. "I am, after all, a detective."

"Have you ever been back to Turkey?"

He shook his head. "One day, I will go. But only when I know that, if I choose, I can stay. I think that once I am there, I will be taken in."

I propped my arm on the table and put my chin in my palm. "Wow."

He raised his eyebrows. "Did you just say wow?"

"Yes. I mean, that's an amazing thing to say. You must know yourself very well."

"Of course. After all, I've lived with myself for a very long time."

"I have too, but I'm still a work in progress. I never know what I'm going to do from one moment to the next." I picked up another almond and examined it closely. "For instance, I never imagined myself asking a man I just met out for a drink."

"Oh? You don't date much?"

"I don't date at all."

He sat back. "Really? But you're an attractive woman. Surely, I'm not the first man in four years to notice?"

I chewed the almond. "Um…ah, well, you see, I work from home, so workplace romance is kind of off the table. Since most of my friends are, you know, married I don't have many opportunities to go trolling for men."

He took it in. "So that is why you don't have anything bad to say about your ex-husband? You're still in love with him?"

I choked on a piece almond and gulped some wine to wash it down. "You really are a detective."

He smiled in response.

"It's complicated," I said. "And you're making it even more so."

"Good. More wine?"

I shook my head. "No, thank you. I'm driving, so I limit myself to one. Besides, I can't stay much longer. I need to get back home."

"Why? Are you worried about something?"

I shook my head but could feel my color rising. I was a terrible liar.

"Why did you ask if Doug Mitchell had ever been arrested? Has he done something that made you think that? Other than lying, that is."

Man, he was good. So again, I tried the truth. "I was just curious. But maybe you should know that he pulled his kids out of school today and shipped them off somewhere."

He frowned. "Really? How do you know this?"

I made a face. "Are you pumping me for information now?"

He shook his head. "No. It's just interesting, that's all."

My wine glass was empty. "My friend, Carol, who works at the library, has a yoga buddy who's the elementary school's secretary. Mt. Abrams is pretty well connected."

"Apparently."

I reached for my purse. "I have to go. I'm sorry. But would you like to do this again?"

"Of course. Next time, a whole dinner?"

I nodded as I got up, and he stood with me. We walked out into the parking lot together, and he waited patiently as I unlocked my car. I felt my heart jump a little.

"Well, thanks."

I could see his smile in the darkness. "You're welcome," he said, and he reached over and drew me towards him. Even with the boots on, I had to stand on my toes, and he bent down to kiss me.

This was not just a pleasant tingle. This was like a jolt of electricity that went right through my boots, into the pavement, and made me grip the fabric of his shirt with both hands. His arms tightened around me, and his strength and heat hit me so hard that when I finally stepped away, I expected to see my clothes fall to the ground in ashes.

"Wow, again," I managed.

"Indeed."

"So, you'll call?" I asked.

"Absolutely."

And I believed him.

There was so much to talk about the next morning that I thought we'd have to walk around the lake twice. Doug had not turned up at the bus stop, and since every mom in Mt. Abrams knew why but didn't want to say anything in front of their children, after the bus left the moms stood in a tight circle, and the speculation ran wild.

I kept my mouth shut. I had a very strong feeling that Doug had run off with his sons because he was frightened of something, and the thought that maybe I was a part of that made me feel queasy. I don't know what he thought I'd done, but somehow, my being in his house set him off.

"Well, you certainly can't blame yourself for any-thing," Shelly said as we trudged up the hill. Boot was walking as far away from the puddles as she could. What a princess.

"We did break into his house," I said. "I mean, nan-ny-cam."

"It's interesting though," Carol said. "He could have called the police. If it was about you being in his house, that's what he should have done. But instead, he went after you himself. Very odd behavior."

"Gee, ya think?" Maggie said. "Ellie was scared to death yesterday. That's beyond odd."

"Actually, Doug was scared to death. I wish I hadn't run away from him. Maybe I could have found out what he was so upset about." I tugged Boot's leash.

The rain had kick started spring. It seemed that everything was a few inches taller than it had been just a few days before. The air smelled clean, and the birds were singing, and aside from the nagging at my conscience about Doug, I felt very happy.

And Shelly, who could read me like a book, decided she couldn't hold it in any longer. "And now I want to hear all about your date. Details, woman. Every last one."

I was smiling. I couldn't help it. "I had a lovely time."

Shelly made a noise that suggested complete and utter disgust. "That is not a detail. That's a non-detail."

We reached the top of the hill and rounded the corner when Maggie stopped short.

"He's back," she said, staring at the Mitchell house, sitting on the other side of the lake.

We all looked. The garage door was down. It was only down when Doug was home. Which meant sometime last night, he had returned without his sons.

"I thought he was staying with the sister too," Shelly muttered as we walked quickly towards the clubhouse.

I almost veered off and went home, but that felt cowardly. Doug and I had both behaved badly, and as much as I would have liked to avoid him for the rest of my life, if he were back, avoidance would be highly improbable. Besides, it wasn't like he was sitting on the front porch, watching us.

"Do you think he's watching us?" Shelly wondered aloud. "Like, from the upstairs window there?"

"Thanks, Shel," I said. "He probably had to get clothes and stuff for the boys."

We hurried along the path for a few minutes, then settled back into our usual pace.

"Okay," Carol said. "You were about to give us a blow by blow of your date with Detective Kinali."

"You first," I said. "Didn't you have coffee with Leon?"

She sniffed. "He has allergies. Coffee tomorrow. Your turn."

I took a breath. "He's very interesting. I like talking to him. We laughed, found a few things in common, I think, and we're having dinner together soon. And we shared a most excellent kiss."

"Then why aren't you doing a happy dance?" Shelly asked.

"I'm a little confused," I said "because of Marc."

Maggie frowned. "What about Marc?"

"Well, he told me he still loved me and that he missed me." I took a few steps before I realized everyone else had stopped in their tracks. I turned, and they were all staring at me. "What?"

"Your ex-husband Marc?" Shelly asked. "That miserable piece of—"

"Now, Shelly," Carol broke in. "It's not entirely uncommon for couples to reconnect."

Shelly whirled to face Carol. "After what he put her through?" She then glared at me. "I hope you told him exactly where he could put *that* idea."

"We never got to talk about it. He kissed me then left."

"Kissed you?" Shelly said, her voice rising about an octave.

"Yes. And it was quite a kiss, let me tell you. If it hadn't been so unexpected, we might well have reenacted our entire honeymoon right there on the living room rug."

She marched forward. "Did you tell him about the hottie?"

"Well," I said, getting in step beside her, "I didn't actually use the word hottie, but I did say I had a date."

"And that's when he kissed you?" she asked.

"Yes." I didn't particularly like where the conversation was headed.

"Hmmm," Shelly said.

I glanced back at Maggie. "What do you think?"

"I'm happily married," she said.

"I'm happily married too," Shelly said. "I'm just older and wiser than you, Maggie. Carol was married forever, and I bet even she's rolling her eyes."

"You must admit," Carol said very carefully, "the timing is suspect. On the bright side, you certainly got enough action this week to keep you going for a while."

We walked the rest of the way around the lake in silence. Although I didn't like to think that Marc would really be the kind of man to mess with my head like that, Carol was right. The timing was, at the very least, suspect.

We were nearing the Mitchell house, and my brain suddenly went off in a completely different direction. "He's still there," I said. "Let's hurry."

We picked up the pace as we walked past the house. I had visions of him bursting out of the front door, screaming. Or maybe he was hiding on the porch and would come up behind me.

"Listen," Maggie said.

We stopped. The house was silent. But there was a quiet rumble coming from the garage.

"What is that?" Carol whispered. "A generator?"

Shelly tightened her grip on Buster's leash and as we walked slowly up the drive. "Does that sound like a car engine to you?" she asked.

"Oh, God," Carol breathed. She ran up to the garage, bent, and pulled the door up and open. Maggie was right behind her.

The smell of exhaust almost knocked us over.

Carol turned, her face white. "Call 911. He's in there."

And then Maggie began to scream.

CHAPTER SIX

W E WERE SITTING ON THE front porch of the
Mitchell house. We might have been four women,
just sitting and enjoying a beautiful spring morning,
but we weren't. We were watching as police cars and
emergency vehicles blocked the road. There was yellow
tape everywhere. We had been asked by the first officer
to arrive to please stay close for questioning.

The whole thing was surreal.

Maggie was still white as a sheet and shaking. Buster
growled at every person who walked by. Carol had
spent twenty minutes on her cell phone finding someone
else to open the library. Shelly left a brief message with
her office, then called her husband Mike and started
crying on the phone.

I felt numb. I was sitting on the porch step, my arm
around Boot's neck, trying not to imagine what was
happening in the garage.

A dark unmarked car pulled up, a flashing light in
the front window, and a very young-looking man in a
dark suit got out of the driver's side.

Sam Kinali got out of the passenger side. He was
wearing sunglasses, so I could only watch as his head
turned to take in the entire scene. Then, his head
stopped turning. He was looking at me.

My arm tightened around Boot, and she whined softly. Carol came down the stairs and walked over to him.

"Oh, thank God, a familiar face," she said. "I'm so glad you're here, Detective Kinali. This is just awful."

He nodded, put his hand on her elbow, and led her back to the porch steps. He took off his glasses and smiled at me. "Are you all right?" he asked.

I nodded several times, but I felt sick to my stomach, guilty and nervous about what he was going to ask, and damn, did he look good in sunglasses.

He reached down, took my hand, and helped me up. Boot growled softly and followed me up the steps and onto the porch.

Carol and I sat down and Sam leaned against the railing. "Ladies, I am Detective Kinali, and this is Detective Monroe. We just need to ask you some questions, and then you'll be free to go."

Detective Monroe took out a pad and pen, looking very serious. Sam smiled.

"Now. Tell me about the morning."

I did not want to be the one to start, so I just huddled further down into the wicker chair, staring at the gray painted floorboards.

Like everything else about the Mitchell house, the porch was picture perfect. A few scattered wicker chairs and Adirondack chairs, painted white, with low scattered tables with potted pansies on them. The perfect place for afternoon lemonade.

"We always walk the same path," Shelly began.

"And you are?" Detective Monroe asked.

Shelly gave her name and phone number, which Detective Monroe copied dutifully. She then turned back to Sam.

"We start at the bottom of the hill after the kids get dropped off from school. We walk across Sommerfield to Morris, take Morris to Davis, and basically crisscross every hill we can until we get up here. We come in from the other side." She pointed to the clubhouse.

"Then we walk around the lake and end up back where we started by the clubhouse. Then we all go our own way home."

Sam looked at the clubhouse, then to the other side of the lake. "How long does it take you?"

"It depends," Carol said. "Usually forty-five minutes to an hour. The hills are steep, and we don't rush. Sometimes the dogs slow us down. If it's cold or looks like rain, we go faster."

Sam nodded. "Fine. So today, was anything different?"

We all glanced quickly at each other.

"Well, we knew that Doug had pulled the kids out of school and had told the secretary he was staying at his sisters," Maggie said.

"And how did you know this?" Sam asked, not looking at me.

"Excuse me," Detective Monroe said. "Your name?"

Sam waited patiently, then smiled at Maggie. "Go on."

Maggie looked embarrassed. "Mt. Abrams is a very small community," she said. "Everyone knows pretty much everything that's going on. The secretary at the school is a friend of Carol's, and Carol told me, and well, once I get hold of information…" She blushed. "I have a big mouth."

"Perhaps," Sam said graciously. "Go on."

"Yeah, well, we knew he had taken the boys, so we were kinda surprised that he was home."

"And how did you know he was home?" Sam asked. "Did you knock on the door to speak with him?"

"No," I said. I cleared my throat. "See, the garage doesn't open by itself. You have to get out and pull up the doors. I know, because my garage is the same. When Doug and Lacey went anywhere, they'd leave the doors open so they could just pull in when they returned. So, if the garage doors were closed, they were home."

"And this morning" Sam said, "they were closed."

We nodded.

"So you were walking past, and what, you heard the engine?" His eyes were on me now, and I nodded.

"It gets real quiet up here if there's no one around," I told him. "We weren't talking, so we heard it. At first, Carol thought it was a generator. Then we went up the driveway and realized it was the car, and Carol lifted the door..."

He lifted an eyebrow. "You weren't talking?" he said with a faint smile.

I smiled back. "It can happen."

He nodded. "Did you try to resuscitate the body?"

The body. I swallowed hard.

"No," Carol said. "I looked in the window. He was gone. I could...tell." Her voice cracked just a little.

Sam looked back to the clubhouse, straightened, and turned around. "Stay here," he said as he walked away.

Detective Monroe followed him around the house to the garage.

I took a deep breath. "I have to tell him about Doug and the car and how he grabbed me, and what he said. It might be important."

"You're absolutely right," Maggie said. "Even if we get arrested for breaking into the house."

"We did not," Shelly said, "break in anywhere. The door was wide open. And I agree. Hottie needs to know."

"Can we not," I whispered, "refer to him as *hottie* right now?"

We sat a few minutes more. Buster had fallen asleep, but Boot was restless and kept tugging at the leash and occasionally barking at passersby. And there were a lot of those. In fact, a tiny audience stood front of the

Mitchell house, pointing at the four of us and whispering. Kate Fisher was there, and Mary Rose Reed was whispering furiously in her ear, probably giving Kate the entire Mitchell history. Kate kept her eyes on the garage.

"Boy," Maggie muttered, "the jungle drums are going to have a field day with this one."

"I wonder why he did it," Shelly said suddenly. "It doesn't make sense for Doug to kill himself. I always thought he was crazy about those boys. Unless he did kill Lacey and was scared he'd get caught."

"He was scared all right," I said. "But I don't think of getting caught."

Boot growled again, and Sam and Detective Monroe came around the corner and up on the porch. My yellow slicker was in Detective Monroe's hand. Sam looked at me.

"This was found," he said softly, "in the backseat of the car. There's a credit card receipt in the pocket, a few weeks old, for a place called Ezekiel's Tavern. A receipt with your name on it, Ellie. Is there someplace we can go and have a little talk?"

I stood up and nodded. "I live right over there. I'll make us all some coffee." I walked off the porch and past Sam, tugging at Boot's leash.

We sat in the kitchen, of course. Detective Monroe took his coffee black, Sam with milk but no sugar. I sat across from Sam at the table. Carol asked to go down to the library, and Sam gave his permission. Shelly and Maggie were with me, hovering by the refrigerator.

"So, Ellie, what is it you want to tell me?"

Everything. I told him everything, about going into the house and finding her clothes gone, about the video camera, about Doug giving me a lift the morning before. Sam sat quietly, his hands folded, listening intently. Detective Monroe took notes. Sam just watched me with fierce concentration.

When I finally stopped talking, I took a long, uneven breath. "I would have told you this all last night," I said, "but I didn't want to get anyone in trouble. And I didn't think Doug would kill himself."

Detective Monroe looked up from his notebook. "What? What happened last night?"

Sam didn't take his eyes off my face. "Ms. Rocca and I had a drink last night. Purely social, John. Nothing at all to do with this case." He finally looked away and turned to John. "Have them look for that video camera. And check to see if any other cameras were hidden in the house. As soon as the sister has been notified, let me know. We need to speak to her ASAP. Have Mike treat this as a suspicious death. Don't just assume suicide."

Detective Monroe stood, fished his cell phone out of his pocket, and walked out onto the back porch.

I leaned forward across the table. "Suspicious death?"

Sam met my eye. He paused for a minute, thinking, then spoke. "Douglas Mitchell was a man afraid of something. So much so that he moved his children to what I imagine he felt was a safer place. And then he killed himself? Does that make sense to you?"

I shook my head. "No, I guess not. But what if he thought he was going to get caught for killing Lacey?"

He shook his head. "You're back to that? Why would he kill her?"

"For five million dollars?" I said.

Shelly spoke up. "It's the only motive for him killing himself that makes sense. If she just left with the money, why would he do it?"

He nodded. "That's true. I made a call after you came to see me, Ellie. Lacey and Doug both inherited. The boys received a million each in trust. The rest was evenly divided between husband and wife." He shrugged. "It was still a sizable amount for both of them. And here's the thing. Their joint account was emptied yesterday. All the money, and there was quite a bit, believe me, was transferred to an off-shore account."

We sat, letting that sink in.

"So, one of them wanted it all," I said.

Sam nodded. "Apparently."

"It couldn't have been Doug," I said.

"Why not?" Sam asked.

"Because the only explanation for Doug saying what he said yesterday is that he gave Lacey his share of the money, but she wanted something more," I said.

Sam nodded. "True."

"How did Lacey's father die?" Shelly asked.

Sam glanced at her. "He was a diabetic. The apparent cause of death was an insulin overdose. By the time 911 was called and he was taken to the hospital, nothing could be done."

Maggie and Shelly both came forward, grabbed chairs, and sat.

"Very Sunny Von Bulow," Shelly said.

Sam, clearly amused, nodded. "Yes."

"Was he alone? When he overdosed, I mean?" Maggie asked.

"No," Sam answered. "His wife, Millicent, was with him."

"Wait," I said excitedly. "I thought we decided she was no longer in the picture."

He threw back his head and laughed. "We? Who's this we?"

Detective Monroe returned. "Detective Kinali?"

Sam pushed away from the table and stood. "Ladies, thank you for all your assistance. We'll put a call out for Lacey's car. She is a person of interest. If nothing else, we need to inform her of her husband's death. We'll find her. We usually do." He smiled down at me and left.

Shelly exhaled loudly. "Lacey is the bad guy. Who knew? I feel so bad now, for thinking all those terrible things about Doug." She shook her head sadly. "Those poor little boys."

"I know," I said. "That's really creepy to think that Lacey came back here and did this."

Maggie shuddered. "Don't say that. I won't be able to sleep as it is. But I gotta say, that is one sexy man."

I grinned. "I know. He's nice too, and interesting to talk to." Something hit me, and I stopped grinning. "Did Millicent kill him?"

"Who? Lacey's father?" Shelly waved a hand. "Why would she? *She* wasn't getting any money."

"Maybe she didn't know that," I said. "Maybe she *thought* she was getting all the money."

"Did she kill Lacey?" Maggie asked.

Shelly looked disgusted. "If Lacey had been killed, don't you think Doug would have gone to the police? Instead of lying to us? No, I think Lacey lit out of here on her own, then came back and killed Doug."

"But why?" I asked. "She already got everything."

We sat there in silence until we heard the sound of a siren. We got up and went to the front door in time to see an ambulance pull out of the Mitchells' driveway.

Good-bye, Doug.

CHAPTER SEVEN

WHEN MT. ABRAMS WAS STILL a baby, rather than a full-grown community, a small town center had gone up, consisting of a post office, a firehouse, and a large public park called, in a complete stroke of originality, Main Park. It was right below Elliot Street, where Josiah had built the second wave of homes. I lived on Abrams Lane at the very top of the hill, and farther from the lake than the Mitchells lived. While the clubhouse was the social hub of the community during the summer, this little bit of quaintness was the year-round center for gathering information, real or imagined.

Over the years, they built a library in Main Park, right where Sommerfield Drive split Main Park in two. The post office was modernized, but the firehouse was deemed too small and inadequate. So a modern firehouse was built along State Road 51, and the original firehouse became the community hall. The Mount Abrams Homeowners Association met there, as well as the Garden Club, Historical Society, a few Girl Scout troops, one church group, Weight Watchers, and a local crafting club. Two book clubs also met there, so as not to crowd out the library. For a 120-year-old building with undependable heat, no air conditioner, and anti-quated toilets, it was a pretty happening spot.

I could actually see the roof of the old firehouse from my back kitchen window and probably looked at it a dozen times every day, but I had forgotten all about the Garden Club until I got a text from Lynn Fahey around five o'clock.

C U at Garden Club 7:30

I texted back.

Maybe not. Doug Mitchell killed self. I found him.

Lynn was quick to respond.

OMG! Terrible. R u guarding the body or something?

I stared at her text.

NO. Happened this am.

Then you can still come

Ah Lynn, the soul of compassion and empathy. I texted her back that I'd be there, then texted Shelly and Maggie, and guilted them into meeting me. Cait was working, so Tessa grudgingly agreed to come with me, promising to sit quietly in a corner and read.

The meeting was not what I needed. I felt physically exhausted and emotionally drained. Doug had killed himself. Or Lacey killed him. Either way, I felt right in the middle of it all, and it was not a pleasant place to be.

Shelly and her husband Mike were already seated when Tessa and I got there. The place was packed. I handed over my fivedollar membership fee and got my official Garden Club card. I spotted Maggie and Viv in the back row. I pushed Tessa towards the small alcove where she could sit and read her book, and then started back towards Maggie, but Kate Fisher suddenly popped up.

"I saw you this morning," she said breathlessly. "You all found him?"

I did not want to talk about Doug and this morning, least of all to Kate. I looked at her.

She was at least sixty, I guessed, with pale hair fading to gray. She was fairly tall and slender, attractive, with blue eyes and an open, easy smile. I could have liked her, if only she'd have kept her mouth shut every once in a while.

"I was there, of course," she went on. "Watching with everyone else. How horrible. They're all saying that you heard the car engine running? It's almost like God sent you to find him. I didn't know them at all, of course, but how tragic. Two little boys, right? And Mrs. Mitchell? Just gone? You talked to the police afterward, didn't you? Did they say anything about finding the poor wife?"

She paused for breath, so I jumped in. "No, Kate, the police didn't say anything about Lacey." Not that I would have told *her* anything if they had.

"That beautiful house, that beautiful family, destroyed by one selfish act. Oh, my heart bleeds, it really does. And to think it happened right here, in quiet Mt. Abrams. You know, when I found this house up here, Paul, you know Paul Malone, my landlord? Well Paul told me that this was the perfect place to live, safe and peaceful. Who knew that something like this could happen? I guess it was lucky the little boys weren't there. Could you imagine? What will become of them now? All that money can't bring their parents back. Poor little lambs."

She had wound down again, so I nodded, murmured something appropriate, and backed away. I hurried to sit with Maggie and Viv.

Maggie was grinning. "Get an earful?"

"Lord, that woman can run her mouth," I whispered. I looked around. "Who are all these people? I don't recognize half of them."

Viv started pointing fingers and naming names. At least a dozen new faces had moved into Mt. Abrams in the past two years, and Viv had handled their transactions. They were mostly younger couples with no children, drawn to Mt. Abrams by its proximity to the train and lower tax rates.

"How did Lynn track them all down?" I asked.

Maggie made a face. "Maybe these are Mary Rose's people."

"No, this is all Lynn's doing," Viv said. "That woman could lead a priest into a whorehouse."

I stared at Viv. "Is that a real saying?"

She made a face. "It is for me."

The meeting started out in a rather orderly fashion, welcoming all the new members (we had to stand up and introduce ourselves) going over the minutes, and handing out the agenda. The library paver question was the fifth item down under Old Business.

"You mean we gotta sit through all this?" Viv groused. "I wanted to just vote and go."

Maggie shushed her. She had lived in Brooklyn her whole life, and found small-town machinations fascinating.

"I mean seriously, what four other things could these people be talking about?" Viv continued. "Mt. Abrams isn't that big."

"Viv," I said, "did you happen to notice when that power of attorney was dated?"

She frowned for a moment. "You're talking about Doug Mitchell? I think it was just the day or two before."

"And it had to be notarized, right?"

She nodded.

There was something stuck in my brain, something that wasn't making sense. "When did he call about putting the house on the market?"

"That Friday. Right after lunch. Why?"

Maggie turned away from Mary Rose, who was standing at the podium arguing about peat moss, and nudged me with her foot.

"What are you thinking?" she asked.

"Okay," I said slowly, thinking aloud. "That power of attorney, he could not have gotten it without her signing as well, right?"

Viv nodded. "That's right. It has to be signed by both parties in the presence of the notary."

"So they were in it together. They had to be. So something must have happened, and they *both* decided to sell the house." I suddenly realized something. "And the bank account. Sam said it had been emptied. They both needed to do that, too." I looked at Maggie. "Do you remember if she seemed different Friday when she got the boys? Think, Maggie. Like she knew she was going to have to leave them?"

Maggie frowned. "I don't know, Ellie. She never seemed excited or upset or very emotional about anything. But nothing struck me funny about Friday afternoon."

The gavel banged, and we all looked to the front of the hall. Mary Rose had raised her voice. Next item— the pavers for the library park.

Mary Rose was a throwback. Her hair was bluish silver and permed, and she dressed in a pantsuit with matching accessories to walk around the block. She had been running the Garden Club for years and grew peonies in her tiny back yard. Until Lynn Fahey had started disagreeing with her, she had pretty much been responsible for every tree, bush, and flower planted in Mt. Abrams. Seven years ago, Lynn suggested that the Garden Club had no right to tell people what they could and could not grow in their own yards, and if Beverly Sutter wanted to plant bamboo, she should plant bamboo, even if it wasn't in keeping with the general look of the community. Lynn and Mary Rose had been at war ever since.

Mary Rose presented a very compelling case. According to her, even a rise in humidity caused the area around the picnic table to become a muddy disaster. Not only would pavers keep the area cleaner, it would visually broaden the walkway and mean less maintenance for Craig, our grounds manager, in that he would not have to move the tables when he mowed the grass. Mary Rose was an excellent speaker, and I found myself nodding in agreement with everything she said.

Then Lynn got up, pointing out that the walkway was already five feet wide, how could there be grass under the picnic tables if Mary Rose kept insisting the area was a dust bowl, and that Craig was *paid* to move the picnic tables when he mowed, so what was the big frigging deal? She then launched into her Death By Rock Salt argument.

Mary Rose did not take it well. New members asked to be recognized, and the discussion seemed pretty fairly divided.

My mind was on other things. "Viv, who notarized Doug's POA? Do you remember?"

Viv nodded. "Sure. It was Mary Rose. She's the only notary in town. You gonna talk to her?"

I nodded. "Yes. Maybe they said something to her. I don't know."

Maggie frowned. "Why is this bothering you so much?" she asked.

"Because I feel like if I had talked to Doug, tried to make sense of what he was saying, I could have helped in some way," I said.

Viv shook her head. "Don't even start thinkin' like that. If Doug chose to kill himself, it had nothing to do with you. If Lacey killed him, it also had nothing to do with you. If anything, Doug took those boys and put them in a safe place because of you. Think about that."

Voices were starting to get louder, so I tried to pay attention. As with all small groups run by people with either big egos or plagued by self-esteem issues, *Roberts Rules of Order* were quickly replaced with name calling and general mayhem. Emma McLaren, self-appointed witch of Mt. Abrams, started telling everyone that the very earth beneath the library had a life of its own and needed to breathe. That was apparently the last straw, because someone finally stood up, and yelling over the raised voices, made a motion that pavers be put down in the library park. I jumped up and seconded the motion.

Mary Rose and Lynn were clearly not through tearing each other's eyes out, but there was a motion on the floor, and they had to shut up. By a show of hands, the motion was clearly defeated. The hydrangeas were safe for another year.

We did not stay for the aftermath. I stood up, motioned to Tessa, and we scurried out of there, followed by Maggie and Viv.

We stood on the street, Tessa and I headed in one direction, Viv and Maggie going down the hill.

"Are you going to talk to Mary Rose?" Maggie asked.

I nodded. "Tomorrow. Come with?"

"You bet," Maggie said, and started walking.

"Can I come too?" Viv called.

"Sure," I answered back.

"That was boring," Tessa said. "This is a boring place to live."

I grabbed her little hand and squeezed it. "Not anymore, baby. Not anymore."

Mary Rose lived in one of the ranch houses that had been built in the fifties, down the hill and closer to Route 51. It was below Sommerfield Drive which was the dividing line between old and new Mt. Abrams.

Among the old guard of Mt. Abrams, living in the new section meant you lacked a certain status, but it also meant you had a real yard, a garage, and an electrical system that could be counted on in all weather conditions.

Mary Rose's yard looked like a cover for *Better Homes and Gardens*. There were daffodils and all sorts of bulbs popping up everywhere, bushes were budding, the Japanese maple was leafing out, and there were no stray leaves or bits of branch to spoil the green sweep of her lawn.

"How does she keep this so clean?" Maggie muttered.

"I don't think she has much else to do," I answered.

Mary Rose opened the door at our knock but did not look particularly pleased to see us. I didn't think she would have been able to see us last night, all the way in the back row, but she did not greet us as fellow paver-lovers.

"Yes? Can I help you with something?" She was dressed in a skirt, blouse, hose, and heels. Her clip-on earrings matched her pin. At nine in the morning. Maggie and I had come straight from our walk, dropped off Boot and picked up Viv, and were still slightly sweaty and disheveled.

"Hi, Mary Rose," I said, smiling. "I know this is going to sound odd, but can I talk to you about Lacey and Doug Mitchell?"

Immediately, her entire demeanor changed. She opened the door, her eyes bright. "Come in, please. I have coffee on."

Her house was immaculate, frozen in the eighties, and there were plastic runners covering the beige wall-to-wall carpet. We followed her into her kitchen, and sat at her round maple table, in matching captain's chairs.

"I must say," she said as she took coffee cups and saucers from the cabinet, "I was quite surprised to see you at the Garden Club meeting last night, Ellie." Having walked past my yard, she was perfectly justified in saying that.

"Yes. Well, Cait may be going to France, and since she's the one who usually looks after the garden, I thought I should maybe get some help." I stumbled over the lie, of course, but Mary Rose didn't seem to notice.

"You have a garden?" she asked. I was so used to drinking coffee from either a mug or a Starbucks takeaway cup that the shallow cup and matching saucer looked antique.

"Sort of. Like I said, I'm going to try to work a little harder at it."

"And you, Maggie?" Mary Rose poured coffee from a Corning Ware coffee pot, pristine white and embellished with a single blue flower. I had never seen one in real life, except at garage sales and thrift stores.

Another legitimate question. Maggie lived in one of the converted summer cottages, long and narrow with roughly twelve inches of yard between her front porch and the curb. Those twelve inches were planted with hostas. The space between her house and the houses on the other side was so narrow that simple pavers had been laid down, creating a dark path barely wide enough to get through. Her back yard consisted of a small deck and two parking spaces.

But Maggie had no qualms about her motives. "I just came to support Lynn. I'm a hydrangea lover."

Viv smiled. "Me too."

Mary Rose sniffed and put the coffee pot back on the stove, giving us her back a little longer than was probably necessary.

She sat with us. "Yes. Well, what were you saying? About the Mitchells? I saw you there yesterday morning, Ellie. You too, Maggie. It must have been awful."

I nodded. "Yes. But I want to ask you about the power of attorney you notarized for them last week."

She took a long sip of coffee and looked thoughtful. "They came to my door just as Fred was coming back, so that was about ten o'clock." Fred was her husband, who every morning, no matter what the weather, walked from Mt. Abrams to the CVS way down on Route 51. It was said you could set your clock by his coming and going, so if Mary Rose said ten o'clock, you could bet she was dead on.

"They were very nervous. Apparently, she had printed off the form on the computer, and they were very anxious to have it notarized," Mary Rose said.

"Excited nervous or scared nervous?" I asked.

Mary Rose narrowed her eyes and thought hard. "Scared. He was scared. In fact, at one point, she put her arms around him, to comfort him. She kept telling him it would be fine."

"What would be fine?" Maggie asked.

Mary Rose lifted her shoulders, then let them drop. "I have no idea. They were very secretive people, you know. I don't think anyone really knew them. I'd invited them to join Garden Club, of course, but Lacey said they weren't joiners." She raised her eyebrows. "Did you know anything about them?"

Viv shook her head. "I sold them the house three years ago, and signed the contract to sell it again, and I don't even think I exchanged ten words with them in between."

"They were not," Mary Rose said, "very good neighbors."

"Was she scared as well?" I asked.

Mary Rose shook her head. "Not so much. In fact, she was in control of the situation. She had the paperwork, had filled in most of it before they got here, and told him where to sign. She seemed in a hurry."

Maggie looked at me. "They sign the power of attorney, call Viv, then what? Why was she in a hurry?"

I had been watching Mary Rose, and she leaned forward. "What do you ladies know that the rest of us don't?"

"Nothing," I said. I stood up. "Thank you, Mary Rose. For the coffee and information."

She got up in a hurry. "Ellie, wait now. What's going on?"

"Nothing, Mary Rose. Honestly. We were just curious about what happened that might have caused Lacey to leave so suddenly."

Mary Rose folded her arms across her chest. "Leave? Who said she left? I'm betting Lacey disappeared because her husband killed her, and then killed himself out of guilt."

I made my way to the front door. "You're probably right. Thank you, Mary Rose."

We hurried down her walk and up the street.

"So, what are we thinking?" Maggie asked.

"I'm thinking that we need to know what happened after the boys got picked up by the bus. Between then and ten, they saw something or heard something that shook them up," I said.

"Or not," Viv said. "Maybe he made it all up. Maybe he did it just to get her to sign, so he could kill her."

"Or maybe *she* made it up so she had an excuse to get the hell outta Dodge," Maggie said.

"But when he was talking to me, he said something like he didn't know she had made friends. That she was using me. If he wasn't talking about Lacey, who else could it have been?" I asked. The more I thought about what had happened, the more confused I got.

"Well, since it's easier to find out if something did happen than if something didn't, where should we start looking?" Maggie asked.

"Oh girl," Viv said. "You have to ask? The post office."

"I have to see my mother this morning," I said. "Do you think—"

Viv grinned. "Leave this to us, Ellie. We've got this covered."

CHAPTER EIGHT

M Y MOTHER'S ASSISTED LIVING FACILITY nestled at the foot of a gently rolling hillside in Sussex County. It was an old mansion that had been carefully converted, added on to, improved, and improved again until it met all the state safety standards, yet still managed to look like a very rich person's gracious country estate. Mom had a room on the second floor. Large and sunny, she had a narrow bed, all her books and pictures, her phone chair and a small television. In the bay window was her dresser and another chair, and that's where I sat, every Friday before going down to have lunch.

We had once been able to go out for lunch, but last year she went to the ladies room at a local Panera, wandered past where we were sitting, out the door, and was found three hours later, sitting in the middle of the freezer aisle of a Pathmark almost a mile away.

Now, we had lunch in the common dining room, which was not a bad thing. Aside from the excellent food, the other residents were more or less delightful characters who put on a never-ending floorshow for their guests.

We sat at a table next to the nimble-fingered Justine Caldwell, who barely had the strength to hold her fork. My mother kept glaring at the poor woman, who, since she was fairly deaf, just smiled and nodded. After lunch we walked around the grounds for about half an hour before going back inside and upstairs. My mother became agitated, as she often did when she sensed my visit coming to a close.

"Justine is taking all my Agatha Christies," she muttered.

"Mom, how is she even getting up the stairs?" I asked.

My mother sat in her phone chair, rocking back and forth. She was still a lovely woman, her thick hair almost completely gray, her big, dark eyes angry and confused. I had inherited her creamy skin and thick, perfectly shaped eyebrows, for which I will be eternally grateful, as well as her stubby fingers and love of eating, for which I was not so grateful. Now, I could feel her irritation growing. Sometimes I just kissed her good-bye and she'd smile happily. Lately though, our partings were getting harder.

"And I don't know why I can't just live with you. I know Marc wouldn't mind."

"Mom, you need to be with somebody all the time now. You know that. I can't watch you. I have to work."

"You work from home," she whined.

"Yes, until I'm off at a conference or a festival or meeting with a client somewhere," I said. My arguments didn't matter to her. She'd heard them all before. She just didn't remember them.

"This is a terrible place. They do bad things here."

"No, Mom, they don't. You love it here."

"And the food is awful. Gruel."

I sighed and picked up my purse. One of the aides, Liz, poked her head in. "Leona," she called loudly, "we're getting ready for cards downstairs. You want to come with me?"

My mother's head snapped around. "Yes. Yes, I love cards." She waved in my direction as she got up. "See you tomorrow, Ellie. Give your babies a kiss for me."

I smiled gratefully at Liz, who took my mother's arm and led her out of the room.

I sat there for a few minutes more. My high school graduation picture was on one of her shelves. I looked at it closely. I was a very pretty girl back then, pretty enough to have had lots of young men offer me beer and pot and sex. In the spirit of the seventies, which was when I had come of age, I took many of them up on their offers.

That was then. This was now. I closed the door behind me when I left my mother's room.

Sam Kinali called while I was walking down to get Tessa at the bus stop.

"How are you?" he asked, like he actually meant it.

"I'm fine. What have you found out?"

"I'm fine too, thanks for asking," he said, laughter in his voice. "I realize it's short notice, but can I take you out for dinner this evening?"

"Cait is working, and on a Friday night on such short notice, getting a sitter for Tessa might be tough." I tried to remember what was in my freezer besides Smart Ones frozen meals, sugar-free ice pops and Cait's chicken potpies. "How do you feel about spaghetti and meatballs?"

"Two of my favorite things."

"I have homemade sauce, and I'll get some salad. About seven?"

"I'll bring wine and dessert," he said, and hung up.

Damn. Dessert.

Tessa and I made a quick run through Stop and Shop, and only spent one hundred and forty seven dollars. That little girl grabbed everything her little arms could reach. When we got home, I pulled the sauce and meatballs out of the freezer, put away everything but the salad fixings and the box of pasta, and quickly dusted the dining room. The girls and I ate in the kitchen, and the weekly housekeeping routine tended to be a little lax.

Cait came down, dressed for work, halfway through the process. "You're dusting? Are we expecting the queen?"

"No. Sam Kinali."

"Do you like him?"

"Do you like Kyle Lieberman?"

"Fair enough," she said, and left without further comment.

The sauce was still frozen when I threw it in the pot, but by ten to seven, it was bubbling gently, and the house smelled amazing. It had been my mother's recipe, and every time I made it I remembered Sunday dinners when my father was alive, and he and my mother were still in love after thirty years.

"Why are we having the policeman over to dinner?" Tessa finally got around to asking. "And why did you change? Is this a date?"

"No," I lied. I did not want Tessa to start getting attached to anyone, or think that I was. "But after we eat, you are going to excuse yourself from the table and go upstairs and watch TV up in the spare room. We may be discussing grown-up things."

"Like that dead Mr. Mitchell?"

I nodded. "Maybe."

"Is there a mad killer on the loose in Mt. Abrams?"

I shook my head. "No, there is not. And if there was, we have the worlds most protective dog to scare anyone away, right?"

She nodded. "Can I bring popcorn?"

"Yes."

"And Oreos?"

"No. Just popcorn. And if you don't behave, I'll return the Oreos and all the other junk you bought today. Understand?"

She nodded.

The doorbell rang exactly at seven. I hurried to answer, opening the door to find Maggie and Viv standing there, looking excited and each holding a bottle of wine.

"What are you doing here?" I asked, trying not to look disappointed.

"Don't you want to hear what we found out today about Lacey Mitchell?" Maggie asked.

Before I could answer, I saw Sam Kinali step up on the porch behind them. He had a bottle of wine in one hand, and what looked to be a bakery box in the other. "I'd love to," he said.

Viv turned around and immediately got it. "Come on, Maggie, we'll come back another time."

Maggie, however, missed all the clues. "Detective Kinali, what luck. We found some very interesting things out today. They might help your case."

My shoulders slumped as Viv poked Maggie with her elbow. "No, Maggie. Let's take our wine to Shelly's house. We'll talk to Ellie later."

"Please, ladies. Don't let me run you off," Sam said, his eyes dancing. "I find all this amateur sleuthing very entertaining. Unless, Ellie, dinner is ready right this minute?"

He was something else. "No. I haven't even put the pasta on," I said. "But it's a beautiful night, let's stay out here on the porch. I'll get glasses and a corkscrew."

"Here," Sam said, openly grinning now. I recognized the box. Pirelli's Bakery. I knew Pirelli's. They made things filled with sugar and cream and candied fruits.

I was doomed.

They were all laughing quite companionably when I went back out on the porch, holding a tray of glasses and a bowl of pita chips. Sam was enjoying himself very much. Viv rolled her eyes apologetically and grabbed the corkscrew, opening her bottle of wine. She poured, and we all drank. I introduced Sam and Viv, but they already seemed like fast friends.

The evening was starting to cool off, but the air smelled fresh and clean, with the faint scent of lilacs, and it was still light. I looked out towards the lake, and of course, the Mitchell house. There was still yellow crime scene tape everywhere.

Sam snagged a pita chip and motioned towards Maggie. "So tell us, what did you find out?"

Maggie cleared her throat. "Well, we talked to Joanie. Joan Dudley, down at the post office. That's kind of the information hub out here, if you know what I mean."

Joan was something over seventy, and had been postmistress for fifty years. She heard every single word that was spoken in the post office, even if it wasn't spoken to her. We often joked that if she could, she'd have tables and chairs in the lobby so that people could sit down and gossip longer. As it was, she pretty much knew everything that was going on in town.

"Lacey came in every morning at the same time," Maggie went on. "I guess right after she came up from the bus stop. Joanie said that she was always polite, never chatted, and didn't get a lot of junk mail. She also said that Doug brought the boys in every Saturday, and that he was much friendlier, but still not much for idle chitchat." She leaned confidentially towards Sam. "Joanie lives for idle chitchat."

Sam nodded encouragingly. "I see."

"Anyway, Joanie noticed that Lacey had a postcard from the library, the ones they send to tell you a book you've reserved has come in, so she thought that's where Lacey went next. So we went there as well."

Sam drank some wine. "And?"

Viv took over. "Carol said that yes, Lacey was there Friday morning. And she did pick up a book. But then something weird happened. Kate Fisher and Lynn Fahey were talking about something, probably the damn Garden Club, and Carol said that Lacey just kind of froze and listened. Kate has a big mouth, just so you know. Not only does she talk a lot, but she's loud. Whatever Lacey heard, Carol said she turned white and practically ran out of the library."

Sam's eyes narrowed. "Really? And Carol—this is Carol Anderson, yes?—didn't remember what the conversation was about?"

Maggie and Viv both shook their heads.

"We were going to Carol's tonight and ask her," Viv said, "but she's got a hot date as well."

Sam grinned, and I gulped my entire glass of wine.

Viv stood up. "Well, hate to leave, but we'll take our bottle here and go tell Shelly what we've learned. Maybe we can all talk to Carol tomorrow, Ellie?"

I stood up, and so did Sam.

"Great idea," I said.

"It was a real pleasure talking to you ladies," Sam said, bowing graciously. Maggie giggled as she and Viv walked off into the evening.

Sam and I settled back down. My solar lights went on. My front porch wasn't as neat and chic as the Mitchells porch. My furniture was older and a bit creaky, but I had painted it all last year, and the cushions had been dusted off. If was cozy and comfortable, and with the view of the lake, it was one of my favorite places on earth.

"This must be a good life for you." Sam said softly. "I can smell your spaghetti sauce from here. Good food, a beautiful lake, and friends who come by with wine."

"Yes," I said. "I'm very lucky. This is a good place to live. I'll put on the pasta. I'll be right back."

Inside the house, I turned up the water for the pasta, lit a few candles, and turned on some music. Tessa made a face at me from her reading chair in the living room, and I stuck my tongue out at her as I went by.

Boot followed me back on the porch. She growled softly at Sam, who patted her on the head and behind her ears, making them friends for life. She hopped up on a chair and sat back, ready to join the conversation.

"I suppose it's terribly unprofessional to talk about an active case?" I asked.

Sam nodded. "It is indeed. But Lawrence isn't too strict about things. The preliminary autopsy shows that Doug Mitchell may have been injected with something prior to his death by asphyxiation. There were no signs of struggle or any other trauma, which indicates he sat there quietly in the car until he passed out. We have to wait for toxicology reports before we can determine what, if anything, was in his system. That will determine whether he either did, in fact, kill himself, or if he was drugged and murdered."

"When will you know for sure?"

"Hopefully by tomorrow. In the mean time, we're looking for Lacey."

"She's a suspect?"

He shifted in his seat. "When a person is murdered, the spouse always gets looked at very closely."

I nodded. A few cars had gone by, and the clubhouse on the lake suddenly lit up.

"What's going on there?" Sam asked.

"That's the lake clubhouse. Every Mother's Day, the Historical Society holds a brunch, a fundraiser for

Founder's Day Weekend. They're over there now, starting to get ready."

"That sounds nice."

"It is. I take my mom every year. The food is good; it's lots of fun for my girls, and you can't beat eating out by the lake on a beautiful spring morning." I stood up. "Ready for dinner?"

We went inside. Tessa was solemn and polite. The dinner was delicious. Sam and I finished the second bottle of wine, and inside the bakery box were perfect little butter cookies that melted in your mouth, and after months of sugar depravation, may have been the best tasting cookies ever. I made espresso, and Sam and I sat at the dining room table, talking and laughing, and when he left, he gave me a goodnight kiss that did more than send electricity to my toes—it sent all sorts of other feelings to all sorts of other parts of my body. This was a man who really knew his way around a woman, and I was pretty sure I wanted him to get to know mine a lot better, and the sooner the better.

It wasn't until I was going to bed that I saw the text from Marc. Asking about Sunday, with a little heart emoji at the end.

CHAPTER NINE

S HELLY CALLED ME FIRST THING Saturday morning.
"How was your dinner? Viv and Maggie came over from your place last night, and we drank ourselves silly."

"My date was terrific. Really. He is a lovely man, and we talked forever, and I had pasta and butter cookies. Pretty much the perfect night."

"Great," she said. "When are we going to talk to Carol?"

The library closed at one on Saturdays, so Shelly and I met up with Carol as she was locking up. She saw us and rolled her eyes.

"Are you here to torment me about the Friday Lacey Mitchell was in the library?"

We fell into step beside her. "Yes," I said. "But first tell us about Leon."

Her eyes lit up. "He's nice," she said. "Almost seventy, widowed for twelve years, golfs three times a week, and thinks John Updike is overrated. We had quite a bit in common and agreed to have a longer date next week. Possibly even dinner." She glanced sideways at me. "And I hear you had some company?"

I nodded. "Yes. Sam Kinali and I are getting along very well, thank you very much, although we did not discuss Updike."

Carol sighed. "Do find out what he reads, Ellie. How else will you know what kind of person he really is?"

"She will," Shelly broke in. "Now what about Lacey?"

Carol lived on Sommerfield in a 1920s Craftsman with lots of beams and a deep porch. We climbed the steps and sat down on weathered teak chairs.

"Can I get you anything?" she asked, and when we nodded, she closed her eyes and took a couple of deep breaths. "She had reserved the Cleopatra biography that came out a number of years ago. I had it brought in from another branch. She checked out the book, and we were standing at the desk, talking about it, when suddenly Kate Fisher laughed very loudly about something; you know how she can be." Carol frowned. "I think Kate and Lynn had been over by the computers in the back, and they were walking towards the front. Lynn was not, I don't think, talking about those stupid pavers. It was something about Mother's Day. The brunch."

She sat up, and her face changed. "Yes. She wanted Kate to help with the brunch, and Kate said something about her own daughter living in California. She had a question about when the boathouse was going to open, and Lynn said next week. Kate started saying she always wanted to learn to sail, and then she was off about boats; you know how she always talks like she knows everything. And in seconds, Lacey turned white and broke into a cold sweat and practically ran out." Carol sighed happily. "That was it. The brunch and the boathouse."

Shelly and I looked at each other.

"What on earth," Shelly said slowly, "could have scared Lacey about the boathouse opening up?"

"Or Mother's Day?" I said. "Lacey was at the last Mother's Day brunch. She sat at our table. My mother thought her little boys were adorable."

Carol shrugged. "I have no idea. Then Kate and Lynn checked out their books, and Lynn made a comment about Lacey rushing off, and Kate asked about her, Lacey I mean, and if I knew her at all, and I told her that none of us knew her very well." Carol shook her head. "I wonder where she is. If she ran away from Doug for some reason, surely she would have come back by now for her sons, no?"

"This hasn't been very helpful," I said. "But thanks anyway, Carol. And good for you and Leon."

She smiled happily. "Yes. Leon. There may be something there. Are you sure I can't get you ladies anything? I can make coffee."

Shelly and I both shook our heads and left. We walked in silence until we turned up towards Davis Road.

"I wonder if Kate's home?" I said, half to myself.

"She's always home," Shelly said. "She has no visible means of support that I know of. All she does is roam around in search someone to talk to."

"Still. I think I'll wander over. Talk to you later." Shelly continued up the hill, and I walked towards Kate's house.

There was something bothering me, but it was so far in the back of my mind I couldn't quite reach it. I stepped onto her tiny porch and knocked.

She opened the door and smiled. "Hello, Ellie. What a surprise! She pushed open the screen door and stepped outside. "Where are your friends? I swear you girls are just like a pack of kittens, running all over town together. All alone? My, is everything all right?"

"I just wanted to ask you, Kate, did you know Lacey Mitchell before you moved here?"

That stopped her. Her mouth dropped open and nothing came out. Then she shook herself. "What a question! Why don't you come on in. I'll make us some tea."

Her house was like a staged photo shoot. Lots of chintz and soft pastels, ferns, and small white candles everywhere. No family pictures. No shoes kicked to a corner or magazines spread open on a side table.

It looked just like the Mitchell house had looked.

Then I remembered something she'd said.

"Kate, how did you know about the money?"

She scooted right by me, off to the back of the house.

"I have this wonderful green leaf tea, so flavorful. I get it from a little specialty shop in Boston. Pricey, yes, but so worth it. I do love a good cup of tea, don't you?"

I followed her into the kitchen. Again, clean and perfect. Even the towels, hanging on hooks, were spotless.

"At the Garden Club meeting, Kate, remember? You said something about all that money not being able to bring the parents back. How did you know about the money?"

"Because it should have been mine, dear. All mine. I was married to that man for years. I really did deserve *something* from that miserable son of a bitch. Why do you think I killed him in the first place?"

I took two steps back and felt my heart in my throat. Her blue eyes were perfectly calm, her smile sincere. But the air in the room had changed, and I was suddenly very afraid.

She took a long breath. "That was probably more information than you wanted to hear," she said. "Honestly, Ellie, I have to tell you the strain of the past few weeks has really taken a toll on my nerves. Now, about that tea. Honey or sugar?"

There were two ways out of her kitchen, back the way we came, through the living room, or through the screened back door. The back door was closer, but I'd have to get past her. Running through the whole house would put her behind me, and I wasn't sure that was a good idea.

I cleared my throat. "Honey. Please."

She beamed. "I love honey too. Put it on everything, even my toast in the morning." She turned away from me again, pulling two pink mugs from the cabinet and adjusting the kettle on the stove. I moved slowly towards the right. The back door was barely ten feet away. God bless old houses and their tiny rooms, I thought. I could easily make it to the door...

I took another step towards the door, and she hit me. It happened so fast I barely registered her lifting her arm as her hand became a fist. I tried to turn away, and I almost made it, but she hit me. Her knuckles went into my cheek, and the pain was incredible. I staggered back, holding my hand to my face. I could feel blood running from my nose, and my eye began to swell.

She shook her hand. Her knuckles were red. "Oh dear, I'm going to have to put some ice on my hand. Will you look at that? I'll be sore for days."

I was trying not to faint. I took a deep breath, counted to three, then exhaled slowly. Again. And again. She had hit me

"Are you crazy?" I blurted. "What did you do that for?"

Her eyes narrowed, and she rushed towards me, her face inches from mine. "Don't call me that," she said, very quietly. "I'm not crazy."

"Then what do you call it?" I hollered, stepping back from her as far as I could. "Why else would you hit me?"

I watched as she carefully rearranged her face, stepped back from me and smoothed down the front of her dress with her hands.

"I'm sorry, Ellie. That was very...wrong of me. But I can't let you leave." She smiled at me, a brittle, frightening smile. No, she wasn't going to let me leave. Ever.

I tried to think. I needed to put her at ease, get her to let her guard down. Right now I could see that she was still so tightly wound that one wrong move, and she'd probably be all over me again.

I pitched my voice down and tried to sound not completely terrified. "Why not, Kate?"

"Well, the whole town is buzzing about you and that very attractive policeman, Ellie. You know how small towns are, by ten this morning we all knew exactly how long he stayed last night. No lights on upstairs while he was there, good for you. Whoring around with a man you hardly know is not the way to conduct yourself, not with two daughters."

The kettle whistled, and she turned and poured the steaming water into the teapot, picked up the teapot carefully, and swirled it gently. "I can't have you telling him about me, can I? I mean, that would lead to all sorts of questions, and frankly, I'm not in the mood right now. Let's give this a few minutes to steep, shall we?" She pulled out her chair and sat down, looking up at me expectantly. "Please, sit down, Ellie. And tell me, I hear your oldest daughter may be moving to France? I love France. Went there with Gerald years ago, when Lacey was in college. We had a wonderful time, although I must say Paris was not very friendly to us. I hear things have changed. I hope so for your daughter's sake."

I glanced at the doorway again. She was sitting, so if I ran, I might make it. Or not. If she caught me a second time, what could she do to me? I felt sure she would use more than her fist. She would try to kill me.

"I wouldn't tell Sam anything, Kate. You can trust me."

She tilted her head and looked very apologetic. "Oh, Ellie, if only I could be sure. But people are terrible liars. Lacey promised me she'd give me all the money that Gerald left her, but she didn't. She said the boys' money was in trust, but I didn't care. She promised me. I don't think she realized how serious I was, so I had to show her. Of course, I tried to get the boys, but I didn't know where Doug's sister lived. So I had to settle for Doug." She lifted the lid of the teapot and leaned over to inhale the steam. "Oh, this smells lovely. Shall I pour?"

I felt sick to my stomach. The pain in my cheek was keeping me focused. I glanced at the table. There was nothing there I could use as a weapon, no carelessly placed paring knife or heavy iron doorstop. I smiled. I could not afford to panic. I needed to do something. But what?

"Oh, wait, I have these lovely scones I made yesterday. Do you bake? I love to. Cookies are my specialty." She got up and moved, coming around the table and behind me. I instinctively hunched my shoulders. What if—

Something came down in front of my eyes and around my throat. I brought my hands up, but it was too late. It was one of the cotton towels, tightening around my neck. I could hear her behind me and feel her hands twisting the fabric. It was impossible to scream. I reached out, hoping for anything to use against her, and my fingers found the teapot. I grabbed the spout with one hand and the handle with the other, and swung my arms up and back, and the teapot smashed into her face. I felt the steaming tea splash against my hair and neck. She screamed, and in that second she broke her grip, and I lunged away from her, knocking over the table in front of me and tearing at my throat as I ran screaming through her living room and straight into Sam Kinali's arms.

"Are you okay?" he asked, his voice shaking.

I stared at him in surprise, then nodded.

"Are you sure? My God, Ellie, what did she do?"

Her tiny living room was full of dark uniforms. There were loud noises everywhere, and I felt cold. He moved away from me, and now the noises seemed far away too, and a very young man in a blue uniform lead me outside and sat me down on one of Kate's shiny white rocking chairs. He was asking me questions, I think, but I couldn't hear very well. Then another young man took his place, and a woman—she looked very kind—was looking in my eyes, and the young man was taking my pulse, and then I stopped shaking, and I could hear everything.

"What's your name, ma'am?" the woman asked.

"Ellie Rocca."

"Good. Now, Ellie, can you tell me what day it is?" The young man put something against my cheek, a cold pack that felt wonderful.

I could hear Kate screaming. Her voice was hoarse, and her words were vile, filthy. She was being taken from the house. I looked down. I could not watch her. "It's Saturday. May fifteenth."

"Good." Her fingers were against my neck, and the skin felt raw and burned. "What was this, a rope?" she asked.

I shook my head. "No. I think she used a tea towel." That suddenly struck me as very funny, and I started to laugh, and I was still laughing when Sam came up on the porch and pulled me up and against him.

Then I started to cry.

The paramedics determined that I did not need to go to the hospital. They gave me a shot of something that took away the pain in my cheek and cleaned my bloody nose. Shelly appeared from nowhere, had a long talk with Sam, then sat with me in the back of the patrol car that took me home. I immediately lay down on the couch. I was aware of Cait, looking horrified, and Tessa starting to cry, and then I was dreaming, odd bits and pieces, Lacey Mitchell and her little boys, waving.

When I awoke, I could tell by the shadows that it was past dinnertime. And I could smell pizza. My mouth felt numb, as did my cheek and eyes. I sat up slowly. My eye was swollen almost shut. My throat felt raw, on the inside and the outside. And I was starving.

"Hey," I called out. My voice sounded weak and strained.

Tessa came in first, running, but when she saw me, she stopped and started to cry. I held my arms out to her, and she crawled in.

Cait and Sam came in together, Cait sitting beside me, Sam across from us on the chair. I looked at Cait over Tessa's head.

"You should be at work."

She shook her head. "Mom, I should be here."

"No. Go to work. Tessa can take care of me. And Sam. You need the tips. Paris is expensive, remember?"

Sam smiled. "I told you, Cait. Go ahead. I can stay."

She looked at me, and her eyes filled with tears. "Are you going to be okay?"

I nodded. "Yes. Really. Go."

She got up and went upstairs. Tessa was down to just sniffles, so we sat there for a few more minutes. I was looking over her head at Sam.

"Thank you."

"For what? You had everything under control by the time I got there."

I shook my head. "She would have come after me. She would have chased me up one side of Davis Road and down the other."

"Perhaps. But I'm sure one of your neighbors would have noticed and at least tried to stop her."

"She's Millicent?"

He nodded.

"She's crazy," I said.

He shrugged. "According to Lacey, she's also evil."

"Lacey? You found Lacey?"

"She found us. She had been in a motel in Harrisburg, looking for a place for her family to relocate. When she heard about Doug, she drove back here. The plan was for him to try to keep things as normal for the boys as possible. He stayed with the boys, because according to her, he thought she was more likely to be in danger once the mother found them. He didn't think he'd be a target." He took a deep breath and shook his head. "She told us about her mother. That's why we happened to be there. We were coming to arrest her."

Tessa slid off my lap and looked up at me. "You look awful. Do you hurt?"

I nodded. "Yes. And I'm starving. Do I smell pizza?"

She brightened. "Yes. Do you want some?"

I nodded again. "Yes. On a tray, please. And water."

She bounced off the couch and was gone.

Sam was looking after her. "Your daughters are both very lovely. And quite entertaining."

I tried to smile. "I bet. Was Shelly here, or did I dream that?"

"Shelly left about half an hour ago. You slept for almost four hours. I have pain pills for you, if you need them. And Shelly said she could come back. With Maggie. And Carol. And just about everyone else in Mt. Abrams."

"She wanted the money," I said.

Sam nodded. "Yes. It was all about the money. She left her husband about ten years ago. No one ever knew where she was or what she was doing. We'll find out, of course. She returned to Fairfax just in time for her husband to die. They're reopening that case as well."

"She told me she killed him," I said. "Killed him for the money."

127

He looked thoughtful. "That's good to know, but I doubt you'll need to testify."

"She followed them back here?"

"Yes. When the will was read, she told Lacey she wanted her share. Lacey took off and came back here. She didn't realize her mother had tracked her down until she heard her voice in the library. She and Doug decided to give her the money and run. They handed over most of it to her, but they couldn't touch the trust."

"She told me. She said she tried to find the boys. She couldn't. She found Doug instead."

"Yes. I don't know what she said or did, but he allowed her to get in the car with him. That's where she stabbed him with an insulin injection. He probably had a seizure before he blacked out. Her fingerprints are everywhere. The autopsy results will confirm. We've got her."

I sighed. "Good."

"It was a very brave thing you did, Ellie," Sam said. He was speaking very carefully. "It was also very reckless. If you had any reason to suspect Kate was a killer, why did you go to see her?"

I looked away from him. "I just wanted to ask her a question. I didn't really *know*, I just…"

Tessa came back, carrying a tray very carefully. She set it down and watched as I sipped some water.

"Does it hurt to drink?" she asked.

I tried to smile. I kept forgetting I shouldn't. "A little. But Sam has pills for me."

I tried to eat the pizza, but it burned the inside of my mouth where my teeth had cut in. So I drank all the water, took two of the pills, and slept again.

I woke up once, in the middle of the night, to go to the bathroom. Tessa lay curled on the couch by my feet. Cait was asleep on the chair. And Sam was in my reading chair tucked in the corner. He was awake.

"How are you feeling?" he whispered.

I knelt down in front of him. "You should go home. I'm fine."

He brushed the hair off my face. "Do yourself a favor. Don't look in the mirror for a few days."

"Gee, thanks. I look that good?"

His eyes met mine. "You're beautiful."

I went to the bathroom, and of course, looked in the mirror. My eye was swollen shut, my cheek and jaw bruised purple, and lips and nose were puffy.

I took another pain pill and climbed back next to Tessa and fell asleep again, watching Sam watching me.

The next morning Sam was gone, and we were all tired and cranky and my entire face felt awful. Tessa attempted to start the morning with a cheerful, "Happy Mother's Day," but it fell a little flat. The good news was that Cait offered to get my mother from the nursing home. The bad news was three texts from Marc, wanting to know if he could come to brunch as well.

I had already bought tickets for the eleven o'clock seating, so that was an easy no. I wanted to blow off the Arboretum completely. This conversation needed more than texts.

I called Marc and told him what had happened. He immediately wanted to come over, but I put him off. If my mother did not remember the orchid show, we'd take her back to the home right after brunch. If she did remember, I'd give him a call.

I showered, put more ice on my face, and found a pretty scarf to put around my neck to hide the redness. I got texts from pretty much every person I knew, asking if I was all right. I drank hot tea with honey and waited for Caitlyn.

My mother took one look at my face and started to cry. "Why did he do this to you?"

I put my arms around her. "Mom, I'm fine. Who do you think did this to me?"

"Marc. Was he drunk? Has he hit you before?"

"Mom, Marc did not hit me. I fell. I'll be fine. Ready to go to brunch?"

She was still crying. "You have to leave him if he beats you. Even though he's such a nice boy."

I patted her back. Tessa and Cait were trying not to laugh. We got her as far as the porch when she started crying again.

"What will happen if he leaves? How will you live? Oh, dear, get a good lawyer." She wiped her eyes with the sleeve of her sweater.

Shelly, Mike, and their two boys saw us, and Shelly hurried over. "Ellie, what is it?" She peered at my mother. "Hi, Leona, remember me? What's wrong?"

Mike was looking at my face closely. "Wow, that crazy lady did a number on you," he said. I tried not to laugh because it hurt, but the situation was getting out of hand.

My mother was telling Shelly about my abusive husband, Marc, and how getting a divorce would send me out into the street. Shelly and Mike's kids wanted a closer look at my black eye, and Tessa was getting hungry. Mike managed to move us all, inches at a time, closer to the clubhouse, and my mother finally got distracted.

"Look," she said suddenly. "There's a sign over the door. Mother's Day! How exciting!"

We sat with Shelly and Mike, and had omelets and French toast, and I chewed all the bacon I could manage on the good side of my mouth. Of course, the entire population of Mt. Abrams knew the whole story of Lacey and Doug Mitchell, and my part in it all, and there was a seemingly endless stream of concerned friends and curious strangers stopping by for a word or six. My mother told all of them I would soon be divorcing, because well, look at her. Everyone smiled and nodded, and after an hour I was exhausted.

"What do you want to do now, Mom?" I asked her.

She patted her hair. "I know you wanted to see the orchids, but you look dead on your feet. Besides, if I have to look at that monster you're married to, I may do him violence. Cait, can you take me back?"

I was so grateful, I almost wept.

Cait and Mom walked back across Abrams Lane, and my mother waved as she got into Cait's car. Tessa and I had stopped to look out at the lake. It was beautiful, and I never tired of it. Tessa put her arms around my waist.

"It's pretty," she said.

"Yes."

"Mrs. Mitchell is back."

"I know." I had seen the Suburban parked in the drive earlier.

Shelly came over and stood with us. "You guys want to come over for the first cookout of the season?" she asked. "A day like this shouldn't be wasted."

I nodded gratefully. "Thanks. Yes, that would be great."

She poked me with her elbow. "You good?"

I nodded. "I will be."

Shelly smiled and followed her family down the hill.

"Mom, if you had a superpower, what would you want it to be?" Tessa asked.

I tightened my arm around her. "To be able to keep you and your sister safe forever."

She nodded. "That's a good one."

"Gee. Thanks. What would yours be?"

"To save all the good days, days like today, so when you were having bad days, you could take them out and live them all over again."

I watched in the distance as Lacey Mitchell came out of her house, got in her car, and drove away.

"That's a good one too, honey."

We turned away from the lake and walked home.

I called Marc again.

"I still love you, too," I said quietly. "But things are confusing right now."

"Your date?"

I nodded, then realized I was sitting on my porch, watching the sunset, with the dog on my lap, and Marc probably hadn't heard me nod. I cleared my throat and said, loudly, "Yes. I like him."

"If he's the one causing the confusion..." Marc began.

"But, he's not. You are."

"Oh," he said quietly.

Boot whined and snuggled in closer. I had managed without the painkillers all day, but knew I'd need them to sleep, and had taken the full dosage a few minutes earlier. I didn't think they'd go to work so quickly, but I felt a sudden heaviness, and my mind began to get fuzzy.

"Can we be friends?" I asked.

"Always."

"Good. I have to go now."

I could hear him breathing. I remembered when we first started dating, and listening to him breathe on the phone was something I'd do every night we were apart. I felt the phone slip into my lap, and I closed my eyes.

I heard Kate's voice, screaming, and then Sam was there, looking angry. Kate was smiling at me, pouring tea. Doug Mitchell was sitting across from me. His smile was fixed, and his skin was blue, and he appeared to be crying.

Sam was there again.

"Good drugs," I murmured. Sam laughed, and I turned towards him and fell asleep.

A FOUNDERS' DAY DEATH

A Mt. Abrams Mystery

by

Dee Ernst

CHAPTER ONE

SUMMER IN MT. ABRAMS WAS heaven for kids. The beach up at the lake wasn't terribly big, so most kids spent the day jumping off the dock and swimming out to the large wooden floats off shore. What beach there was had happy toddlers running all over it, with a corner carved out for the sun-worshipping teen girls. There was sailing on the other side by the boathouse and fishing every morning in canoes and rowboats. Lake Abrams wasn't big—barely one hundred and seventy acres—but it was large enough that the swimmers and the sailors and the fishermen never seemed to crowd each other too much.

Of course, adults liked the lake too. In the summer, the clubhouse was open until eleven, and on its wide screened-in porches, mahjong and martinis reigned. Behind the clubhouse, on a slight rise, ancient maples provided shade that kept picnic tables and wooden chairs cool and comfortable, even in the humid New Jersey summers. Yes, it was practically perfect.

But that was Mt. Abrams for you. Practically perfect.

Small communities were like that, or at least that's what the residents all said. Mt. Abrams had all sorts of things going on behind closed doors, the same sort of things that happened in the big cities, but it wasn't

135

talked about. And since no one was staggering down the street drunk or openly beating their kids, we could all pretend bad things didn't happen here.

But sometimes bad things had a way of raising their ugly heads and waving their broken arms, and no amount of looking away could make it stop. Like what happened in Emma McLaren's garden.

No matter how hard everyone tried to say otherwise, something bad had happened there. And it wasn't going away.

I'm Ellie Rocca. I didn't live directly on the lake, but I did have a lovely view of it from the front porch of the house I kept after my divorce. I sat there every morning with my coffee and watched my ten-year-old daughter Tessa walk to swim practice. The summer had been a cool one, and I knew that the early morning lake water was brisk, but she loved it. She was like a little guppy, swimming like a mad thing, jumping and diving and coming out of the water only for food and bathroom breaks. All summer she was brown from the sun and wrinkled from being in the water, her fingertips looking more like raisins than anything else.

I usually walked my spaniel, Boot, around the lake while she was at practice. Carol Anderson joined me most mornings before she headed off to open the library, and my best friend Shelly walked on the mornings she could slip away from her kids.

I heard Carol coming up the hill before I saw her, because of the very lively discussion she was having with Mary Rose Reed, President of the Garden Club, and Emma McLaren.

Every community had one. You know—the crazy cat lady. Mt. Abrams had more than one, because Mt. Abrams had a lot more crazy people in general than most small towns. Emma McLaren, however, was more than just a crazy cat lady. She was also a self-proclaimed witch. She lived in a tiny Victorian, built in 1901, with a side yard barely big enough for her Prius. But years before, the house next door to her had burned to the ground. She bought the double lot (most lots in that section of Mt. Abrams were barely thirty feet wide, just enough for a small cottage and a tiny side yard) put an eight-foot–tall stockade fence around it, and a little bit at a time, turned it into a large and quite fabulous garden. We could only speculate what was going on behind the tall battered fence, especially after she installed a lock on the gate after being vandalized a few years ago. But she opened it to the public during Founders' Day weekend, and I never missed going in. It was a wonderful mix of practicality and whimsy, with beds of herbs and medicinal plants and berries of every kind, as well as zinnias, roses, and exotic vines growing up arches and over benches that were tucked in every nook and corner. There was still a rather wild-looking side to the garden, where the previous owners put in row of lilacs and nothing else, and Emma was content to let a few wild flowers and weeds grow there. It was an enchanted place, and if you were lucky, after your walk through she would read your palm and give you fresh-brewed mint tea.

Every one loved Emma. She was always bringing tonics to sick children and bouquets of dried herbs to neighbors and friends. Even her cats were loved. Biscuit was the only outside cat, and she would often walk along with you if you happened to be going in a suitable direction. Rasputin, Frito, and Delphine stayed indoors, gazing out Emma's front window as the world went by. She had lived in the same house for thirty-some years, long enough for her home to be called the McLaren house. She was one of the Mt. Abrams elite.

She also had a long-standing argument with Mary Rose.

Every year, the second weekend in August was set aside for the Mt. Abrams Founders' Day Celebration. In the 1870s when Mt. Abrams was a small summer community owned and populated by Josiah Abrams and his family, the weekend was the unofficial end of the summer, and an excuse for the Victorian ladies to get all dressed up. Over the years, as the community grew from a tiny summer enclave to almost a full-grown town, Founders' Day grew as well. Now, it lasted all weekend. There was a dance and carnival at the clubhouse for the kids and teens Friday night. Saturday morning started with a parade, and the rest of the day included a boat race, a fishing contest, and a sandcastle-building contest. Saturday night was a huge potluck on the lake, with fireworks and dancing for the old folks.

Sunday was Open House Day; that was what the argument was about. Mary Rose had, for years, been trying to corner Emma McLaren's secret garden as part of the Garden Club's paid tour. It was a major fundraiser for the Garden Club, and every year, hundreds of outsiders streamed into Mt. Abrams to tour the old homes and the tended gardens of the residents.

Just as a point of information, my house was not on the tour. Neither was my yard. If you could see either of them, you would understand.

Emma refused to be part of the tour, allowing anyone and everyone to view her garden. She was a hard nut to crack, but that didn't mean Mary Rose didn't try every year.

Carol rolled her eyes at me as the trio climbed my porch. She was older than I by at least ten years, tall and lean, with a shock of silver hair cut short and four or five earrings in each ear. She was a lovely woman. Most of the time.

Her mouth was in a thin line. "Ready?"

I nodded, then smiled at Emma and Mary Rose. "Are you ladies walking with us this morning?"

Mary Rose tightened her jaw and shook her head. "No. What would be the point? Emma once again refuses to participate in a very important community function, putting the Garden Club, as well as the entire Founders' Day fund raising effort at risk for possible dissolution."

Emma was short, barely five feet tall, round everywhere, with white hair streaming almost down to her waist and washed-out blue eyes. Today she wore her hair was in a single braid down her back, and she sported a bright orange T-shirt over her jeans.

"Good Lord, Mary Rose," she said. "Your Garden Club has managed without me on the tour for as long as there's been a tour. Don't try to guilt me, young lady. Go away before I curse your rose bushes."

Mary Rose turned and stormed off. I looked at Emma and raised my eyebrows. "Can you do that? Curse her roses, I mean?"

Emma smiled. "No, but I can sneak in there at night and pour vinegar at the roots; the acid'll kill them in no time."

Carol finally relaxed and laughed. "She followed us all the way up the hill and never stopped talking. That woman is a royal pain."

"Yes," I said. "But she's our royal pain. Let me get some bags."

Boot tended to stop every five feet to pee. It was amazing how much her tiny bladder could hold. She also liked to spread her poop all around the lake. She was at least a three-bagger, and my pockets bulged with recycled shopping bags.

"How are you, Emma?" I asked as we set out. I knew her, of course, but not well. She was more Carol's friend. But she was always delightful company.

She smiled. She was one of those people in a perpetual good mood. "Good. Thanks to the cool weather, my arthritis had practically vanished, which is why I can join you ladies this morning. The berries are doing well, and I have enough blueberries for quarts and quarts of jam. Would you like a jar?"

"Of course," Carol and I said together. Emma's homemade things were legendary.

We rounded the clubhouse, and I could hear the kids laughing as the coach coaxed them into their drills.

"So," I asked Emma, "are you ready for Founders' Day?"

She made a face. "Well, I've been trying to put in a koi pond. It's a lot of digging, of course, and some days I just can't do it. I was hoping to have it done by this weekend, but now I'm not sure. And then, well, you know." She dropped her voice. "The Canadians."

She didn't have problem with any real Canadians. Her issue was with the lesbian couple that lived on the other side of her garden and had, for years, been trying to claim part of the property as theirs. Aggie Martin and Rita Ferris lived in another Victorian, slightly bigger than Emma's. They also had parking for one car next to their house. What they wanted was a driveway on the other side, so they could park the second car there, rather than down by Rt. 51 in a large parking lot, owned by the Mt. Abrams Homeowners Association, where residents could park for a yearly fee. They floated the idea that a section of the original lot had been theirs, and that section of Emma's garden was actually on their land, and had been nudging her for years to agree. But like I said, Emma was a hard nut to crack.

Why did she call them Canadians? No one knew. No one dared ask. I knew Aggie and Rita well enough to talk to, and after living in Mt. Abrams for almost fifteen years, they were just another couple who walked their dog and sailed their boat and pretty much minded their own business. Being gay was no big deal, and I had never heard Emma refer to any of the other gay residents, male or female, as Canadian.

"What's going on?" Carol asked.

Emma sighed. "They want me to pay for a new survey of the garden. And I won't. I had a survey taken when I bought it, and if they don't think the lines are in the right place, well, they can pay for a second opinion." Her legs seemed to be going twice as fast as Carol's, who had legs up to her neck. "I think they're getting into the garden at night."

Carol made a noise. "Don't be silly, Emma. You've got that place locked up tighter than Fort Knox."

"Yes. Well, that's what I thought, too. But things have been happening. You know I'm trying to put in a koi pond. By the lilacs. My wheelbarrow and shovel were stolen. The form I had bought for my pond was damaged. Yesterday, I went in and all the sunflowers were gone. Cut off at ground level and lying there, dying."

"Groundhog?" I suggested.

"No. Biscuit sleeps in there at night. She keeps the critters away. Besides, I don't think a groundhog would be interested in my wheelbarrow."

"Well," Carol said, "unless they both grew wings, I don't know how Aggie and Rita are getting in. Sorry about those sunflowers. I liked getting a handful of them every once and a while."

After that, the conversation wandered. It usually took me about thirty to forty minutes to walk around the lake, depending on Boot, the condition of the path, and general laziness of the day. With Emma on board, it was almost an hour. Not because she was a slow walker, but it seemed like every five feet, there was an interesting flower or plant she wanted to look at. She even found a fabulous spider web. I'm not a fan of spiders, generally. I'm on a definite live-and-let-live basis with them, but this web was spread between several fallen branches and had just enough of the morning moisture still clinging to it to look like a diamond necklace thrown casually upon the ground.

Emma was a wonder at finding stuff like that.

I invited them in for coffee, but both Emma and Carol declined. I checked for texts, made another cup of coffee, and then went to work.

Work was upstairs in a tiny sunroom over the porch. I was a freelance editor, working on my laptop, sometimes in my pajamas, sometimes in the middle of the night. There were lots of upsides to working for yourself, and just as many downsides, like having to pay for your own health insurance and never getting invited to the office Christmas party. But I was doing okay.

I had a cozy mystery to edit. A sixty-year-old quilter with a nose for murder. I just loved those kinds of books.

Carol texted me Friday morning saying she couldn't walk with me, but could I come down to her? I grabbed Boot and her bags and headed out.

Mt. Abrams was built on the side of a fairly large hill. The lake is at the top, and behind it is the small mountain for which the community is named. Right around the lake are the oldest homes, the original Victorians built by Josiah Abrams for his family in the late 1800s. As you move slowly down, the houses get smaller and smaller, until you get to Sommerfield, which divides old Mt. Abrams from new. South of Sommerfield are large craftsman style homes, and Dutch colonials built during the twenties, then the Cape Cod houses from the fifties, and then, along Rt. 51, the bi-levels and ranches of the sixties and seventies.

Carol lived on the new side of Sommerfield in a fabulous Craftsman with a yard large enough for lots of trees and a spacious back yard. But before I made it down to her house, I got sidetracked—along with everyone else who happened to be out that morning.

There were two—yes, *two*—police cars on Davis Road, which is a long and narrow road, lined with the original tiny summer Victorian cottages. It was where Emma lived, and the police cars were directly in front of her house, lights flashing. That was where Carol was, standing opposite Emma's porch, looking worried. She saw me and flagged me over. I had to walk through about a dozen people, which for Mt. Abrams, was the equivalent of a horde.

"What's going on?" I asked.

Carol's mouth was in a thin line. "I was coming up this way to see if Emma wanted to walk with us again and saw this. I hope she's okay."

Emma was just fine. She appeared then on her porch, followed by three officers, and she led them directly into her garden. She left the gate open, so Carol immediately moved forward to take a look, and you'd better believe I was right behind her.

Her garden was a mess. Blueberry bushes were pulled up by their roots, as were her roses. One arbor was on the ground, smashed, and another was leaning crazily against the fence.

"Oh, no," Carol breathed. "How awful."

Emma was obviously upset, but keeping it together. She was nodding, listening to whatever the policeman was saying, and I thought about how calm and cool she was.

Then, she wasn't. "They did it. The Canadians," she screamed. "They finally went too far!"

Carol sighed and hurried forward. "Emma, honey, I don't think you should be making those kinds of accusations," she said.

Emma turned to her, face red. "You know they've been after me for years! Well, if they think they can get me to sell after this, they are very mistaken."

One of the officers, a young Denzel Washington look-alike, looked at me and asked quietly, "Do you know about these Canadians? Are they here illegally?"

"Ah…" Boot suddenly caught the scent of something interesting and pulled me forward. "They aren't really Canadians. She's talking about the couple next door." I nodded at Aggie and Rita's pale-blue house peeking up over the side of the fence, mostly hidden by the lilacs.

He pulled out his pad. "They aren't from Canada?" he asked, scribbling.

I shook my head. "No. They've lived there about twelve years now." Boot was straining at the leash. I let her go. In the fenced-in garden, she couldn't get out to the street without going past me. Besides, she seemed intent on the mounds of soft dirt under the lilac bushes.

Emma had her hands on her hips. "It was them. Who else? Everyone loves my garden."

"Well ma'am," one of the other policemen was saying, "we'll go over and talk to them. You say the garden is locked at night?" He had lots of curly dark hair and looked a little like Paul Michael Glaser, so he became Starsky, of the old television series *Starsky & Hutch*.

Emma nodded. "Yes. Six years ago, kids kept getting in. They'd planted marijuana plants next to my basil, and they made a mess whenever they, well, harvested. So I put the lock on."

Denzel was still scribbling. "Was it locked this morning?" he asked.

She nodded. "Yes. I come early to let my cat out. Biscuit. She sleeps here during the summer to kill off the rabbits and ground hogs." She sniffed. "She bolted out the minute I opened the gate, and this is what I found." Emma's lip started trembling. "They tore up my blueberries. And look at my Louise Odier!" She burst into tears.

Carol put her arms around Emma, looked over the sobbing woman's head and said, "Louise Odier is the name of a rose, not a person."

Starsky nodded wisely.

By now, a small crowd Stared into Emma's garden. Carol frowned and made shooing motions, and they backed away, except, of course, for Mary Rose, who shouldered her way in to stand beside me.

"Do you think she can put this back to right by Sunday?" Mary Rose asked.

I looked at her, disgusted. "Really? The poor woman had someone break into her beloved garden, tear all sorts of things up out of the ground, and you're worried about Open House Day?"

Mary Rose shrugged. "We could all help. I mean, I know she was trying to put a pond in there by the lilacs, and we probably couldn't get that done, but the rest…"

I shook my head and stepped away. There had been lots of digging around the bushes, and there was a pile of puddingstone and some piping lying on the ground. I didn't know much about the pond project, but I imagined that Emma had put a lot of time and energy into it. Boot found the whole mess irresistible and was nosing around happily.

Aggie Martin came into the garden, Rita right behind.

"Emma, is everything okay?" Aggie asked.

Aggie was average height with dark hair and glasses. Rita was taller, with very straight hair and the kind of boobs that started conversations. They were both in their early sixties, both schoolteachers in Bergen County, and both said they had known each other since college. They both wore jeans, winter and summer, and vintage T-shirts. Both looked concerned, and as they gazed around the garden, shocked.

"This is terrible," Rita said. "What happened?"

Emma flew at Rita, her hands slashing like tiny claws. Luckily, Carol already had her arms around Emma, and she pulled Emma back before any eyes got scratched out.

"You know perfectly well what happened!" Emma screeched. "You did this! You've ruined my garden! I could kill you both for this!"

Denzel quickly suggested we move out of the garden and into the house. Carol, her arm still around Emma, left the garden, Denzel right behind. Hutch corralled Aggie and Rita and lead them out. Starsky walked around to look at the torn up blueberry bushes. I went over to grab Boot's leash.

Boot had been digging. She had quite a hole started. And there was something in the hole that did not look like it had anything to do with building a pond. Instead, it looked like one of those skeleton hands you buy in the party store for Halloween, to scare the pants off little children.

"Officer..." I called faintly.

He came over. "Can I help you with something?" he asked politely.

I pulled Boot away from the lilac bushes.

He followed my stare. Then he got closer, dropped to one knee, and looked carefully.

"Is that..." I asked, backing away slowly.

He nodded. "Yes, I think it is."

"Do you think it's attached to something?"

He turned and looked at me, rolled his eyes, and spoke into his walkie-talkie. I kept backing away, pulling Boot with me, until I was out of Emma's garden. Boot whined softly and gazed up at me.

"Bad dog," I told her.

CHAPTER TWO

I DIDN'T GET BACK HOME until almost noon.

I texted Caitlyn, my older daughter, telling her where I was, and that the police weren't going to let me go quite yet. I texted the nursing home where my mother was living to tell them I wouldn't be there for my weekly visit. When I finally did climb the steps of my porch, it looked like Nemo had not only been found, but his entire family was hanging out for a party.

"This looks great," I called, fighting my way through a curtain of fake seaweed.

Founders' Day weekend was the pride and passion of Mt. Abrams. People built floats for the parade. Sure, there were marching bands, and we even had bagpipers and a juggler, but the residents built elaborate floats, all working in extreme secrecy, each float-building team hoping to take home the top prize. Yes, there were trophies. Of course there were. And they were coveted by all.

My own daughters, thank God, did not allow their competitive natures to be influenced by dreams of the Best Large Area Float trophy, or the Best Theme Float trophy, of even Best Decorated Bike trophy. No, they always set their sights to win Best Decorated House.

I know. Decorated House? How do you decorate a house for Founders' Day? Well you can go with the Founders' Day Theme (this year, Underwater Wonderland), or you can go traditional, with hanging paper lanterns and candles and balloons. Then there's the ever-popular live action, where Mt. Abrams finest talents danced, sang, or otherwise worked their ways into the hearts of many, all for the sake of, yes, another trophy.

My daughters neither danced nor sang. They had been, for the past two weeks, painting fish on large pieces of cardboard, fabricating fake seaweed from crepe paper and shredded fabric, and even found fishnets to string across the porch. They compiled a playlist of ocean-related music, from "Under The Sea" to "Octopus' Garden" to play during the critical judgment hour, and were still working on their special-effects lighting. Cait, by the way, was twenty-four, and had not walked away without a first place trophy in over fifteen years. Expectations were high. The effort had been huge. The results were spectacular.

Which is what I came home to.

Caitlyn stuck her head out of the kitchen. "You found another body? What is this, a habit now?"

In all fairness, when Doug Mitchell's body had been discovered earlier in the year, there had been four of us. So I did not, technically, find it myself.

I glared at Cait. "It's Boot's fault. She was digging in the wrong place."

Tessa came running to me, peanut butter all over her mouth. "Is Detective Sam on the case?"

Caitlyn had probably figured out that Detective Sam Kinali and I were more than just casual acquaintances. Tessa probably figured it out as well, but chose to ignore the possibilities and just looked at him as the nice policeman who occasionally stopped by and took us out for ice cream. Well, *her* out for ice cream. I still had fifteen pounds to lose, so I had fat-free–sugar-free frozen yogurt, which was *not* the same as ice cream. At all.

"No, baby," I said giving her a hug, then wiping peanut butter off my shirt. "Somebody else came. Sam was probably busy solving some other crime."

"Will this effect the judging?" Caitlyn asked, worried.

Entrants in the House Decoration Competition had to have the entries done by one in the afternoon, and the decorations had to stay in place all weekend. Judges, whose identities were kept secret due to the unfortunate Earl Calhoun Bribery Scandal of 2005, could walk by at any time, so day and night viewing had to be considered. Our house would look better at night, provided the strobe lights and the fans going at the same time didn't short-circuit the house's sketchy electrical system.

I collapsed on the couch, and Boot crawled into my lap. I felt a bit skived out, considering where her paws and nose had recently been. "I'm sure," I said, pushing Boot firmly away, "the judges will come by. You know how serious this is taken. Nobody is going to let a little thing like a decomposed body delay Founders' Day."

"Okay," Cait said, sinking into a chair. "Daddy will be here at seven."

Their father, my ex-husband of almost five years, never missed Founders' Day. He came by Friday evening to help the girls with the house. He sat with us to watch the parade, and came back Sunday to walk the girls through Open House Day. For the past few years, Founders' Day had been the only time Marc and I saw each other. Last spring, when Cait applied to a fellowship in France that would take her away for two years and Tessa threw a bit of a tantrum about it, he and I found each other alone in the same room for the first time in a very long time. That was when he had kissed me and told me that he still loved me, and that he missed me. You'd think that since I was still madly in love with Marc, it would have been a fairly thrilling moment in my life. However, I had just told him I was going on a date. My first date since the divorce. And *that* was the moment he chose to tell me all this? You can see why I was suspicious of his intent.

That date was with a smart, funny, and sexy police detective named Sam Kinali. Sam and I had recently, oh, how should I put this? Taken our relationship to the next level. Yes, that would be a good way to put it. We had started bonking each other like teenagers. Now it could have been all those feel-good endorphins racing through my body, or maybe it was that first flush of excitement and anticipation in a relationship that I hadn't felt in over twenty years, but being with Sam made the whole still-in-love-with-Marc thing fade a bit into the background.

Sam would be here at six. Marc at seven. Hmmm...

"And I invited Kyle over for dinner," Cait said, trying to look nonchalant.

Kyle was Kyle Lieberman, who had been her best friend in grade school, a gawky, nerdy boy who had recently graduated Wharton with an MBA and now looked every inch the buff, successful financial wizard. He and Cait had reconnected a few months ago, and although Cait and I shared a don't ask, don't tell policy about the men in our lives, clearly Kyle was starting to be something more than just the kid from third grade.

"We've got plenty," I said. Founders' Friday night dinner had become a tradition. I'd started the pulled pork in two separate Crock-Pots at seven that morning, and Caitlyn and I had made a huge bowl of potato salad that was now resting in the fridge. Coleslaw was a last-minute fix.

Pretty much all of my friends in Mt. Abrams walked their kids up to the dance at seven-thirty, then came to my porch for something to eat, and of course, drink. I wasn't directly on the lake, but from my yard you could easily see across the street to the clubhouse and the beach. It was a perfect spot for all things Founders' Day—the Friday night dance, the parade, and the Saturday night fireworks over the lake.

Tessa was bouncing on the couch, something normally not tolerated, but after all, it was Founders' Day weekend, and a lot of things slid by. "Jerome is going to be my partner tomorrow for fishing," she said.

I looked at her. "What about your daddy? He's going to be so upset."

She shrugged. "He can catch his own fish. Jerome and I are going for a ten incher."

Lake Abrams was stocked every spring, and by late summer, the fish were practically jumping out of the water and into rowboats as they came by. Years ago, Marc and I had bought a canoe, and it was still over in the boathouse. I sometimes took it out at dusk and just sat in the middle of the water, watching the sunset. Cait confessed she and her friends used to take it out to get stoned, which was actually pretty smart if you were going to break the law. This was the first year Tessa could take it out by herself, providing there was somebody with her.

Cait smiled. "Is Jerome your boyfriend then?"

Tessa made an elaborate show of rolling her eyes in complete disinterest. "Of *course* not. We've just known each other *forever*." That was true. But then, she had known all of her friends in Mt. Abrams forever.

So Tessa was, obviously, still mad at her father. She had counted on him to stop Cait from going away, and when he failed, she decided to blame him for the situation rather than Cait. I could see her reasoning, of course. It was much easier to stay angry with someone you saw twice a week than at someone you lived with.

Boot lifted her head and wagged her stump of tail, and Shelly Goodwin came through the door.

Shelly was my best friend in Mt. Abrams. She was five years younger than I, a pretty woman with carefully dyed reddish hair that fell to her shoulders and a body that looked like a floorboard, long and flat. My hair was carefully dyed also, but for necessity rather than vanity. Left on it's own, my dark, wavy hair would take on the color and texture of a very used Brillo pad.

"Ellie, honey, are you okay? My God, it looks like *CSI* down there. The whole street is blocked off; there are cars and vans everywhere, and they've set up a tent in the middle of Emma's garden. Mary Rose is apoplectic, because three of her houses on the tour are right there on Davis. I'm worried for her health." Shelly stopped talking long enough to grab Tessa in a hug. "The porch looks amazing. You guys are *so* going to win this year!"

Tessa grinned. "Want to hear the music?"

Shelly nodded. "Go ahead. But I'll stay here with your mom, okay? I'll still be able to hear it, right?"

Tessa nodded and vanished on to the porch. Shelly sat down next to me as "Yellow Submarine" blasted through the open window.

"Is Sam in on this?" Shelly asked.

I shook my head. "No. Another detective came. Before I left, they were starting to dig up the body."

Cait crouched down next to me. "So it was a body? Like, a whole person was buried there?"

"I think so," I said.

"Did they know how long it had been there?" Shelly asked.

I shook my head again. "No. But it had to be from, like, way before that house burned down, right? Who used to live there?"

"The Mallecks," Shelly said. "She was a doll. He was an asshole. They were living there when I moved in, and that was twenty years ago."

"I didn't know them at all. When did the house burn down?" I asked.

"2001. So, what, fourteen years ago? The year after Walt Malleck left," Shelly said.

"What do you mean, left?" Cait asked.

"Left Paula. She said he was sleeping with some young girl, and that the two of them ran off without a word," Shelly said. A funny look crossed her face. "Unless he never left at all."

Cait lowered her voice. "Dum-da-DUM."

I patted Shelly's hand. "Calm down, girlfriend. That body is most likely a hundred years old, probably some faithful retainer, buried by one of the original Abrams."

"Well, maybe we can ask Paula herself," Shelly said. "Both her kids are still sort of around, and they come for Founders' Day, and Paula is usually with them. They hang out with somebody down on Blackburn."

"What are you going to ask her? Hey, Paula, do you know who put that body under your lilacs?" Cait grinned at her warped sense of humor.

"I can be discreet," Shelly said. "This is really going to put a damper of Founders' Day."

"I don't know," Cait said. "Founders' Day can use a little shaking up. And I bet there's going to be lots of press around, and all sorts of people are going to want to come out here and check out little old Mt. Abrams. We'll be famous."

Shelly sighed. "At least that will make Mary Rose happy." She looked sideways at me. "Did you invite Sam over for the evening?" she asked.

I nodded.

"And, is Marc going to be here?"

I nodded again.

"Can I watch?"

I swatted her with the back of my hand. "I may charge you extra for the floor show."

She grinned happily. "I'll bring cash."

CHAPTER THREE

BECAUSE THE FRONT OF MY porch had been transformed into a Deep Sea Wonderland, the tables and chairs were set up in the side yard. As I lived in one of the larger Victorians that Josiah Abrams had originally built for his children, I not only had lots of square footage inside the house, but I had a lawn and garden space on the outside. Well, I use the term garden loosely. Marc had planted all sorts of things, and Cait tried to keep them alive. My entry into the Garden Club earlier that spring had been a preemptive move in case Cait left, as she was the only thing that stood between green, flourishing plants and a desert wasteland.

But I digress. To the left of my house was the drive and detached garage. On the right side was a beautiful maple that provided constant shade in the summer and bags of red leaves in the fall. That was where we set up shop. Cait and I moved the kitchen table out, as well as a few folding tables and pretty much every chair in the house. The food would be set up on the small side porch, and people could spread themselves out wherever they could find space.

Kyle Lieberman came by at about four with a keg of beer and lots of ice. He'd been an awkward kid back in elementary school, all knees and elbows, the classic geek who always got picked last for dodge ball. He and Cait reconnected, and although I didn't ask many questions,

I knew what was happening from a mile away. He was smitten. Well, of course he was. Cait had grown into a gorgeous redhead with brains and a sense of humor and a fierce loyalty to those she loved. He'd grown into a tall, good-looking guy with a shiny new MBA from Wharton and a high-paying job in finance. He was considerate and funny, and also still a little shy and awkward, which just added to his general adorableness.

Too bad Cait might be going off to France for two years.

I made coleslaw and took the buns for the pulled pork out of the freezer. I managed to *not* eat any of the chocolate chip cookies I had bought at Costco. I set out two pitchers of tea to steep in a beam of sunlight, went upstairs to shower and change, and came back down just in time to take the pork butts out of the Crock-Pots to cool and shred. I could hear Tessa on the porch singing along with "Three Little Fishes." Cait and Lyle were in the yard, drinking beer and gazing into each other's eyes. I poured myself a glass of wine. Time to start the festivities.

"Mom," Tessa called. "Detective Sam is here."

I grabbed my wine glass, struggled through the seaweed, and met Sam on the front walk.

He was gazing at the house, shaking his head in amazement. "Is this what you people really do here?" he asked.

I gave him a kiss. "Yes. Every year. Didn't you believe me when I explained it to you?"

He grinned. "Hearing about it and seeing it are two very different things. Now I can't wait to see this parade you've been talking about."

Sam Kinali was a very sexy man. That was the very first thing I noticed about him when we first met three months ago. He was tall and broad, with thick hair turning silver and very white teeth that flashed out of his dark and handsome face. He was Turkish, and my early fantasies about him involved tents in the desert and mutual grape feeding. Now that I knew him better, I could add that he was also very smart, with a dry sense of humor and the ability to talk to anyone about anything. He was intensely curious about the world, which made him an excellent police detective. He was also excellent in the sack. Just sayin'.

I put my arm through his. "Come around to the side. We've got plenty of beer. Cait and Kyle are here, and tonight you'll have the pleasure of meeting Marc."

He threw back his head and laughed. "Oh, my, that should be interesting. Does he know about us?"

"Yep. Although like you said, hearing about something is quite different from seeing it in person."

He shook hands with Cait and Kyle, then sank into a lawn chair. Cait liked him, I knew, but he made her a bit uncomfortable. Probably for the same reason Kyle made me uncomfortable.

I handed him a red plastic cup full of beer, sat next to him, and then nudged his foot with mine. "So, do you know what happened in Emma's garden?"

He grinned. "Why did I know that would be the primary topic of conversation?"

"Hey, you've been around long enough to know the excitement level here in Mt. Abrams," Cait said. "Come on, Sam. This is hot stuff."

He settled back in his chair. "I don't know much. I'm not working the case, but I do know that the FBI has been called in to help with forensics. They're still down there, apparently getting an earful from the residents because the street will probably be cordoned off all weekend."

"Really?" I asked. "Davis Road is on the parade route. Oh, I bet Sharon is having a fit." Sharon Butler, who grew up on Sommerfield and now lived in an expanded cape on Dogwood Lane, was this year's president of the Founders' Day Committee. I didn't know her that well, but I liked her.

"Yes. Apparently, there's already been a series of very forceful phone calls to the mayor's office. But after all, a body had been found. Surely, people recognize that this investigation is a priority?"

Kyle made a rude noise. "Sam, you forget. This is Mt. Abrams. The Founders' Day parade has had the same route for over a hundred years. That's the only priority people consider around here."

"One hundred years?" Sam echoed. "That's how long this has been going on?"

"Well, the parade part. The actual weekend started as just a big barbecue at first in the late 1870s, I think. The parade wasn't added until the early 1900s."

Sam chuckled. "This small-town living is quite extraordinary."

"Well, all small-town living certainly is," I said. "But I think Mt. Abrams is at the very deep end of the extraordinary pool."

He nodded. "Yes, you may be right. I'm fairly certain that things happen here that happen no place else on earth."

How right he was.

The thing about Friday night of Founders' Day weekend was that lots of people got free meals. Practically everyone with an entry for the Best Decorated House had some sort of food or drink available for visitors, because walking around and looking at all the houses and noshing at each entry was a generally accepted practice. Nobody was denied, because you never knew who was judging. This fact was taken advantage of by several less than honest Mt. Abrams residents who had no interest in house decorations at all, but were simply trolling for free food and drink. Certain individuals were notorious. Gary Koch, for instance, was known to ask for Tupperware containers, so he could take food home with him. Louise Lombardi was usually so drunk by the time she made it to my house that she would often pass out on my couch. I always found a thank-you note taped to the refrigerator door when she left in the morning.

So Friday night often found me surrounded by people I didn't know very well, because if I say so myself, my pulled pork was something of a local legend. My friends would all be there of course, having walked their kids up to the clubhouse and dropped them off. The little ones stayed on the beach and lawn, where there were games and booths and even pony rides. The older kids went up on the screened porch and waited for the DJ to crank up the music, which usually happened around nine. From my yard, you got a bird's eye view of everything that was happening, which made it a perfect place to hang out.

This particular Friday night was made special by the appearance of Madam President herself, Sharon Butler. I thought she was just there for the food, but it turned out, she was after Sam.

Living in a community as small as Mt. Abrams, there were very few secrets, and pretty much everyone knew that I was seeing a police detective. Sharon, having no luck with whoever was in authority at the scene down on Davis Road, was obviously trying to get some assistance through more personal, if indirect, means.

She shamelessly introduced herself to Sam, lowered herself into a wicker chair right next to him, and then went to work.

"Sam, I know we've just met, but I'm president of Founders' Day, and I could really use your help. The police officers at Emma McLaren's refuse to tell me when they will be out of there, and there's a parade scheduled for ten o'clock tomorrow, and I need Davis Road clear." She was open, honest, and completely sincere. She was just barking up the wrong tree.

It was still light out, although my solar lights were starting to flicker on. I could see Sam's face. He looked sympathetic and obviously amused.

"Sharon, it's a pleasure to meet you, but I'm afraid I can be of no help. I am not involved in what's going on down there, and even if I was, the FBI has now stepped in. As local law enforcement, I'd have little or no say. Sorry."

She made a face. She was very pretty, weighed close to three hundred pounds, and always looked like she'd stepped out of a magazine. Even tonight, in eighty-degree heat, and after running all over Mt. Abrams checking on things, her makeup was perfect, her hair sleek and bouncy, and her linen outfit relatively unwrinkled.

"But Sam," she said, leaning toward him, "it's Founders' Day. Didn't Ellie explain to you how important this weekend is?"

Sam chuckled. He had been drinking beer for a few hours now and was probably as close to drunk as I'd ever seen him. Not that he was slurring his words or anything, but he was…relaxed, his usual high-energy demeanor was dialed down. "Ellie explained everything to me. Several times, in fact. I'm still in a state of disbelief over some of the things she has told me to expect. So I sympathize with you. Really. But I'm not so important that I can tell anyone, let alone the FBI, what to do."

Aggie Martin and Rita Ferris had come by earlier and were standing with my good friend Shelly Goodwin. All three of them immediately stopped talking as soon as Sharon made her pitch, and I could tell they were hanging on every word.

"Sam, really," Rita said. "Can we at least get them to turn off those spotlights? I don't know how we'll get to sleep tonight. We live next door, and it's like daylight outside our window."

Sharon looked over at Rita. "Oh, that's right. You're next door to Emma."

Aggie nodded. They had eaten a bit of pulled pork earlier and had a few beers. They had never hung out at my house before, usually just came by to see what the girls had done to the porch, but I wasn't going to question them lingering. I had a hunch Aggie was a judge. She had looked very carefully at the way the girls had set up the lighting.

Sam shrugged. "Ladies, you do understand that a *body* was found? It's being treated as a crime scene until what happened there can be positively determined."

"That body is probably a hundred years old," Aggie said.

Sam leaned back and laced his fingers together. His body language changed slightly, and I could tell he'd slipped into a slightly more official mode. "I doubt that. Those lilac bushes, they're not as old, surely? And the body was not buried all that deep. If it had been there a hundred years, the body would have been discovered when those lilacs were first planted."

"Sam," I said accusingly, "you stopped to look?"

He grinned. "Of course. Professional curiosity. And I chatted with Martin Feltz, the detective in charge."

"What did he say?" Sharon asked, somewhat breathlessly.

"That they were trying to find the previous owner of the house," Sam said.

"Oh, we know where she's living," Rita said. "Jupiter, Florida. We still get a Christmas card from her every year. Paula was so nice to us when we first moved in. She used to bake us cookies every Sunday. But you can probably find her this weekend down on Blackburn staying with the Millers. Betty and Paula were great friends, and Paula comes up every year for Founders' Day."

Sam nodded encouragingly. "Really? On Blackburn?" He looked at me, half smiling. "People come back here for Founders' Day?"

"All the time. She was a very nice woman," Shelly said. "He was a real piece of, well, whatever."

"Oh yeah," Aggie said. "He was cheating on her. With someone in Mt. Abrams. Well, that was the rumor anyway. She was the one who planted those lilac bushes. I remember helping her. That side yard was full of rocks. He never lifted a finger to help her. She did everything in that house. Remember, Rita?"

Rita nodded. "He was always down at Taylor's. That was a bar next to the train station. It was a real dive before Zeke bought it and turned it around. Walt Malleck was a mean drunk."

Sharon made a noise. "He was more than that. He was perverted. Evil."

Sam tilted his head. "That's pretty strong."

Sharon shifted in her seat. "I grew up here. I knew all about him. He was a selfish bastard."

"Hey, no swearing in front of the innocents," Marc called. He came into the yard with Tessa, Jerome, and Shelly's youngest son, Greg. He'd picked them up from the carnival and walked with them through town, looking at the other house decorations.

Tessa ran up to me, excited. "We are going to take first place. Absolutely. Nobody comes close."

I kissed her. "Really? You're not just a *little prejudiced*?"

Marc stood by the keg, pouring himself a beer. "No, I think the girls have it wrapped up again this year. Right, Jerome?"

Jerome, his mouth full of chocolate chip cookie, nodded.

Marc grabbed a folding chair and swung it around to join Sam and Sharon. "So, Sam, what do you think of this circus?"

I had been watching the two of them all evening, and they were perfectly polite to each other. Each had known the other would be there, of course. I had no worries about Sam. Marc, I knew, could charm the leaves from the trees if he wanted, but he also had a small but vicious jealous streak. And since he had recently told me that he still loved me, I was a bit concerned. But he had either forgotten that fact or never meant it in the first place, because he and Sam got along like long-lost brothers.

Sam took a long drink of beer. "This is like nothing I have ever seen before. You people should have your own reality show."

Shelly giggled. She'd been drinking here for a bit and was in a great mood. "I know, right? The Real Housewives of Mt. Abrams."

Aggie shook her head. "No, please. You don't want all your dirty little secrets to come out, do you?"

Shelly giggled again. "Dirty little secrets? Sorry, I got nothin'. You Ellie?"

"I inhaled," I said.

Marc made a rude noise. "Is that all you're going to confess to?"

I kicked him and grinned. "For now, yes."

Aggie looked at Sharon. "How about you, Sharon? You've lived here your whole life. I bet you know all the dirt."

It was almost dark now, but I could see Sharon's face, and she didn't look comfortable. "I know enough," she said. "Not that I would repeat anything. Loose lips sink ships, as they used to say."

Rita threw her arm around Aggie's shoulder. "I'll tell you mine if you tell me yours."

Aggie rolled her eyes. "What possible secrets could you tell me I don't already know about?"

Rita made an elaborate show of thinking hard. "How about the night I looked out the window and saw..." She paused, obviously for dramatic effect, "...who was digging a grave under the lilacs."

We all laughed.

Aggie jostled Rita with her elbow. "Talk about loose lips. Rita, you're going to get yourself into trouble."

"Well," Sharon said, getting up. "I obviously will have to sort this entire mess out myself. The mayor is useless; you all just sit here, and the parade starts at ten tomorrow." She seemed visibly upset. "After years and years, to have this happen. And during my year."

"Sharon, calm down," I said. "People will understand. No one can blame you for something like this." I said it, but I'd lived in Mt. Abrams long enough to know that lots of people would, in fact, blame her. "You can reroute the parade across Elliot."

She shook her head "And have all those people who sit in Main Park not see a thing?" Her voice was actually trembling, and she hurried off into the darkness.

Sam turned to me. "Is she really that upset?"

I nodded. "President of Founders' Day is a very elite position around here."

Shelly nodded. "Seriously. This could ruin her social standing."

"Social standing?" Sam asked.

Marc snorted. "I'm with you there, Sam. It's ridiculous how narrow-minded everyone is around here."

"Not everyone," Aggie said.

"No," I said, a little louder than probably was necessary. "Not everyone." I glared at Marc.

He shook his head. "Let me say goodnight to the girls. Where's Cait?"

I was feeling prickly. Marc had not liked living in Mt. Abrams. It had been our longest, and ultimately, final battle. In the end we had both won. I stayed. He left. "She's at Kyle's, I think."

He nodded. "Well, okay then, I'll just find Tessa." He held out his hand. "Good meeting you," he said to Sam.

Sam rose and shook Marc's hand. "The same." They shook, and Marc walked off towards the clubhouse.

"My, my," Shelly murmured. "How civilized we all are."

"Oh, shut up," I growled.

Sam reached down, grabbed my hand, and then pulled me up and into a hug. Then he kissed me. "I'll go back down to Davis Road and see if there's anything to be done. I doubt it, but I'll try." He looked at Rita. "Should I have Detective Feltz come up and question you? About what you saw out your window?"

Rita's jaw dropped. "I was kidding," she squeaked. She pointed to Aggie. "She'll tell you. I sleep like a log. I'm never looking out my window at night."

Aggie nodded. "True that. You've got to learn to keep that mouth shut, Rita."

"I was just trying to be funny," Rita said. "We'll come with you, Sam. Thanks, Ellie. And the house looks great."

"Good. Glad you could come by." I stood there and waved, then looked around my yard. I could see Tessa and Jerome walking back from the lake. Shelly and her husband Mike were slow dancing to the music that drifted in from the clubhouse. Maggie Turner and her husband Derek were lying on the grass, pointing out things in the sky to each other. Carol, who had arrived rather late and had stayed quiet the entire evening, came up to put her arm around my shoulder.

"What do you think?" she asked.

"I think it's a perfect Founders' Day Friday night."

She nodded. "Yeah. Me too."

Chapter Four

Louise Lombardi slept on my couch again. She had wandered over after eleven, when there were just a few of us still sitting around the keg, and had kept Shelly and Mike, Carol, Maggie, and me in stitches. She was another of the Mt. Abrams Old Guard. She had grown up on the new side on Sommerfield, gone away after college, then moved back in to one of the tiny houses on Morris after her divorce. She was childless, worked on Wall Street, and was a first-class drinker. She was one of a kind in Mt. Abrams, a high-powered, hard-partying, working woman who had a string of men in and out of her home at all hours and was totally unapologetic about it.

She was kind of my idol.

Usually she rolled out earlier than the rest of us, but when I came down, she was still snoring on the couch. Boot, who had been given a doggie Prozac the night before to keep her from barking her head off, was curled at Louise's feet. I smiled at them both and made coffee, and then brought up a chair from the side yard up to the porch to sit among the starfish and seahorses to watch the sun come up over the lake.

My porch was one of my favorite places in the world. I could look across Abrams Lane to the spread of green sloping down to the lake. The clubhouse, which had been Josiah Abrams's original grand summer home, was off to the right, and beyond the lake stood Mt. Abrams, barely a real mountain at all, but enough to make for spectacular sunrises.

At this hour of the morning, the loudest thing you could hear were the birds chattering back and forth. The sky was a clear blue. The saying went that in never rained on Founders' Day, and in all my years of living here, I had come to believe it to be true.

"Hey," Louise said groggily from the couch. "Anybody?"

"Out here," I called. "Grab some coffee."

She slouched out a few minutes later, mug in hand, her hair disheveled. Lou was tall and very thin, a body kept taut and toned from daily workouts and bronzed from her membership at the tanning salon down on Rt. 51. Her sundress was made of that crinkly material, so it didn't look any worse for wear after she'd slept in it. She looked around. "Chair?"

I pointed to the side yard.

She carefully put her mug on the floor, went to get a chair, pushed aside a swath of fake seaweed, then sat. She sighed. "God, I love this ridiculous little town."

I nodded. "Me too. I think Founders' Day Weekend is the best thing there is, right after Christmas. Last night, Shelly said we should have our own show. The Real Housewives of Mt. Abrams."

Lou grinned. "Now, that would be worth watching. Underneath all this Pollyanna BS is a lot of dark and serious shit."

I laughed. "That's what Aggie said. That all the dirty secrets would come out."

"Well, there are plenty of them. You wanna bet that body in Emma's yard is Walter Malleck?"

I stared at her. "Seriously?"

She nodded. "Oh, yeah. My mom was good friends with Paula, Walt's wife. He just disappeared, you know? No note, nothing. Paula just assumed he'd run of with whoever he was sleeping with, because there seemed to be no other explanation."

"Who was the mystery woman?" I asked. "Did she disappear too?"

Lou shrugged. "Don't know. No one ever knew who she was. Probably the best kept secret in Mt. Abrams *ever*. But no woman in town up and disappeared when Walt did. So I bet Paula got tired of his shit, smacked him over the head, and buried him right where she could keep an eye on him."

"You're making this up," I accused her.

She shook her head. "Nope. Bet you a buck."

"Yeah, but when the house burned down, everyone said Walt came back and did it."

She shrugged again. "*Somebody* set fire to that house, sure, but not Walt." She glanced at me. "So, Marc and I had a nice conversation last night."

"Oh?"

"Yeah. He likes Sam, but said that you two were getting back together."

"He said *what*?"

She grinned. "I thought that might surprise you."

I glared into my coffee cup. Ever since Marc walked out, I'd fantasized about him coming back, telling me he'd made a terrible mistake, and begging me to let him come home. I still loved him. Of course I did. He had been my soul mate. And he had, in fact, told me he still loved me. That was months ago. Since then, he had not said another thing about it and had not kissed me again. True, we were much friendlier, talked to each other more, and spent more time together in the same room. But not alone, and certainly not as anything but exes.

Just who did he think he was, anyway?

Lou got up. "You watching from Maggie's?" she asked.

I nodded. The girls tended to wander off during the parade, but I sat on Maggie Turner's front porch and drank Bloody Marys as the parade went by.

Lou nodded. "Maybe I'll see you there." She went into the house, and came out a minute later, minus her coffee mug. Boot followed her out and stood on the porch, wagging her stumpy tail as Lou went down the walk, turned on to the street, and then waved good-bye.

Marc told her we were getting back together?

What a snake.

Maggie Turner lived on Morris Street before the corner where the parade route came up Morris and turned onto Davis. It was a prime location, and seating on her tiny porch was coveted. To be honest, my porch was lots bigger, but the view was not as good. The parade was basically over by the time it turned on to Abrams Lane, with everyone heading up to the Clubhouse, not passing my house at all. So for years, Marc and I had joined Maggie and Derek, along with Viv Brewster, the Goodwins, and Carol Anderson. Only the adults sat on the porch. The kids were on the narrow street, hands open, hoping to grab the candy that the parade marchers traditionally threw. Tessa and I had an agreement. She could eat all she wanted in one day, as long as I got all the Tootsie Rolls. She conceded it was worth the sacrifice. This year would be tough. I still had fifteen more pounds to lose before hitting my fighting weight, or at least a size ten. I'd been super good about no sugar. Maybe if I didn't eat dinner…

Boot and I walked down after breakfast. Davis Road was clear. I wasn't sure Sam had anything to do with it, or it was just the gods of Founders' Day at work again. I turned in and went by Emma's garden. There was crime scene tape everywhere, and one police car half up on the curb. Emma's house was shut tight. I peeked into the garden and saw a lone officer sitting on a bench.

"Are you on trespassing duty?" I asked.

He nodded grimly.

"Well," I told him, "there's going to be a very cute parade going by here in about an hour, if you want to move the bench up here. At least it will be something to watch." He smiled and nodded, and I went out of the garden. Rita and Aggie were setting up their porch, and Aggie waved. Everyone on Davis was setting out chairs, and there was already the buzz of voices on the street. People around here took their parades very seriously.

I had gotten a text from Sam. He was running late and would meet me at Maggie's to watch his very first Founders' Day Parade. When I explained that all the floats and bands were put together by residents, he looked very confused.

Most people do. This is not the sort of thing that other small towns do. Mt. Abrams was a one-of-a-kind community.

Sitting on Maggie's porch at nine-thirty on a Saturday morning was just about the best way to spend a Saturday morning. All of her chairs were comfy wicker; she was on the east side of the street, so there was no sun in your eyes, and she always had the most delicious Bloody Marys. She made them with real horseradish and lots of Worcestershire sauce, and put a spear of dill pickle in instead of the usual celery. Totally amazing. She also had warm quiche and homemade cinnamon buns to keep the alcohol from going directly to your head and making you totally useless for the rest of the day.

Boot started whining with excitement as we came down toward her house, and I knew that meant Marc was already there. I often thought that Boot missed him more that Tessa and Cait did. I could see him, standing on the street with Derek, Maggie's tall, very fit and incredibly handsome husband. Derek was African-American and had been college basketball player. He still had the lazy grace of an athlete. His hands were beautiful, with long, slender fingers. He was a graphic artist and also had a daily cartoon that was very sly and funny, and although it wasn't in any conventional newspapers, it was very popular online.

I let Boot off her leash, and she ran to Marc, practically jumping up into his arms. He grinned and hugged her squirming little body. I let him enjoy the moment, because I was about to tear him a new one.

"Hey, El. Mornin," he called.

I marched up and glared at him. "What did you tell Lou last night?"

Derek held up both hands and took a step back. "I sense you two need to be alone."

"You can stay," I snapped. "In fact, maybe you'd better. That way, you can tell the judge I was perfectly justified."

Marc let Boot slide to the ground. "I don't know why you're upset," he said in a calm, soothing voice.

"What?" My voice was pitched so high I think a window cracked somewhere. "You don't know why I'd be upset that you told Lou we were getting back together when I have a boyfriend, and you just met him, and you and I have never even *discussed* the possibility?"

Boot whined. Maybe her ears hurt.

Marc leaned in. "I told you I still loved you."

"Yeah? So?"

He looked hurt. "Ellie, I made a mistake. You and I both know we're perfect together."

"No, I don't know that. The year before our divorce, we were pretty imperfect together. In fact, I think we were miserable together." I could see Derek out of the corner of my eye, stepping slowly backward. "Derek,"

I snarled, "don't even think about moving. I told you I may need a witness."

"Mags," Derek called. "Help."

I pointed my finger. "Saying you still love me may mean something to you, but to me, it's just a bunch of words. You think we should get back together? Fine. Prove to me you're worth my time. Only I gotta tell you, Sam takes up all the extra time I've got these days, so you'd better start doing something pretty special." I wasn't exactly sure I meant that, but I was fuming inside and had to say something. I thrust the dog's leash at him. "And you keep the dog today." I whirled around to face Derek. "Good morning. Happy Founders' Day." I stood on tiptoe, kissed him on the cheek, and then went up onto the porch.

Maggie stuck her head out the door. She was young— just thirty-six—and had five tattoos, my favorite being a tiny musical clef on the inside of her left wrist. "Is it too early for a drink?" she asked.

I settled deep into a chair and continued to glare at Marc. "It's never too early."

She popped back out seconds later with a tray loaded with mason jar glasses and a tall clear pitcher filled with smoky red liquid. "Allow me," she said, pouring a glass and adding a pickle spear. She poured one for herself, and we clinked.

"Happy Founders' Day," we said in unison, then laughed.

She nodded to Marc and Derek, still in the middle of the street, now deep in conversation. "Although it was very civilized of you and Marc to arrange for joint custody of your friends, doesn't it feel awkward sometimes?"

I nodded. "Up until now, we really only spent any time together on Founders' Day. And it was all very polite. Marc didn't really like the people here." I flashed her a grin. "After all, we're a unique bunch. But he did make a few friends. And he knows the girls love it here."

She nodded. "True. So what was this all about? You mentioned Lou. Lou Lombardi?"

"You know she always crashes on my couch, right? Well, this morning she told me that Marc told *her* we were getting back together."

"No!"

"Yes." I stared into my drink. "She also said she thought the body in Emma's garden might be Walt Malleck."

Maggie's eyes popped open. "Really? Wow. That was before my time, but boy, I remember when I moved in, that was still the thing everybody was talking about, him running off, and then the house burning down."

"You've been here that long?"

She nodded. "We moved from Brooklyn twelve years ago this December."

"Wow."

"Yeah. We were such hipsters, two artists looking for a simpler life. Now, we're full-blown suburbanites, with a kid and a mortgage, just like everybody else."

I stared at her, her head shaved on one side, the short hair on the other side bleached blonde. Then I looked at Derek, his entire left arm tattooed in some sort of hieroglyph, dreadlocks to his waist, his earring glinting. "You guys will never be like everybody else," I told her.

"Thank you," she whispered, and we laughed again.

Vivian Brewster was coming up the street, a huge basket draped over her arm. She always brought her homemade biscuits with a jar of wild clover honey. She saw us on the porch and started yelling.

"Girl, you started without me? You crazy!" She was a realtor and had probably handled every real estate transaction in Mt. Abrams in the past six years. She and Maggie were best of friends. As she reached Derek and Marc, she gave them both a kiss. Her skin was lighter than Derek's, but not by much. Her face was beautiful. She looked like a queen, but when she started talking, any illusions of royalty fell quickly to the side.

"Can you believe this drama?" she asked, dropping her basket on the table and reaching for a glass. "We don't need no more dead bodies 'round here. Hard enough gettin' people to look at houses up on the hill. Folk think we're a cult or some such bullshit." She shook her head. "Although I did just find a new renter for that Davis Road house. You know, Kate's old place?"

Kate Fisher had vacated a cute little place on Davis Road, one of the few rental houses in Mt. Abrams, after she was arrested for murdering her son-in-law. She was, it was generally believed, a bit off her nut. Since she had tried to strangle me with a tea towel, my feelings about her were much stronger.

"Family? Another divorcée?" Maggie asked.

Viv took a long drink and shook her head. "No. One fine-lookin' gentleman. I never mix business with pleasure, but I will absolutely make an exception for Mr. James Fergus. He is fine, and I want him *mine*." She burst into laughter, and Maggie and I joined in.

"Great," I said. "But you're going to have a lot of competition. There are lots of single ladies up here."

Viv shook her head. "Not quite like me though, right?"

We laughed again and waved at Rita Ferris as she trotted up the hill.

"Where you going?" Maggie called.

"I left my phone up at the Clubhouse last night. At least, I think that's where it is," she said.

"It might be locked," I said.

"I got the key," she said.

"Better find it quick," Maggie said. "The parade starts in, like, fifteen minutes."

Rita grinned and picked up her pace. Viv opened her basket, and I reached for a biscuit. I could see Sam coming down the hill, and he spoke briefly to Rita as they passed each other. Off in the distance, I could hear the blast of a siren, signaling all that the parade, lined up in Lower Main Park, was about to start. Maggie's daughter, Serif, came running out of the house, clutching a plastic bag to collect her candy.

The Founders' day Parade was about to begin.

CHAPTER FIVE

A NOTHER SIREN SOUNDED TO OFFICIALLY start the parade. Between the first siren and when the parade participants finally made their way to Maggie's corner, Cait and Kyle came by to say hello; Tessa came and dragged Marc off to sit with Jerome and his family up on Davis Road, and Mike and Shelly Goodwin arrived, carrying extra folding chairs and a French toast breakfast bake. Also in that time Sam refused to tell me anything about the body in Emma's garden.

"I'm not attached to the case," he kept saying.

"But you went down last night, right? And talked to whoever was in charge, right? So, he must have told you *something*."

Sam just grinned. He was a big man, not just tall, but broad shouldered and muscular. He was wearing a white polo shirt tucked into khaki shorts, with scuffed Docksides and no socks. He looked absolutely yummy. I could have eaten him right up if I wasn't so aggravated at him. I recklessly poured a second Bloody Mary.

"At least, do they know how long it's been there?"

He shook his head. "No idea. This is real life, Ellie, not *Bones*. We have no forensic expert who can simply look at the body and determine fifteen separate and completely accurate facts. Tests need to be done. It takes time. There was one body, probably male, and since there appeared to be clothing remains, probably not in the ground more than twenty years." He bit into a cinnamon roll and smiled from pure bliss. "Please, don't ruin this for me. This is the most extraordinary thing I've ever tasted."

Since I had to admit that Maggie's rolls *were* extraordinary, I kept my mouth shut until he had swallowed the last bit and licked his lips.

"So, maybe it was Walt Malleck?" I asked.

His shoulders slumped. "Ellie, stop, please."

Viv laughed. "Give your man a break, girl. He is *not* working today. Let him sit and enjoy his very first Founders' Day parade. You know that as soon as anyone knows anything, we'll *all* know it."

She was right there.

I gazed longingly at the French toast. It smelled amazing. But, if I wanted even one Tootsie Roll, I was going to have to control myself. I bit down on the pickle in my drink. I knew for a fact that pickles had practically no calories, whereas one bite of baked French toast would instantly add at least two inches to my hips.

"Here they come," Serif called excitedly. Derek stood beside his daughter in the street to prevent her from running into the middle of the parade in search of candy.

The first group to round the corner was the Historical Society, or, as Viv affectionately called them, The Mt. Abrams Hysterical Society. They were all dressed in Victorian garb, and I had to admit, looked pretty spectacular. Lynn Fahey was up front in a lilac and white number, complete with shirtwaist and bustle, and carried a parasol. Viv made gagging noises, and the rest of us tried not to laugh. Sharon Butler was in the Historical Society, but as president of Founders' Day, was not walking with them. Her husband was there. They had been high school sweethearts, and to me they were a very odd couple. Sharon was big, not just physically, but she had a personality that tended to take over the room. David was a thin, short man who didn't talk much and rarely smiled. Right now he looked completely miserable, sweating in striped pants, suspenders, and spats.

We watched a few Girl Scout troops, the Garden Club, and then real fun started.

First came the decorated bikes and strollers. The kids always had fun with this, and both of Shelly's boys had their bikes decked out. Strollers were also cute, particularly for the sleeping baby cuteness factor. Music came next. The older kids usually put together some sort of marching band, and this year there was a kazoo choir of fifteen- and sixteen-year-old boys, some of them contributing percussion through various manufactured burping and fart noises. Gotta love the willingness to participate.

Finally, the floats. The Newsome family, numbering into the hundreds some years, had an elaborate homage to King Titan, with six-year-old Thomas rising from a Plaster of Paris shell, complete with beard and trident, surrounded by little girls in mermaid costumes. Six adults were needed to pull the platform along, each sweating grown-up wearing a "We Serve The King" T-shirt. Thomas threw candy from a large basket cleverly disguised as a block of coral.

Sam looked on in amazement. "They did that themselves?"

Maggie and Viv burst into giggles. I nodded and poured another drink.

And so it went, a total of eight floats by Mt. Abrams's best, brightest, and most competitive families. I put my money on the Gastons, who had managed to create a very convincing submarine being attacked by a giant squid.

Last came a mounted police officer, followed by the Wyatt sisters dressed as clowns and carrying a broom, shovel, and bucket, in case the policeman's trusty steed decided to anoint any of Mt. Abrams's streets.

Sam stood as they went by to applaud. The policeman smiled and waved. Sam remained standing and clapping even as the Wyatt sisters disappeared up the hill.

"I have never in my life seen anything like that," he said at last. "Now what? I cannot wait."

"Now, we go back up to the lake for the boat races and the fishing contest. That's when they'll announce the House Decoration winner. This may look like a happy community celebrating together, but it's really all about who brings home the biggest trophy."

I tried to help Maggie clean up, but she waved me away, so Sam and I started up the hill. Aggie Martin yelled as we passed Davis.

"Have you seen Rita?"

I shook my head. "Not since earlier. She was heading into the Clubhouse."

Aggie looked thoroughly pissed off. "Is that where she went? She just said she forgot something and took off, and I haven't seen her since. And her parents have been sitting on our porch pretending they like me this whole time. I'm going to strangle her."

I started to say something, but the wail of a siren cut me off. I glanced up at Sam. He was listening.

The siren got louder. I could almost track it as it came up Rt. 51, turned onto Blackburn, and then came up the hill, heading for the clubhouse.

"Let's go," Sam said quietly.

We hurried up the hill and headed toward the clubhouse. Something was wrong. My first thought was that someone had collapsed while pulling one of the floats up the last hill. I could see a police car and heard more sirens. Surely an ambulance was moments away.

It was a second police car, driving past the clubhouse to the docks.

"Stay here," Sam muttered.

"Seriously?" I asked, and he shook his head as I followed him, weaving in and out of the floats that had pulled over on the grass beside the beach.

More sirens. Two policemen were keeping the growing crowd back from the beach. One officer was standing on the dock where the rowboats had been lined up in preparation for the race. Sam showed his badge, and we walked through the crowd and up to the dock.

Sam turned to me. "I mean it. Stay here."

I nodded and watched as he walked up the dock, flashed his badge again, and spoke to the officer standing there. Then he went over to one of the rowboats, crouched down, and looked. He looked for what seemed to be a long while. Then he stood up and came back to me.

"It's Rita. She's in one of the boats. Someone bashed her head in with something, probably an oar. Get the girls and go home. Founders' Day is over."

My porch was back to normal, the fish and seaweed hastily pulled down and stuffed into plastic bags. Because all the activity at the clubhouse could be seen from my yard, that was where we gathered. There was food everywhere, brought over in hastily packed plastic containers and reheated in my kitchen.

Marc asked if I minded if he stayed, and I told him, of course not. Tessa was a mess, and spent most of the afternoon on his lap on the couch in the living room, Boot curled at her side.

I sat and watched the crowd that stood huddled under the trees behind the clubhouse. That was as close as anyone was allowed to get. There was an odd, unnatural quiet hanging over the lake. Death had visited Mt. Abrams before, but never on Founders' Day. I wondered what upset people most, what had happened to poor Rita, or the fact that Founders' Day had been so abruptly cancelled.

Sam was at the crime scene. He was tall enough that I could track him as he moved from the dock to the clubhouse and back again. He had sent me a brief text—he was on the case.

At one point, Sharon came up on the porch and asked for something to drink. She had been with the police, of course, and for the first time that I could remember, she did not look perfectly put together. Her face was flushed, and her makeup was streaked with sweat. Her long linen tunic was wrinkled, and one corner of the bottom was twisted as though she had been wringing her hands in the fabric. Poor Sharon—what a Founders' Day.

Shelly sat with me on the porch. Immediately after the body was discovered, Mike ran up to the lake, scooped up the boys, and they were now at the movies, along with probably half the children in Mt. Abrams. She was sitting, nursing a red plastic cup of beer, watching the crowd intently.

"Do you think this has anything to do with what happened in Emma's garden?" she asked.

I let out a long breath. "It kinda looks that way, doesn't it? I mean, it could just be a giant coincidence, but I doubt it."

"That means that maybe the body was Walt Malleck. And maybe somebody killed him and buried him there. And maybe that somebody is still around, and that's why Rita is dead," Maggie said. Derek was on the other side of the lake with Serif, fishing is a small cove out of sight of the clubhouse activity.

Carol Anderson was also with us, sitting on the first step, leaning against the porch rail. "That's a lot of maybes," she said.

"Where was Emma today?" I asked her.

She glared at me. "Why would you ask that?"

"Because, she wasn't around," I shot back. "Just a question."

Carol shook her head. "Sorry. I have no idea where she was all day. And I'm thinking what you're thinking. She did tell about half the world yesterday that she'd wanted to kill Aggie and Rita both."

Shelly snorted. "Emma? Kill someone? Maybe by magic potion or by long pins stuck in a voodoo doll, but hitting someone in the head? For one thing, she'd have to have been on a chair to hit Rita on the head. Unless Rita obligingly laid down first."

I had to smile. "True."

"But, it's a little odd, Paula Malleck being here, and finding the body, and then this happening to Rita," Carol said.

"But Paula's been coming to Founders' Day for a while now," I said.

We were quiet for a few minutes. Sam was in deep conversation with a group of men who had pulled up in a black car. They were all in suits, and I immediately pegged them as FBI. I quickly texted him.

R they the Feds?

I watched him as he pulled out his phone to glance at my message. Even from a distance, I could see the flash of his teeth as he smiled. He texted back.

I'm working
And you're looking hot
U R distracting
Good

He lifted his head and looked toward the porch, shook his head, and put his phone away.

Shelly had been watching me. "What did Sam say?"

"Nothing. He's very much a stickler about this sort of stuff."

"About what sort of stuff?" Marc asked. He had come out of the house and was standing behind us, leaning against the front door jamb.

"Official stuff. He doesn't give too much away. How's Tessa?"

He shrugged. He was thin and slight, his once flaming red hair going gray. "She fell asleep. What a day. Where's Cait?"

"With Kyle," I said. "Where else?"

"What's going to happen when she goes away?" he asked.

I shook my head. "No clue. She doesn't talk to me, and when I ask she gets upset. I think Kyle is a very unexpected development for her, and she's not sure what to do."

"Poor things," said Carol. "Kyle is such a lovely young man. When he was just a kid, he would hang out at the library and help me out after school. He was so polite and helpful. Of course, being the geekiest boy in Mt. Abrams may have had something to do with it. I don't ever remember him playing sports. He and Caitlyn were thick as thieves there for a while. I believe they had a secret club."

Marc smiled. "That sounds like Cait. She's a big lover of the underdog."

"Well," Maggie said, "Kyle's not much of an underdog anymore. He's cute and rich and kind and very smart. He's almost good enough for her."

"Good," Marc said. "Being the smart, geeky kid finally paid off for someone."

Carol stood up and stretched. "Leon was coming over tonight, but it looks like we'll have to change our plans. She looked at us. "Anyone for dinner at Zeke's?"

Shelly shook her head. "No, thanks. Mike's had the boys all day. His brain will be fried."

"Maybe Viv and I will meet you," Maggie said. "I'm pretty sure Derek will want to stay in."

I shook my head. "Can't say right now."

Marc looked at me. "Why don't you come with me? It'll be fun."

I opened my mouth to say something vaguely off putting, then stopped. I had pretty much challenged him to put his money where his mouth was. Was this him stepping up? Was this a *date*? "Sure, Marc. If Cait can watch Tessa."

He grinned. "I'm off to find her. I'll ask. Should I meet you there, or pick you up?"

Zeke's was at the bottom of the hill, across from the railroad station, a ten-minute walk for me. "I'll walk down with Carol and Leon."

He nodded, waved, and sauntered off the porch. Shelly, Carol, and I watched him turn onto Abrams Lane and disappear around the corner.

"So, are you two having a date?" Carol asked.

I shook my head. "I have no idea."

"What will Sam say?" Maggie asked.

"I have no idea."

Shelly sighed. "Do you know what you're doing?"

"I have no idea."

When Sam finally made his way to my front porch late in the afternoon, he looked drained. He threw himself into a wicker chair and closed his eyes. "Can I just stay here forever?"

"Sure," I told him. "Beer?"

He opened his eyes and shook his head. "No, thank you. I have to go back over there."

"So, what happened?"

He let out a long breath. "Whoever did this must have been desperate. She was killed just minutes before she was found. And she was killed in the clubhouse and dragged down the path and into the boat. Who would do that in broad daylight, when in any minute, dozens of people were going to round the corner and would see what was happening?" He shook his head. "If it was premeditated, I'll be very surprised. I think someone saw an opportunity and went for it."

I nodded. "Rita would ordinarily not have been up here at all. She came up looking for her phone."

"Really?"

I told him about Rita running by, and what she had said.

He ran his hand through his silver-gray hair. "Yes, I passed her myself. So, she was coming up this way? That just creates more questions. Did someone follow her? Was she meeting someone? And of course, motive is a mystery. Who would want to kill her? When someone is killed, we immediately look to the spouse or partner, but Aggie never left her porch. There are dozens of witnesses."

"What about Emma?"

He made a noise. "Yes, well, that's where Martin Feltz is looking. First, a body in her garden. Now, her neighbor is dead after Emma publicly threatened to kill her."

"Do you know who the body is?"

He gave me a sidelong glance. "Tentatively identified as Walter Malleck. We're questioning his wife now."

"Lou was right," I muttered.

"About what?"

"She said the body was probably Walter's."

Sam sighed. Loudly. "You know, my first instinct as a police officer would be to be fairly suspicious of someone who could guess the identity of a body, especially when the body could have been anyone."

I waved a hand. "Sam, I think the idea that the body was Walter's crossed everyone's mind here in Mt. Abrams. After all, he disappeared without so much as a note to Paula. Didn't take money or even his car."

Sam frowned. "Did she put in a missing person's report?"

I nodded. "I think so. But I think once she told the police he had a girlfriend, they kind of figured he went off on his own."

Sam shook his head. I'll pull the old report." He tapped his fingers against the arm of the chair. "Any idea who the girlfriend was?"

I shook my head. "Nope. Paula insisted that it was a local girl, but when Walt left and no one from Mt. Abrams left at the same time, well, that sort of fell flat." I looked over toward the lake. Spotlights were being set up, and I could here the rumble of a generator. "Poor Paula. She comes back to enjoy a pleasant Founders' Day, and her husband's body is found. How awful."

He nodded, as if to himself. "Yes. Indeed. I'm going to be tied up the rest of the night."

"It's okay," I told him. "Marc and I are meeting some people down at Zeke's." I spoke very naturally. My voice didn't squeak or anything, but Sam still gave me a funny look.

"You and Marc?"

I shrugged. "And just about everyone else that was on my porch today."

He got up and stretched. "Okay. Have fun."

I stood, and he gave me a very nice kiss before setting off toward the clubhouse. I didn't know if I was happy that he was so comfortable in our relationship that he didn't consider Marc a threat, or a little disappointed that he wasn't worried that my rampant sex appeal might spark something.

I went inside and looked for something to wear.

I had a wonderful time with Marc.

I remembered about how, particularly in the last years of our marriage, we could barely find something to talk about besides the kids. We had planned our days around avoiding each other. When he left, I was devastated, but I had to admit, also relieved, because living with him had become exhausting.

After so much time living with him under such stressful conditions, I had forgotten how charming he was. Funny and sarcastic and a terrific listener. We sat across from each other at one of the big tables in the corner of Zeke's, and ate and laughed and drank beer and laughed some more.

Leon, Carol's date, was a very short, fairly stout man with thick horn-rimmed glasses and a wicked sense of humor. When he and Carol came in together, I choked down a snort, because they looked like Jack Spratt and his wife, but in reverse. He gazed at her all night in undisguised admiration, and she never stopped smiling.

Maggie and Viv came in after Carol and Leon and didn't notice the difference in height until Leon got up to go to the bathroom.

Viv stared after him, finally blurting, "How are you two in the sack?"

Carol smiled demurely. "Just fine. Thanks for asking."

The main topic was, of course, Founders' Day. If I listened hard enough, I'm sure it would have been the main topic of conversation at every table, as Zeke's was filled with Mt. Abrams residents who normally would have been up at the clubhouse, eating pot luck and dancing to the oldies.

Once I told them that the body in Emma's garden was probably Walt Malleck, Maggie and Viv started dreaming up impossible scenarios as to who might have killed Walt and why. They fluctuated between Paula knocking him out in the kitchen and dragging his body out in the middle of the night bury him, and his young lover waiting for him by the back door, bashing him with a nearby hammer when he tried to call it off. We discussed the pros and cons intensely, and then Viv would say something totally ridiculous, and we would burst into laughter. I know, we were talking murder, but remember, we were all a bit drunk.

We didn't talk about Rita. That was still too fresh and raw. We had been on my porch when Rita's parents came racing up to the dock, and we watched as her mother dropped to her knees, screaming, as the body went by on a gurney.

It was almost midnight when we left, and Marc was the only one who had a car. He offered to take us all up the hill, and we said no. Then he offered to take *me* up the hill, and I still said no. Then he grabbed my hand and pulled me toward him, whispering in my ear that maybe he was a little drunk and should probably not drive at all, and why didn't he just spend the night with me?

I pulled away from him and shook my head. Carol and Leon were already across Rt. 51. Maggie and Viv were waiting for me, standing a discreet distance away.

He grabbed my hand again. "Hey, El, come on. Wasn't tonight just like old times?"

Yes, it was. I felt all warm and fuzzy. I could imagine us together. We had always been...combustible. I shook my head again.

"No, Marc. Don't. This isn't fair."

His arms went around me, and he nuzzled my hair. "Fair? Come on, Ellie. Since when is life fair?" He didn't have to stoop to kiss the back of my neck. "I'm talking about you and I tonight. What's so bad about that?"

I jerked away from him, turned, and started walking. Fast. Before I threw myself at him and started peeling his clothes off right in the parking lot. Before I started beating him about the head and shoulders for even *suggesting* we have sex. I was burning up with so many feelings I could barely see straight. But I didn't need to. Maggie and Viv were on either side of me, and they stayed there all the way up the hill to home.

CHAPTER SIX

IT RAINED ALL DAY SUNDAY.

It was the first time in memory that it rained on Founders' Day weekend. It was almost as though the weather gods knew there would be no Open House Day and figured it was safe to let loose. There was thunder and lightning, and the rain was so fierce at times I could barely see the yellow-coated figures still working around the lake. Tents had gone up the night before, but everything and everyone looked soaking wet.

My phone never stopped chirping. Texts came in from just about everyone I knew. Paula was still at the police station. Emma had been found and returned home, where she was being questioned. The body was Walt Malleck. He had been shot. He had been stabbed. He had been hit over the head with a blunt object. Aggie had stormed over to Emma's and accused her of murder. Emma had cursed Aggie with one hundred years of bad luck. The police dragged Aggie away, screaming. Paula had returned from the police station and accused Emma of being Walt's lover. Emma responded by saying that Walt's lover had been a man, then she cursed Paula with two hundred years of bad luck. Paula had been dragged from Emma's house, screaming. The police were putting Emma in protective custody. Aggie was taking out a restraining order. Paula had been arrested. Emma had been arrested. Aggie had been arrested.

In other words, no one knew what was happening.

I knew they were all waiting for Sam to come by to give me the official story, so I could then pass it along. But the rumors were so amusing, even if Sam did tell me anything, I wasn't about to end the rampant speculation.

Cait, who hated the gossip that was so much a part of Mt. Abrams, was offended at first, but even she had to admit that things were getting pretty entertaining.

I finally got a text from Carol that made me stop laughing.

At Emma's. Can u come down?

I texted back, grabbed my slicker, and then yelled at Cait that I'd be back in a few.

The dock and clubhouse were still surrounded by yellow tape, but there was only one police car idling in the rain. I hurried down the slick street, and as I came to Emma's house, I took a quick look in the still open garden door.

I almost cried. The whole one side of the garden had been trampled; there was yellow tape around a gaping hole, and there was mud everywhere. I heard a pitiful cry and saw Biscuit huddled under a bench, trying to keep out of the rain. I crouched down and called her, and the poor thing shot out and jumped into my arms. I turned and hurried to Emma's porch.

The door was open, and through the screen I could see Emma and Carol sitting in front of the fireplace. Emma got up when she saw me and opened the door, taking Biscuit from my arms and scurrying back to the kitchen. I shook off my slicker, hung it on a frail-looking coat rack, and then sat next to Carol.

"What's going on?" I asked in a low voice.

"Emma has a theory," Carol said.

"About what? Walt? Rita?"

Carol nodded. "Both. She said the police didn't appear very interested, but since you know Sam…" Carol shrugged. "She wants to talk to you."

Emma came back into the living room, cuddling Biscuit, who was bundled in a kitchen towel. She sat in a faded flowered armchair by the fireplace, and her other cats immediately swarmed her, finding comfy spots on the arms of the chair, along the back, and of course, on her lap. Her hair lay gathered in an untidy bun at the top of her head, and she was wearing a pale green chenille bathrobe. The perfect picture of a crazy cat lady.

"Thank you for coming, Ellie," she said somewhat breathlessly. "I think the police need to find Walt's lover. I think whoever it was killed him and buried him under those lilac bushes. I also think that when word got out about my koi pond, whoever killed Walt tried to discourage me from digging by trashing my garden. And I think that poor Rita saw whoever it was *in* my garden, and that's why *she* was killed." She was vigorously drying off Biscuit as she spoke, and when she was done, she shook Biscuit out of the towel. Biscuit jumped down, looked mildly embarrassed, then began to groom herself. The other cats all watched with interest.

"That's actually a very good theory," I said. "The police didn't like it?"

She smoothed the damp towel on her lap and began folding it. "No. Apparently, they have no faith in psychic intuition or dreams."

"Oh? You dreamed this?" I asked.

She nodded. "Yes. Last night. I couldn't see the person's face, but the figure was tall and very thin. It could have been a man or a woman, I couldn't be sure. And Walt was hit over the head with the shovel that Paula had been using to in dig her lilacs." She sniffed.

"You know that Paula was away the weekend Walt disappeared? She was moving her son, the oldest, to Delaware. He was going to college down there, you see. He hated his father. Couldn't wait to get away. The younger boy was with them. So Walt was alone."

I glanced at Carol. Her face was perfectly neutral.

"I didn't know that. Did you tell that to the police too?" I asked.

Emma nodded. "Yes. They already knew that. Paula is up here, did you know? Both of the boys live close. But she told me she knew he had run off and good riddance to him." She sniffed again. "Walt was not a very likable man."

"Well," Carol murmured, "*someone* liked him."

"No one we know," I said. "Do you know anything about the fire?"

Emma shook her head. "I just remember waking up, and the smoke was everywhere. I don't know who called the fire department, but they were there by the time I got downstairs. And thank God, too, or that fire would have taken my house as well. Poor Paula. She'd had a rough time, moneywise, after Walt left. She was going to have to sell the house, you know." Emma leaned forward and dropped her voice. "For a while there, I thought maybe Paula did it. But the investigators couldn't find any proof of arson."

I frowned, thinking. "I thought the rumor was that Walt came back and burned down the house."

Emma sat back and looked smug. "I started that one."

My jaw may have dropped. "Oh?"

"I didn't want people to think Paula did it," she explained.

I cleared my throat. "Well, Emma, although dreams are not necessarily, um, always reliable, it's a good theory. The problem is Rita was killed very spur of the moment. She never should have been up at the clubhouse in the first place. So the killer was either following her around or was very lucky to find her alone by the docks."

Emma frowned slightly, then shrugged it off. "Then he or she followed her. Rita, I mean. The dream wasn't to clear about that part, but I definitely saw Rita getting hit with the same shovel that killed Walt."

"There was no shovel found. Sam thinks she was hit with an oar," I said.

Emma looked hurt. "After all, dear, it was a *dream*. And there's a great deal of symbolism in dreams. The shape of the shovel, the shape of the oar…."

"Of course." I stood up. "Well, thank you for telling me this. I'll be sure to speak to Sam."

"Will you?" Emma looked up at me hopefully. "I'd be so grateful. This is very bad for our neighborhood, all the negative energy, and I'd hate to think about poor Walt's soul wandering in my garden, searching for closure."

"Was he wandering before?" I asked. Carol, who had stood up with me, poked me in the side with her elbow.

Emma just frowned again. I may have said the wrong thing. I pulled my slicker off the rack to put it on. "I'll talk to Sam," I promised on my way out.

Carol's umbrella was on Emma's porch, and she shook it open. "Have you seen the garden?" she asked.

"Yes. It broke my heart. Do you know Paula?"

Carol shrugged. "Vaguely. From years ago when she'd come into the library."

"We need to talk to her. Any ideas?"

Carol thought a moment. "Viv? I bet Viv knows her."

I nodded. "Good idea. I'll give her a call. Thanks for texting me. Some of Emma's *dream ideas* might be sound."

"I thought so too," Carol said. "Let me know if you talk to Paula. I'd like to be there."

We stepped off the porch together and into the rain, Carol turning one way, me heading up the hill toward home.

Sam listened very patiently to me after dinner. I'd made fried chicken, and we had leftover potato salad and sliced tomatoes. Cait and Tessa stuffed themselves then curled up to watch *The Sound of Music*. Again. Sam and I sat out on the porch, listened to the rain, and talked about Rita and Walt Malleck.

"When Walt disappeared, questions were asked, of course," Sam explained. "Paula was with the boys, so there never any suspicion cast on her. There still isn't. Not for Walter, anyway, although it's pretty clear that the two incidents are connected.

Incidents. A woman was bashed over the head in broad daylight in what people insist is a safe and happy community, and it was considered an *incident*.

"I talked to Emma this afternoon," I said.

He glanced at me, a smile playing along his lips. "She had a very interesting theory," he said. "It might have been better received if she hadn't told us that it came to her in a dream."

"That doesn't change anything," I said. "It makes a lot of sense. We need to find who Walt was involved with."

"We? Again with the we?" He shook his head. "Ellie, please, you're dealing with a very desperate killer. Look at what happened yesterday. In the middle of the morning like that? Anyone who's willing to take that kind of risk needs to be left to the professionals."

"Yes, of course," I said. "But let's face it, I could do a much better job of rounding up all the little pieces of information floating around. Somebody saw something; they just didn't know at the time it was important. Whoever killed Rita walked up to the dock, and then walked back down the hill. There are all sorts of people running around before the parade, but not up by the clubhouse. I just need to—"

"Leave it to the professionals," Sam said slowly.

I rolled my eyes. "Yes. I said yes, and I will leave it to you. But I can still ask questions, can't I?"

He grinned. "What are you working on?"

Since I was a freelance editor specializing in mysteries and thrillers, who occasionally got wrapped up in whatever I happened to be reading, it was not a completely random question. "I just started a new author. Murder-mystery. Amateur sleuth."

"Living in a small town?"

I grinned back. "Yes. And she knits."

He threw back his head and laughed. "I wish you would learn to knit."

"Please. I'd end up stabbing myself in the eye with a needle."

He stood up and pulled me up against him. We stood there for a few minutes, getting quite, ah, close. He finally stepped back.

"I have to go to work tomorrow."

I cleared my throat. "Okay. So, I'll talk to you."

He reached out and stroked my cheek. "Yes."

He was halfway down the walkway when he turned. "By the way, how was your dinner? With Marc?"

I swallowed. "Fine."

I saw him nod, and he got onto his car and drove away.

It was raining again on Monday. Tessa was, at eight-thirty, already whining about having nothing to do. I had to finish my current project, respond to at least four new requests, and oh yes, talk to as many people as I could about Saturday morning.

Cait had taken the weekend off from work, so I knew that she had picked up at least two lunch shifts to make up for her lost time. I knocked on her door, and when she grunted, I stuck my head in.

"I'll pay you twenty dollars to take Tessa somewhere."

She rolled over and looked at me with one sleepy eye. "Like, the Meadowlands?"

I closed my eyes and shook my head. The Meadowlands she was referring to was not the sprawling sports complex, but rather the legendary dumping ground for unwanted bodies. "I was thinking more like the mall. Or the movies. Or the FunPlex. Anywhere but here. I have to work."

She yawned dramatically. "You're lucky I'm not working. But if it's raining tomorrow, you're on your own. I have to go in by eleven."

"That's fine. I just really need today."

"Twenty plus expenses."

"Of course. Starting right now."

"I need a shower."

"Take her in with you." I shut the door gently and went into my office.

My office had multipaned windows on three sides, and I usually needed the white sheers that covered the windows to keep out the sun. Today, I pushed them open and stared moodily out into the rain.

There was still one police car across the street by the lake. Yellow tape was still everywhere. There were three tents, one on the dock in front of the boat where Rita had been found, one where the dock met the shore, and one on the pathway to the clubhouse. I shifted my gaze from the dock to the clubhouse. Rita had come up this way to find her phone. Had she? Or was she interrupted before she had a chance to even look for it?

Sam had said I could ask questions. Well, no, not exactly. But he hadn't said I *couldn't* ask questions. I didn't want to interfere, because he was right. Whoever killed Rita was fearless and desperate, not the kind of person I should go running after.

Sam had said Rita had been hit with an oar. Who would bring an oar into the clubhouse? Whoever did it wasn't waiting for her, because none knew she'd be there. So, they had seen her, grabbed an oar off the dock, and followed her into the clubhouse.

I had to find out who, if anyone, was in or around the clubhouse Saturday morning on Founders' Day business.

Who would know that information?

Well, Sharon would. She had been running the whole show, and I was pretty sure she was the type of person who tracked her minions very carefully.

One of the problems was, of course, that I didn't know Sharon very well. Just like I didn't know Paula Malleck, another person I really wanted to talk to. But I knew a few people who might.

So I sent a text to Shelly, Maggie, Carol, and Viv, inviting them for a little Monday night wine on the porch. I hinted at leftover cookies.

The good news—four yeses in four minutes.

The bad news—I had to drive out in the rain for more cookies.

CHAPTER SEVEN

O F COURSE, THE FIRST THING everyone wanted to talk about was Marc. Shelly, in particular, having missed my big date with him on Saturday night, wanted not only details, but also complete analysis and all possible speculation. I wanted to talk about anything other than Marc, because I was still fairly confused and pissed off and hopeful and disgusted and pretty much a complete mental jumble about him. And him and me. And Sam and me. And who I wanted, what I wanted, and who I wanted it from.

"Remember," Shelly said, quite firmly. "He is the man who broke your heart and left you bleeding, alone, in the gutter. I love him; you know that. But I do not want to see him back in your life."

Carol sighed. "Seeing them together was like seeing them back in the good old days," she said. "Remember how cute they always were? The finishing each other's sentences gets old, but they still *get* each other."

Viv did not know Marc. She had moved in when our marriage had started to go south and had no memo- ries of our "good old days." She just remembered me sobbing, drunk and miserable, telling everyone what a lousy husband he'd been. She waggled her finger at me. "Girlfriend, you have a good man in Sam. I never knew Marc the charmer, or Marc the soul mate. I just knew Marc the prick. And a leopard does not change his spots. Just because he's back to being all sweet and lovey dovey, don't mean he isn't still a prick."

Maggie lifted her wine glass. "Here, here."

"Listen, everyone, I know what Marc is, okay? After all, I was married to him. We had dinner together. I think he really does want me back, but that doesn't mean *I* want us back together. Can't I just enjoy his company while he makes his case?"

Viv settled back and shrugged. "Just be careful."

"I will. I promise." I looked around at them. It had stopped raining, and the moon was rising over the lake, and the night was cool and pretty spectacular. "I want us to talk about what happened this weekend. About Rita."

Shelly leaned forward, her eyes bright. "Yes, I thought that might be what this was about. Anything from Sam?"

"I spoke to him tonight. She was hit with an oar. They found it, but there were no prints. The killer rubbed it clean with something; there are fibers they're analyzing. She was hit in the front room of the clubhouse. Blood was found. She was dragged to the boat and dumped in." I looked over to the clubhouse and tried to visualize what happened in real time. "She had been looking for her phone, which was why she was there in the first place. Someone came up behind her, hit her, and dragged her. The first two boats had gear in them, so she went into the third boat, which was empty. The killer went back, cleaned the oar, and threw it into the nearest boat. It only took seconds."

"Wait," Maggie said. "I think we're picking up this story in the middle. I have to think that Rita getting killed had to do with Walter Malleck being found. Shouldn't we start there?"

"But that was years ago," Shelly said. "Nobody is going to remember details about the night Walter disappeared. But I bet people will know exactly where they were Saturday morning."

"And what about Emma's theory?" Carol asked, " I thought it was pretty sound."

"What theory?" Maggie asked.

Carol explained quickly, saving the part about it being a dream for last.

Shelly rolled her eyes. "She dreamed this?"

"Yes," I said. "But it makes good sense. It might not be hard to find out if anyone saw someone going into Emma's garden. Just like we need to find out who saw Rita coming up the hill. And who else they saw. Nobody was supposed to be in the clubhouse, right?"

Viv made a face. "I helped out the year before last with setup. The same group who clean up Friday night gets everything ready for Saturday night. All the tables are clean and set, floor's cleaned; it's all set to go. So when the Saturday night dinner starts, the doors are unlocked, and everything is ready. The porch is open, of course, and the bathrooms. Maybe somebody was cleaning the bathrooms?"

"We need to ask Sharon," Maggie said. "I bet she knew where every volunteer was every single second."

"That's what I thought," I said, drinking wine. "But I just don't know her well enough to just dive into the conversation." I looked around. No one was jumping up to volunteer.

"Well," Carol said, "she and Mary Rose are pretty tight.'

My shoulders slumped. Mary Rose Reed was president of the Garden Club, and I had gotten on her wrong side earlier in the year by voting against her during the Great Hydrangea Debate. "That doesn't help me," I said.

"There's a Founders' Day meeting tomorrow night," Shelly said. "They called an emergency session. I'll go with you. We can get Mary Rose talking, I'm sure. You know how nosy she is. And I'll bet she grabs Sharon, and we can listen in."

I drained my wine glass. There were still cookies left, lots of them. "Good idea. I'll bring down these cookies, so I won't be tempted to eat them all by myself. But we need to talk to everyone who lives between Rita's house and the lake. *Everybody* was out. Someone had to have seen something."

"The problem," Maggie said, "is just that. Everybody was out and about. How are we going to decide who was out waiting for the parade and who was stalking Rita Ferris?"

"We need to think about this some more and narrow our focus," Shelly said. "Maggie is right. This started with Walt's body. We need to find the connection between that and Rita."

"We also need to talk to Paula. Viv, do you know her?"

She shook her head. "Sorry, no." Viv picked up a cookie and broke it in half. "What we need to do is be careful. The reason Rita was killed was probably because she heard something or knew something about Walt's murder. If we find out what she knew, we'll be next. And I do not want to end up in some rowboat."

"We're on guard," Maggie said. "We'll be careful."

Viv waved the cookie at Maggie. "We'd better be."

The sun was shining the next day, and all the yellow tape around the lake was gone. The rain had washed away anything that might have been missed by the police, Sam explained, so there was no point in keeping people away. But by noon there was no one on the beach. Tessa had grabbed her bike and said she was off to Jerome's. Cait left for work. The day was sunny and beautiful and deathly quiet.

I texted Carol.

U working?

Not until one.

Perfect. I could use the company. *Going to walk Boot down to Main Park. Want to come?*

Pick me up.

Walking down to Main Park would mean walking down Blackburn Road. Which was where, coincidentally, Paula Malleck was staying with the Millers.

Carol was waiting for me at the corner of Sommerfield and Blackburn. We walked into the park and sat on a bench, looking down the hill and toward the Miller's house.

Main Park was divided, more or less in half, by Sommerfield. Upper Main had a few houses on the north end, as well as the library and post office. But Lower Main was nothing but trees and a wildflower meadow and all the wonders of nature, all the way down until it smacked into Rt. 51. The Miller house was an expanded cape cod style house that backed onto Lower Main.

"Are we waiting for Paula to come out and sit on the deck?" Carol asked.

"Wouldn't that be nice?" I ran my fingers through my hair, resisting the urge to pull at the roots. "I don't know, Carol. How do we do this? Just go up and knock on the door and ask her who she thought her husband was sleeping with?"

Boot jumped up on the bench beside me and leaned against me, panting. Carol and I sat for a few minutes, waiting for divine intervention.

And it came.

"Look," Carol said.

The back door of the Miller's house opened, and their small white dog came scampering out. Boot's ears perked.

"Would Boot eat it?" Carol asked in a whisper.

I shook my head and let go of the leash. "Nope. Too small."

Boot took off like a shot down the hill. I counted slowly to three, then took off after her.

Carol was right behind me, screaming, "Hey, get your dog!"

The back door opened again, and a woman hurried out and down the deck. Carol and I arrived just as the two dogs finished their ceremonial butt sniffing and were actually chasing each other in circles.

I grabbed the leash. "I'm so sorry, she just got away."

The woman came down and scooped up the little white dog. "No harm done. Good thing though, Mary would have killed me if I let anything happen to Snooks."

"Hello, Paula," Carol said easily. "It's good to see you."

Paula had changed quite a bit since I'd seen her last, fourteen years ago. She was thinner, her hair an improbable shade of red, and she was dressed in a bright linen sundress. I had remembered her as old and rather frumpy. She had gotten younger looking over the years.

"Hello, Carol. And is it Ellie?"

"Yes. You look terrific, Paula," I said. "Really. I wouldn't have known you."

She grinned. "Thanks. Yes, it's amazing what life without a miserable husband will do for your looks."

Wow. Okay, Paula, let's just put it out there. "Ah…"

She laughed. "Please, Ellie, no need to try to be polite. Walt was a horror to live with. I was so glad when he left, I could barely contain myself. Knowing that he hadn't left me but was killed instead is just icing on the cake. I hated that bastard. Murder was what he deserved. Although, I do feel sorry for poor Aggie. She and Rita were a wonderful couple. I hate thinking that Walt's death all those years ago has come back to haunt so many people."

Carol had eased her way up the steps and was standing right next to Paula. "What do you mean?"

Paula leaned in and dropped her voice. "She did it."

I came closer. "She?"

Paula waved us onto the deck, dropped Snooks to the floor, and motioned for us to sit. "Everybody is afraid to say anything around me. Like I'll be offended or reminded of my heartbreaking loss. But whoever Walt was screwing around with probably killed him. And chances are she never left Mt. Abrams. Or if she did, she came back. All these people do. So it only makes sense that Rita saw something or did something after the body was found, and it made her a target." She sat back and folded her hands. "Stupid. Tragic, but stupid. Rita was always saying ridiculous things that got her into trouble."

"Paula, did you have any clue who it was?" I asked. Might as well go for broke.

She looked at me very carefully. "Do you know that you're the only person who has ever had the nerve to ask me that question? I always thought it was Lou Lombardi."

I tried not to let my jaw hit the ground. "Really?"

She nodded. "Her mother and I were pretty good friends, and Ellen was always going on about what a wild child Lou was. And she was worried about her sleeping around. And I knew Walt thought *quite* a lot of Lou. Well, she was a beautiful girl, wasn't she?"

"But did you ever hear or see anything from Walt? About Lou, I mean," Carol asked.

Paula shrugged. "No. I guess not." She frowned.

"What?" I asked.

"Walt lost interest in having sex the year Danny was born, which was fine with me. He was a lousy lover. I was actually kind of surprised he was going after someone else." She shook her head slightly. "He'd say he was going out for a bit of the Irish. I always thought he was going down to Taylor's to drink. But when he'd come back, he wouldn't be drunk. Once I asked him straight out if he was sleeping with another woman, and he laughed so hard I thought he'd bust a gut."

"He'd walk?" Carol asked.

Paula nodded. "Always. He didn't like to drive. We barely used that second car."

"Paula, what about those lilacs?" I said.

She smiled. "The boys bought them for me for Mother's Day. Two little plants. That's when I decided to line the whole drive with them." She made a bit of a face. "And to block the view. I liked Aggie and Rita, but they spent a lot of time looking down into our yard, such as it was. So I bought two more plants early in the summer and started to plant them. If I had known it would be so much work, I'd have stuck them in a pot had been done with it. Lots of rocks. After I planted them, I put the rocks back around them, to try to keep the weeds down."

"So whoever buried Walt would have had to move the rocks, then dig a hole, put the body in, cover it up, put all the rocks back...that must have taken all night," I said slowly.

Paula was watching me closely. "I was gone all weekend." She narrowed her eyes. "Are you girls playing Jessica Fletcher here?"

Carol waved her hand. "Don't be silly. It's just that there's usually not a lot going on in Mt. Abrams. You have to admit, this is kind of huge."

Paula smiled. "Well, let me know if you need any more information. The police want me to stick around, so I'll probably be here all week."

Carol smiled back. "Why, thank you Paula. That's very good to know."

We chatted. The dogs sniffed each other's butts again, and Carol and I said good-bye, and then we continued walking down the hill. Somewhere, on the other side of Rt. 51, was Dunkin' Donuts. Even Boot knew where we were going and tugged on the leash.

"Well, if I didn't already know they were not the happiest of couples," Carol said, "I'd be a bit shocked at her attitude."

"She's not exactly the grieving widow, is she? So we're looking for a young girl, Irish, who still lives here or came back?"

"Yes. And she apparently spent an entire weekend digging a grave for her dead lover."

We waited for the walk sign, then crossed Rt.51. Carol went in to Dunkin' and got us coffee, while Boot and I sat at one of the picnic tables.

Carol blew on her coffee to cool it, then fished out a Munchkin from her bag and tossed it to Boot, who deftly caught it, swallowed it whole, then sat patiently. She had at least half a dozen more Munchkins in the bag, and I was trying not to drool.

"Paula was gone all weekend, so our little Irish lass came over, killed him, hid the body until nightfall, moved all the rocks, dug, came over the next night and dug some more, buried him, then put all the rocks back?"

Carol raised her eyebrows. "Sounds positively exhausting. Maybe it was a little Irish lad? Walt lost interest in sex; he was bad at it in the first place, and he laughed at the idea of a woman."

I stared at her. "Oh, my God, Carol. Do you think? Well, crap. You've just doubled our suspect pool."

She shrugged. "Just a thought. I don't think it will help to find out what was going on years ago. We need to focus on what was happening on Saturday. That's our best chance of figuring out who did this." She took a bite of a powdered sugar Munchkin. "Should I give Boot another?"

"Sure," I sighed. "At least one of us should be enjoying them," I said. "It might be worth our while to find out who was trashing Emma's garden."

"Whoever was doing that was doing it in the middle of the night," she pointed out. "Most people are asleep."

"But those who weren't probably noticed somebody carrying a ladder around. Unless we're looking for someone with wings."

"Which would also be noticeable," she grinned.

"Yep." I held out my hand. "Give me one of those. A chocolate one. All this thinking made me hungry."

She spilled one perfect Munchkin into my hand. Boot whined softly.

I didn't even feel guilty.

The Old Firehouse was a large, drafty building that was abandoned back in the '60s when a shiny, new firehouse was built on Rt. 51. Rather than tear it down, the Historical Society raised enough money for it to be restored and used as a community center. Everyone from the Girl Scouts to the Garden Club used it for meetings and such, and that was where the Founders' Day committee was holding it's emergency meeting. I felt terrible for Sharon, huddled with her closest cohorts. The crowd that gathered was angry and confused. Never, in the history of Mt. Abrams, had Founders' Day been so rudely interrupted.

Sharon started with the good news. The winners of the House Decorating Contest would be posted on the bulletin board in front of the library, and the prizes could be picked up at Mary Rose Reed's house, over on Grant Street.

She got very quiet, and she gripped the podium with both hands as she spoke. "It has been suggested that next weekend we finish the Founders' Day activities as they had originally been planned. I personally think that would be disrespectful. However, this is for the community, and I will put this to a vote. All in favor of continuing Founders' Day next week, raise your hand."

About half a dozen hands went up.

"Opposed?"

Everyone else, at least fifty of us, raised our hands. Sharon looked relieved.

"Motion defeated." She took a long breath. "The police are investigating, but there is not a lot of progress being made. Detective Feltz is here tonight, and would like to speak to you."

Martin Feltz was tall, thin, and bald. He was dressed in a dark suit and was all business.

"We are asking for anyone who may have seen Rita Ferris, or anyone else for that matter, up around the Lake Abrams Clubhouse Saturday morning to please get in touch with me at your earliest convenience. Any information you give will be kept in the strictest confidence. We could really use your assistance in this matter. As of right now, we have no clues as to who may have killed Rita Ferris. Thank you."

He nodded and stepped back. Sharon came forward and cleared her throat. "We'll have our next regular meeting two weeks from tonight. Thank you all for coming."

She stepped down and practically ran out of the firehouse.

I stared at Shelly. "That's it?"

Shelly looked thoughtful. "Well, I guess there was nothing else to say." She twisted in her seat to look back where Sharon had left the building. "Very unlike her to run like that. She's a natural born talker. I wonder what's up?"

I sighed. "I don't know, but I think we need to talk to her. Any ideas?"

Shelly lifted her shoulders, then let them drop. "Mary Rose?"

I sighed. "I was afraid you were going to say that."

I walked home, took Boot for a quick walk, then sat on the porch and waited. It was Marc's night with the girls, and he had picked them up before dinner. During the summer, they were usually out until pretty late, so I stared at the lake and thought about the book I was working on. The writer had a great voice, but her plotting was all over the place. She also had about a dozen red herrings, which confused the hell out of me. Almost as much as Rita's murder was confusing.

Marc pulled up, and instead of just letting the girls out, he turned off the car and walked them to the house. He kissed them goodnight, then sat beside me.

"How are you?" he asked.

I nodded. "Good. You?"

"I'm sorry."

"Oh? About what?"

"About being a jerk the other night."

I was quiet. Yes, he had been a jerk. I wasn't sure I was ready to forgive and forget. On the other hand, I didn't want to be a jerk either. "Sam and I are good right now," I told him. "It's not like there's nothing going on in in my life, and you can just drop back in."

"Are you in love with him?" he asked.

Good question. "It's too soon. We're still figuring things out."

Marc ran his fingers though his hair. "I like him. I just don't think he's your type."

"And what, exactly, is my type?"

I could see him grin in the darkness. "Charming literary types with pink hair?"

I laughed. "Not pink yet, but starting to fade, that's for sure." I stopped laughing. "If you never stopped loving me, why did you leave?" I had never asked him that before. My heart was in my throat, waiting for him to answer.

He took his time. "You weren't ...yourself. You'd become angry and sad, and I don't know, awful. I couldn't talk to you anymore. You stopped making me laugh. You stopped caring about what I was doing. You stopped caring about me period."

That hit me. Hard. "You're the one who stopped caring," I blurted. "I was fat and unemployed and had a newborn baby and a teen and you were off living your life as though nothing had changed, and anytime I said anything about it you just closed up and walked away."

He exhaled loudly. "I think we both...stopped thinking about the other person. We were too focused on our own pain."

We sat quietly for a few more minutes, then he got up, touched my hand, walked out to his car, and then drove away.

Chapter Eight

M ARY ROSE REED AND I were not friends. I was not friends with all sorts of people, so it didn't really bother me all that much. Mary Rose was pretty much involved with every single organization in Mt. Abrams and had been for years. Lynn Fahey was giving her a run for her money as Most Socially Active Mt. Abrams Resident, but Mary Rose still held the lead.

Mary Rose didn't like me much, but she did love to gossip, and for that reason I had no problem walking down to her house the next morning to knock on her door. Once she knew I wanted to talk about what happened over the weekend, I knew she'd welcome me with open arms. Besides, I had a perfectly valid excuse to see her. My daughters had won Best Decorated House. Again.

Her yard, in late summer, was beautiful, not a leaf out of place, no blade of grass leaning too far to the left. She lived below Sommerfield, in the so-called new section, which meant her house had a front and back yard, a driveway that actually held two cars, and plumbing that did not need a sacrifice to the gods once a year to work properly.

"Ellie, good morning," she said from behind her tightly closed screen door. "What can I do for you?"

"I just checked the board, and my girls are due a trophy."

She smiled and opened the door. "Of course. Come in. Where are they? I would think they'd want to get it themselves."

"Cait took Tessa down to Sandy Hook," I lied.

"Well, it's a beautiful day for it."

I followed Mary Rose into her dining room. Mary Rose was a throwback to the fifties. She always dressed in an outfit—tops and bottoms that matched, with coordinating accessories, polished shoes, and when the weather turned cold, panty hose. Today she wore a denim skirt, red checked sleeveless blouse, bright red Keds, with a white bead necklace, and matching clip-on earrings.

She had the trophies and ribbons carefully arranged on the table. She checked her list, then handed me the biggest, most gaudy trophy of them all.

I beamed as I took it. Cait and Tessa were going to be thrilled.

"Thanks." With anyone else, I would have carefully thought of a gracious segue to Rita, Walt, and the whole situation in general. But with Mary Rose, subtlety was not needed.

"Who do you think did it, Mary Rose? I'm sure you have a few ideas."

She lit up like a Christmas tree, pulled out two chairs from under the dining table, and then motioned for me to sit. "Aggie and Rita were both very active in the Historical Society, you know. I really loved those girls. Such hard workers, you know? Aggie is just devastated. She hasn't a clue as to who could have done it. Rita had no enemies. Sure, she ran her mouth a bit too much, and maybe some of her jokes fell flat, but she was sweet."

I nodded sympathetically. "Yes. But surely her murder was tied to finding Walt Malleck, don't you think?"

Mary's face got dark. "Walt Malleck was an evil man and a terrible drunk. Whoever killed him did the world a service."

"True, Mary Rose, but still. It was murder. Someone must have gotten pretty anxious when Emma started digging around."

Mary Rose shuddered. "Yes. That koi pond. It would have been so beautiful. Emma's garden is ruined now, have you seen it? I have no idea how she'll ever bring it back."

"She said someone had been getting in," I said, watching her face.

She frowned in concentration. "Yes. She told me that."

"Have you heard any ideas about who might have been responsible?"

"No," she said shortly.

"Has anyone said anything about being up at the clubhouse? I can't believe nobody saw anything."

Her face relaxed. "I know. It's very strange. On Saturday morning, everyone was getting ready for the parade. Nobody was paying attention to who was going where. And if anyone *had* been up there, it was probably a committee person, checking up on things, so nobody would have given it a second thought." She leaned forward. "People are funny, Ellie. They see what they want to see. A man could have been walking around carrying a machine gun, and folks would have looked and thought, gee, that guy must be in the parade, and just gone on their way. Or they don't see at all. The expected is always invisible."

"You're right, Mary Rose, " I said slowly. I looked down at the trophy in my hand. "You're right. Thank you. You've given me lots to think about."

"Oh?"

I smiled. "Yes. Let me go. Thanks again."

I went out and started up the hill. The expected *was* invisible. She was right. Nobody noticed the UPS guy, or the JCP&L truck. The school bus was never seen. On Saturday, it would have been expected that people would be running around, and in places they wouldn't normally be. Nobody would have paid attention to who was at the clubhouse because everyone knew that, at some point during the day, *somebody* would be there.

Well…poop.

Clearly, I'd have to start looking at this from another angle.

I turned the corner and started into the post office. I usually didn't bother getting my mail every day, but I was right there, and Joan Dudley, postmistress and gossipmonger extraordinaire, was out front watering the flower boxes that hung in the post office windows.

"Morning Joanie, how are you?"

She turned, scowling. Joan was not a terribly happy person. She constantly complained about how unappreciated, overworked, and generally abused by post office patrons in general she was. What kept her going, Shelly once joked, was the constant influx on information she received by merely listening to what folks said to each other while collecting their mail.

"Oh, Ellie, hello. I'm doing all right, I suppose. My back, you know. And people are in such terrible moods. Everyone is angry and upset. Poor Emma is beside herself. Not only was that man found in her yard, but her garden is completely destroyed."

I nodded. "Yes, I know. We should all pitch in and help her put it back together. After all, everyone loved Emma's garden."

Joan sniffed. "Not everyone."

Perfect. Just what I wanted to hear. "Oh?"

She carefully plucked a dying petunia leaf and dropped it to the ground. "You know those two who lived next door?"

"To Emma? You mean Aggie and Rita?"

She nodded. "Oh, yes."

"Did they say anything to you?" The "to you" part was a courtesy. Joan made note of everything that was said in her little kingdom, whether it was said to her or not.

She glanced around. Elliot Street, which could be affectionately called the commercial center of Mt. Abrams, was deserted. The library, a few doors down, had its door open, but no one was sitting out front. The Old Firehouse was shut and still. The houses on the street were quiet. Midday in the summer was a very quiet time in Mt. Abrams.

Nonetheless, she lowered her voice. "They ran into Harry Floyd and asked to borrow his ladder." She raised her eyebrows. "He said they could have it as long as they wanted."

She turned and marched into the post office.

I didn't know who Harry Floyd was, but then, I didn't know lots of people who lived in Mt. Abrams. But somebody I did know could undoubtedly point him out, and maybe he would be willing to tell me what Aggie and Rita needed a ladder for. I followed Joan into the post office, dug in my pocket for my box key, and pulled out a few bits of mail. I was going through the motions, trying to figure out what to do next, when one envelope jumped out at me.

It was addressed to Caitlyn. From Lyon, France.

Her acceptance—or not—to a two-year fellowship in a strange place very far from home.

Seriously too much for my brain to handle.

I held the envelope up to the light, as though trying to read whatever was inside.

"Joanie" I called. "When was this?"

She appeared in her window. "When was what?"

Honestly—what were we just talking about? "When did they talk to Harry Floyd?"

"When did who talk to Harry Floyd?"

Oh my God. "Aggie and Rita?"

"Oh!" She looked thoughtful. "About six weeks ago. It was the same day Sharon told Lynn Fahey she was divorcing her husband."

I stared at her. "Sharon Butler? Divorcing her husband?"

Joan glanced around. The post office lobby was empty except for me. Who on earth was she looking for? "Yes. Apparently, he's gay. Has been for years."

I remembered what Carol said, about Walt and an *Irish lad*. Butler was an Irish name. David had lived in Mt. Abrams all his life. He and Sharon had gone through school together. Had she known then?

If she had, what did that mean, exactly?

I clutched Cait's letter and the Best Decorated House trophy to my chest and practically ran home.

Oddly enough, Sam was not nearly as excited about my information gathering as I thought he should be. In fact, his reaction was downright negative.

"Didn't I tell you to leave this to the professionals? Meaning me and the police, not to mention the FBI? Did you not hear me say that? We're dealing with a very dangerous person here, Ellie. What did you think you were doing?"

"I thought I was getting some pretty helpful stuff. Like maybe Aggie and Rita were trashing Emma's garden."

"And why is that helpful, exactly?"

We were out to dinner. Cait and Tessa decided to celebrate their newest trophy by feasting at Qdoba, followed by homemade ice cream at Denville Dairy. While my stomach was jumping up and down with pure excitement at the possibilities, my head remained focused on those last pounds to lose. So after I gave the girls some money and waved good-bye, I called Sam and suggested a quick dinner at Zeke's, where I knew I could get a great Thai chicken salad. He said yes. Dinner was lovely. The after-dinner coffee was where things got sticky.

"Look, Sam," I explained patiently. "We thought that Emma's garden getting vandalized was related to the possibility of her digging up Walt, which is what happened. And Rita getting killed was also related to Walt. If you take the vandalizing part out of the equation, everything changes."

He exhaled very loudly. "Who is the *we* in this? Because the police have several theories, including the possibility that the events are totally unrelated."

I sat back. "What? Are you kidding? Of course they're related."

"Ellie, Walter Malleck was a much despised drunkard who was hit with a blunt object and buried under newly-planted lilac bushes that may or may not have been planted for the express purpose of creating a convenient grave. His disappearance was reported after his family returned from a weekend trip that gave them all alibis. Rita Ferris was generally liked and respected. She should have been sitting on her porch Saturday morning, but was killed in a place no one knew she would be, on the spur of the moment, by either an extremely lucky or very clever killer. Why are they necessarily connected?"

I stared into my coffee. I hated when he got logical. "It's just a feeling," I muttered. "What about David Butler being gay?"

He sat back and threw up his hands. "What about it? That's not a crime, you know."

"Yes, I know. But what if he was the one Walter was having an affair with? Paula said he had no interest in sex, and David was young and lived right in town…"

"So was Louise Lombardi, young and living in town."

I narrowed my eyes. "Lou?"

He looked uncomfortable. "I told you, I'm naturally suspicious of anyone who can play Name the Body and win."

"You like Lou Lombardi as Walt's killer?"

"Shhh." He looked around. "Ellie, please. I should not be talking to you about this at all. I just want to make it clear that you need to stop poking into things. We have some pretty exceptional people looking into this. Don't make waves. Please."

"Okay," I said. But I was thinking that what I *really* needed to do was talk to Sharon Butler.

Thursday did not start well. The lake was still closed off as a crime scene, and Cait had a lunch shift. I had not heard a word from her about what was in her letter. She had taken it from me without a word and carried it upstairs. I had thought about going through her room while she was at work, but decided that was a dishonest, not to mention childish, thing to do. Besides, Tessa was up my butt all day. I finally talked her and Jerome into a *Star Wars* marathon, allowing me to at least get some work done.

I texted Shelly after lunch.

We need to talk to Sharon Did u know David was gay? They're getting divorced

It took her less than a minute to get back to me.

I know! No way! Says who?
Joanie
Of course. Ill b up after dinner
That made me feel better.

I sent my edits off to my new author and read a bunch of emails. I tried to keep focused on work, but my brain was going in too many directions. I finally decided I needed to go out, but what about Tessa and Jerome?

"Do you want to walk Boot around the lake?"

"No."

"How about going to the library?"

"No."

"We could walk down to Dunkin' Donuts, and I'll buy you Munchkins."

Tessa glared at me. "You made us sit and watch these movies, and now you want us to go outside? Make up your mind. Besides, it's cool in here and gross out there. What's for supper? Can Jerome stay?"

"Hot dogs. Yes." She had a point. The humidity had soared overnight, and just opening the front door let in a blast of air so humid my hair immediately frizzed up to my ears.

"I'm taking Boot for a quickie. Stay here."

Tessa rolled her eyes at me before returning them to the TV screen.

Boot wasn't too thrilled about going out either. We walked over to the clubhouse. I looked over the taped-off areas again. What had happened here?

Rita had walked up onto the clubhouse. No one would have been there, but maybe someone had seen her? She wouldn't have been alarmed if she *had* seen someone. After all, any number of people had a reason to be up there. She was the one who didn't belong. She was there because she'd left her phone.

I walked up to the screened-in porch. It was huge, running the length of the clubhouse, with more than a dozen round glass tables with six to eight chairs around each. Glass-front doors led into the house. It was all taped off, of course, so I walked around to the boathouse.

The boathouse had been built in the forties, a squat, ugly building that served as a massive storage spot for all the rowboats canoes, and outdoor furniture that belonged to the lake association. The double doors were usually padlocked, but I saw the chain was loose, and the doors were open a crack. I pushed them open further and walked in. Boot sniffed happily. "Hello?" I called.

Silence.

It was a huge cavern of a place, with canoes and kayaks hung on the walls and large coils of rope in the back corners. The sunlight barely reached in a few feet from the doorway, and most of the interior sank back in the darkness.

It was cool and smelled damp and moldy. Kind of creepy.

"What are you doing here, Ellie?" A quiet voice asked.

I looked around. There, coming out of the shadows, was David Butler.

I jumped about a foot in the air. What was *he* doing here? "Just looking around. Trying to imagine what Rita did up here before she died."

He moved closer. He was dressed in denim shorts and a polo shirt, and was wearing scuffed sneakers. "Not died. Was murdered," he said.

I felt something run up my spine. "Yes. That's right. Murdered. And what are you doing here?"

He shrugged. "Just seeing if there are any Founders' Day remnants we may have forgotten. Sharon is a little, well, obsessive about stuff."

I tried to smile, but my lips were very dry. "Yes, I can imagine her being that way about certain things."

He stuck his hands in his pockets and looked away from me. "About all things."

He was not a terribly attractive man, rather thin and scrawny, with that brownish hair that looked like no color at all. His eyes were gray or light brown or some nondescript shade, with pale brows and no eyelashes. I knew he was in his early thirties, but he looked older. More…worn. He perfectly fit in to the odd and slightly unnerving feel of the boathouse. I was suddenly reminded of the movie *Psycho* and how Tony Perkins managed to perfectly match the weird house behind the motel.

Had he been Walter Malleck's lover fourteen years ago? He would have been in high school. He and Sharon, according to local legend, were already in love and planning to wed.

"Has she always been like that? So organized, I mean." I tried to keep my voice cheerful. "You've known her a long time, right?"

"Forever." He must have realized that he sounded a bit unenthusiastic, so he smiled woodenly and added, "and it's been wonderful."

"High school sweethearts, right? You two are kind of legendary up here."

He nodded. "Yes. I asked her out our sophomore year. We really hadn't dated all that long, but she had staked her claim. We've been together ever since."

"Yes." That was a rather strange way of putting it. Staked her claim. Almost as though he really hadn't much to say about it all. "How's Keith?" Their son, I knew, was around eight.

His face transformed. His eyes lit up, and he looked almost happy. "Keith is great, just great. Bummed out about last weekend, of course, but I'm taking him to Beach Haven tomorrow. Just the two of us."

"How nice."

He nodded and walked closer to me. "I always take the week after Founders' Day off from work. It's nice to get away after all the fuss and bother. Keith gets a little stressed out. Sharon has a tendency to, well, micromanage the weekend."

I had a feeling that Sharon micromanaged just about everything in their lives. Boot had been waiting somewhat patiently, but now she strained at the leash. "Well, I guess I should go."

"So, what do you think *did* happen?" he asked me suddenly. His Keith-face was gone. He looked old and a little creepy again.

"Ah, you mean with Rita? Well…" I took a few steps back and was out of the boathouse and once again in the light. I took a deep breath, and realized I had been frightened. Of David? Really? He was so skinny, if he had tried to grab me I would have easily body blocked him and knocked him to the ground.

"She made it into the clubhouse. She looked around and found her phone. Whoever killed her was very lucky, don't you think? To be there at the same time?" I moved closer to the dock. "Whoever did it had grabbed an oar, then followed her in, hit her, then dragged her back out." I frowned, thinking. "Why not leave her in the clubhouse? Why risk being seen dragging her to the boat?"

David had moved and was suddenly right beside me. "Indeed." Boot whined and tugged again at the leash. "Why do you think she was followed in?"

I searched his face. It was perfectly smooth, his small, almost colorless eyes hooded and still. "How else could it have happened? There's no way anyone could have been waiting for her, is there?"

He turned abruptly, closed the doors, and picked up the chain. He snapped the padlock shut. "You're right," he said. "Have a good day, Ellie."

He walked away quickly, hands back in his pockets.

CHAPTER NINE

CAIT CAME HOME FROM WORK and went straight upstairs. I was deciding whether to grill everything outside or remain in air-conditioned comfort when she came back down, the letter in her hand.

"They said yes," she blurted.

My heart dropped. Of course, I wanted what she wanted. And living in France had been a dream of hers for years. I looked at her face. "Why aren't you happy?"

She swallowed hard, and tears welled up in her eyes. "I think I'm in love with Kyle."

"Oh, baby." I crossed the kitchen and put my arms around her. She was taller than I was, but she was still my first-born little girl. "Oh, Cait. Honey. I can't even imagine how hard this must be."

She wasn't exactly crying, but she hugged me back, and I felt her trembling. There was nothing I could say or do except wait for her.

She finally stepped back, her eyes red. "I'm afraid if I go we'll lose our chance at happiness. I can't expect him to wait. Real life isn't like that. But if I stay with him, I'm afraid I might resent him later for keeping me from doing something I've wanted my whole life." She slumped down in a chair. "What should I do?"

I shook my head. "That's not fair. You know I want you to stay here, because Tessa and I will miss you terribly if you go. I can't give you objective advice, Cait." I sat down next to her. "What does Kyle say?"

She crumpled the letter in her hand. "Kyle wants me to go. He says he can fly over every couple of months, and that nothing will change between us. But it will. It's still…new between us. If I stay here, we can take our time and see what happens. We can grow together. We have a chance of seeing if this is real. If I move to France, everything becomes artificial. Everything we say and do when we are together for those few days will be because we *aren't* together the rest of the time. Does that make sense?"

I nodded. "Yes. And you're absolutely right. Long distance relationships are all about urgency and making up for lost time. You're a smart girl, Cait. At least you're looking at this with a very clear eye."

"So how am I supposed to decide?"

"Make a list. And stick to what you know absolutely, not what you want or think will happen. If you go to France, you will study and live in a country you've always wanted to live in. That's what you know. Don't write down that you'll love living there, and you'll meet amazing people. That's a wish. If you stay here, you and Kyle will have a chance to grow this relationship. That's a known. You will get married and live happily ever after? That's a wish. Got it?"

She nodded, then made a face. "That's what it's come down to? Deciding my life based on a list?"

I shook my head. "It's all I got. Sorry."

She smoothed out her letter and stared at it. Then she nodded. "Okay," she said. "Got it."

She got up and left the kitchen. I sat for a few minutes more, then put water on the stove to boil the corn. I had no energy left to even try to light the outside grill.

Shelly Goodwin and I had been friends for a long time, since two weeks after Marc and I moved to Mt. Abrams. She and I had been through a lot together, and had long ago reached a point where we had to be polite with each other. So when she appeared in my kitchen without so much as a knock, a call of hello, or even Boot bothering to bark, it was fine. It was more than fine. It was what real friendship was all about.

"So, how do we know David Butler is gay?" she asked, opening my refrigerator, pulling out a bottle of white wine, and then pouring efficiently.

"Joanie heard Sharon telling Lynn they were getting a divorce."

"I never would have guessed. Not that gay men are instantly identifiable, because of course, they're not, but…" Shelly shook her head. "I'd divorce him because he's a little odd and creepy."

"Very odd and creepy," I said, taking a long gulp. I told her about what had happened at the boathouse. Her eyes grew wide.

"You have to tell Sam," she said when I was done. "Immediately."

"Sam does not want me sticking my nose in. Besides, tell him what? That I was snooping around, met someone else snooping around, and got freaked out?" I slumped in my chair.

"Drink," she said.

We sat there in silence for a while.

"Cait says she's in love with Kyle and doesn't know if she should go to France," I told her.

"Oh, the poor kid," she said. "True love versus life's dream. That really sucks. What did you tell her?"

"I told her to only consider the reality. Is it really true love, or just the possibility? Is it really a life's dream, or a result of years of imagining what it would be like?"

"That's actually good advice."

"Yeah, I get it right sometimes." I poured some more wine. "Who do we need to talk to?"

"You mean besides Sharon? And every single person between Rita's house and the clubhouse?"

"Maybe just the Olsens," I said. The Olsens lived at the beginning of Abrams Lane, where the parade swerved off the road into the drive to the clubhouse. They were an older couple who spent most of their time sitting on their porch, watching the world go by.

"Another good idea. But one I'm sure the police have already thought of."

"True. The thing I can't get my head around is how lucky this guy got. He wasn't just there, you know. Rita had to have been followed."

"Exactly. We know that, because we know that no one knew she'd be there in the first place."

"But somebody did know," I said suddenly. It hit me so hard I almost couldn't breathe.

Shelly grabbed my arm and gave it a shake. "Earth to Ellie. What are you talking about?"

"Rita had the key to the clubhouse," I said.

Shelly looked blank, then the penny dropped. "Oh, my God. Who gave her the key?"

"Who *has* a key?"

"Well, Noah Bishop is president of the lake association, he'd have one, and the maintenance guy, what's his name, George something?"

I nodded. "Yes, but I don't think George would have motive for killing Rita."

"Sharon would need a key, right? As president of Founders' Day, she'd need to get in and out of the clubhouse all weekend."

We looked at each other. Sharon?

"David had a key to the boathouse padlock," I said slowly.

"He's on the lake association board," Shelly said.

"And he lived here back when Walt was killed, and he's gay, and Butler is an Irish name."

She frowned. "What has that got to do with anything?"

I repeated Carol's theory about Walt and his lover being a man. She nodded thoughtfully.

"So, we have opportunity, because he gave her the key and knew she'd be here. But why kill her? Even if he killed Walt, why was Rita a threat?"

"Remember Friday night? When we were talking about the Real Housewives of Mt. Abrams? And secrets? Remember what Rita said?"

"What, about seeing who was digging in the Malleck's yard? But that was a joke."

"Maybe. But Sharon was there. And she heard it. And she left before Rita admitted it was a joke. Maybe she thought it was true, maybe she told David."

We were quiet again. Shelly poured herself another glass of wine.

"You need to tell Sam," she said at last.

"Oh, I know. I'll call him tomorrow morning."

She fiddled with her wine glass. "Are we still going to talk to Sharon?"

"Oh, yes."

She grinned. "Excellent."

Fridays I visited my mother.

Mom was in a nursing home and had been ever since my father had died. It was interesting. When she called me, which she did every week, she knew exactly who I was and pretty much remembered everything about me and the girls. She still thought I was married to Marc, even though in the past few months she had been convinced that he beat me, beat the girls, was cheating on me with her cousin, Isabel, and had abandoned his family and moved to Dubai.

Visiting her was another story. She was always glad to see me, and knew I was not a casual visitor, but she didn't always remember my name. When the girls came with me, it was even harder, because although I could sometimes convince her I was her daughter, she never believed I was old enough to have children of my own.

This never upset Cait and Tessa. They enjoyed visiting their batty grandmother, who could always make them laugh and gave unsolicited and often outrageous advice.

I had begun to compartmentalize. This bright but dotty Leona was no longer my mother. She was, instead, a sometimes sweet, sometimes difficult person in my life. That way, I stopped mourning for the loss of the person I had loved, and instead began to enjoy this bewildered, familiar stranger I could no longer count on to share anything with me other than the here and now.

Tessa drove up with me on Friday morning. She was a great favorite of the residents, who were drawn to her bright energy and limitless patience. My mother did not mind sharing Tessa, except with poor Justine Caldwell, who my mother had marked as Public Enemy Number One and accused her of everything from petty theft to global conspiracy.

Mom was not having a good day. She did not know who I was. She completely ignored Tessa. Then, she thought Tessa was ten-year-old me and started to get frightened.

We left after fifteen minutes.

I sat in the car, looking down at the dashboard. Tessa was very patient, but finally suggested that maybe I should start the car.

"And maybe we could have lunch with Detective Sam instead?"

What a brilliant child. I called Sam, he said he would meet us, and off we went.

"Mom, will you be like that someday?" Tessa asked.

"I don't know, sweetie. I hope by the time I'm Gram's age, there will be a cure for what has happened to her."

"What did happen to her?"

"She got old."

She looked at me skeptically. "Do you really think anyone is going to find a cure for that?"

"No, but maybe they'll find a cure for dementia. That's what Gram has." I glanced over at her. "It's not her fault."

"I know. Do I really look like you did when you were little?"

I nodded. "Yep."

"Good. Then I know I'll be pretty when I grow up."

I really shouldn't have a favorite child, but sometimes...

Sam met us at the local Applebee's, where a cheerful person seated us, another cheerful person gave us water, and cheerful Heather promised to come back and get our order. Tessa, who knew the menu by heart, still carefully read every laminated page.

"Sam. I need to talk to you about Rita."

He lifted his eyes from the menu. "Ellie, really?"

"Sam, the clubhouse was locked Saturday morning. Rita walked by Maggie's porch and told us where she was going, and I told her it might be locked, and she said she had gotten a key."

He immediately put the menu down. "Say that again."

I did. He narrowed his eyes. "There was no key found on her body." He glanced over at Tessa, but she was oblivious. "We did find her phone."

"Also, Aggie and Rita borrowed a very tall ladder."

He flipped a hand. "We know all about that. They were getting into the garden. They were trying to get Emma to sell them half the lot."

"What! You didn't tell me."

His mouth twitched. "Last time I checked, you were not actively investigating this case."

I was a little annoyed. "Sam Kinali, you know perfectly well I am *very* actively investigating this case."

He threw back his head and laughed out loud.

Tessa looked up. "What?"

"Your mother is a very honest woman, Tessa," Sam said. "Even when she shouldn't be."

Cheerful Heather took our order, and I sat back and glared at Sam. "I bring you important information, that you never would have found out, and you don't even have the courtesy—"

"Ellie, now calm down."

"No, I will not."

He sighed and folded his hands together. "All right, then. You tell me what you've got, and I'll tell you what I've got." He shot a look at Tessa. "And you will repeat none of this."

She rolled her eyes. "I'm just a kid. Who would believe me anyway?"

Sam grinned. "True." He turned to me. "Rita and Aggie had been climbing into Emma's garden at night. They hid the ladder on the other side of the house during the day. They just wanted to discourage her from doing any more work, because they wanted her to sell them part of the lot. Malicious mischief, but Emma has declined to press charges."

"What about Walt?"

"Cause of death was a blow to the back of the head, probably the sharp edge of a shovel. Death probably instantaneous. There are still tests to do, but chances of finding any physical evidence are pretty thin. Wife and sons have alibis. The so-called lover is the only other viable suspect, but that could be anyone."

"Whoever it was, they were Irish."

He nodded. "Yes. We got that from the wife." Drinks were delivered. Sam sipped his coffee and nodded at me. "Your turn."

"I ran into David Butler in the boathouse yesterday, and he had the keys to lock it back up."

"Why were you in the boathouse?"

I made a face. "Because the clubhouse was still off limits."

He chuckled. "Of course. Who else would have keys?"

I shrugged. "You'll have to talk to Noah Bishop. He's the president of the lake association. Sharon may have a set, to get things going for the weekend. She could have gotten them from David, who's on the board. Or he may have gotten them from her." I glanced at Tessa. She was staring up at the television screen over the bar. "What if David was Walt's lover? He's gay. Butler is an Irish name. Rumor has it, he and Sharon are splitting up."

Sam took out a little notebook and was scribbling things down in it. He glanced at his watch. "This is all very helpful." He looked up from his notebook. Thank you, Ellie."

"You're welcome. You should also talk to the Olsen's."

"We did already. They saw Rita."

"Go back and ask them about David Butler."

Cheerful Heather appeared with our food. I stared at Sam's cheeseburger, dripping with cheese and bacon, surrounded by fries, and looked down at my salad, which looked disgustingly healthy and low-calorie, but not nearly as appetizing.

"Why?" he asked, before taking a bite.

"Because the reason they noticed Rita was because she shouldn't have been there. But David is on the board of the lake association. Seeing him around the clubhouse might not have registered because seeing him there was expected."

He chewed thoughtfully. "That's an interesting theory."

"It's not mine. Thank Mary Rose." Tessa was dipping her chicken tenders into a sweet and spicy smelling sauce. I speared a cucumber and chewed thoroughly. "Is everything delicious?" I asked.

Tessa nodded, because her mouth was full of crispy chicken. Sam nodded because he just bit down on three French fries, with ketchup.

"Yeah," I sighed. "Mine too."

I GOT A CALL FROM Shelly right before dinner.

"Hey, I don't know if this is good or creepy, but I ran into Sharon and told her we wanted to talk to her about last week."

I pulled my marinating chicken out of the fridge. "That's good," I said.

"She said she'd meet us in the boathouse around eight."

"That's creepy."

"That's what I said. What do you think?"

I thought I wanted to call Sam. He was coming by anyway, probably around nine. I also thought he'd not be pleased if I asked him to hide behind the boathouse to hear what Sharon had to say.

"Can you come up?" I asked.

"Yep. See you at eight."

Why the boathouse? Why the same place I had run into David?

Dinner was easy. Grilled chicken legs, corn, and sliced tomatoes. Cait was working, so Tessa and I ate outside by the grill, then she packed up to spend the night at Bennett Fahey's house, along with six other girls, all celebrating Bennett's eleventh birthday. Knowing Bennett's mother, Lynn, I imagined there would be games, a craft, healthy snacks, and finally, a politically correct yet little-girl friendly video to lull the girls to sleep. Lynn was even more organized than Sharon Butler.

I walked Tessa down Carver Road to the Fahey house, and on the way back, saw Lillian and Jack Olsen sitting where they always sat, in twin rockers on their front porch. We were neighbors, not really friendly, but stopping for a chat on a lovely summer evening wasn't totally out of line, was it?

"Evening, Lillian, Jack. How are you both?" I waited on the street, calling to them with a wave.

"Evening, Ellie. We're good. How did your girls make out?"

They always walked down to see how the girls decorated the porch. I took this as encouragement and moved from the street up the walk.

"They won. Again. The shelf is getting crowded."

Lillian beamed. I never knew my grandmothers, but I always wished that at least one of them would have been like Lillian—kind, sweet, always concerned about others. Jack was a bit of a scoundrel. He had a wicked sense of humor and liked to watch the ladies, but he was also a generous man who never said no to helping a neighbor.

"Too bad about Saturday," Jack said. "Just a shame that had to happen to that poor girl on Founders' Day."

A-ha. There it was. "Yes. Saturday was just awful." I made my way up to the bottom of their porch steps. "Poor Rita. Why, I bet you two could have seen who did it and never realized it."

"Well, that seems to be what the police think," Jack said. "Your boyfriend was here just a bit ago, asking more questions."

"Sam? Really?" He certainly had moved fast.

Lillian nodded. "He's a very attractive man, Ellie." She wagged her finger at me. "Hold on to that one."

Jack cackled. "I told him to make sure to hold on to *you*. You're quite a looker yourself these days, Ellie."

I felt myself blushing. "Thanks, Jack. So, what did Sam ask you?" That seemed a perfectly normal next question, right?

"Who we saw going up to the clubhouse," Lillian said. "Again. This time, he asked us if we'd seen David Butler. Now, why would he ask a thing like that? David would never hurt a fly."

CHAPTER TEN

I had to force myself to not rush up onto the porch and shake Lillian by the shoulders. "Can't imagine. So, did you?"

Lillian shook her head. "Of course not."

"Funny, though," Jack said. "He didn't ask about Sharon."

"Who didn't ask? Sam? Why would he ask about Sharon?"

"Well," Lillian said. "She was up at the clubhouse. But way before Rita. I'd forgotten all about it until Jack and I were just talking. But Sharon had been up there all the day before, hadn't she? I mean, she was pretty much everywhere on Saturday."

My heart started pounding very hard. "Yes. Of course she was. So you didn't tell Sam? About Sharon?"

"Why, no. Do you think it's important?" Lillian asked.

"If it is," Jack said, "Ellie can tell him. Spice up the pillow talk, right Ellie?"

"Oh, Jack," I sputtered, while Lillian swatted his arm with multiple shushes.

I stepped back. "Yes, I'll be sure to tell him. Well, good night."

I practically ran back to the street and up to my own house. I had my phone out before I got to the porch. "Sam, I just stopped at the Olsen's."

He chuckled. "Didn't you trust me?"

"Of course. But here's the thing. They saw Sharon."

"What?" he asked sharply. "Where?"

"Up at the clubhouse. Before Rita got there. They'd forgotten."

"Listen to me, Ellie, I—"

Someone jerked the phone away from my ear. I whirled, and there was Sharon Butler, holding my phone, shaking her head. She turned my phone off and set it carefully on the railing. "Oh, Ellie, what have you done now?"

She looked very sad. "Ellie, was that your boyfriend on the phone?"

I nodded. "Yes." My voice came out as a croak. Her hands were empty. She had no weapon with which to hurt me, but then, she was used to improvisation. She could probably kill me with my potted plant.

She shook her head. "Then I guess we don't have much time."

I cleared my throat. "For what?"

She sighed. Deeply. "What else were you going to tell him?"

"Nothing he didn't already know," I said. I was a terrible liar, but since my voice was shaking anyway, she might not be able to tell. "You killed Rita."

She opened my front screen door. "Let's go inside and talk about this."

Boot ran out, barking. She even looked slightly fierce. Sharon just smiled at her, and I went into the house, and Sharon walked in behind me.

There was one room on the first floor with a lock, and that was the powder room behind the stairs. All I had to do was cut left, leap over the couch, and skirt the bookcase by the stairs. I knew that Sharon was pretty fit. She may have had weight issues, but I'd never seen her out of breath, and I was fairly certain she could grab me and throw me down without breaking a sweat.

"You killed Rita," I repeated. "Why?

She looked close to tears. "Because she saw me bury Walter."

"Walter Malleck? You killed Walt too?"

"No, of course not. David did. But I buried the body, and she saw me. She said so right here, remember? I couldn't have her tell anyone, not after keeping David's secret for so long." She was pacing back and forth in front of the fireplace. "Why did she have to say that? She never should have opened her mouth."

Oh, poor Rita. Her attempt at a joke had made her Sharon's target.

"Sharon." I was trying very hard to keep my voice even, but my adrenaline had kicked in, and I was practically jumping out of my skin. "Why did David kill Walter Malleck?" I had made my way to the end of the couch, but she was watching me closely.

"It was an accident. No, not an accident, exactly but David never meant to kill Walter. He loved him. But Walt was ending it, and David got upset, and they argued, and Walt was walking away, and David picked up the shovel and hit him. He was angry. He just wanted to keep him from leaving." She ran her hands through her perfectly blown-out hair. "He wanted to go to the police, but what if he was sent to jail? We were going to be married. I couldn't let him go to jail." She looked at me, desperation in her eyes. "I was the fat girl in high school. David was the only boy who was nice to me. I loved him. I knew he was gay, but I didn't care. I loved him. And who else would love me? I had to save him."

"So you buried Walter?"

She nodded. "Yes. I did it in the middle of the night. It was awful, and his body…" She grew very still. "I can't have you telling my secret."

"The Olsen's saw you go to the clubhouse, Sharon. Sam will figure it out." I had a sudden picture flash through my mind of Sharon, coming to my house on Saturday afternoon. "Your shirt. The linen thing you were wearing on Saturday. You wiped off the oar with the hem, didn't you? That's why it was all twisted. They found fibers. They'll put you at the crime scene. I won't have to tell anybody anything."

Boot was barking again. She had been left out on the porch, and I recognized her happy bark. Somebody I knew was coming. Let it be Sam, let it be Sam…

Sharon picked up the poker by the fireplace. Her face was calm, almost peaceful. But I saw her eyes, and there was a spark of madness there. I told myself she wouldn't kill me here in my own home, that she wouldn't take that risk. But she had killed Rita and dragged her body from the clubhouse to the dock even though anyone might have seen her. She didn't care much about risk.

I took a few steps toward the stairs. "Sam is coming, you know," I told her.

"So?" She moved closer to me, the poker hanging loosely in her hand. "Where do you think you're going, Ellie?"

She moved so quickly I barely had time to react. She swung the poker hard, and I felt it hit my shoulder as I ducked. I rolled behind the couch and struggled to my feet, but she was right behind me, I could feel her, and I was afraid to look because I didn't want to see it, the poker, as it came down on me…

"Sharon? What the hell are you doing?"

Boot was running around the couch, barking like a mad thing. Sharon had looked away, toward Shelly's voice, and I reached up and grabbed the poker. She pulled back hard, and I fell against her, and the two of us crashed into the side table, the lamp hitting the floor as we wrestled for the poker. Shelly was screaming, and

Sharon and I were on the floor. She was on top of me, and the poker we were both holding was pressed hard against my chest. I'll never live through this, I thought wildly. She'll crush me to death. And then I saw Viv Brewster, standing over Sharon's shoulder, holding the fallen lamp in both hands and swinging it hard against the back of Sharon's head.

Sharon stopped struggling and lay still on top of me. I made a giant effort to push her off me, and then sat up, breathing hard. Boot was in my face, licking me, tail thumping wildly. Viv and Shelly stood together, looking down. I could hear sirens.

"You okay?" Viv asked.

I nodded and took Shelly's hand, and she pulled me to my feet.

"She killed Rita," I said. I was finding it hard to catch my breath.

Viv took my arm and led me to the couch. "Sit. Put your head between you knees. Now, just breathe deep."

I did as she said. The sirens were louder now, and my living room was suddenly crowded. Boot was barking hysterically. I looked up and grabbed her, holding her on my lap as the room filled with officers in blue. Shelly was sitting next to me, and Viv was talking to one of the policemen. My shoulder hurt. I could feel across my chest where the poker had been pressed against my flesh. Then I saw Sam hurrying through the front door. He gave me one look, and his shoulders slumped, and he shook his head.

He knelt in front of me. "Are you okay?"

I nodded.

His hands were on my face, wiping tears I didn't realize I was shedding. "Good. You cannot do this again. Ever. You're killing me, Ellie, you really are."

I nodded again, pulled Boot even closer, and sat back, eyes closed.

The police were still there when Cait came home. She sat beside me, tight lipped, and listened to the whole story. When I was done I could see her jaw clenched so tight I thought her teeth were going to shatter.

"What if Tessa had been home?" she asked. "What would have happened?"

I had been successfully avoiding that thought for hours, and hearing her say it brought another wave of anxiety and fear.

"I know, Cait. I know. This was just...who knew Sharon would come here?"

"Why did you have to butt in in the first place?" Cait asked, her voice getting louder and shriller. "That crazy woman almost strangled you last time. What is wrong with you?"

Shelly put her arm around Cait's shoulders. "Everything turned out fine, honey. Really."

Cait turned to her, her face flushed with anger. "This is not her job. It's not yours either. Are you encouraging her?" She got up and glared at Sam. "Are you?"

Sam shook his head. "No, Caitlyn, I told your mother to stay out. She just has a habit of...attracting the wrong sort of attention."

She stormed upstairs. I could hear her door slam.

"She's just upset," Viv said. "She loves you."

"I know." I covered my face with my hands. I had never felt so tired in my whole life.

Sharon had come around, saw the police surrounding her, got up calmly, and proceeded to tell Sam everything. He read her her rights and asked her repeatedly if she wanted a lawyer, but she insisted on going on. The words came out in a rush, like a great unburdening.

Walt had seduced David. David told Sharon what had happened. Sharon had already planned her life around

David and could only watch helplessly as he became more involved with the older man. And then, one night, they fought. Walter was ending it. They quarreled in the house, Walter walked out into the yard, and David followed him. He grabbed the shovel and hit Walt in a rage.

Then he went to Sharon.

They dragged the body back into the house, and Sharon returned the next night to bury Walter Malleck. But for months she worried that Paula would find the body, so she finally started a fire in the garbage cans and watched as the house burned to the ground.

Sharon and David got married. They stayed in Mt. Abrams. They had a son. And then Sharon heard Rita talk about who she saw digging in the Malleck's yard.

"But she was just joking," I blurted. "Rita didn't really see anything."

Sharon sighed. "How do you know, Ellie? How could *I* know? After all that time, I certainly wasn't going to take any chances."

The house was finally quiet. Sam was gone. He had Sharon to process at the station. And David.

Shelly, Viv, and I sat in front of the fireplace. The poker had been put back in its place. I stared at it while Shelly poured some wine.

"Drink, Ellie. It will help you sleep."

"Thank God you came," I finally said. "Thank you."

"Thank Viv here for insisting on coming along. I probably would have just stood there and screamed while she crushed the life out of you."

I looked at Viv and smiled. "You were pretty awesome," I said.

She smiled. "I usually am. You gonna be okay tonight? Is Sam coming back?"

I nodded.

"Okay then. Shelly, you ready to go?"

"Sure am. I'll call you in the morning, okay Ellie?"

I nodded, and they let themselves out. I sat for a few more minutes and heard Cait coming down the stairs.

She sat next to me, picked up the wine bottle, and drank directly from it. "I'm sorry for what I said."

"I know."

"I was upset."

"You had a right to be."

She drank again. "I'm not going to France."

I turned and looked at her. "Because of Kyle?"

She shrugged. "Partly. I have a chance to teach French at the Montessori school if I tell them I'll go for my teaching certificate."

"That would be exciting."

"Yes."

She pointed her finger at me. "And someone has to keep an eye on you. A woman your age should not be getting herself into this kind of trouble."

"My *age*?"

"Yes, Mother. At your particular time of life, you should be taking things slower, not throwing yourself in front of every homicidal maniac in the state."

"You make it sound like I'm a doddering old lady."

"You're not. But you need to stop doing crazy shit if you ever hope to become one."

Boot pawed my leg. I started scratching her ears. "I know, Cait. I really do."

We were silent for a few more minutes.

"Daddy wants the two of you to get back together."

I drained my wine. "I know that too. He should not be talking to you about that."

"I told him that. I think he was expecting me to be on his side."

"You aren't?" I asked, surprised.

She shrugged. "He left us. That's hard to forget."

"Yes, it is."

She stood up and stretched. "Are you coming up?"

I shook my head and took the wine bottle from her hand. "Sam is coming back."

"I like him."

I smiled. "Me too."

She bent down to kiss me. "Love you. G'night."

"Night, baby."

I poured another glass of wine and sat with Boot, staring at the empty fireplace, until Sam came through the door

A Killer Halloween

A Mt. Abrams Mystery

BY

Dee Ernst

CHAPTER ONE

I DID NOT LIKE HALLOWEEN.

I hadn't liked it since I was nine years old, and my brother and I went trick-or-treating, and the Coopersmiths gave us mealy apples, and all the other kids in the neighborhood told us they were poisoned apples. Even though my mother insisted they were *not* poisoned, I didn't see her offering to take a bite to prove her point, so I was convinced from that evening on that Halloween was just a giant ploy to kill off small children.

I know. That was over forty years ago. You'd have thought I'd have gotten over it by now.

But I never did.

When Halloween rolled around in Mt. Abrams, where everyone knew everyone else, where kids felt safe to run up and down the streets and ride bikes to the lake unsupervised, the entire community became involved. There was dunking for apples and a few spooky-themed games and a haunted house. There was a Best Costume contest at the old firehouse. People decorated with pumpkins and ghosts and witches, and for days, the air rang with spooky sounds coming from hidden speakers.

Normally, I loved my community. I was involved. I had even joined the Garden Club earlier in the year, partially as a favor to Lynn Fahey to disrupt Mary Rose Reed's evil plan to kill of the hydrangeas in front of the library. But eventually I found that I liked the Garden Club and was actually learning a few things that might keep my so-called garden alive.

Then Halloween reared its ugly head, and Mary Rose Reed, Garden Club president and Mt. Abrams organizer extraordinaire, got the great idea of holding a scavenger hunt this year, instead of the usual hanging out by the clubhouse, playing a few games, and generally letting the costumed segment of the population run wild.

As I said, it was a great idea. But then she had to start telling us more details, and the idea went from great to awful. Obviously she had never been involved in a *real* scavenger hunt. Those poor kids would be bored to tears.

So, I raised my hand. And opened my mouth.

I should have known better. One reason I normally don't join community groups is *not* because I don't play well with others, but rather, I think I can do a much better job all by myself, without all the hand raising and discussion and *voting* on things.

By the end of the meeting, I was in charge of the scavenger hunt.

Now, that wouldn't have been all that bad, but Mary Rose was never one to cede power gracefully, so while I was in charge of planning the hunt, she would be responsible for hiring the entertainment. Specifically, Mr. Scarecrow, a professional clown and juggler that she insisted would be a perfect addition to the festivities.

After what happened to Mr. Scarecrow, you'd better believe I never raised my hand at another meeting again. Ever.

My best friend, Shelly Goodwin, got quite a kick out of the whole situation.

"Tell me again?" she asked. It was the morning after the Garden Club meeting. We were walking up Carver Road, where we walked every morning after the school bus picked up the kids. My daughter, Tessa, was now eleven. Seemingly overnight, my being on the same planet with her was cause for embarrassment. So she walked to the bus stop alone. I had a second cup of coffee to fill in the time usually spent with her while I silently argued with myself the pros and cons of an expensive boarding school. Shelly would text me, and I'd be off down the hill, meeting her and Maggie Turner and Carol Anderson for a quick turn around the neighborhood.

Shelly's son was the same age as my daughter, and he didn't feel it was a crime to be seen with his mother, but that was one of the many differences between boys and girls. Having already raised one girl to complete womanhood, I knew that Tessa would eventually see me as a human being once again, but it would take a while.

My cocker spaniel, Boot, was seriously investigating a possible chipmunk infestation under a fallen log. We stopped walking and watched her sniffing furiously. Shelly's dog seemed totally unconcerned.

"Mary Rose had these really terrible ideas," I explained. "She wanted the kids to find, like, thirty different items, stuff like, an acorn or a red leaf. What kind of crap is that?" I looked at Shelly accusingly. "If you had been there, you could have stopped me."

Maggie had recently dyed the unshaved portion of her hair a bright blue. "I doubt that," she giggled. "I've seen you in action, Ellie. Once you've gotten something between your teeth, you don't let go."

Carol, tall, graceful, older, and infinitely wiser, smiled. "When all else fails, try Pinterest. What have you got so far?"

Boot had moved past chipmunks and was now nosing the ants, so I tugged on her leash, and we went on up the hill. "Well, teams. We can't have all those kids just running around by themselves. So, teams of three or four, with an accompanying adult."

Shelly turned around and walked backward. She ran marathons in her spare time and wasn't above a little showing off. "Teams? That's good. But you know that no matter how successful you are, Mary Rose will find a major problem somewhere. And don't you hate Halloween?"

"Yes, you know I hate Halloween. And you're right. Mary Rose will tear me to shreds over something. She's still involved, of course. She's hiring a scarecrow."

We turned onto my street at the top of the hill.

As always, the lake looked beautiful. Lake Abrams wasn't very big, but it was wide and quite lovely, and the vivid fall colors on the small mountain behind it reflected on the still water. I saw this view several times a day, and it never failed to make me grateful to be alive.

"What do we need a scarecrow for?" Maggie asked.

"Good question," I said as we started around the lake. "She says he's going to be entertainment."

Carol made a rude noise. "That's her nephew. Or stepnephew. Something like that. She was telling me a few weeks ago at the library. He and his brother are breaking into show business."

"Well, that's certainly taking the long way around," Shelly said. "But trust Mary Rose to turn a community event into a personal gain for herself, one way or another."

It's not that we hated Mary Rose. In fact, she could be a very nice person. Sometimes. But she was one of those people that loved to gossip. In turn, she generated quite a bit of gossip herself.

Carol, as head librarian of the Mt. Abrams branch of the Lawrence Library system, managed to pick up quite a bit of information, but was much more responsible about spreading it around. Except to us, of course.

"Her brother remarried," Carol explained. "And the new wife has two grown sons. They've tried stand-up, a little acting, and are now doing parties. Clown stuff and magic for the one. The other son is a singer, plays a few instruments, that sort of thing."

Shelly's dog, Buster, stood stock-still. Boot, a few seconds behind, stopped as well. We looked, and there, barely visible in the trees, was a light-colored, very lean, and mangy-looking coyote. Buster began to grow. Boot, who had the courage of a newborn lamb, stayed silent.

"Well, he's ugly," Maggie said loudly, and the coyote vanished.

"A lot of cats are going to go missing this winter," Carol said as we walked on. "We should post something on the bulletin board."

I nodded. "Along with a call for volunteers. I'm going to need lots of adults to make this scavenger hunt work. Although, I did get an offer of help right after the meeting."

Shelly glanced at me. "Who?"

"James Fergus."

"Why, you sly dog," Carol murmured.

James Fergus was the newest Mt. Abrams resident, a fine-looking gentleman who was renting a house on Davis Road. He was tall and of an indeterminate age, but most guesses put him around my age, fifty. He was good looking in a movie star sort of way—thick, dark hair, blue eyes, an amazing body, and charm oozing from his very pores. He was a landscape architect, so his appearance at the Garden Club meeting was cause for a ripple of excitement that wasn't just for his looks.

And after the meeting, he grabbed me and offered to help.

"Don't tell Viv," Maggie warned.

Vivian Brewster, our good friend and local realtor, had her eye on James.

I grinned. "Of course I'm going to tell her. How else would I get her to help me out?"

By the time I'd finished our walk, I was in a pretty good mood. I was a freelance editor, specializing in mysteries and thrillers, so I was pretty confident I could come up with an exciting hunt that would challenge the imaginations of every child—and adult—in Mt. Abrams. Something clever enough for Sherlock Holmes but tame enough for Miss Marple, witty enough for Archie Goodwin, with the charm of Richard Jury. A piece of cake.

By the end of the day, I had nothing.

So much for my good mood.

My oldest daughter Caitlyn was twenty-four and quite beautiful. She was also very, very smart. She had passed up a fellowship in France and was instead teaching French at a Montessori school. It wasn't the opportunity to teach that kept her home. Rather, it was Kyle Lieberman, her childhood friend who was now a handsome, successful young man who had managed to keep his awkward adorableness while holding down a mid-six-figure job on Wall Street.

She thought the whole scavenger hunt thing was a hoot.

"Mom, you hate Halloween," she said, after laughing hysterically for about seventeen minutes.

"Yes, I know. But you know how I love mysteries, and a scavenger hunt is like a mystery, and I thought I'd be really good at this, and I'm not."

I stared down at my dinner. Broiled boneless chicken breast, roasted cauliflower, and sautéed zucchini. I had gained five pounds over the three-day weekend by making—and eating—a huge pot of chicken and dumplings and an apple pie. I also spent most of that weekend in bed with Sam Kinali, my extremely smart and funny and sexy boyfriend. Tessa had been with her father. Cait and Kyle went to Delaware. Sam and I indulged in all sorts of pleasures, including eating, lots of wine, and sex. I know that in theory, sex can burn calories, but apparently not as many as long brisk walks and weight training. So I had some catching up to do in the weight-loss area.

"You've got over a month, Mom. I'm sure you'll think of something." Tessa was eating mashed potatoes with her chicken. With lots of butter. She looked like me— dark, curling hair, dark eyes, round, pretty face. She was also going to be built just like me when she became an adult—short-waisted, big boobs, no hips, and having to fight a round middle all her adult life. But for now, she ate mashed potatoes with lots of butter.

Her momentary burst of civility quickly passed. "You'd better, 'cause I don't want all the kids talking about how lame you are," she said.

"Well, Tessa, I'll keep that in mind. Heaven forbid your friends think I'm lame." I stabbed my chicken. "Do they think I'm fat?" In my mind, it was a hypothetical question. But Tessa…

"Not any more. You dodged the bullet on that one, Mom."

Oh, you little…

Cait stepped in gracefully. "What's with the scarecrow?" she asked.

I took a cleansing breath. "A Mary Rose idea. Her nephews? Stepnephews? Something like that. Todd someone and his brother. Apparently, they're an act."

"Todd Richter? I went to school with his brother, Doug," Cait said. "Doug had an amazing voice, and played all sorts of instruments. Really talented guy. Todd was a year or two younger. Kind of a screwup, but with great tattoos. He did magic. Kyle and Doug are still friends."

I nodded and moved some zucchini around. "That sounds right. Todd is going to be juggling, making balloon animals, that sort of thing. Won't that be fun, Tessa?"

My youngest daughter rolled her eyes. "Maybe. As long as he's not lame."

Again with the lame.

Cait came to the rescue. Again. "What kind of scavenger hunt would *you* want, Tessa?"

Tessa made a curling road through her potatoes as she thought. "I'd want to be with my friends. Not by myself. And not, like, a gazillion things to find. And it should be fun stuff. Maybe each thing could be its own prize. No going behind scary houses. And maybe popcorn and cider."

Cait raised her eyebrows. "I'm impressed, Tessa. Those are good ideas. Right, Mom?"

I was still seething a bit over the "fat" thing, but had to agree. "Great ideas. I already thought about teams. Maybe you could help me?"

She rolled her eyes. "Really? I didn't ask for this, you know. And now you want me to *help*?"

I swallowed my chicken.

"I'll be glad to help, Mom. And I bet Kyle would love to, as well," Cait said.

Eventually, Cait would be moving out of my house. Tessa would be on her own. Things, I knew, would get dicey, because Cait was often the only thing between her sister and...

"Thank you, dear," I said. I stabbed the chicken again. And reached for the mashed potatoes.

I finally had it all figured out. There would be twelve stations, with a specific item to find at each location. The clues would be given in random order, teams would find the correct station—a front porch, a backyard, an empty lot, whatever—and collect the item, as well as being checked off by a trustworthy volunteer. It's not that I honestly believed that anyone would actually cheat at a simple scavenger hunt, but I knew that to some parents, winning trumped personal ethics, and I wasn't taking any chances.

Emma McLaren was going to let us use her garden as one of the stations, as well as a spot for cider and doughnuts. Her garden had been badly trampled that summer when Boot accidentally dug up a body in the exact spot where Emma's koi pond was supposed to go. At the end of the summer, a bunch of us got together to help her rake, transplant, and generally repair the damage. An early hard frost killed off anything left alive, so she threw down lots of straw and said we could use the space.

It was there Mr. Scarecrow would be doing his act.

Mary Rose had brought him around the week of Halloween, so he could look everything over. Mr. Scarecrow was indeed Todd Richter, a tall and lanky young man with lots of tattoos up and down his arms and several piercings. He would juggle, do tricks, make balloon animals, and generally entertain anyone who stopped by Emma's for a doughnut and hot cider. Since the whole point of winning the hunt was to figure out the clues and find everything in the shortest time, I didn't really think any kids would be watching him for very long, but I wasn't about to mention that to Mary

Rose. The woman was on a mission, and that involved a check for Mr. Scarecrow.

Vivian Brewster had graciously offered to be my right-hand woman, and she and I walked Todd through the neighborhood, gave him a general rundown as to how things would work, and tried to draw him into any type of conversation. He nodded and grunted a lot, but as far as sentences went, he was loath to give them up. He followed us around for twenty minutes, then got into his Honda and drove away.

Viv and I both waved as he drove down the hill.

"That is one ugly man," Viv said. "He doesn't even need a costume. He could scare the bejesus out of small children just the way he is now."

"And he didn't seem very jolly. Aren't clowns supposed to be jolly?" I asked.

Viv shuddered. "Honey, I just remember that evil clown from that Stephen King thing, you know, the one who lived in the sewers? I've always thought clowns were creepy."

"You should mention that to James," I said, "so he can protect you from the big, bad scarecrow."

She grinned. "He'd be very good at protecting, I'm sure. In fact, I'm sure he'd be good at all sorts of things."

I never heard the rest of James's very useful qualities, because Mary Rose appeared from nowhere. "Isn't he wonderful?" she gushed.

Mary Rose was a throwback. She wore outfits that matched, low heels in all seasons, and always had on lipstick that was the same color as her nail polish. Her hair was permed in a short gray helmet, and her earrings were clip on. Standing next to Viv, who was tall, black, dressed in leggings, over-the-knee black boots and a colorful fringed sweater, Mary Rose looked like she belonged in a 1950s sitcom.

Viv turned to Mary Rose and tilted her head. "Thank God he's got a costume, or he'd be scaring the kids outta here faster than—"

"What Viv means," I interrupted quickly, "is that his piercings are very unusual."

Mary Rose sighed. "Yes. His brother, Doug, is quite different. Doug is a singer. Very talented. They're having a bit of a disagreement right now, but I'm sure that they'll iron everything out by the weekend. Doug helps out, you know? Gets things set up. Todd would be lost without him."

Viv raised an eyebrow. "Disagreement? I can't imagine anyone not getting along with someone as warm and friendly as Todd."

Mary Rose looked confused for a second, then laughed nervously. "Oh, you're just being funny, Viv. I know that Todd can come across as, well, a bit distant, but once he puts his mask on, he's a whole other person. Well, see you ladies later."

She scurried off, and Viv shook her head.

"Just what Mt. Abrams needs for Halloween. Dr. Jekyll and Mr. Hyde."

I poked her with my elbow. "Stop it. It won't be that bad. So tell me, what else do you think James would be good at?"

She laughed and told me as we went back up the hill.

Chapter Two

FRIDAY WAS MY DAY TO visit my mother. She lived in a lovely assisted living facility, A beautiful old mansion that had been converted and improved so it met all the state standards, but still looked like an elegant country home. Mom had recently been fitted with an ankle bracelet after walking out the front door, down the driveway, and out onto the highway. Now, if she chose to walk out the door, bells and whistles would sound, and she'd be turned around before clearing the parking lot.

Sometimes she remembered who I was. Lately, she thought I was just a caseworker, checking up on her situation. She would recite a litany of complaints—bad food, not being allowed to read, being locked in the same room with petty thieves and general scalawags, and being given drugs that immobilized her for hours at a time. I sat and listened, pretended to take notes, and made generally sympathetic noises. She did not invite me to have lunch with her, and when I made the suggestion, she looked embarrassed.

"My dear young woman, I'm sure you're a perfectly nice person, but I'm waiting for my daughter. I'm having lunch with her. I hope you understand."

Liz, her aide, managed a tight smile. I swallowed the lump in my throat and nodded. "Sure. I understand perfectly." I stood up and kissed her on her forehead.

Liz patted my mother's hand. I walked out into the brisk fall air with my heart down around my knees.

I called Sam. "Can we have lunch?"

"Isn't today lunch with Mom day?"

"Apparently not. She's waiting for her daughter."

"Oh, Ellie, I'm sorry. Sure. About an hour?"

I arrived early and thought about either having a drink or eating an entire basket of bread sticks. Luckily, Sam came in before I was forced to choose.

Sam Kinali was a big man—tall, broad across the shoulders, and arms that strained slightly against the fabric of his suit. He was a senior detective on the Lawrence Police Department, and in the five months I had known him, he always managed to generate a little jolt in my gut. He was also a great listener. Which is what he did for the first twenty minutes while I vented about everything from my mother to my bratty daughter, from Halloween to what the hell I was going to do for Thanksgiving this year.

"Thanksgiving?" he asked when I finally wound down. "Isn't it a bit early to think about Thanksgiving?"

I shook my head and stabbed my chicken Caesar salad with my fork. "Right after Halloween, there's about three days until Thanksgiving, then you blink, and it's Christmas. It's one giant rush of buying food and gifts and bad weather and cranky kids. Marc wants us to have Thanksgiving together with his family, which would be great because I wouldn't have to cook, but then I'd have to have him at *my* house for Christmas Eve, and I would have to invite his *family*, and his mother never did like me… Maybe I could just run away from home?"

He threw back his head and laughed. "And where would you go?"

I sighed. "Good point."

"Do you need help with Halloween?"

"Yes, I do. I need someone I can trust to be at the finish line, to add everything up, determine the times, and not cheat."

He looked at me quizzically. "Cheat?"

"Never underestimate the lengths at which a parent will go to have a child in first place."

He laughed again. "I'll take your word for it. So, we've gone through Thanksgiving and Christmas. What about New Year's Eve?"

I shuddered. "Worst holiday ever. I stay home, guzzle champagne, and watch the ball drop."

"Would you consider going away for the weekend? With me?"

I looked at him. His eyes were twinkling. "Where?"

"There's a bed and breakfast in Vermont. A friend of mine from law school has taken the whole place, and has arranged for a murder-mystery weekend."

I started to laugh. I had promised Sam on the heads of both of my children that I would *never* again become involved in any kind of crime solving. Sharon Butler had almost killed me, and it had caused a rift between us, mainly because he had warned me to back off from investigating the murder of Rita Ferris, and I hadn't listened to him. "You're inviting me to play detective?"

He shrugged elaborately. "Since you like it so much, yes. And in a completely controlled setting, I'll know that you'll be perfectly safe. And you'll get to spend time with my friends for a change."

"Okay. It's a deal." A bed and breakfast. A weekend with Sam. And murder.

It sounded perfect.

Saturday morning was clear, and the temperature was predicted to stay in the high 50s. Halloween had become something of a crapshoot in New Jersey. One year brought a freak snowstorm that caused trees to fall, roads to be blocked for days, and extensive power outages. Then there was Hurricane Sandy. The past few years everyone held their collective breaths to see what October 31st would bring.

Saturday, we got lucky.

Cait and Kyle were to act as runners for me. All my other volunteers would keep in touch via cell phone, but in case anyone needed supplies or help, I could stay at my post in front of the library to keep things going while Cait and Kyle sprinted all over the neighborhood. So they were there with me when Mr. Scarecrow reported for duty.

He was dressed in tattered jeans and an equally tattered denim shirt, and appeared to be as sullen and uncommunicative as before. With him was his brother, Doug, who made me rethink the entire science of genetics.

Doug was also tall and lanky, and dressed in almost identical denim. He was very handsome, grinning from ear to ear, with no discernible ink or piercings. He and Cait hugged, he and Kyle performed an elaborate handshake, and he took my hand warmly.

"Good to meet you, Ellie. I'm just here to tote and set up for Todd. He's the real star," Doug said.

The real star shot Doug a look full of poison, grudgingly acknowledged my existence, and headed off toward Emma's.

Cait looked after him. "Everything okay, Doug?"

Doug shrugged and looked embarrassed. "I have a gig tonight, and Todd usually helps me with the setup. Because he's working too, he's trying to back out. It'll be fine. We fight about this all the time."

"Where's the gig?" Kyle asked.

"Hoboken," Doug said. "I'm in a jazz trio, vocals and bass. You should check us out." He touched his finger to his forehead in salute. "See you all later."

I watched him as he trudged after his brother. "They're brothers?"

Cait giggled. "I know, right?" Cait wore a Wicked Witch of the West costume, her long red hair stuffed into a pointy hat, pale green makeup and swirling robes. Kyle was a flying monkey, his wings flapping awkwardly. He was sweating under his brown fur.

"You must really love my daughter to be wearing that around," I remarked.

He grinned. "I sure do." Cait turned bright red under her patina.

James Fergus came around the corner, Vivian Brewster at his side. I glanced at my watch. 4:35. The hunt was starting in less than half an hour, but there were already small children milling around.

"Are we ready?" I called to Viv.

She sported a brightly colored native costume I knew she had brought back from Trinidad. With her black skin and dazzling smile, she looked like Caribbean royalty. James wore a kilt. Seriously. Full Scottish regalia including a sword, and a little black tam on his handsome head. I almost swooned.

Vivian beamed. "Let's go."

Once the kids got lined up, things moved quickly. Tessa and Jerome teamed with Shelly's two boys. The four of them were zombies. It was, generally speaking, a big year for the undead. Tessa stood out by being a zombie princess, her last year's costume of pink tulle carefully shredded and splotched with fake blood.

My ex-husband Marc walked her down from the house, then acted as a team leader for another group. Parents were generally okay with the fact that if their child was on a particular team, they could not be the leader of that team. I got a few arguments, but James just straightened up and put his hand on his sword. He was at least six-two and was quite an imposing figure.

My hero.

I carefully recorded all the start times. Sometime in the next forty-five minutes or so, teams who had collected all the clues would check in at the old firehouse, where the incorruptible Sam Kinali would mark their finish time. As soon as all the teams checked in, the adding and subtraction would begin. Until then, I could sit back and relax.

Or not.

About thirty minutes into the hunt, while I was checking in the last of the teams, Carol Anderson sent me a text.

Mr. Scarecrow is very popular, but left for bathroom break 15 mins ago. Have u seen him?

Cait and Kyle were down at the school bus stop helping Marie Wu get down the dill pickles hanging in her tree. I had put them up there myself, forgetting that Marie was barely five feet tall. She was having a hard time reaching them and didn't want any other adult to mess around with her clues. I didn't blame her, but now I was runnerless.

"James, could you go up to Emma's, and see if you can find Mr. Scarecrow? He's apparently taken an extended pee break." I was sweating beneath my costume. I was a tea bag, which meant I was wearing a huge muslin bag stuffed with oak leaves, with a red Lipton tag dangling from my neck.

He straightened his sash, or cloak or whatever he had draped dramatically over his broad shoulders, and headed off. Vivian watched him walk away. I did too. It was something to see.

"Hot man in a kilt," she breathed.

"Amen, sister," I said, and handed out the last of the clues to the very last team. I sat back and sighed. "Thanks, Viv."

She reached into her tote bag to pull out a thermos. "Gin?" she asked, then proceeded to pull out two martini glasses, a jar of olives, and made us each a very tasty martini, which hit me like a ton of bricks coated in fairy dust.

James appeared and confirmed that Mr. Scarecrow had returned. Viv found another glass and poured him a drink as well. It was getting dark, and a little cooler, and the three of us were having quite the evening.

"Is that the kilt of your clan?" I asked James.

He nodded. "Yes. I could give you my entire clan history, from about the twelfth century, if you'd like."

I shook my head. "That's okay. Some other time. So we did a great job here tonight, thanks so much. You're becoming part of the neighborhood, James."

He held out his glass for another drink, and Vivian poured carefully.

"Yes." He ran his fingers through his dark hair and pulled it so it stood up on end. "It's nice to feel a part of something." He smiled. "And the people here are terrific."

I tried not to grin, and was seriously considering another drink when I got a text from Sam. The first of the teams had arrived at the finish line.

I hauled myself up and shook out my tea leaves. "Gotta go." I gathered my clipboard and phone, and started down the hill, leaving James and Vivian sitting comfortably, glasses in hand.

Tessa and her team did not win. They didn't even come close, because Jerome misunderstood one of the basic rules of the hunt and ate all four of the mini-muffins that were in fact Clue #6. One team of older girls lost one of their members when she took off with her boyfriend and missed checking in to all but three checkpoints. There were a few more minor tragedies, but all in all, everyone seemed to have enjoyed the scavenger hunt very much. Mr. Scarecrow received mixed reviews. While some parents applauded his juggling and general goofiness, other parents complained that he did nothing but play Simon Says and sing silly songs. The scavenger hunt winners were announced, then the winners of the Costume Contest.

Tessa and her friends won First Place, Group Division.

At that point, I was fairly done with the evening. Cait and Kyle agreed to go back to the house to give out candy, while Sam and I walked around making sure all of our checkpoints had been cleaned up for the night. We saved Emma for last, because I knew she would need the most help.

Poor Emma. We found her sitting on her porch, her cat, Biscuit curled on her lap.

"Ellie, dear, I haven't the energy to do another thing." Her long gray hair had been pulled up in a bun, but it was now tumbling down around her face, adding to her usual crazy cat lady vibe.

"Can we leave the table and chairs in here?" I called from her garden.

"Please don't," came a faint reply.

I looked at Sam. "I borrowed these from the clubhouse, and it's locked up. I guess I can get the car and move them up to my house for the night?"

He shook his head. "You look beat. Let's call it quits. Why don't we just move them next door? Then we can take them up to the clubhouse in the morning with my car." Sam drove a Suburban, which technically, was kind of a car, but more of a moving van.

"Good idea." Next door was Aggie Martin's house. It was dark and empty now, the "For Sale" sign planted bravely out front. "We can just stash everything on the porch. That puts it all out of the way."

Sam and I started closing up the folding chairs. Emma had hung paper lanterns everywhere, and the cider bowl was empty. The trashcan was full of empty paper cups, and broken pieces of doughnuts scattered the ground. Her spooky sound machine was blaring from the corner, emitting loud shrieks and hollow laughter.

"Here, let me help," Carol Anderson called, coming in from the street. Carol and Emma were good friends, and I knew that she had been helping earlier with Emma's station. She grabbed two chairs. "Where are we putting these?"

"Thanks, Carol. On Aggie's porch. How did it go here?"

"Great. Mr. Scarecrow was a big hit. He had some great tricks. But he bolted out of here as soon as the last kid left. He didn't even take off his mask, he was in such a hurry. Did he even get paid?"

I shrugged. "Mary Rose will see to it, I'm sure."

Carol carried the chairs out, and Sam and I turned the folding table over. One of the legs was jammed, and after three seconds of struggling, I threw up my hands. "Help, I need a big, strong man."

Sam laughed. "If I see one, I'll send him over."

I put my hands on my hips. "Oh, ha-ha."

He kicked at the leg, and it folded obediently. "There. Anything else?"

I looked over his shoulder. Carol was back. Her face was white.

"Ah…"

"What? Carol, what's wrong?"

She closed her eyes. "It's Mr. Scarecrow. He never left at all. He's lying on Aggie's porch. I think he's dead."

Sam moved quickly, and I was right behind him. Out of the garden and around to Aggie Martin's front walkway.

I stopped and watched as Sam walked cautiously up the steps. He stepped past the folding chairs that Carol had propped under the window. He was looking down, into the dark, far corner of the porch.

"Sam?" I called.

He had his phone out. "Yes. He's dead. Don't come up here." He spoke into his phone. I could feel Carol behind me, her hand on my shoulder.

"Well?" she whispered.

I shook my head.

Poor Mr. Scarecrow.

CHAPTER THREE

IT WAS AFTER MIDNIGHT, AND I found myself in the highly unimaginable position of being Mary Rose's best friend in the world. Carol and I had walked down with one of the first police officers to arrive at the scene to tell her what happened. As it happened, her brother, Steve, and his wife, Kim, were there. Apparently, they had been there all evening. They had arrived after Todd and Doug, had been out and about looking at the decorations, and had stayed for dinner. I had met them both over the course of past Mt. Abrams events. They had helped Mary Rose with last year's St. Patrick's Day Pancake Breakfast and had stood next to me, doling out green pancakes and bacon. I didn't know either of them well, but my heart broke for them nonetheless.

Mary Rose immediately broke down and had not stopped crying. Sometimes it was just a broken sobbing. Sometimes in was full out bawling. She kept grabbing my hand and thanking me for being with her. Her husband Joe made phone calls and brewed endless pots of tea, which Mary Rose drank between bursting into tears and running to the bathroom.

Kim, Todd's mother, didn't cry at all; she just…shrank. She huddled into a corner of the couch, her face white and blank. Only her eyes showed her anguish at the loss of her youngest son. Steve's face was also a blank. He sat next to her, holding her hand, not saying a word.

What could he say?

The night had become surreal.

Doug finally arrived. He had been tracked down at a club in Hoboken, and got to his aunt's house after eleven. Mary Rose's living room was bursting with family and friends, not to mention two police officers that were taking statements from the family. Sam had been there earlier and suggested quietly that everyone might want to go to the police station. Mary Rose stopped crying long enough to insist that she could not allow her family to be dragged into a cold, impersonal room to be questioned, when obviously what they needed was the warmth and support of familiar surroundings.

Sam knew Mary Rose well enough to let it drop.

By unspoken agreement, all trick-or-treating in Mt. Abrams stopped at nine o'clock. That meant everyone was still out in the streets when the sirens started, and once again, the whole community crowded onto Davis Road to watch yellow tape go up and hear the crackle of walkie-talkies as police and technicians swarmed another tiny Victorian house. I had texted Cait to tell her what happened. She wanted to come down, but I asked her to stay, so she could be home when Tessa returned. Then I texted Marc, who had taken Tessa and her friends around the neighborhood. I asked him to stay away as well.

The very last thing the situation needed was a bigger crowd.

Carol finally left, and I tried to hide in a corner, but Mary Rose would not let me be. At one point, she looked at me with teary eyes and said, "You'll find out who did this, won't you, Ellie? Please?"

I shook my head. "Mary Rose, let the police do their job. Sam is here. He's the best."

She shook her head. "No, Ellie, *you're* the best. You found out who killed Doug Mitchell. And poor Rita. Promise me?"

I'm a terrible liar, and as I nodded, I was sure that a bolt of lightening was going to come for me, straight down through Mary Rose's ceiling.

I had promised Sam Kinali that I would never again stick my nose into anything that remotely looked like a crime. I had also sworn the same to Caitlyn and Marc. After Sharon Butler tried to kill me with my own fireplace poker, all three had felt an intervention was needed, and I didn't put up a fight. I may have gotten a thrill playing detective, but my family had to come first. And I wasn't about to jeopardize my relationship with Sam for an adrenalin boost.

"Don't worry, Mary Rose," I told her. "I'll take care of this."

Sam came back, took one look at me, and escorted me outside. "You need to sleep. Now."

I leaned into him and sagged as his arms went around me. "Oh, that poor kid. This is so awful."

I felt his lips in my hair. "Do you need a ride home? I'll get someone to take you."

I stepped back. "No. I'm fine." I was still a tea bag and suddenly realized I'd spent the entire night shedding leaves all over Mt. Abrams. It struck me as funny, but I was too tired to laugh. "Call me?"

He smiled gently. "Of course."

I turned and started up the hill to home.

Todd Richter was killed when a small, blunt instrument, probably a hammer, hit him on the back of the head. The attacker was close to the same height, and considering the force of the blow, was either very strong or very angry. Todd was killed somewhere else, possibly in Aggie Martin's tiny back yard, and hauled up on to the empty porch after the fact. There were no fingerprints found. The weapon was not found. The time of death was put between six-thirty, as that was the last time anyone saw him alive, and seven–forty-five, which was when Carol found him.

The body had still been warm.

There were no immediate suspects, although Todd apparently had lots of enemies. He was involved in drugs, and aside from using pot and cocaine, he dabbled in illegal pain meds from both the using and selling sides. He was in debt to his mother and his brother, as well as a few major drug dealers and/or loan sharks.

For a clown, he had a real dark side.

Since he had posted all over social media where he was going to be Halloween night, anyone who wanted to kill him knew exactly how to find him. With so many people wandering the streets, children as well as adults in costume, it would have been easy for anyone with a rubber *Scream* mask to wait for Todd, and no one would have blinked. Usually, in Mt. Abrams, strangers stuck out like sore thumbs, but on Halloween, it was easy to get lost in the crowd.

Sam told me this, of course, over the few days after Halloween. Mary Rose called me every day asking if I'd found out anything new.

I was getting better at lying.

Then my daughter Caitlyn made a request.

It was after dinner, and I was waiting for her to go out and meet Kyle, but she announced that he was coming over instead, and they both wanted to talk to me.

I narrowed my eyes at her. "Both of you?"

She nodded.

"You're making me nervous. Are you pregnant? Getting married? Breaking up?"

She rolled her eyes and shook her head. "No, no, and no."

I exhaled loudly. Thank God.

Kyle, when he arrived, looked tired and also nervous, and the two of them sat next to each other on the couch.

"Okay," I said. "What is this about?"

Cait tugged on the ends of her curling, red hair. "The police are asking Doug a lot of questions about Todd's death."

Sam had not mentioned that to me, but since I wasn't actually part of the official investigation, I wasn't surprised. "And?"

"Well, he didn't do it," Kyle blurted. "He couldn't have. Doug is a gentle guy, and he loved Todd, even if Todd was a screwup."

"I believe you, Kyle. But what has any of this got to do with me?"

"Could you, you know..." Cait cleared her throat. "Look into this?"

I sat back and stared at her. "Excuse me?"

Cait shot Kyle a look that clearly said *I told you so*, but went on bravely. "Let's face it, Mom, you kind of have a talent for figuring things out. We need you to find who killed Todd and get Doug off the hook."

I closed my eyes, mentally counted to three, then opened them slowly. "Did you not, in this very room not so long ago, tell me I should never get involved in another murder?"

"Yes, but—"

"And did you not," I continued, my voice getting a little louder and slightly more high pitched, "warn me that putting myself at risk was bad enough, but dragging Tessa in, not to mention yourself, was inexcusable?"

She squirmed. "Mom, this—"

"I believe threats were made, by Sam and your father, and oh yeah, *you*, as to what might happen if I *did* stick my nose into something?"

She sat back, shoulders slumped.

"I believe a strong case was made that perhaps I needed professional help if that sort of thing was repeated? And you yourself mentioned taking Tessa out of harm's way?"

She looked at Kyle, shook her head, and sighed. "Yes."

Kyle swallowed hard and looked straight at me. "But Ellie, what if Doug gets arrested, and then he gets convicted and spends the rest of his life in jail for a crime he didn't commit, while the real killer just goes free, and maybe kills someone else? And what if you could have prevented it?"

Did I mention that Kyle had the biggest blue eyes this side of Elijah Wood? And that he had a strong, handsome face? And that he was sweet and still dorky, a slightly irresistible combination?

"I cannot poke my nose into this," I said at last. "First of all, Todd may have died here, but he didn't live here. I know nothing about him or his life, and I can't go poking around and asking questions of people I don't know." I took a deep breath. "But you two can."

Cait sat up. "What do you mean?"

I shrugged. "Well you two know Doug. It wouldn't seem too out of line if you asked a few questions. Talk to Todd's friends, find out who he was close to, who his enemies were. Sam told me Todd was into drugs, and owed money. Maybe somebody knows who he owed money to. If you told me, I could push Sam in that direction."

The two lovebirds looked at each other. "We could do that," Cait said.

"I know you could. But just be really careful. Don't talk to any of those drug people yourselves, for God's sake. Remember, one of them might be a killer."

Cait looked relieved. "Thanks, Mom. I promise we'll take care. And we'll bring everything straight back to you."

Kyle smiled. "Thanks, Ellie. Doug is a good guy. I appreciate this."

I sniffed. "Yeah, well, take care of Cait. If she gets in too deep, I'm counting on you to be the smart one."

Cait stuck out her tongue. "Gee, Mom, thanks."

"You're welcome."

The weather had turned cold. Well, it was November in New Jersey, so it wasn't an entirely unexpected event. It meant bundling up a little more than usual for my morning walk. As soon as the temperature dropped below thirty, or it snowed, or became icy, slushy, or in any other way unpleasant, the morning walks would be called off entirely. Carol Anderson valued her comfort, and Shelly and I were basically wimps who just went along with whatever Carol decided.

Maggie Turner, who was usually our fourth walker, was off on tour. She played with a fairly famous chamber group that practiced locally for eight months out of the year, which made Maggie's life a breeze. But then there came four months of touring, starting November 1st, finishing the end of February. During that time, she was lucky to fly home once a week, and had never spent a Christmas day with her daughter, Serif.

"Where's Maggie this week?" Carol asked as we started up the first hill.

"Detroit," Shelly said. "I bet it's really cold there." She looked sideways at me. "How's Todd's murder coming along?"

"I wouldn't know." I shifted the leash from one cold hand to the other. "I've sworn off murder, you know that."

Carol had been smart and wore dark gloves of lined leather. "But surely, after Mary Rose, aren't you doing *something*?"

"No. I swore to Cait and Sam and Marc, and I'm staying out. But Caitlyn is doing a little snooping around."

"Cait? Really?" Shelly, who ran marathons in any weather, was wearing some sort of high-tech super outfit that clung to her fit but flat body like a second skin. "What's her interest?"

"Doug graduated with her and Kyle," I explained. "He and Kyle are still friends, and apparently the police are looking hard at Doug to be the killer."

"So, what has Cait told you so far?" Carol soothed her short, gray hair behind her ears. "Anything useful?"

I shook my head. "Not a thing. Most of what she's gotten so far has been from Doug. Todd was in trouble. Drugs. He owed money. He did a little dealing. He and Todd had formed a legal partnership, and Doug wanted out because Todd was spending every cent they made on coke."

"And Mary Rose invited him to entertain our children?" Shelly's jaw tightened. "How could she?"

"He was," Carol said gently, "a very good clown. He had those kids in stitches. He was pulling pennies out of their ears and juggling mini-pumpkins. Why, he even balanced a spinning plate, you know, on his nose? With one of those long poles? And then he had them singing and playing the silliest Simon Says game I ever saw. Emma and I were in stitches. Those kids didn't want to leave, scavenger hunt or no."

We were rounding the lake. Most of the leaves had fallen in the past few days as a result of the cold. Boot and Shelly's dog both had their noses in the leaves, sniffing happily.

"So, Carol. Did Todd seem distracted at all?" I asked casually. "Or did he receive a call or text on his phone that seemed to upset him?"

"I knew it," Shelly said gleefully. "You can't keep a good woman down."

"I'm just asking a simple question," I said.

Carol shuffled through the leaves. "He didn't interrupt his performance," she said, "even when his mother came by to watch. But at one point, there were no kids around, and he checked his phone, then told us he was running to the bathroom. He was gone a long time for a simple pee break, so maybe he did make or receive a call. When he came back, he was perfectly fine, didn't seem upset at all, and started the kids singing *Row, Row, Row Your Boat*, and he made them sing faster and faster until everyone was hysterical. He stayed until there were no kids at all, and I went out and saw that the street was pretty empty, and he was gone, like a flash."

"What time?"

She pursed her lips. "I told the police six-thirty. That's about right. The first of the kids got there right after five, and the break came about half an hour later. He was gone about twenty minutes. I remember because that lovely James Fergus arrived just as Todd returned, and I took a picture of them together, and my phone said five-fifty." She was smiling, a dreamy, faraway kind of smile that was usually associated with young girls and Justin Bieber.

"Did you see in what direction he went? Todd, I mean?"

Shelly made a noise. "Just asking a simple question?"

I glared at her. "Just confirming what Cait told me. Doug arrived in Hoboken just after seven, so he must have left as soon as Todd was done."

"But we never saw Doug," Carol said.

I stopped walking. "What do you mean?"

"Well," Carol said. "He was there helping Todd unload the car. All his stuff was in this large duffle bag, and Doug drove the car to Emma's, unloaded, then took off again. When Todd left, he threw everything back in the duffle, but I didn't see Doug come back. I just assumed Todd walked back down the hill. Doug was parked in the lot by Route 51."

"But the bag wasn't found," I said slowly. "Not with the body."

"So, Todd went to the car, dropped off the bag, then came back up to meet someone, and then he was killed?" Shelly shook her head. "That makes no sense."

"It also makes no sense that Doug would just leave his brother there," I said. "Something is not right here."

"I'll say. Too bad you're not looking into this," Shelly said. "I bet if you asked a few questions, you could get a much clearer timeline."

"I'm sure the police have a perfectly good timeline," I said.

"Well, if not, you just let me know." Carol looked smug. "I never told anyone *I* was swearing off crime solving. I find the whole thing rather exciting. And I'd be happy to share any information I happened to pick up."

I grinned at her. "Why, thank you, Carol."

She grinned back. "Well, dear, that's what friends are for."

CHAPTER FOUR

IT WOULD HAVE BEEN EXTREMELY helpful if I knew everything the police knew. The good news was, I had a direct contact. In fact, I was sleeping with the very man in charge of the investigation. The bad news was, I couldn't ask him anything without him becoming, quite understandably, upset. So I turned all of that over to Caitlyn. And she was very subtle in her methods.

"So, Sam," she asked him after dinner Thursday night, "are you going to arrest my friend Doug Richter?"

Tessa, who was helpfully clearing off the table, stopped dead in her tracks. "Yeah. What about that? Did you find out who killed Mr. Scarecrow?"

Sam looked around the table, his eyes bright. "What a group of nosy women I've become involved with. Ladies, this is about a murder. I'm not supposed to be discussing this with strangers."

Tessa put down the plates she was holding and folded her arms across her chest. "Sam, really? Strangers? You're practically family."

My heart jumped a little. I knew that she and Sam got along, but for her to say something like that…

I glanced at Sam. I could see Tessa's words hit him as well.

"Thank you for saying that, Tessa. It's a wonderful thing to be thought of as family. Especially *this* family. However, I'm sure my bosses would not approve."

"Well, we won't tell them if you don't," Cait said.

Sam looked at me. I kept my face neutral.

"I'd love a cup of coffee," he said, to no one in particular.

Tessa picked up the plates and hurried into the kitchen. Cait, ever the smart one, hurried after her.

"Ellie…"

I held up both hands. "Sam, I swear to you. I've asked one person a few questions. That is it."

"Who and what did you ask?"

"Carol. After all, I see her every morning, and she was with Todd most of the time he was there. So I asked how long he stayed, if he got any calls or texts, and when he left."

Tessa came bustling in with the sugar bowl and a clean spoon. She looked at Sam, then me, and went back into the kitchen.

"They're still talking," she said in a whisper loud enough for both Sam and me to hear.

Sam chuckled. "Your girls certainly do take after you."

"I know. Isn't it great? So, I'll show you mine if you show me yours?"

He waggled his eyebrows. "Maybe later?"

I burst into giggles as Cait and Tessa returned, Tessa carefully carrying a steaming cup, which she placed in front of Sam.

"Thank you."

"You're welcome. So, are you going to tell us or what?"

Sam threw back his head and laughed. "Fine. Sit down." He picked up his spoon and pointed it at Tessa. "And not a word of this to the station commander."

She nodded solemnly. "I swear."

He stirred his coffee slowly, sipped, and then added some sugar. "Suppose you tell me what you know, Ellie."

I cleared my throat. "I know that Todd was gone for about twenty minutes. Carol said he took a bathroom break, but he checked his phone before he left. She also told me that Doug had dropped Todd and his duffle bag full of goodies off in the car, but when Todd left for the night, he carried the duffle bag himself, and Doug was not around. That makes me think Todd walked down to the parking lot, dropped off the bag, then came back up the hill, which narrows down the time of death. That would have taken him about fifteen minutes to walk, round trip. So he was killed between six–forty-five and seven–forty-five."

"Which eliminates Doug as a suspect," Cait said. "Doug arrived at the club in Hoboken just after seven. There's no way he could have killed Todd here at quarter to seven, then made it down there at seven o'clock."

Sam nodded. "Yes. Doug claims Todd met him at the car, threw the duffle bag in the truck, then told him to go. Doug was angry about possibly being late, so he didn't ask any questions and just took off. And you're right, Cait, the timeframe makes it a very improbable that Doug had the time to kill Todd, bring him back up the hill, and still arrive in Hoboken when he did."

"So, what's the theory?" I asked.

Sam sipped more coffee. "Todd met someone, possibly someone involved with his drug, ah situation, behind the Martin house. We have convincing evidence. Obviously, whoever did this wanted the body to be found sooner, rather than later. Although the porch is fairly screened from the street by the shrubs, if the body had been left in the back, it could have stayed there, undiscovered, much longer."

"Which says what about the killer?" I asked.

Sam shrugged. "The killer may have wanted to send a message. Although, drug enforcers don't usually hit people with a blunt instrument." He glanced at Tessa, who was sitting, wide eyed, and drinking in every word.

"Well," I said brightly, "I think that wraps up today's briefing. Tessa, love, finish the table and get to your homework, okay?"

She looked at me, suddenly remembered that I was The Parent, rolled her eyes, and then slowly, painfully, and with obvious reluctance, picked up three forks and a paper napkin and walked into the kitchen.

Sam brought his coffee into the living room, and we sat together very companionably in silence for a bit, until Tessa and Cait both went upstairs.

He smiled. "So, you're really not snooping around?"

"No. I'm not." I was having Cait, Carol, Shelly, and as soon as I made the phone call, Vivian Brewster do the snooping around for me.

"This is a tricky one. Doug had the motive, but since he couldn't be killing his brother and driving across Route 80 at the same time, he's off the list."

"Motive?"

"It would appear that Todd siphoned off money from their business account. Lots of money. That's always a motive."

"But they were brothers."

"People are rarely killed by strangers, Ellie. It's hard to work up the passion, or hate, needed to murder someone, let alone someone you barely know."

"Can I pass this on to Mary Rose? She's been calling me and texting me, grabbing me in the street, sending smoke signals…"

He laughed. "Yes. Of course." He looked thoughtful. "Did she ever talk to you about her brother and his new family?"

I shook my head. "No. Why?"

"Steve Wyzinski is a very cool customer. He didn't seem broken up at all about Todd's death."

"I imagine it's hard to form a relationship with adult stepkids."

"Possibly. Am I really practically part of the family?"

"Well, I'm thinking that if you can crack a hard nut like Tessa, you're in."

"How nice," he said, kissing me lightly on the lips.

How nice indeed.

The next morning, after walking around the lake, I dropped Boot back at the house, and Shelly, Carol, and I walked down Davis Street to look at Aggie Martin's house.

There was still yellow tape everywhere. The sky was gray, and the wind was kicking up leaves, and the once perky little Victorian looked sad and lonely.

"Let me get Emma," Carol said, and walked past the walled garden.

Shelly and I went up Aggie's driveway. Sure enough, in the back corner of the tiny yard, there was more crime scene tape.

"So, maybe Todd just wanted to use his cell in private, came around here, and the killer, what, waited for him? Followed him?" Shelly got closer to the corner and leaned in. "Whoever it was could have been hanging out right behind Emma's fence here, and when Todd came around, jumped out and hit him."

There was a thick hedge of some sort of evergreen between Aggie's yard and whoever lived behind it. I peered through. "Do you know who lives there?"

She shook her head. "No. They're new, and the kids are younger. Carol would know. Or Emma."

Dale and Martin lived on the other side of Aggie's. I didn't know them at all, not even their last names. They'd moved in two years ago and had no children. They kept to themselves except on Founders' Day weekend, when they cruised the neighborhood in search of free food and drink.

Emma and Carol came around the corner. Poor Emma, she looked a fright, her hair long and wind-blown, with a fringed shawl wrapped around her stout body.

"Wait," she said shrilly, stopping cold and holding out one hand, as though to ward off a blow. "There is evil here."

Shelly and I exchanged glances, but Carol leaned in, looking concerned. We waited for several seconds. Emma took a deep breath, closed her eyes, and began to sway back and forth.

"Emma?" Carol asked.

"Wait. Wait." Emma said.

We waited. Emma McLaren was Mt. Abrams own self-proclaimed witch. She was a lovely woman who made herbal potions and could read your palm, but at times I found her connection to the spirit world very tenuous.

She opened her eyes. "He died here."

Carol nodded patiently. "Yes. We know that."

Emma frowned and looked around. "He was meeting someone else."

I had explained carefully to Shelly that I was not going to actively involve myself in trying to solve Todd's murder, and that I was counting on her to pick up the slack. I nudged her.

She looked surprised, thought a moment, then asked. "Who was he expecting?"

Good job, Shelly.

Emma was still frowning. "A dark man. A bad man."

Shelly ran her hands through her short hair. "Well, Emma. That's who he met, isn't it? A good man wouldn't have killed him."

Emma looked slightly put out. "Good people do bad things all the time, Shelly. He was desperate. He was worried about *his* mother."

"Todd?" Carol asked.

"Who else?" I said. "Although, the killer could have been worried about his mother."

"So maybe Todd was worried about his mother, and that caused him to do something that got him killed?" Carol tried valiantly to get Emma more focused.

Emma shook her head. "I don't know. But there was a problem between Todd and his stepfather. A big problem."

Carol looked over at me, eyebrows raised. "Steve Wyzinski? Mary Rose's brother?"

I shrugged.

Emma sniffed. "Bad blood. Very bad blood."

Shelly sighed. "Time to talk to Mary Rose."

Carol stayed back with Emma as Shelly and I walked on. I rattled off a bunch of ideas and questions for Shelly to ask Mary Rose, and Shelly listened intently, then shook her head.

"Forget it, Ellie. Mary Rose wanted you, not me. She's not going to pay attention to anything I say."

"True. But try, okay? Once she gets going, it'll be easy." I took a deep breath as I knocked on the door.

Normally, Mary Rose is not necessarily happy to see me, but when she opened her door, she actually threw her arms around me.

"Oh Ellie, thank God you're here. Come in. Have you heard anything?"

I disengaged and glanced over at Shelly, who was trying very hard not to laugh out loud. "Yes, I have some news, Mary Rose."

She ushered us in, past her immaculate living room and back to her kitchen, which, like the rest of her home, had been meticulously decorated in the 1980s and not touched since. We sat around her maple table, on captain's chairs.

Shelly, I could tell, was still struggling with the outburst of affection that had greeted me at Mary Rose's door, so I immediately got serious.

"Mary Rose, I've spoken to Sam, and it looks like your nephew has a good alibi."

"He's not my nephew," she said. "But, thank you. The police haven't been very forthcoming with information."

Hmmm. Saturday night she was devastated by Todd's death, and today Doug's *not* her nephew? Shelly picked up on that quickly.

"Mary Rose," she asked, "how long have Steve and Kim been married?"

"Four years. We were very excited, of course. Steve's wife had passed over years before, and we were thrilled that he'd found someone. Especially someone with children, even if they were grown. We couldn't have any, you know."

Mary Rose was married, but Joe was never around, and when he was, he faded into the background and didn't say a word. So when she said "we," I had to remind myself that she wasn't using the royal we.

Shelly made encouraging noises, which was all Mary Rose needed. "Todd was always a problem. Drugs. And Doug was such a lovely, talented boy. Have you heard him sing?" She clasped her hands in front of her. "Doug is very loyal. He won't even admit that Todd is dragging him down and ruining the business." She stopped and closed her eyes. "Was. Todd *was*." She leaned forward and dropped her voice to a whisper. "He stole from their company, he stole from his mother, and he tried to steal from Steve. But Steve wasn't having it. In fact, he told Kim that if Todd stayed, he was going."

I was trying to process two things. First, did that give Steve a motive? And second, why was she whispering? Who else was there? I glanced around. Nope, no one.

Shelly whispered back. "Really?"

Mary Rose nodded. "He'd already left her once. He was serious."

I couldn't help it. "Why are we whispering?"

Mary Rose straightened and cleared her throat. "Anyway, I'm sorry for what happened to Todd, but I'm certain that Kim is the only person truly sorry to see him gone. Her, and all the drug dealers who depended on him."

Shelly and I exchanged glances. Back to drug dealers again. Or maybe not.

"Mary Rose," I asked, "what was Kim's reaction to Steve's ultimatum?"

She shrugged. "She was going to choose her son, of course."

"Steve must have been pretty angry about that," I said.

The penny dropped. She glared at me. "What are you suggesting, Ellie?"

"When did Steve and Kim get here Saturday night?"

She patted her permed hair, a bit nervously. "Early. Before five. The two of them walked around for a bit. Kim wanted to watch Todd, so Steve came back here a little earlier, and when Kim got back, we had supper."

"Was Steve here the whole time?" I asked.

"Of course," she snapped. Then she dropped her eyes. "Well, no. After supper, he walked up to Emma's. To see if Todd needed help."

Shelly leaned forward again and dropped her voice. "And?"

Mary Rose stood up abruptly. "I think you should go now."

Shelly and I stood up and walked to the front door. Mary Rose was not behind us. I turned and saw her, still standing at her kitchen table, staring down at her hands.

Shelly and I let ourselves out.

CHAPTER FIVE

M Y MOTHER HAD BEEN IN an assisted living facility
for so long now that I'd almost forgotten she
had raised my brother and I in a brick ranch on a
sunny suburban street, within walking distance of
the elementary school. But she hadn't forgotten, even
though she sometimes didn't remember that I was her
daughter, and she kept asking, everyone and anyone,
for a ride home.

She was sitting in the group living room, playing
canasta with four other women. I knew she had trouble
with numbers, but with those cards in her hands, she
was still sharp as a whip. I watched them all for a few
minutes, before I approached and said a general hello.
They all said hello back. After all, I knew them, and
they all knew me. Or at least knew my face.

Mom looked up immediately and smiled broadly.
"I've been waiting for you."

My heart jumped. "Really? How nice. How've you
been?"

"Just fine, but you know you promised to take me to
Dogwood Lane today. I'm going home, isn't it wonderful?"

My heart stopped its jumping. No, she didn't recognize me after all. I was just the driver.

"I don't think that was today," I said.

The ladies continued to play. When my mother's turn came, she pounced on the center pile, shuffled though all the cards, and put out three four-of-a-kind and a five-of-a-kind, a red three and a natural canasta.

"There." She said triumphantly, discarding a black three, leaving her hands empty. "I think I've won!"

A tiny redhead with lots of green eye shadow swore very loudly. She had just had her eighty-fifth birthday, but still talked like an obnoxious teenaged boy. "Leona, I'd swear you were cheating, but I know you can't remember how."

Mom waggled her finger. "I don't need to cheat. I'm a natural." She looked up at me. "I still have to pack. Can you help me?"

I smiled brightly. "Do you have your pass?"

Mom frowned. "What pass?"

The redhead, Connie, glanced up at me. "Leona, the pass from the director. You know you need one to leave."

Peggy, blind in one eye, was the scorekeeper. She was slowly counting cards and writing down numbers in a loopy scrawl. "Can't leave without it, Leona. You know that."

Mom sat back, her lower lip pushed out. "I forgot."

"That's okay," I said, still smiling. "Maybe we can have lunch instead."

"Winner pays," Connie cracked. "You remember that, don't you?"

My mother rolled her eyes. "Yes, Connie, of course I remember. Winner always pays. I just can't believe I forgot about that blasted pass. This means I have to wait another whole week." She looked up at me. "You do come every week, don't you?"

Connie cackled, pushing her hair off her forehead with tiny, claw-like hands. "Course she does. She's a good girl."

My mother sighed. "I guess I can wait."

She was still beautiful, my mother, her hair thick and wavy around her face, her skin still glowing softly, her dark eyes bright. Lately, she'd been complaining about a sore back and was getting a massage a few times a week. I envied her at times, caught in a world where the days were spent playing cards and imagining a younger, brighter life. Not to mention massages and good food and whirlpool baths.

"So, lunch?"

She nodded. We were early in the dining room, and chose a table for four, a tacit invitation for others to join us. Mom and I had little to talk about these days. She no longer knew my daughters. In her mind, *she* was the one with children to raise, in a little brick house on Dogwood Lane. Sure enough, Connie sat with us, and the two of them talked about growing up in Newark, taking the train to New York for a nickel, living only ten blocks away from each other in a quiet Italian neighborhood. I listened, imaging her young and lovely, not owning a pair of stockings until she was twenty and World War Two had been over for years.

Then I kissed her good-bye. She clung tightly to my hand.

"You won't forget next week? You promise?"

I patted her hand. "Of course I promise."

Then I drove home.

Caitlyn had kept her part-time job as a waitress in a very lovely and expensive French restaurant, because the money she made there in tips was almost as much as her full-time teaching job. Friday nights she was usually at work, and if she wasn't working, she was with Kyle, so I was a little surprised when she announced she was staying home.

I looked at her with raised eyebrows. "Is everything okay?"

She nodded. "Yes. Kyle is coming over. With Jonah."

"Who's Jonah?"

"A dealer that Todd owed money to."

I had to think about that one. No, it couldn't be. "Drug dealer? You've invited a drug dealer to my house?"

She didn't look the least bit phased. "Yes. He wanted to talk in some bar in Dover, but you told me not to do anything dangerous, so I asked him to come here."

"Are you crazy?" My voice got a little higher. I may have been screaming. "A *drug dealer*?"

"Mom, calm down. It's fine. Doug knows him. Kyle too."

"Kyle? Kyle deals drugs?" My mind was going way too fast for my mouth. I found it impossible to put all of my feelings into sentences. "Kyle? Drugs?"

She patted my hand. "Mom. Kyle smokes pot. So do I. So, I seem to recall, do you."

"That was a long time ago. Now, it makes me hungry, then puts me to sleep. That's beside the point."

"Jonah is not a scary kind of dealer. He's sort of the ice cream man of the local drug trade. Drives around with some fun stuff, takes cash, has his regulars. But he knew Todd really well, and knew who else Todd was working with. He could help us narrow down a killer."

Tessa, thankfully, was with Marc. He was taking her to spend the weekend in the Poconos at his brother's family lake house. It was too cold for swimming or boating, not cold enough for skiing, but Tessa got along with her cousins and always had a good time. I'd been thinking about a romantic evening with Sam. Looked like that was off the table.

"Sam will be here at eight. Would he consider this Jonah person an ice cream man?"

Cait looked worried. "Can you call him? Have him come later?"

"How much later?"

"Like, after twelve?"

We'd been standing in the kitchen, but this was too much. I sank into a chair. "What time is Jonah coming?"

"Sometime between nine and ten. Maybe later."

I was trying very hard not to show too much of how I was feeling. "You didn't think, since it is my house, that you should have asked about this first?"

She shrank back a little. Maybe it was my clenched teeth. Or the heavy breathing. Or my face, which was probably beet red with steam coming out of my ears.

"Mom, it just happened really quickly. Doug is bringing him over, and this was the only time…I'm sorry."

"Doug? He's coming too?"

She nodded.

"It would be good to talk to Doug."

She brightened. "That's exactly what I thought."

"But I'm not supposed to be *doing* any of this, remember? You're the one who's supposed to be asking the questions, not me."

"I know. So, if you want, you can just hang out at the top of the stairs and listen to us talking, and that way…" She arched her eyebrows. "You're off the hook."

"I don't think," I said slowly, "that Sam would consider me off the hook."

"Maybe we could have Sam here, after all. Like, unofficially. So he can hear what Jonah has to say too. I'm sure we'll get a whole lot more information out of him than Sam would."

Hmmm…

"Let me call Sam."

I went right to voice mail, so I left a brief message, then went upstairs to finish up some work. My favorite client was publishing a series of shorts, and the schedule was tight. As a freelance editor, the good news was that I didn't have to answer to anyone but my clients. The bad news was, if I was behind, there was no one to help me out. I was in the zone, so I didn't hear my cell phone until about the third or fourth ring.

"Sam? Hi. I have a hypothetical for you."

"Oh?"

"Yes. Suppose a young man was murdered, and he had associates that were involved in an illegal activity. And suppose you had the opportunity to eavesdrop on someone else questioning one of those associates. Would you consider that a good thing or a bad thing?"

Silence.

"And suppose your girlfriend had absolutely nothing to do with the setup, other than owning the house where the questioning was taking place?"

"Ellie...what?"

"Doug Richter is bringing Jonah the ice cream man by for a conversation with Cait and Kyle. They're going to be talking about who Todd owed money to and who might have wanted to kill him because of it. We've been invited to sit at the top of the stairs and listen in."

"Is ice cream man some kind of euphemism for drug dealer?"

"Yes. Apparently Jonah is the nice, helpful kind."

"We've already interviewed several of Todd's, ah, connections."

"Anyone named Jonah?"

"No. And you swear this is not your idea?"

I actually pulled the phone away from my ear to stare at it before answering. "You're kidding, right? Me, sitting down with someone like that?"

He chuckled. "It's not a totally outrageous supposition, Ellie, and you know it."

"I swear to you, Sam, this was all Cait's idea. Kyle is Doug's friend. They want to figure this out."

He sighed. "I have some paperwork. I was going to try to get there by nine. Is that good?"

"Yes. We can talk to the kids about strategy."

"We?"

"Okay. You."

He laughed. "Sure."

And hung up.

Because I have a weakness for all things crime/murder/thriller related, I was a huge fan of *The Wire* when it ran on television. So I naturally expected Jonah to look like Idris Elba. Or maybe I *hoped* he'd look like Idris Elba.

Instead, he looked like a young Woody Allen, with more hair. And hipster glasses.

He and Doug rang my front door bell a little after ten. Sam and I had been having a spirited discussion with Cait and Kyle about drugs in general—what were the most damaging, most addictive, what should be legalized, how drug use should be treated—and it had been quite an education for me. Coming of age in the 70s, I'd tried pot and cocaine, ate a mushroom or two, and even pulled all-nighters during college finals with artificial aid. But as a grown up adult, the occasional hit off someone else's joint at a party was as wild as I got.

Cait and Kyle had pretty much the same experience I had, only they couldn't understand why, in this day and age, pot was still illegal. Sam had lots of facts and figures, but in the end, he couldn't understand it either.

The problem was that Todd's relationship with marijuana hadn't been the problem. It was the prescription painkillers that got him hooked.

"Really?" I said, looking at Cait. "What is wrong with people? I mean, there are happy endings with that stuff. Everybody knows that."

Kyle shrugged. "Todd had been on and off the stuff since high school. And that's as long as Doug's been trying to get him clean. A couple of stints in rehab...it's tough. It was tough. Now, it's over."

Sam settled back in the couch, his arm around my shoulders. "It must have been a great relief, then," he said.

Kyle stiffened a little. "Doug would have kept on trying. He never would have given up."

"And what about Steve?" I asked. "How did he feel about his stepson's ah...problem?"

Kyle looked over at Cait, frowning, as though trying to figure out what to say next. "It wasn't good. Steve wasn't very supportive. I think it caused a real problem with Kim."

Sam glanced at me. "Ellie?"

"I'm sure you've interviewed Steve already," I said.

Sam nodded. "Yes. He said he walked up to Emma's around six-thirty to see if Todd needed any help. Todd was gone already, so he just turned around and walked back down." He shifted his weight. "We're looking at him. We're looking at everyone."

On cue, Doug and Jonah arrived.

Doug looked pale and exhausted. Jonah looked like he was always picked last for volleyball in school.

"Ellie, thanks so much for this," Doug said as he grabbed my hand. "Really. This is Jonah. He said he'd help."

Jonah ignored me and was staring at Sam, who looked innocent enough in khakis and a rugby shirt, but there must have been a cop vibe coming from somewhere.

"Why is he here?" Jonah asked the room at large.

"He's my boyfriend. We were just going upstairs, so you guys can talk privately." I smiled at Jonah. "But can I get you something to drink first?" I almost offered chocolate milk.

Jonah shook his head and actually wrung his hands. As many times as I'd read that in a book, I'd never seen a person do that in real life.

"As long as I'm guaranteed immunity, he can stay. In fact, maybe it's better that he's here. I wouldn't want anything I say to be repeated incorrectly."

Sam stood up. He was a large man, but next to Jonah, he looked like Hagrid from the *Harry Potter* movies. "I'd be happy to hear what you have to say in a completely unofficial capacity."

Jonah nodded. "Excellent. In that case, a little red wine would be nice. Maybe a nice Pinot?"

Cait nodded. "Sure. Anyone else?"

We all sat down, arranging ourselves around the fireplace, which by now had a small but happy fire blazing away. Boot came shuffling down the stairs, barked a few times for show, then jumped up on the couch next to me. She curled up, her head on my lap, and promptly fell asleep.

Jonah eyed her skeptically. "That's one ferocious watchdog you've got there."

I scratched Boot behind her left ear. "It's past her bedtime," I explained. "If this were ten in the morning, she'd be all over you."

"Good to know. Oh, thanks, Cait." Jonah reached for his glass of wine, sipped, and nodded. "Good. Now, what do you want to know about Todd?"

I clenched my jaw. After all, I was out of this, right? I raised my eyebrows at Cait, who took a deep breath before starting.

"We need to know who Todd owed money to, and for what, and who might have wanted him dead," she said.

Jonah pursed his lips. "He was into me for about five grand, and you know that what I sell is rated PG." He shifted toward Sam. "I deal mainly in marijuana. A little hashish, maybe some oxy, but mostly pot. It's just a matter of time before it's legalized in this state, and I'm trying to build a reliable client base."

Sam nodded. "Sound thinking."

"Exactly. Which is why I handle distribution myself. Too many middlemen will only hurt me down the line. I'm not trying to be greedy. I'm just trying to maintain a nice lifestyle while putting away a little something every month so that, when the time comes, I can go wide. Kiosks. I'm thinking at least one in every mall in the state."

Kyle grinned. "Great plan, Jonah. Seriously."

Jonah looked modest. "It's been a dream. Now, back to Todd." He turned in his chair. "Dougie, I love you like a brother, you know that. But Todd was in serious shit with very bad people." Jonah glanced at Sam. "I won't mention names. But—December, 2013."

Sam's eyes flickered. "Really?"

Jonah nodded, then refocused on Doug. "These are the kinds of people that kill for fun. But a ball peen hammer is not their preferred MO. In fact, a rather large handgun at close range is how it usually goes."

"But, Jonah," Kyle interrupted. "It was early evening. There were tons of people around. Would they risk someone hearing the gunshot?"

Jonah sat back and shook his head. "Are you kidding? These guys wouldn't care if it was the middle of Bloomingdale's at lunchtime." He drank some wine. "I'd like to help you, but if you're thinking this was a drug-related killing, you're barking up the wrong tree. This was personal." He glanced at Doug. "Maybe you were right? About that girl?"

"What girl?" Cait pounced.

Doug looked thoughtful. "He hadn't mentioned her in weeks."

"What girl?" Cait asked louder.

Doug ran his hands through his shaggy brown hair. "Todd was seeing her, sleeping with her, whatever. Eve somebody. She told him she was pregnant, and he dumped her. Insisted it wasn't his. She was…angry."

"Did you tell the police about this girl?" Sam asked.

Doug shook his head. "No. I'd actually forgotten about her."

Kyle leaned forward. "What do you know?"

Jonah pushed his glasses up off his face and into his curly dark hair. "She's a junkie. Todd had every reason to doubt her claim. She turns tricks on the weekend, waits tables during the week in a pizza place in Montclair. She shouldn't be hard to find." He drained his wine and set the empty glass on the coffee table, wiped his face with both hands, and then put his glasses back in place. "Nice meeting you," he said to Sam and me. "I hope this was helpful," he said to Cait. He stood up, nodded to Doug, and walked out.

"Interesting character," Sam murmured.

Doug stood up as well. "Anything helpful?"

Kyle nodded. "Yes, well, the drug thing looks to be off the table, but Eve is a possibility, right, Sam? A strung out, pissed off girl could have done it easily, right?"

I looked at Sam. "But where would she get a hammer?"

He nodded. "Exactly."

"But you're not sure it was a hammer," Doug protested.

Sam shrugged. "We're pretty sure."

Kyle stood, kissed Cait on the lips, and then waved. "I'll take Doug home. Thanks, guys."

They left. I rearranged Boot, so I could lean against Sam. "Well?"

"This is complicated," he said softly. I could feel his lips in my hair.

Cait stood. I heard her say good night. I closed my eyes and snuggled in closer.

"Where would *anyone* get a hammer?" I asked.

"Exactly," Sam said.

Shelly Goodwin sometimes went to church on Sunday mornings. I did not. I'd offered to take both of my girls to church, and a younger Cait took full advantage. Catholic, Methodist, Presbyterian, Unitarian—she sampled them all. Then Buddhism and Islam. Judaism. She dabbled in Paganism. She settled on nothing, but she really tried.

Tessa went to church with Marc on the big days—Christmas and Easter. She was not at all curious, which was fine with me, because I liked spending Sunday mornings on the couch surrounded by coffee and the *New York Times*.

When Shelly came by, she wasn't in church clothes. She was in sweats and sneakers and looked like she hadn't slept. She grabbed some coffee and pushed the newspaper to the floor.

"First, tell me about the drug dealer."

I settled back. "He looked like a sixteen-year-old nerd. And not the sexy kind, the pocket-protector kind. He has a business plan and is putting aside a little something every month. He'll probably have the first pot-selling franchise in New Jersey."

She snorted. "So, he didn't arrive with a scary-looking posse?"

"Nope. And he pretty much took all the other drug dealers out of the picture. Apparently, no self-respecting drug kingpin's hit man uses a hammer."

"So we're back to no suspects?"

"No. Doug mentioned Todd's old girlfriend." I told her about Eve.

"So, we have to go to Montclair and eat pizza," Shelly said. "We could do that."

"*You* could do that," I said. "Remember?"

"Of course." She took a deep breath. "Listen, I have something to tell you."

"Okay. Shoot."

"Mike and I are splitting up."

I stared. I felt like someone had hit me in the stomach. Hard. "What?"

She took a long gulp of coffee. "You know we've been having problems."

"Wait a minute. You told me, like, a few weeks ago that you were arguing, but that's marriage. That's not problems."

Her eyes suddenly filled with tears. "It's gotten bad. Suddenly. And it's my fault."

I shook my head. "No, Shel, don't say that. It takes two people to break up."

"No. It's me. I…"

I leaned forward and gently took the mug out of her hands and placed it on the table. "What?"

"I think I'm in love with somebody else."

I felt something wash over me. Anger? Disappointment? Regret? She was *in love* with someone else? "Shel, you're married. How do you fall in love with somebody else?"

"All at once, like falling off a cliff." She wiped the tears that streamed down her cheeks. "I didn't mean for it to happen. We just started talking one day, and everything just clicked in my head, and I hadn't felt so happy in, like, years, and all I wanted to do was spend more and more time with him, and before I realized what was even happening, it was too late. I've never felt this way, Ellie. Never about Mike, even when we were first in love. This is…overwhelming. When I'm not with him, I'm miserable. When I am, I'm so happy I can't even breathe."

Her words tumbled out in a rush. I closed my eyes tightly. What was I supposed to say to her? My best friend, who was walking away from over twenty years of marriage to a good, honest man, with whom she had two boys and built a home and a life. For what? "Shelly, maybe if you and Mike saw someone?"

She sniffed and shook her head. "Wait."

She got up, went to the downstairs bathroom, where I heard her blow her nose. Several times. I stared out the window and remembered all the things she had said to me when Marc and I were splitting up. But that was Marc walking out, not because of another person, but because the two of us had grown so far apart that we couldn't stand being in the same room together anymore. We had both been so unhappy. I hadn't wanted Marc to leave, and had been devastated when he finally did walk out, but there had also been a sense of relief.

Shelly and Mike were a completely different story, and I could find very little to relate to. Or sympathize with. Shelly was leaving her husband for another man. That was hard for me to support.

She came back out and sat. "This is so hard. It's finding out that every single thing I believed about my life isn't true anymore. I'm miserable about this. I don't want to hurt Mike. He's my best friend. But Jamie—"

"Who?"

She looked right at me. "Jamie. Fergus."

"Jamie Fergus as in James Fergus who's renting the house on Davis? Are you kidding me?"

She shook her head.

"Well, you can stop worrying about what's going to happen, because Vivian is going to kill you when she finds out."

She cracked a smile. "She knows. Jamie told her all about us."

I slumped back against the cushions. "He's only lived here a couple of months. How long has this been going on?"

She made a face. "Four weeks?"

"You're going to throw away an entire life after just four weeks? My God, Shelly, really?"

"I know," she wailed, and burst into tears.

I put my arms around her and let her cry, trying to figure out what to do and say next.

I kept reminding myself this was the real world. I spent most of my time reading books, and in books, things like this ended either in a bloody murder or happily ever after. While I couldn't see any actual blood being spilt, I also could not imagine everyone shaking hands and agreeing to play nice. Mike loved Shelly, adored his boys, and must have felt like the world had been jerked out from under him. And Shelly...what the hell was she thinking?

"Have you slept with him?" It kind of just came out.

She shook her head violently against my shoulder. "No. I would *never* do that. I'm married!"

"Well, that's good, anyway. You need more tissues." I pushed Shelly gently away and went to the bathroom for the box of tissues. I also quickly texted Viv a simple *HELP*.

"Here. Blow some more," I said when I sat back down. Shelly nodded obediently and blew her nose, wiped tears, blew again and finally took a long, deep breath.

"Better. Thank you." She had the tissues gripped tightly in her hands. "You think I'm a terrible person, and I should be shot, don't you?"

"You are one of the best people I know. I just don't think you're seeing this very clearly. You don't know him, Shelly. How can you be so in love with a man who you haven't spent any time with? I mean, granted, he looks great in a kilt. And if this were a Sarah MacLean book, that would be enough. But you've got a real life here, honey, and you're putting everything at risk."

She carefully put the tissues on the table. "I know. It's so crazy. I haven't slept in days. I felt so guilty I couldn't even look at Mike. I finally told him everything last night, and he's so upset. He says he's willing to move out temporarily and let me decide, but he will only do that if I agree not to see Jamie."

"That is very generous of him."

She sighed. "Yeah, that's Mike all right. He's such a good guy, but I don't know how I'm going to stay with him after meeting Jamie. It's like living in a cozy valley, and you think you're fine and safe, and you are, you really are. Then one day someone leads you up to the top of the mountain and you realize there's a whole other world, and it's grand and beautiful, and the fresh air fills you up, and you're feeling things for the first time. After that, how do you go back down to the valley?"

There was a knock on the door. Thank God. "Come in," I yelled.

Vivian Brewster came in, took one look at Shelly, and then sighed. "Oh."

"Viv," I pleaded. "Help me. I have no idea what to say."

She threw off her brightly colored poncho and sat on the other side of Shelly. "This is a mess," she said to me. "Shelly is pretty wrapped up in this. But so is James. He and I have talked this through, and I gotta tell you, the man is completely in love. He cannot see straight. So even though I usually start smacking people around about this sorta stuff, in this case, I think maybe it's real."

Shelly nodded. "See? It's not just me."

"But the boys…" My shoulders slumped. "Shelly, this will kill the boys."

Her eyes filled with tears again. "I know. I know. Everything about this is so awful, Ellie, but what am I supposed to do? Spend the rest of my life with Mike and the boys and always want to be with someone else?"

"Well…" I looked over at Viv, who shrugged her shoulders.

"I got nothin'," she said.

I sighed and looked at Boot. She wagged her stump of a tail, but didn't offer help. I looked out at the lake.

The colors were fading; the leaves had been dropping in the sudden cold, but the sun was shining off the water, and as always, something in my heart lifted.

"We can figure this out, Shelly." I said. "Of course we can. But please, don't do anything just yet that can't be undone, okay?"

She sniffed. "Of course."

Viv nudged her, and when Shelly turned, Viv wagged her finger. "No sleeping with him. And I *know* how badly you must want it. But no. Ya got that?"

Shelly turned beet red. "Do you know how hard…"

"Yes," Viv said.

"Yes," I said.

And we all started to laugh.

I got a lot of work done Sunday afternoon. Once I put Shelly out of my head, I found myself in the zone, that imaginary place where everything comes together. I even worked through lunch. And that hardly ever happens.

When I finally did stop, my head was spinning and my stomach was growling. I found my phone and scrolled through some texts. Marc was on his way with Tessa. Cait was spending the night with Kyle. Sam sent a little emoji blowing kisses.

I made a peanut butter and jelly sandwich, wrapped myself in a throw, and then sat on the front porch. The sky had turned gray, and the wind was picking up, but the fresh air, plus the kick of carbs, felt great.

Who killed Mr. Scarecrow?

Somebody who knew where he'd be. That was anyone who could have looked at any of his social media. So pretty much anyone in the world.

Somebody who wanted him dead. That was sticky. Was a junkie of an ex-girlfriend a viable candidate? Not really. At least, I didn't think so. But I also thought it had to be someone close to Todd. Someone with a personal connection. Someone Todd would let get close enough to hit him with a hammer. Like his stepfather, whose marriage was in jeopardy. Or his brother, whose career was being dragged down.

According to Sam, Todd had two calls come through before he was killed. One from a throwaway phone and one from Doug. Neither had left a message. Todd called both numbers back during his break.

Doug said he was just checking up.

The call from the throwaway—was that the call that took up all Todd's time? Was it from one of his dealers? The ex-girlfriend?

"It would be good to know who that second call was from," I said aloud.

There was a squirrel that had been running up and down the tree in my front yard. He stopped at the sound of my voice and looked at me, tail twitching.

"I bet that was the call that set up the meeting behind Aggie's house. But why would he walk all the way down to the parking lot to drop off his bag, then walk back up to meet someone twenty feet from where he *just* was? Why didn't he just take the bag with him? Or leave it with Emma?"

Squirrel made a noise.

"That makes no sense. It's really bothering me."

It must have bothered him too, because he scampered up the tree.

Marc's car pulled in, and Tessa bolted out of the car and ran to me.

"Dad says I can spend winter break with Uncle Paul and go skiing."

I pulled her in for a hug. "That sounds like an amazing idea."

Marc loved to ski. I did not. In fact, I was generally against any activity that required me to spend lots of time outside in the cold and the snow. He had taught Cait and Tessa, and they both loved it. I had spent many married weekends curled up in front of a fire somewhere waiting for Marc and Cait to return from the slopes. During our divorce, when things could have turned ugly, Marc went out of his way to take the girls skiing on winter weekends. The fact that his brother owned a place just twenty minutes from the ski resort made those weekends more affordable than they would have been otherwise.

Marc had her overnight bag with him as he came up. "I hope you don't mind," he said. "She and her cousin Lara sort of organized the whole week."

Tessa's eyes were bright. "It's okay, right? Uncle Paul can't be there, but Aunt Suzie and the kids will. Dad said he'd stay the whole week too."

I looked past Tessa to Marc and raised my eyebrows. Marc thought his sister-in-law was a brainless, selfish bimbo who only lived for shopping and bragging about how superior her own children were compared to the world's children in general.

"It sounds great. Why don't you take your stuff upstairs. It's just you and me tonight, so I thought sushi?"

She nodded, grabbed her bag from her father, and was gone.

"You, Suzanne, and four kids in a log cabin with no cable." I shook my head. "Oh, to be a fly on the wall."

He sat next to me, leaned over, and kissed me on the cheek. "You could come with us."

"I'd end up killing Suzanne and burying her under a snow drift."

He chuckled. "Yeah, she can be a little hard to take sometimes, but Tessa and Lara were really into it. Maybe Cait and Kyle could come."

"Kyle skis? I didn't know that."

"Yes. You should think about coming, El. It would be nice to have the family together." He grabbed my hand and laced his fingers with mine. "We really should be spending more time together, you and I."

I looked at him very carefully. This was the man who made me believe in soul mates. From the moment I had met him, I knew that he and I were meant to be together.

Just like Shelly said she felt with James Fergus.

I was older now, wiser, and a bit more cynical. Was that why what had happened once between Marc and I seemed to be something completely far-fetched and illogical now?

Sam and I were very happy together, but as much as I felt a strong attraction to Sam on many levels, I wasn't calling it love. I didn't know him well enough. Or perhaps I knew myself *too* well.

"Marc, we've been dancing around this for months."

"I know. And I don't know why we're not doing more things together. Or sleeping together. We still love each other, Ellie. You know that."

"I'm doing things with Sam." I swallowed. "I'm sleeping with Sam. And I'm too old to be having sex with two men at the same time. I gave that up in my twenties, when I realized what a bad choice it was."

"It sounds like you're choosing Sam over me." He wasn't looking at me. He stared out at the lake.

"Shelly and Mike are having problems. He's moving out for a while."

He turned to me, surprised. "Really? That's too bad. I thought they'd be one of the couples who made it."

"She says she thinks she's in love with someone else."

He swore. Marc was a man of words. He loved them, and used them carefully, but sometimes nothing was right for the moment but a good, old-fashioned f-bomb. "What has that got to do with us? Are you saying *you're* in love?"

"No. I'm just saying that things happen. It's hard to know what's the best thing to do. Who's the best person to spend your life with. Sometimes, you just have to wait until the dust settles."

He nodded. "And that's what you're doing?"

"I guess."

He brought our joined hands to his lips and kissed the back of my hand. Hard. "I can wait," he said, got up, and drove away.

Chapter Six

ONDAY MORNING IT RAINED HARD, so I knew there would be no walking around the lake. I waved good-bye to Tessa and took Boot for a quick walk up and down the street. Just letting her out the front door was not an option. She had been known to poop on the front porch rather than get her feet wet. She also had a habit of tearing off after any particularly suspicious-looking squirrel. Boot was one of those dogs that really belonged on a leash.

Shelly texted me.

Home from work. Mental health day. Viv is in the mood for pizza. You in?

So here was the dilemma. No, I wasn't supposed to be actively looking into Todd's murder, and that meant not looking for the ex-girlfriend. But going out to lunch in Montclair wasn't necessarily an extreme event. I'd had lunch there lots of times. And if Viv wanted pizza, who was I to argue?

I texted her back.

We can take the train. Leaves at 1045

I loved the train. I had a fantasy about taking a train cross country, seeing the Rockies from the comfort of a dining car, complete with gourmet food and high-priced cocktails. Taking the NJ Transit commuter into Montclair wasn't exactly the same thing, but I still felt like it was an adventure.

The rain slowed to a drizzle by the time we got off at the Montclair station. Shelly wore a bright yellow slicker and had opened up her Met Museum umbrella. Viv had on a long trench coat. I almost expected her to whip out a fedora.

"Where to first?" Shelly asked.

I squinted at my phone. "According to Yelp, there are seventeen pizza restaurants in Montclair."

Viv looked thoughtful. "No way I can eat seventeen slices of pizza."

"I can't either. But I think we can eliminate the nicer restaurants that happen to serve pizza. I doubt Eve is working at place with tablecloths and a wine list."

"True," Shelly said. "Let's find the closest place, sit down, and make a list."

We found a very clean but no-frills pizzeria. Our waitress was named Chloe. She didn't know anyone named Eve. The slice with Coke I ordered was perfectly fine.

"The good news is we've narrowed down the list," I said. "Only six to go,"

"That's the good news?" Viv looked doubtful.

"What are we going to do with all that pizza?" Shelly asked.

"We'll take them to go," I told her. "Our kids will love us."

Viv tapped her brightly colored fingernails on the table. "Is this how Stephanie Plum started out?"

I shook my head. "No. We're blazing a new trail here."

We found Eve after the fourth slice. She was a very thin, pretty girl with natural-looking blonde hair and a paisley tattoo that ran from her bony shoulder down to her wrist. Her hair was pulled up in an untidy knot on the top of her head, and her dark eyes were outlined in black liner.

"Need menus?" she asked after we sat down.

This called for an extended stay, so I manned up and ordered two slices. Viv managed one. Shelly, more health conscious, asked for a small salad and water.

"She doesn't look pregnant," I said after she left.

"Doesn't look old enough to drive, either," Viv murmured.

"How are we supposed to start a conversation with her?" I wondered.

"We could try the straight-ahead approach," Shelly said, watching Eve behind the counter. "You know, hey, Eve, did you kill Todd Richter?"

I gave her a look. "Shelly, you're supposed to be honing your skills."

She sighed. "Sorry, Obi-Wan. I'm in a pizza coma."

"I say we just go for it," Viv said. "I'm tired and cranky, and I need a nap. And I'm done with pizza."

Eve returned with our drinks. It was after two, and the place was empty except for us. As she turned away, Viv cleared her throat.

"Listen, Eve, We're hoping you can help us out."

Eve turned, her eyes narrowed. "With what?"

"Well," Shelly said. "We're from Mt. Abrams."

Eve shrugged. "So?"

We glanced at each other. She was either an excellent actress, or she'd never heard of the place.

"The place where Todd was killed?" Viv said gently.

Eve's lips tightened, and her jaw clenched. "The police have already talked to me. I was working Halloween night. Right here. I didn't kill him."

"Of course you didn't," Viv soothed. "We were just going to ask you about his other friends. You know, was he fighting with anyone?"

Eve shook her head. "No. I mean, no more than usual. Todd rubbed a lot of people the wrong way. He wasn't... nice." She was looking down, twisting the corner of her red apron between bony fingers. "He wasn't nice to me, anyway."

Shelly made sympathetic noises. "When you heard he was killed, did a name jump out at you? Did you suddenly think, wow, so-and-so finally did it?"

Eve nodded. "Of course."

Shelly leaned forward. "Who?"

"Doug. His brother, Doug."

"You know what bothers me the most?" Viv asked.

We were back home. Well, almost. Tessa had texted that she was staying after school, so we'd stopped in at Zeke's. Viv was having a martini, while Shelly and I opted for white wine. Zeke's was a low-key neighborhood place, right next to the train station. It had good food, cheap drinks, and because we could walk home, no one needed to be the designated driver

"Tell me," I said.

"Why did Todd walk all the way down to the parking lot just to drop off his stuff? I mean, he was meeting somebody, right in Aggie's back yard. Why didn't he just walk out of Emma's and go next door?"

I stared into my wine. "That bothers me, too. Obviously, he planned to meet someone there. It just doesn't make sense."

"What does Sam say about it?" Shelly asked.

I drank some wine. "Sam and I aren't discussing this, remember?"

Viv snorted. "You gotta tweak your pillow talk, girlfriend."

"Maybe he wasn't planning on going to Aggie's at all," Shelly said. "Maybe he was walking down to the parking lot and met somebody who said, hey let's talk."

Viv leaned forward. "So, they were in the parking lot, and Todd said, hey let me drop this bag off and we can go somewhere more private, and that's how he ended up back up the hill."

"Then, it had to be a Mt. Abrams person," I said slowly. "Someone who knew that Aggie's house was empty."

"But Doug said he saw Todd, and that he dropped off the bag and headed back," Shelly said. "He must have run into whoever on his way down to the lot."

"We need to find somebody who saw Todd walkin'," Viv said. "'Cause you know somebody did. In fact, I bet a whole lotta folks saw all sorts of things without realizing what they were lookin' at."

"There aren't too many houses down that way," I said. "Most of the trick-or-treat action is above Sommerfield. Who do we know down there who we can talk to?"

Viv raised her eyebrows. "You mean, besides Mary Rose?"

"Somebody on Morris," I said. "Way down by Route 51."

We thought. Well, I thought. Shelly and Viv *looked* like they were thinking

"Lynn Fahey," Shelly blurted. "She's down on Carver."

I pulled out my phone. "That's right. Good job. I forget about Lynn sometimes."

Viv made a rude noise. "How is that even possible? The woman has her fingers in every little pot."

I texted Lynn.

R u around? Have ??? about Halloween.

"You know what else bothers me?" I said, watching my phone for a reply. "The hammer. If this *was* a crime of passion, then you have to accept that the killer used whatever was around, and a hammer just happened to be in Aggie's back yard? If it was premeditated, don't you think the killer would have spent a little time looking for a better weapon?"

"Better than what?" Viv asked. "Seems to me that hammer did a fine job. But I see your point. It's a little odd."

"On the way home, let's stop and talk to Emma. Maybe she was doing work in her garden and left a hammer laying around." My phone sat there, silent. Lynn was not getting back to me. I picked it up and stared at it. Still silent.

"Which means the killer was not just a Mt. Abrams person, but a Mt. Abrams person whose kid was drinking cider and eating doughnuts in Emma's garden," Shelly said.

We looked at each other.

"Well, that sucks," Viv said, and drank the rest of her martini.

Emma, of course, wanted to give us tea and home baked cookies, and normally, that would have been perfect on such a gray and chilly afternoon. But Viv had begged off halfway up the hill, and Shelly wanted to get home and enjoy the rest of her afternoon by napping. Being the good friend that I am, I completely understood.

"Emma, we're just here for a couple of questions," I explained. She had a cozy fire going, and all her cats were curled up on one over-stuffed chair. She sighed, and we all sat down.

"I tell you, I'm very upset about what's been happening around me the past several months," she said, pulling her sweater closer around her. "I think some sort of all-out purification needs to happen. Mt. Abrams is in a very bad way."

"You may be right, Emma," Shelly said. "But right now, we're confused about the hammer that was used to kill poor Todd. Had you been working on anything in your garden? Repairing one of your benches or a trellis?"

She took a quick breath in. "Are you suggesting that *my* hammer was a murder weapon?"

"No, of course not," Shelly said.

"But we were wondering where a hammer may have come from," I said.

She settled her shoulders indignantly. "It did not come from my toolbox, I'll tell you that. First of all, when I am done with a project, I put everything away. And I know for a fact my hammer is where it should be, because I used it last night." She leaned forward. "I can't believe you would think something like that of *my* tools."

Obviously, her tools had minds of their own.

"Sorry, Emma," I said. "We were just trying to tie up a loose end."

She sat back and sniffed. "Of course. If you ask me, it was probably his own hammer that killed him."

Shelly and I glanced at each other.

"Todd had a hammer?" I repeated slowly.

"Yes. He had one in his duffle bag. His brother was helping him set up, and one of the table legs was stuck, and he went into the duffle bag and pulled out a hammer to bang the table open."

"Yes," I said. "When Sam and I were taking it down, Sam had to kick it closed."

"So, Todd had a hammer with him," Shelly said to me.

"I wonder if Sam knows it," I said back to her. "I wonder if he found it in the duffle bag, or if it's missing."

"You have to ask," Shelly said.

I nodded. "I know."

Emma cleared her throat. "Ladies, I'm still here. Is there anything else you want to ask me?"

"No, Emma." I smiled at her gratefully. "That little bit of information was very helpful. Thank you."

"He wasn't evil, you know," Emma said as we stood up.

"What?" I stopped to look at her.

She was staring into the fire. One of her cats jumped up on her lap, and she stroked it absently. "He wasn't evil, although he did an evil thing. He felt like there was no way out."

"Do you mean Todd?"

She shook her head slightly. "They were both very sad. Too sad. Brothers are supposed to bring comfort to one another."

Shelly looked at me with her eyebrows raised.

I sat back down slowly. Emma called herself a witch, and at times like these, I almost believed her. "Emma, do you know who killed Todd?"

She closed her eyes. The cat shifted slightly on her lap, and I could hear it purr. "So sad. And angry. It's hard to hide that kind of anger for so long."

"Emma, do you know who killed Todd?"

She opened her eyes. They were filled with tears. "No. But his brother does."

Caitlyn was not impressed. "She's a crazy cat lady, Mom. She should stick to her peppermint oils and homemade cough syrup."

"Sometimes she's said some very uncanny things," I reminded her. "Remember when she told you in high school to buy a dress for the prom a week before Jack Humphries asked you?"

She rolled her eyes.

"And she knew where you lost Grandma's watch. And that Walt Malleck had been killed by his lover. And—"

"Yeah, well, she's wrong this time. Doug has been telling Kyle about Eve. She's practically psychotic."

I sighed. "No, she's not. I don't even think she's pregnant. I talked to her today. She seemed very normal and was working all Halloween night."

Cait looked impressed. "You tracked her down? Really? Way to go, Mom."

I tried to appear modest. "Yes, well. The police have talked to her already. I'm sure she's not a suspect."

Cait pushed her dinner plate away. Tessa had run upstairs to do her homework, and Cait and I had waited for her footsteps to fade before we started talking. The kitchen was totally quiet. Years ago, we had a wall clock that ticked loudly, and I'd always been somehow comforted by the sound. Now, the LED clock on the oven offered nothing but silence.

"Does Doug have a day job?" I asked her.

"Yes. He works for that big music store in Rockaway. He knows a lot about guitars. I think he gives lessons there."

"What about Todd?"

She stood and started clearing the table. "Todd's day job was getting high and hanging out in some dive bar in Newark."

We cleaned up the kitchen together. She seemed distracted, but I knew better than to push. Finally, she folded her arms across her chest and leaned against the refrigerator.

"The thing is, I don't think Doug is so innocent either. He's...nervous. Kyle knows him a lot better than I do and insists that Doug is fine, but I think Doug is hiding something."

"Like what?"

"Well for one thing, he told the police that the whole time Todd was at Emma's, he was sitting up by the lake. But I never saw him there, and Kyle and I were both hanging out on the porch waiting for trick-or-treaters."

"Have you asked him about it? Doug, I mean."

She looked uncomfortable. "Kyle thinks I'm being ridiculous, and that Doug could have easily been on the other side of the lake where we couldn't see him."

"Well, that's true."

"Sure. It makes so much more sense to traipse through weeds and stuff to sit on a wet log instead of walking up the drive to the clubhouse and sit on a nice, comfortable bench."

"Honey, you can't let your loyalty to Kyle get in the way here. Have you talked to Sam about this?"

She shook her head.

"Do you want to?"

She took a deep breath. "Yes. I think it might mean something. Where else was he? And why did he lie?"

I walked over and hugged her. "Maybe he didn't, baby. But we'll talk to Sam, okay?"

She nodded.

But the both of us kind of forgot about it, because the next day, Steve Wyzinski was arrested and charged with the murder of his stepson, Todd Richter.

I was upstairs working, on the phone with one of my favorite authors. Usually, all communication between me and the authors I work with is via e-mail, but there are a few that I've known for so long, I can just pick up the phone, and we can talk about what we're working on.

Content editing is hard. The words an author puts to page are like their children and telling somebody that their child is screwed up and doesn't make sense requires a certain amount of tact. I may blunder through my personal life, but as an editor, I treat authors with firm but velvet-covered hands.

But I cut the conversation short as soon as the pounding on my door began, and Mary Rose's voice filtered upstairs. I ran down to find Boot barking hysterically, and Mary Rose standing in my living room, tears streaming down her face, screaming my name.

I grabbed her by the shoulders and shook her, hard. "What happened?"

She clamped her hands over her mouth and squeezed her eyes shut. I could see her pulling herself together as the wrinkled forehead relaxed, the eyes opened slowly, and her hands dropped to her side.

"They arrested Steve," she whispered. "This morning. They found the murder weapon in his garage."

I did not see that coming.

I guided her to the couch and pushed her down gently. "The hammer? It was in his garage?"

She nodded.

"How did they know to look for it there?"

Her eyes widened. "I have no idea."

"Does he have a lawyer?"

She nodded. "Kim is getting one."

"Okay. That's good." I took a breath. "Did Sam…was he there?"

"I think so. That's why I came to you. You have to tell Sam he's made a mistake. Steve wouldn't kill anyone. Not even Todd."

I let a few seconds pass. "What do you mean, Mary Rose? Not *even* Todd."

Her jaw tightened. "That boy was wicked. He was ruining them. He was dragging them all down."

I thought about what Emma had said. *"He wasn't evil. He just did an evil thing."* She had been right after all. But…

"Where's Doug?"

She frowned. "What does that matter? They took Steve. In handcuffs, Kim said. Just like a criminal."

I glanced at my watch. "Okay, Mary Rose. Tessa will be home soon, so I can't go with you right now.

Cait gets home from work around four. As soon as she walks through the door, I will drive down to the police station. Why don't I meet you there? Or you can wait for me. That might be a better idea. I'll pick you up, and we'll drive there together."

She smoothed her gray hair with both hands. "Joe can drive me. I need to get there right away.

"Right." I kept forgetting she had a husband. "Then I'll meet you there as soon as I can."

She stood up and fixed her eyes on me. "This is a terrible mistake, Ellie."

"I'm sure it is."

"I'm counting on you to make it right."

I shook my head. "Mary Rose, don't do that. I can't be responsible for what happens now."

She lifted her chin and walked quickly out of the house.

I slumped back into the couch. Steve? How on earth…

Cait was stunned. "They arrested him? But…how?"

I had changed from my usual work clothes—yoga pants and a fleece pullover—to jeans and a cashmere sweater. I even had lipstick on, and not just because I was going to see Sam, although I always tried to step up my game a little bit when he was around. Mary Rose would be dressed in her best intimidation outfit, which would probably include pearls, kitten heels, and pantyhose. Solidarity comes in many forms.

I pulled on a Ralph Lauren blazer I had rescued from Goodwill. "I have no idea how long I'll be down there. There's a meatloaf ready to go in the oven. I'll be home when I can."

"Mom, listen."

I turned.

Cait chewed on her lower lip. "Kyle texted me."

I waited.

"Doug…Doug told him that he thought, Doug, I mean…" She finished in a rush. "Doug told Kyle that maybe his stepfather did it."

"When was this?"

"Last night."

Okay. So far, Doug had gone from a drug dealer to Eve and now… "He keeps pointing his finger at different people, Cait. And every time he does, it's a false lead. Why would he do that?"

She shrugged.

"It's like he's trying to send the police after one suspect after another."

"Well, it looks like he was right this time," Cait said.

I shook my head. "I don't think so, Cait. And you don't either."

"It's just that Kyle is so sure about Doug being innocent."

"And you're not? Can you tell me why?"

She ran her fingers through her long red hair. "I don't know Doug very well, but he's said some things. I don't think he liked his brother very much. In fact, it sounds like they kinda hated each other."

I gave her a quick hug. "I've got to go. Talk to Kyle about this. He has to understand that even good people can do bad things, and he can't blindly defend Doug. Don't get emotional about it. Stay calm and logical, okay?"

I grabbed my purse and headed out.

Mary Rose and her husband Joe were with Kim Wyzinski in a small conference room. An officer showed me in and closed the door behind me, and Mary Rose jumped up and grabbed my hand.

"Thank you, Ellie. Thank you for coming. I feel so much better now that you're here."

Kim looked exhausted and very frail. I edged my way around the table and sat next to her.

"You found a lawyer for Steve?" I asked.

She nodded. She was picking at the skin around her thumb, and I could see the cuticle was raw and bleeding. I put my hand over hers and squeezed gently. "What happened?"

She stared at our hands. "They came with a warrant for the house and the garage. The hammer was in the garage. Sitting right on the tool bench. Steve says he doesn't know how it got there, and I believe him. It belonged to Todd. Todd marked all his tools with some kind of symbol, like, he burned it or stamped it or something. He did it to keep people from walking off with his stuff." She looked up, her eyes full. "Steve didn't do this."

I patted her hand. "What did Steve say?"

She shook her head. "That he didn't know anything about it. He hadn't been in the garage for a couple of days. There's no room for the cars, it's just for storage, you know? Anybody could have put it there."

"Is there a regular door to get in, or do you need to open the garage doors?"

She sniffed. "There's a regular door."

"Is the door locked?"

She shook her head. "No."

"Okay. That's good."

The door opened again, and Sam came in. He stopped short when he saw me, but his expression did not change. Behind him was his partner, John Monroe. The room was getting crowded.

John sat down across from me, glanced up, and then did a double take. "Ellie?"

I waggled my fingers at him. "Hey, John. How's the family?"

He nodded. "Good. And the girls?"

Sam cleared his throat. "Ellie? Are you related to this somehow?"

I smiled brightly. "Just a friend, Sam. Is that okay?"

He exhaled slowly. "We'd like to speak to Ms. Wyzinski alone, if that's all right with you?"

I stood up. "Of course. We'll be just outside."

I pushed Mary Rose and Joe out of the room, and we sat on stiff metal chairs in the hallway.

"What's he asking her?" Mary Rose whispered.

"Probably going over the timeline for Halloween night. You told me that Steve left you, and went up to see if Todd needed help."

She clenched her jaw, but didn't say anything.

"Mary Rose," I said, "you need to tell me."

"Steve left about six-thirty," Joe said. "Walked up the hill. Came back around seven and said that Todd had already gone."

That was the longest sentence I had ever heard come out of Joe Reed's mouth. Ever. He was a tall man, lean and muscular from all his walking, with an average face and thinning gray hair. Because Mary Rose was such a forceful presence, most people forgot that Joe was even around.

Mary Rose looked at her husband with narrowed eyes. "He wasn't gone that long," she snapped.

Joe nodded calmly. "Yes, Mary Rose, he was. And you even commented on how long he'd been gone."

Mary Rose folded her arms under her breast and hugged herself. "I don't remember," she muttered.

"Well, I do." He leaned forward to look at me around his wife. "About half an hour. Said he'd met somebody and was talking about the Halloween decorations."

"That's good, Joe. See, Mary Rose, we need to find out who he spoke to. That will help with his alibi."

She stood up abruptly, gave her husband a cold look, and walked off down the hall.

"Where's she going?" I asked Joe.

He shrugged. "Who knows? She'll find someplace to sit by herself and stew."

It was almost an hour before the conference room door opened, and Kim shuffled out. She looked, if possible, even more defeated. She was tall and thin, and her clothes hung off her body like rags. Joe stood up immediately and hugged her. Sam looked down at me.

"Still here?"

I nodded.

He held the door opened and motioned with his head for me to go in. "John, can I have the room? Find Mrs. Reed. We need to talk to her as well."

John shot out of there, closing the door behind him.

"I thought you said you weren't involved in this," Sam said. I could tell he was trying very hard to keep his temper in check.

"I'm not. But Mary Rose—"

"I don't care about Mary Rose," he snapped. "You promised me, and your daughters, that you would not put yourself at risk any more."

"I know Sam, but Steve Wyzinski does not make sense for this. There's more to this case, and I think—"

"It doesn't matter what you think. We have motive, opportunity, and the weapon was found on his property with his fingerprints on the handle."

"How did you even know where to look?"

He put his hands in the pockets of his trousers. "Anonymous tip."

"What? Are you *kidding*? Oh, Sam, come on now. If that doesn't—"

"Ellie, I'm only going to say this once. Stay away from this. You have no stake in this. Stop interfering. I mean it."

We stared at each other.

There was a part of me that was so angry with him I could have smacked him over the head for being so stubborn and totally unreasonable. But he was right. I had told him I wouldn't meddle around in murder, and here I was, breaking my word. There was another part of me that recognized that there was more at stake that just finding Todd's killer, and that he and I had yet to weather any storm. What loomed ahead could be treacherous for us both.

I turned and walked out, slamming the door behind me.

CHAPTER SEVEN

Shelly and Viv got to the house after nine, both looking grim and determined. Cait and Kyle were there as well. We needed to get organized fast. The longer Steve sat in jail, the harder it was going to be to prove his innocence.

"How do we know he didn't do it?" Kyle asked.

"We don't," I told him. "But remember what you said about Doug? Same applies here. If he didn't do it, we can't let him go to prison. We need a plan. Any ideas?"

Viv, the perfect guest, had brought her own cocktail shaker, the extra-large one, filled with vodka, ice, and a drop or two of vermouth. She offered it to us all, and found a taker in Cait, who iced the glasses and found the olives with her usual efficiency.

Viv sipped thoughtfully. "You're the idea person. We're the faithful troops, remember?"

"We have to find whoever Steve said he was talking to," Cait said.

I shook my head. "Already asked Mary Rose. Steve didn't know his name. Whoever it was was a tall man, gray hair, with grandkids."

"What were the kids dressed as? Maybe we can find out who he was that way," Shelly said.

I looked at her. "Very good, grasshopper. Okay, we find out what they were dressed as, and that will be your mission. Find those kids. I think somebody from the Historical Society taped the entire costume contest. That will help."

She reached over and took Viv's glass off the table, took a sip, then made a face. "How do you drink that?"

Viv smiled. "Very carefully. What about me?"

"Do you know who bought the house behind Aggie?"

She nodded. "I didn't handle it, but someone from my office did. The Giancomos. He, she, and two grade school kids. They both work, I think. I helped them with the inspection, so they know me. I'll call them tomorrow and ask them…what?"

"If they saw or heard anything in Aggie's yard. I doubt it. Emma's noise machine was really loud, and that hedge is super thick, but we might get lucky." I looked at Cait and Kyle. "You realize that getting Steve off the hook might turn the heat on under Doug again?"

Kyle shook his head. "Doug did not do it. In fact, I'll ask Doug if I can take a look in that garage, see if anything looks odd."

"Or maybe we can ask a few of Steve's neighbors if they saw anything. Or anyone." Cait finished her martini and waggled her glass. Viv graciously refilled it.

"What are you going to do?" Shelly asked.

I didn't want to do anything. I didn't want the divide between Sam and I to get any wider. But… "I'm going to talk to Steve. I need to hear his version of things, not Mary Rose's."

"Sam won't like that," Shelly said.

"Sam *really* won't like that," Cait said.

I nodded. "Yeah. I know." I stared into my water glass, wishing it was something stronger. Then I looked wistfully at Viv's shaker.

"Come on, girl," Viv said, grinning. "It cures what ails you."

I was looking at the shaker, trying to remember. "Viv, when you and James were sitting in front of the library Halloween night, how long did you stay there?"

"Until we heard the sirens. We were talking." She glanced at Shelly, who turned red.

"The most logical route to Emma's garden from Mary Rose's house was right up Blackburn. Did you notice Steve come up that way?" I asked.

Viv put her drink on the table and leaned forward, palms on her knees, frowning. "I'm not sure. I don't know him that well. I might not have even recognized him. But Lou Lombardi was right at the corner, wasn't she?"

Right. Lou had one of my scavenger hunt stations, a booth in Upper Main Park, where kids had to stick their hands in all sorts of slimy, scary goop to capture plastic spiders. "You're brilliant, Viv. I'll call her. Lou notices everything."

Shelly snickered. "Everything male."

I kicked her. "Be nice. And Viv," I drained the water out of my glass and held it out. "I think I'll try a bit of that after all."

I texted Lou the next morning, and she called me back right away.

Louise Lombardi worked on Wall Street, and could have probably lived in Manhattan if she wanted, but she'd been born in Mt. Abrams, and moved back after her divorce. She also had a place in Cape Cod where she spent most of June and July. She worked hard for her money and spent it freely. She also had no interest in men as far as relationships went. But as far as men in general, she was an unabashed supporter of the One Night Stand. She liked men. A lot.

"So, what do you want to know? Did I see who?"

I moved the phone to my other ear and settled into the cozy chair in my office. "Halloween night. Did you see Steve, Mary Rose's brother?"

"Yes. He and his wife, what's-her-name, Kim, stopped and we chatted for a few minutes."

"Can you give me a time?"

"Five-thirty-ish? Maybe? Kim got bored pretty quick and left him with me for a few extra minutes."

"How about later in the night? Like, after the hunt was over?"

"Hold on." I could hear her speaking to someone in her office, margins were mentioned. I was completely ignorant of most of what she did for a living, but I imagined she was very good at her job. "Okay. I'm back. Sorry. So, after? Yeah. I saw Steve. He was alone, wandering up Davis. We didn't speak."

"When?"

"About an hour later."

"Did you see him come back down?"

"Nope. But I was packed up and gone in, like, ten minutes."

"Thanks." I hung up. So, Steve had gone back up to see Todd, just as he said. How long would it have taken him to get to Emma's house, realize Todd wasn't there, and come back down? Surely, not ten minutes.

I walked down to the Upper Park.

I stood in the cold in the exact spot that Lou had set up her station on Halloween night. I checked my watch and began walking, across Blackburn to where Davis turned off to the left. I then walked down towards Emma's house, trying to imagine Steve doing the same thing. Would he have been hurrying? If he had every intention of murdering Todd, that might have put some extra speed in his step. If not, he would have been taking a nice, leisurely stroll.

I opted for leisure. I went past Emma's porch, stopped in front of her closed garden gate, counted slowly to ten, then walked back.

Twelve minutes. So Lou might have just missed him.

I walked back to Emma's house and stood in the middle of the street.

Mt. Abrams has a lot of hills, but all the streets running east to west are relatively flat, and from where I stood on Davis Road, I could see all the way across to where Lou had set up her station, and all the way in the other direction to where Maggie's house stood at the crook in the road. Steve would have been able to see as well, and he could have seen Todd walking away, towards the parking lot, using the easiest and most logical route. Did he see him? Did he follow him? And did anyone see him?

I trudged back home, got in my car, and drove to the police station.

Steve was surprised to see me. I was surprised they let me see him. He was also, understandably, confused as to what exactly I was doing there.

"I need to hear from you exactly what happened that night," I said to him. We were in a tiny room, across from each other sitting at a bare metal table with a very nice-looking officer standing silently in the corner.

He sighed. "God, Ellie, it seems like I've told this story a hundred times in the past twenty-four hours."

That wasn't good. I didn't want him to just recite back whatever he told the police. "Okay, then, let me sort of guide you. Don't answer automatically, Steve. Think about what you're saying. So, whose idea was it to go to Mary Rose's in the first place."

"Kim. She wanted to see Todd as a clown."

"She'd never seen him before?"

He shrugged. "Yes. Lots of times. But she was insistent."

"Okay. What time did you get there?"

"A little after four."

And what did you do?"

"We sat on the front porch. I had a beer with Joe. Mary Rose was explaining the scavenger hunt."

"Did you see Doug or Todd?"

He shook his head. "No."

"Did they know you'd be there?"

"Of course. We had talked about giving Todd a lift so Doug wouldn't have to worry about his gig later that night, but Doug said it was fine."

"Good. Now, who decided it was time to get up and walk around?"

"Kim."

"So tell me where you went. Think about it. Where did you stop first?"

It was excruciating. First of all, I always thought that Steve was a perfectly nice man, but he had struck me as a little boring. Now, I realized he was *very* boring. His voice was a monotone; when he spoke, he looked down at his hands, and he sighed. A lot. Granted, we weren't having a conversation under ideal circumstances, but... it was all I could do to keep from putting my head down and taking a quick nap.

We finally got to the part of the narrative I'd been waiting for. "So, Steve, when you went up to see if Todd was done, you didn't see him anywhere?"

"No."

"Not even walking down the street? Towards the parking lot?"

For the first time, there was a crack in his composure. " I told you, I never saw him."

"No, you didn't tell me. You may have told the police, but not me." I leaned forward. "I walked from Mary

Roses' house, up Blackburn, and then to Emma's. I know how long it should have taken you. But you were gone a long time, Steve."

"I told you, I stopped to talk to somebody."

"A man."

"Yes."

"Gray hair, with little kids."

"No. I mean, yes, he was."

I sat back. "What were they dressed as? The kids?"

"I don't know."

"What was the man wearing?"

"I don't know."

"Steve," I said carefully, "this man is your alibi. You stopped and talked to him. Surely you noticed the kids."

He was quiet.

"They would have been impatient, right? Wanting to go to the next house. Or wanting to go home and look at their candy."

He looked around. Everywhere but at me.

"Steve?"

"There was no man," he whispered.

I took a long breath. "Then you lied?"

He nodded.

"So, where were you all that time?"

"I got to the end of Davis, turned the corner, and sat on that bench there." He looked up at me, and his eyes were huge. "I didn't want to go back to Kim. I knew she'd just start on Todd again, how we need to help him. She'd be mad at me because I didn't find him."

"Did anyone see you? Sitting?"

"No."

"So, there is no alibi?"

"No. But I didn't kill Todd. I didn't want him dead, just out of our lives."

"But Kim would never let that happen, would she?"

The door banged open, and Sam stood there, his lips in a tight line. "Officer, you can take Mr. Wyzinski back to his cell. Please."

Steve stood, opened his mouth to say something, then shook his head and left. Sam closed the door, and we were alone.

"What are you doing here, Ellie? I told you to stay away."

"The last person who got to tell me what to do was my father," I said, looking at him steadily. "And you're not my father."

"You have no business being here."

"I'm just trying to get something straight in my mind. I think you have the wrong person."

"He has motive and opportunity. The weapon was found on his property. His alibi is so thin you could blow it away."

"He just told me he has no alibi at all. But I still think there's something off."

"Yes, well, what you think is not relevant to this case. You have gone past meddling. You are now interfering with an investigation. You have to go." His face was white. I had never seen him angry, not at me, anyway, and it sent a chill through my backbone.

"You're wrong," I told him.

"No, I'm not," he shot back.

I stood up and left, closing the door quietly behind me.

After dinner, I texted Shelly that there was no need for her to try to find two kids and their grandfather. Viv called. The Giancomos had not seen or heard a thing. Cait came home late. She had gone directly after school to Doug's and had talked to a few of the neighbors. No one had seen or heard a thing. The garage, Cait said, faced the street, and anyone breaking in could have easily been seen.

"Unless it was the middle of the night," I said.

She shook her head. " Maybe. Doug let a few things slip. Steve really had it out for Todd. Wanted him out of the house."

"I know. Things aren't looking too great for Steve right now."

"So, maybe he did it?"

I didn't want to think about that. Mary Rose would be devastated, and although there were plenty of times I'd have loved to see her brought up short, I wouldn't wish something like this on anybody. I also didn't want to think about Sam. Yes, I had promised him I would stay away from murder. But he was wrong. Surely, that was cause for some sort of exemption, right?

I was brushing my teeth for bed when I got his text.

R u asleep? Can we talk?

Yes. Where r u?

The doorbell rang.

I ran downstairs and reached over to turn on a light as I opened the front door. Sam stood there, hands in the pockets of his trench coat, head down.

"We need to talk," he said.

I let him in.

He stood by the fireplace, turned away from me. The silence was killing me.

"Did you buy that directly from Columbo?" I finally asked.

He turned, looking surprised, then looked down at his coat and laughed. "No. But it's a good look, right?"

I nodded.

"And while we're on the subject, that's an interesting look you've got going on."

I looked down at myself. I was wearing SpongeBob SquarePants jammie pants that I had bought for Tessa, but they had been mislabeled and were way too big for her, so I kept them for myself. I also had on a faded XXX-sized black T-shirt with the words "All first drafts of anything are shit" printed on the front in lime green.

"Yeah, well, this is my going to bed outfit," I said. "Unless I'm going to bed with you."

His mouth twitched. "Is that your opinion of first drafts?"

"Pretty much. And Hemingway's. Sit."

He did. "You're right. Everything about this stinks. It wasn't my decision to arrest Wyzinski. It came from above, and the logic was sound. It just feels completely wrong."

I sat across from him. "As crazy as it sounds, I think Doug is the killer."

Sam nodded. "Me too. Unfortunately, there's no way Doug could fit in the timeline. There was no time for him to kill Todd and make it to Hoboken when he did."

The idea that had been cowering in the corner of my brain finally broke free. "Sam, what if Todd was killed earlier?"

He sat back and rested his head against the couch cushion. "What are you taking about, Ellie? Todd was alive at six-thirty."

"No. Mr. Scarecrow was alive at six-thirty."

He lifted his head.

"Mr. Scarecrow was wearing a mask," I said.

He sat up. "And?"

I swallowed. "What if Doug killed him? No one saw Doug after he dropped Todd off. And Cait says that Doug claimed to be sitting up at the lake while Todd was putting in his show, but she and Kyle never saw him up there. So what if Doug put on the mask and gloves and pretended to be his brother? They're built exactly the same, and with the mask on, who would know?"

Sam opened his mouth to say something, shut it, then swore. "Yes. Of course."

"Mr. Scarecrow got a phone call from Doug. He said he needed a break and was gone for twenty minutes. When he came back, he started singing songs. Prebreak Mr. Scarecrow was doing magic."

Sam leaned forward and clasped his hands. "So, he tells Todd to meet him behind Aggie's house. Why?"

I shrugged. "Could be anything. To apologize?"

"How would he get the hammer?"

"The hammer was in the duffle bag, and Emma said he used it to bang open a table leg that was stuck. Probably the same leg that you fixed, remember?"

He nodded. "Who used it? Todd or Doug?"

"We can ask Emma. But Doug had access to it. He could have easily slipped it under his shirt or something."

"Right." Sam rubbed his hands together. "So, Todd meets him, and they argue. That sound machine, wouldn't Emma have turned it off?"

"Probably while Todd was performing, yes. But if Todd weren't there…"

"The noise of any arguing would have been drowned out. Doug hits Todd, takes the mask and hat and gloves, walks around the corner and plays at Mr. Scarecrow. When all the kids are through, he dodges around to Aggie's yard, drags the body on the porch, walks down the street, and drives to his Hoboken gig. Could it really be that easy?"

"Why wouldn't he just leave Todd's body where it was?"

Sam sighed. "I interviewed Doug twice. He obviously loved his mother. He was really concerned about what Todd was doing to her and her marriage. I think he put the body on the porch so it would be found right away, rather than have his mother have to wait through a search once Todd was found to be missing."

I felt suddenly cold. "Emma was right. She said Doug knew who the killer was. Oh, Sam, this is awful."

"Yes, especially since it will be very difficult to prove."

"What do you mean? All the pieces fit."

He smiled gently. "Do you realize how far-fetched it sounds?"

I hugged myself. "Can't you do anything?"

"Well, the easiest thing to do would be to test the inside of that duffle bag for DNA. Once it's established that the hammer was in the bag, then it's easier to tie it to Doug."

"So, do that."

He leaned back again. "I can't get a warrant for something like that if there's already a plausible suspect in custody."

I shivered. "Man, that sucks. What are you going to do?"

He shifted on the couch and opened up the front of his coat. "Well, I could start by warming you up."

I got up, walked over, then carefully straddled him on the couch. He wrapped his coat, and his arms, around me.

"Better?" he asked.

I snuggled in a bit more. "Yes. So you agree it's a viable theory?"

He nodded. "Yes. It makes more sense than the drug connection."

"Which was Doug's idea, by the way. As was Eve. But seriously, how did he think anyone would believe her to be a killer? I bet she's not even pregnant. As skinny as she was, believe me, I'd notice."

He raised an eyebrow. "Oh. You saw Eve?"

I tugged at his tie. "It was Shelly's idea. She had the day off, and Viv wanted pizza. I can show you the text."

"And you went to Montclair because there were no pizza places closer?" he was trying not to smile.

I pulled the tie off. "We like the train ride. Now, what if we can prove it was Doug under that scarecrow mask?"

"And how exactly would we do that?"

"Someone must have seen something."

He shook his head. "We talked to a lot of people, Ellie. No one saw Mr. Scarecrow without that mask on."

"Yes, but you're the police."

He was silent, and his hands were making their way under my T-shirt. "And you're not?" He said at last.

"What can it hurt?" I began unbuttoning the top button of his shirt. "Doug thinks he's in the clear. It's not like he'll even know what I'm doing. I will not be in any danger." I leaned forward and kissed the v-shaped patch of skin at the base of his throat.

"I suppose," he said, kissing me right behind my left ear.

"I can just talk to a few people." His shirt was unbuttoned, and I ran my fingers down the center of his chest.

"Fine. Focus on the sliver of time when the two of them were together," he murmured, pulling my T-shirt up over my head.

"Who knew brainstorming a murder could be so sexy?" I asked.

He grinned.

Then we stopped talking altogether.

CHAPTER EIGHT

I TOLD SHELLY AND CAROL my plan the next morning. Shelly was so excited that she started running in tiny circles.

"Doug? Oh, my God. Ellie, you're amazing." She was bouncing, her short ponytail bobbing up and down.

"That's so awful," Carol said. "But it makes sense. I thought Mr. Scarecrow changed up his act because he was just getting tired of the magic tricks. The voices were so similar, there's no way I would have said they were two different people."

"Well, to be honest, my idea could be all smoke and mirrors. Maybe Steve Wyzinski was tired of his wife putting up with Todd. Maybe Steve *did* kill him. But it doesn't feel right. And Doug spent so much time and energy accusing other people, you know?" I shivered. Why didn't I ever think of gloves?

Carol nodded. "Todd and Doug were dressed almost the same. Well, jeans and a denim shirt. Maybe there were differences, but none that I could see. They both had on work boots. Todd had a T-shirt on under his denim shirt, I do remember that. But when he pulled his mask on, it came down to the middle of his chest with all that straw sticking out, so there was no way of noticing if Mr. Scarecrow Number 2 was also wearing a T-shirt. And then there were those ridiculous glasses that he wore over the mask, and the hat, and the gloves…it could have been any tall, skinny guy under there, Ellie. How are we to prove anything?"

Shelly was now jogging circles around Carol and I. Buster was dragging his feet a little, and Boot was trying to follow.

"Shelly, stop that. We're getting all tied up here." My cell phone made a noise, and I pulled it out. "It's Lynn. I texted her the other day to see if she saw Mr. Scarecrow. We should talk to her?"

Shelly untangled Buster's leash. "Yes. For sure. We can get her on the way back."

"Okay," I said, and texted Lynn back.

Lynn Fahey was giving Mary Rose a run for her money for the Most Involved Mt. Abrams Volunteer award. There wasn't a real award, of course, but you wouldn't know it to watch the two of them go toe to toe in the Let Me Do It department. Lynn had her age working against her. Mary Rose had quite simply been doing it longer. But Lynn firmly believed she had a fighting chance.

Today, Lynn's long hair was coiled on top of her head, and she was wearing a long denim skirt, Birkenstocks with argyle socks, and a Fair Isle sweater. As early as it was, her house smelled like vanilla and sugar.

"Are you baking?" I asked as Shelly and I came in. We had dropped off the dogs and left Carol to get ready for work. Shelly, I knew, didn't have to be at work until later.

"Just some shortbread," Lynn explained. "Can I get you some? With tea?"

My mouth was watering, but I shook my head. "No, thanks. I just wanted to ask you about Halloween. Were you walking the kids around, or giving out candy? Did you by any chance see Mr. Scarecrow at all?"

She nodded. "Sure, I saw him. He was practically running all the way down the hill. I was worried he was going to trip and roll all the way to Route 51."

"Did he still have his mask on?" I asked.

She nodded. "Yes, and I thought it was pretty strange. It had to be itchy, right? With all that straw and stuff?"

Shelly sighed. "Yes. Well, that's that."

"What are you looking for?" Lynn asked.

I glanced at Shelly. I did not want anyone to know I was still poking around in this. If it got back to Mary Rose, she would hound me to death. And if it somehow got back to Doug...

"Just curious. His car was parked in the lower lot. Did you see where he cut over?"

She nodded. "At the Carson driveway, three houses down. Come on, what's going on?"

"They arrested Mary Rose's brother," I told her.

Lynn's jaw dropped. "Oh, how terrible. When?"

"Yesterday. I'm trying to prove a theory, but I'm not having much luck," I started for the door. "Thanks, Lynn."

"Go down and talk to Heather," Lynn said. "She's home now, and I know she was home Halloween. Her husband took the kids, and she gave out candy."

I thanked her, and Shelly and I left. We walked out to the middle of Carver Road. Shelly looked down the street.

"We're here," she said. "We may as well."

I nodded. "Do you know Heather?"

"Well enough. Let's go."

Three houses down was a tiny Cape Cod with a bright red door. We rang the bell. A dog barked, and seconds later, a baby started screaming. Shelly and I exchanged looks.

The door opened, and a disheveled young woman in a flannel shirt and leggings stood there, holding a little boy who looked about three and was howling, his baby face red with anger or frustration.

"Yes?"

"This looks like a bad time," Shelly said quickly.

Heather Carson made a face. "It's always a bad time. Come in."

The living room was decorated with a couch, two over-stuffed chairs, a flat-screen television, and the entire Fisher-Price section of Toys R Us. Heather set down the toddler, who immediately threw himself on the floor and cried even harder.

"That's Dylan. He wants to paint the dog green," she explained. "It's an ongoing issue. This way."

The kitchen was neater and quieter. She sank into a chair and a small, furry dog immediately jumped in her lap, whining. "Hi, Shelly. And you're Ellie Rocca, right? You're kind of famous around here," she said.

"Ah, oh. Well." Really?

"So, what's up?" Heather looked about thirty, pretty, and exhausted.

"About Halloween night," Shelly said. "You were home?"

She nodded.

"Did you see Mr. Scarecrow?"

She nodded again. "Gizmo here went ballistic." She hugged the dog. "I looked out, and he was coming up my drive. Lots of folks do. The parking lot is just behind me. We're used to people taking the shortcut."

I took a breath. "Did he have his mask on?"

"No. In fact, he must have just taken it off, because he was stuffing it into this canvas bag he was carrying."

Shelly made a squeaking noise.

Heather grinned. "Okay, what's going on?"

"Did you see his face?" I asked.

"Well, I guess I did, but nothing really registered. I mean, it was getting dark, and he was moving pretty fast."

Shelly sighed. "Thanks, Heather. We were just... fishing around."

We walked back through the living room. The screaming had abated somewhat, but there was still a great deal of kicking going on. Heather let us out, and we walked up her drive, across her small back yard. From there, we could see across an empty lot to the parking area.

"So, I guess Sam questioned everybody and his brother about who saw what down here Halloween night, right?" Shelly asked.

"Yep. Nobody saw anything."

"So, who else can we talk to?"

"I don't know. Maybe James?"

She turned deep red. "Why?"

"Because he was up here at the time when Doug became Mr. Scarecrow. He may have noticed something." I glanced at her. "What's going on there?"

She stuck her hands in her pockets, and we started walking back up the hill. "Mike has found a place. He's moving out this weekend."

"Do the boys know?"

She nodded. "It was...bad."

"And you're still sure this is the right thing to do?"

She shook her head. "No. Not at all. I only know that if I don't at least *try* to see what my life would be like with Jamie, I'll never forgive myself." Her voice was tight.

"Want to come with me now?"

She cleared her throat. "No. I have to get ready for work. But he's home today. Go ahead and talk to him."

We walked up Morris. Shelly veered off to her house, and I went on up to Davis Road.

He invited me in. "Coffee? I just brewed some."

Brewed? People still brewed coffee? In the age of Keurig? "Sure. Thanks."

He took my jacket. I was dressed in jeans and a faded LBI sweatshirt. If I had known I'd be having coffee with James, I would have seriously rethought my morning walking outfit.

When Kate Fisher had lived in the little rental house on Davis Road, it had been furnished with pastels, chintz, and potted ferns. James had taken a very different approach. The walls were a deep, rich blue, the trim a glossy white, and there were English hunting prints in elaborate frames on the walls. Decidedly masculine. Very attractive. Just like James.

I sat in his dining room, and he brought out a French press coffee pot on a tray with mugs, cream, and sugar. He poured, and we stirred and sipped in silence.

"Are you here about Shelly?" He asked.

"No. I'm not. But if you'd care to talk, I'm happy to listen."

He tapped the fingers of his left hand against the mahogany of the tabletop. "I'm completely...smitten," he said. "I haven't felt this way in thirty years, since I was a kid. I feel awful. She's willing to break up her marriage for me. I've got nothing to lose here, and everything to gain." He had been staring down into his mug. When he lifted his eyes, they were filled with tears. "I can't believe two people falling in love can cause so much pain."

"Oh, James. I'm so sorry for you both. And, well, I'm happy too. I mean, happy you're in love and all that, but..."

He nodded. "I know. Vivian says I should be grateful for the gift and let the rest roll away."

"Vivian? My Viv? Wow, that's pretty enlightened for Viv."

He cracked a smile. "She and I have had a few discussions. She's become a good friend."

"Well, you are very lucky to have her on your side. Believe me, that is one person you do not want for an enemy."

"I hear you. So, what's this all about?"

I took a drink of coffee. It was delicious. "About Halloween."

"Ah." He sat back. "Okay. What can I tell you?"

"Everything that happened when you got to Emma's."

He pushed away his mug and laced his fingers together. "Emma and Carol were in the garden, and there were a few kids there as well. Emma was serving them doughnuts, and Carol was talking to a few of the parents there. I came into the garden, and Carol came up and asked me if I'd seen Mr. Scarecrow. I said no, and asked her which way he had gone. Now, if you're in the garden, all you can see is which way someone turned when they left, up or down the hill. Carol said up the hill, so I went back out and he was standing right there. I asked him if he was okay, and he said yes. He saw the kids and immediately went into character, talking in a kind of funny voice, hopping around. He had everyone singing in like two minutes."

"So, he had his mask on?"

"Yes. And his hat. And those silly glasses. He was having trouble with gloves, though."

"Gloves?"

"Yes. Like they were too small."

Something in my brain clicked. This was important. Why? "Did you notice his tattoos?"

"What tattoos?"

I thought hard. Todd's hands, his wrists. "Was there an arrow coming down from his wrist, ending in the middle on his hand?"

James shook his head. "No, and I probably would have noticed."

"Did he get the gloves on?"

"Eventually. We had a few photo ops first, then he got them on. It seemed strange that they were so tight."

"Because his hands were bigger," I said, half to myself. "How the heck am I going to prove that?"

"Prove what?"

"James, it wasn't Todd you were with. It was Doug. Todd was already dead, right next door."

He raised both eyebrows. "What?"

"Todd had very distinctive tattoos on his arms and wrists. Doug didn't. Now, how to prove it?"

"At least three different people were taking pictures and videos. Maybe one of them?"

"You're brilliant! Of course. Do you know who any of those people were?"

"Well, Carol for one. I'm sure she'd know who the others were."

I got up, went over to him, and kissed him in the middle of his forehead. "Truly brilliant. Wait until I tell Sam. Thank you, James."

I grabbed my jacket and bolted out the door. I was at the library in under three minutes.

Carol took one look at my face and motioned me into her tiny office.

"What's wrong?"

"Remember you said you took a picture of James? Did you take one with him and Mr. Scarecrow?"

"Ellie, is this relevant to anything at all?"

"Yes. Do you have the pictures?"

"Of course." She pulled her purse out of her desk and found her phone. She spent a minute flicking through the photos before she handed it to me. "There. Is this what you need?"

It was a picture of James and Mr. Scarecrow. James photographed very well. Mr. Scarecrow looked... scarecrow-ish. I could not see his hands. I swiped. The next picture was James alone, with his head turned, looking to the left. Swipe. James alone. Laughing. Swipe.

Mr. Scarecrow, reaching up to adjust his hat. The sleeve of his denim shirt was pulled back. His wrist and forearm were bare.

"Bingo," I whispered. The date and timestamp were across the bottom. I sent the picture to Sam with a simple message.

No tattoo.

Then I sent copies to my business e-mail, my phone, and my personal e-mail. It wasn't that I didn't trust technology; it was just that I didn't trust *me* with technology.

I handed Carol back her phone. "We just solved this case," I told her.

She smiled. "Ellie, dear, was there ever any doubt?"

Now, there was only one more person to see.

Mary Rose was not at home, so I texted her to call me whenever she could, and trudged back home. I was freezing, so I made a cup of tea and started a fire in the fireplace. Boot, seizing the opportunity, made a nest for herself under the throw in the corner of the couch, her butt pressed firmly against my side. I kept staring at my phone. Surely, Sam would call, congratulating me on my expert detection technique. Or Mary Rose, so I could tell her the good news/bad news about Todd's death. I tried to imagine myself in Kim's shoes, but couldn't.

I don't know how long I'd been asleep, but Boot was barking and someone was knocking steadily on my door. I scrambled up from the couch and threw open the front door. There stood Mary Rose and Kim Wyzinski.

And Doug was right behind them.

"Ellie, I got your text. What did you find out?"

I stepped back, and the three of them came in. Kim looked completely done in. Doug seemed nervous, and looked like he hadn't slept in a while. He walked over to the fireplace and stood with his back to the flames.

"Listen, I was in the middle of a phone call to one of my authors," I babbled. I have always been a terrible liar. I snatched up my phone. "Let me just finish up, okay?"

I scurried up the stairs, calling Sam as I did.

"Ellie, I got your picture. We're discussing a warrant right now."

"Sam, Doug is here. With Mary Rose and Kim. What should I do?"

Sam swore. Loudly and for what seemed to be a long time. Finally, he said, "I'm on my way."

I walked slowly back down stairs.

Doug was still there by the fireplace. Mary Rose was on the couch, scratching Boot's ears. "Well?" she asked.

How to stall. "Were you all at the jail?"

Kim, sitting next to Mary Rose, shook her head. "No. We've been talking to the lawyer. He says the evidence isn't all that strong." She was wearing a short red jacket. Her hands stayed in her pockets, and she was rocking back and forth. "It's a lot of money. But he thinks he can get Steve off." Her voice was soft and broken.

"That's good, right?" I said. I edged my way around the couch.

"It would be better if we could just find out who really did this," Mary Rose said. "What did you want to tell me?"

"Nothing. I mean, I'd been asking around to see if I could find anyone who saw Todd before or after he met Doug."

Doug's head swiveled, and he stared at me.

"Just to see if anyone saw who it was that Todd met, that's all," I said in a rush.

"The police already did that," Doug said in a hushed voice. "They couldn't find anyone. Could you?"

"No. Nope."

"Then why did you text me, Ellie? You made it sound as though you found out something important." Mary Rose stood and brushed a stray dog hair off her coat. "I was hoping at least you found out who made that call to the police about the hammer. If we knew that, we'd know who the real killer is."

"An anonymous call is just that," Doug said. "We'll never know who made it."

"Don't be too certain," Mary Rose said smugly. "Ellie has a way of finding out all sorts of things."

Doug had been watching me. He stepped away from the fireplace. "What sort of things?" he asked softly.

He knew that I knew. What would he do with his mother and Mary Rose in the same room? Nothing. I was sure of it.

"There's a picture," I said. "Of Mr. Scarecrow. Without any tattoos on his wrist."

Doug closed his eyes briefly, then turned away.

"What?" Asked Mary Rose. "What are you talking about?"

Kim stood up. "Doug?"

Mary Rose grabbed Kim's arm and shook it. "Kim, tell me." She looked at me. "Ellie, what has a tattoo have to do with anything?"

"It proves that whoever was Mr. Scarecrow between five-fifty and six-thirty wasn't Todd." Doug's shoulders slumped.

Kim took a step. "Doug, please."

"I don't understand," Mary Rose said shrilly. "What do you mean, it wasn't Todd?"

Doug's shoulders started to shake. "Simple, Mary Rose," I said. "By five-fifty, Todd was already dead. And Doug took his place."

Kim reached out her hand. "Son…"

Mary Rose stared at me, then at Doug. "My God, *Doug*? He killed his own brother?"

I nodded. "Yes."

Doug turned. Tears streamed down his face.

He shook his head. "No."

CHAPTER NINE

"DOUG," KIM PLEADED. "DON'T."
He shook his head. "I can't. I can't anymore."

Kim went to put her arms around him, but he shook her off.

Wait. What was wrong here? I took my eyes from Doug's anguished face and looked at Kim. Her jaw was clenched, and her eyes were suddenly hard.

"Kim, was it *you*?" The idea hit me so hard I couldn't even breathe.

She ignored me. "Doug, you know what we said."

Doug began to sob, a harsh, ugly sound.

Mary Rose turned white and dropped down on the sofa.

Kim put her hands in her hair and tugged, hard. She was muttering to herself, and I felt suddenly sick to my stomach.

Boot lifted her head and began to bark. There was a quick knock on the door, and Sam came in, John Monroe right behind him. Sam looked at the scene quickly, and his hand dropped from his hip.

"Ellie, can you tell me what's going on?" he asked calmly.

"Kim," I whispered. "Kim did it. She killed her own son."

"I didn't mean to," she said, very loudly. Her head was still down, her hands still pulling at her hair. "I just couldn't do it anymore. I couldn't. And he just made me so angry…" She dropped her hands. She didn't look beaten or fragile anymore. Her eyes narrowed in anger. "He went after Doug with that damn hammer. I couldn't let him hurt Doug. He'd done so much damage already, I couldn't. So when Todd dropped the hammer, I picked it up. I didn't mean to hit him that hard." She spat the words. "Do you really think I set out to kill my own son?"

Sam had been watching her face. He glanced at me, then nodded to John Monroe, who walked over to Kim and reached for her arm.

"You have the right to remain silent," he said quietly. He fastened the handcuffs around her one wrist. "Anything you say can and will be used against you in a court of law." He cuffed her other wrist and turned her around. Her shoulders were stiff, and she held her head high, chin out. John walked her out of the house.

Sam looked at Doug "You need to come with us."

Doug nodded. "I'll be right behind you," he choked out.

Sam nodded and left.

Doug lowered himself stiffly into the chair by the fireplace and buried his face in his hands. I sat next to Mary Rose and watched him as he wept.

He finally wiped his face, took a long, shuddering breath, and then slumped back in the chair, his eyes closed.

"What happened, Doug?" I asked.

"Todd couldn't come to my gig because he had to be somewhere else, paying off a ten thousand dollar debt. He didn't have ten thousand dollars, of course. Mom was going to give it to him. She called me, said she had the money, and I called Todd. We were going to meet him in back of the house next door. It was going to be so simple. Mom would give him the cash, and he'd go back to being a clown. But when we got there, he said he needed more money." Doug shifted in his seat. "I went after him. I wanted to kill him, I really did. But he pulled his hammer out of nowhere. I mean, I don't even know why he had it. I hit him with my fist, and the hammer flew out of his hand, and Mom picked it up."

Mary Rose made a sniffling sound.

"She was so calm. She looked down at him and didn't even cry. She took the mask and the gloves off the ground and told me I should go out and be Mr. Scarecrow. No one would know the difference, she said. I was to make sure that people thought he was alive for as long as I could. That way, we would all have an alibi. She said that the police would think somebody killed him over drugs."

"That almost worked," I said.

He nodded. He was looking into the fire. "Then I tried to get the police interested in Eve. That didn't work either. So Mom got desperate and called the police about the hammer."

"She put it in the garage?" Mary Rose asked, her voice shooting up an octave. "She did that? When she knew they'd go after my brother?"

"She said there wasn't enough to convict him. That he'd get off. And by the time the trial was over, Todd's murder would just be another cold case." He unfolded himself from the chair. "Sorry, Mary Rose, but I couldn't just let my mom go to prison." His eyes shifted to me. "Why did you have to go snooping? It almost worked out perfectly."

"Why did you move the body, Doug?"

He looked surprised at the question. "Todd was my brother. I couldn't leave him out there, all alone."

Mary Rose covered her mouth with her hands.

"You'd better get down to the station, Doug." I said. "They're going to want to talk to you."

He nodded and left, shutting the front door gently behind him.

Mary Rose was shaking. I grabbed the throw from where it had bunched up behind the dog and drew it around her shoulders. She looked at me. "What just happened?"

"A very sad story just ended," I said.

By the time Tessa came home from school, Mary Rose had left to wait for her brother to be released from jail. I was upstairs, trying to work. Tessa came and went, first to have a snack, then off to do homework.

Tessa was not a problem. Cait, on the other hand, was going to be tough.

I heard her bounding up the stairs. She stopped in the doorway of my office.

"Anything new?"

I motioned to the battered chair in the corner next to my desk. "You might want to sit down."

Her coat slid off her shoulders and landed in a heap on the floor, on top of her purse and tote bag. She sat, watching my face. "What?"

"Kyle was right about Doug. He didn't kill his brother."

"Do you know who did? Was it Steve? Oh, no, that's awful."

I shook my head. "No, honey. It was Kim."

She looked away, and I could almost see her brain turning. "His mother?"

"Apparently, Todd was going after Doug, and she hit him to stop the fight."

"If it was an accident..." She looked back at me. "Doug covered it up?"

"Yes. He put on the scarecrow mask and pretended to be Todd. That moved the time of death. It gave his mother an alibi."

"Wow," she whispered. "So all this time I thought he did it?"

"He was protecting his mother."

She stood. "I need to tell Kyle right away. This is, well, unbelievable."

"It's sad. That poor family."

She bent down and gathered up her things from the floor. "Is Doug going to be in trouble?"

"Probably. He's an accessory to a murder."

"Oh." She stood there, looking miserable, her arms full of coat and purse, and I wanted to gather her into my lap and tell her that everything was going to be just fine.

But it wasn't going to be just fine. For Kyle's good friend Doug, the world would never be fine again.

She turned and left, and I spent the rest of the afternoon staring at my computer, thinking about being a mother, and trying to imagine what the world for Kim Wyzinski was going to be like for the next forty years.

Sam came by late. He looked tired and unhappy, and he sat in front of the fire, nursing a scotch, not talking, while I sat in my reading chair and didn't say anything. When he finally motioned for me to sit beside him, I curled up in the crook of his arm and sank into him, grateful for his strength and warmth and the feel of his fingers in my hair.

"This one was bad," he said.

I nodded.

"Thank you for what you did. It…helped."

"Good."

"And I have to admit, I was impressed at your self control."

I smiled against his shoulder. "Well, luckily I have minions."

He raised his eyebrows. "Minions?"

"Yes. Everyone I knew was asking questions, so I wouldn't have to."

He threw back his head and laughed. I loved his laugh. It came from the very center of his chest, and rolled up and out like champagne from a bottle.

"So, I shouldn't be impressed by your self control as much as I should be impressed by your powers of manipulation?"

"I prefer to think of it as project management."

"Oh, well then." He kissed the top of my head. "I confirmed the reservation for New Year's Eve. Are we still good for that?"

"Yes. It sounds wonderful. You and I, a romantic inn, a body…"

He laughed again. "Yes. And absolutely no chance of you getting into trouble." He drained his scotch and sank further into the couch.

"What will happen to Doug?"

Sam sighed. "He'll cut a deal. He'll have to. If he gets a sympathetic judge, he could walk."

"And Kim?"

"A mother killing her child? That's a tough one. Doug backs her story, that Todd went after him, so she'll be charged with manslaughter. It depends on the jury."

I pulled away and looked up at him. "How do you do this all the time? Deal with such damaged people?"

"Someone has to speak for the dead. Someone needs to find the truth, and hopefully, dispense justice."

"It's late."

"Yes." He sighed. "I should probably get going."

"Why don't you stay?"

He looked down at me in surprise. He had never spent the night at my house with the girls home. "Are you sure?" he asked.

I nodded. "Cait's an adult, and Tessa has sleepovers all the time. I even have extra toothbrushes."

"Thank you. I would love to stay."

We sat there a bit longer, until the fire had burned down, and Boot had curled up in her bed, then I turned off the light, and we went upstairs, together.

Made in the USA
Charleston, SC
19 October 2016